SHADOW CREEK

JOY FIELDING
SHADOW CREEK

**SIMON &
SCHUSTER**

London · New York · Sydney · Toronto · New Delhi

A CBS COMPANY

First published in the USA by Atria Books, 2012
A division of Simon and Schuster, Inc.
First published in Great Britain by Simon & Schuster UK Ltd, 2012
A CBS COMPANY

1 3 5 7 9 10 8 6 4 2

Simon & Schuster UK Ltd
1st Floor
222 Gray's Inn Road
London WC1X 8HB

www.simonandschuster.co.uk

Simon & Schuster Australia, Sydney
Simon & Schuster India, New Delhi

A CIP catalogue record for this book is available from the British Library

Hardback ISBN 978-1-47111-218-8
Trade paperback ISBN 978-1-47111-219-5
Ebook ISBN 978-1-47111-221-8

Printed and bound by CPI Group (UK) Ltd, Croydon, CR0 4YY

To Warren

ACKNOWLEDGMENTS

As always, my sincere thanks to Larry Mirkin and Beverley Slopen, great friends and wonderful critics who graciously read my manuscripts during various stages of completion, and offer invaluable advice and encouragement. Thanks also to my terrific agent, Tracy Fisher, at WME Entertainment for her continuing guidance, hard work, enthusiasm, and wisdom. To my editor, Emily Bestler, her assistant Kate Cetrulo, copyeditor Tom Pitoniak, and everyone at Atria, thanks for all your assistance. A special thank-you as well to Kristin Cochrane, Nita Pronovost, Adria Iwasutiak, Val Gow, and everyone at Doubleday, Canada, as well as to my many foreign publishers and translators. I may not always understand you, but you're clearly doing something right.

And a big virtual hug to all my readers, especially those who e-mail their appreciation of my efforts, those who show up at my various speaking engagements and public appearances, and those who read my monthly newsletters and follow me on both Facebook and Twitter. In what has been an occasionally difficult year—those who read my monthly newsletter and follow me on Facebook and Twitter will understand what I'm talking about—your support was, to borrow a much used and abused word, awesome.

And lastly, some words of thanks and, above all, love to my husband, Warren, and our daughters, Shannon and Annie. (An extra-extra-special thank-you to those who purchased Shannon's CD, *No More Cinderella,* through her website, Amazon, or iTunes. Those of you who haven't as yet, please go to her website at shannonmicol.com and do so immediately. Sorry—what can I say? I'm a mother!)

And a grandmother! So, thank you, Courtney, for being such a great dad to my gorgeous grandson, Hayden, and to Hayden, for being the sweetest little boy who ever lived.

SHADOW CREEK

PROLOGUE

"IT WAS A DARK and stormy night,'" Ellen said, reciting the infamous opening line of some long-forgotten novel. The sentence had the dubious honor of having once been voted the worst opening line of a book ever, although Ellen didn't think it all that bad. If pressed, she was fairly certain she could come up with worse, although admittedly, her once-prodigious memory was no longer what it was. But then again, she decided with a laugh, what was?

Her laugh was surprisingly youthful for a woman her age, more like the giggle of a teenage girl than that of a woman who had recently celebrated her seventieth birthday.

"It certainly is that," her husband of almost fifty years agreed. Stuart Laufer embraced his wife with unusually muscular arms for a man closing in on seventy-five, and together they stared out the window of their old log cottage at the surrounding trees, whose branches were being whipped into a veritable frenzy by the formidable winds.

It had been raining for almost five hours, the downpour having started at just past three o'clock that afternoon. A series of dark, menacing clouds had appeared out of nowhere, crowding the sky and quickly overwhelming the weak sun. Large, heavy pellets of rain followed almost immediately, bullets from a celestial machine gun. Then came the wind, accompanied by loud bursts of thunder and wild streaks of lightning, then more wind, more lightning, more bullets. Beautiful, Ellen had marveled. Terrifying, too, as beauty often was.

I was beautiful once, she thought.

"This is way too violent to last very long," Stuart had said earlier, as if to assure them both. "Guess I was wrong," he'd later admitted as the afternoon stretched into the evening and was swallowed by the ever-darkening sky. The lights in the small cottage began flickering on and off, casting vague, animal-like shadows on the white walls. "I better light a fire in case we lose power," he said now.

"'I'll huff and I'll puff and I'll blow your house down,'" Ellen whispered to herself, recalling the fairy tale of the three little pigs and the big bad wolf, which her mother used to read to her when she was little. Unexpected tears suddenly filled her deep-set blue eyes. Amazing, she thought. Here she was, seventy years old and still crying for the mother she'd lost almost twenty years earlier. As if she were still that little girl curled up in her mother's lap, wrapped in her protective arms. How much she still missed her—her mother's absence almost as strong as her presence had once been. Ellen could still feel the softness of her mother's lips against her forehead, still see the pride in her eyes whenever she looked her way, still hear the drama in her voice as she read aloud from the Brothers Grimm. Ellen had always assumed she'd read those stories to her own children one day, and after that to the grandchildren who would surely follow. But neither of her sons had ever shown much interest in fairy tales and they rarely sat still long enough for her to get out more than the obligatory "Once upon a time." They'd squirreled out of her lap whenever she'd tried to corral them, preferring toy airplanes to books, and later, girls to just about anything else. Both boys, now grown men of forty-three and forty—was it really possible?—had married women they'd met while away at college—Berkeley for Todd, Stanford for Ben— and moved to the opposite side of the country. Neither marriage had lasted more than a couple of years, and both men had married again, Ben several times, the latest to a pole dancer from Russia. The various marriages had produced five children, three boys and two girls—Mason, Peyton, Carter, Willow and Saffron—where did they get these names?—all of whom were now young adults and none of whom had any connection to their paternal grandparents back east. Ellen couldn't remember the last time she'd spent significant time with any of them. For years she'd sent money at Christmas and at birthdays. Sometimes she received a thank-you note. More often than not, she didn't. She'd complained to her sons, but they claimed to be powerless. "Ex-wives," Ben had said with a shrug, as if this explained everything. Ellen had recently tried communicating with her grandchildren via e-mail, but her brief inquiries into their health and well-being had gone unacknowledged. She doubted that any of them would bother showing up for the fiftieth-anniversary party she and Stuart were planning for the fall. Whatever happened to "happily ever after"? she wondered now.

Ellen heard Stuart grunt and his knees crack as he bent

down to arrange the logs in the old stone fireplace. She studied his weathered but still handsome face, his soft brown eyes narrowed in concentration, his wide brow furrowed, as his fingers, their knuckles swollen with arthritis, struggled to light a long match. Despite the years, the man was still a sight for sore eyes. Even after all this time, he still made her heart flutter. Amazing, Ellen thought, wondering at her good fortune, and feeling guilty she hadn't been able to pass that same luck on to her sons.

Except that marriage was as much about hard work as it was about luck, she understood. And it hadn't all been wine and roses, peaches and cream. There had been days, sometimes even weeks at a stretch, when the thought of Stuart disappearing under the wheels of a bus had been more than casually appealing. There had been times when she'd considered leaving him, once when she'd actually had her hand on the telephone, the phone directory on the kitchen counter open to the listing of prominent New York divorce attorneys.

But then she'd remembered a piece of advice her own mother had given her, about when times got tough to remember the reasons she'd married Stuart in the first place, and she'd thought of his sweet smile and his sly sense of humor, and the way his gold-flecked brown eyes lit up whenever she walked into the room. Soon she was recalling various random acts of kindness, thoughtful gestures, and the gentle way he always touched her, how she loved his keen mind and his open heart. And soon, the yellow pages would be back in the drawer, and she'd be cooking him his favorite dinner of macaroni and cheese. Which was something else she loved about him—that he was so easy to please.

It didn't hurt that their sex life had always been active and fulfilling. Even now, at their advanced age, they still made love often and enthusiastically. While the acrobatics of their youth may have disappeared, their ability to please one another had not. "You know what the most common form of sex is among senior citizens?" Stuart had once asked, looking up from the morning paper he was reading. "Oral sex," he'd continued with a wink. "Are you saying they just talk about it?" Ellen had quickly countered. How they'd laughed.

She laughed again now, marveling that so many of their friends had all but abandoned lovemaking in the latter years of their marriages, some seemingly without regret. Not that she and Stuart had very many close friends anymore, other than Wayne and Fran McQuaker, she realized sadly, having lost several friends to cancer and others to the simple vagaries of time. The laugh quickly died in her throat.

It probably hadn't helped when they'd decided to abandon city life for the rustic cabin they'd bought as an investment property years earlier. Ellen had always considered herself a real city girl, so when Stuart first brought up the idea of a cabin in the woods, she'd balked. But after her initial concerns subsided— the bugs, the wild animals, the isolation—she discovered to her shock that she actually enjoyed the peace and quiet of the country. She loved the scenic drive through the Adirondacks, the way the roads twisted and turned up the mountains, the way the tall trees surrounded them protectively as they drove, the noises of the city becoming fainter the higher they climbed, then disappearing altogether, replaced by the singing of birds and the sound of water gurgling from nearby creeks. The thought of putting the property up for sale became less and less attractive the more time they spent there, and eventually they'd given up the idea altogether, selling their house in White Plains instead, and settling in the cottage full-time two years ago. Their son Ben had strongly advised against it. But then Ben, a lawyer, had left his second wife, also a lawyer, for a Russian pole dancer he'd met at a strip club called CHEATERS, so Ben's judgment was somewhat suspect. "What are you going to do if there's an emergency?" he'd asked.

"We have a telephone and a computer," Ellen had reminded him. "It's not as if we're that far from civilization."

"It's a lousy idea," Ben had countered, although he'd never actually set eyes on the place himself. "Just the name freaks me out. Shadow Creek," he'd pronounced with a shudder, referring to the narrow creek that ran behind the old log house. "Besides, Katarina hates mosquitoes."

"As opposed to the rest of us who love them," Ellen muttered now. And it was true—there were lots of mosquitoes. Especially now, in July. And spiders. And snakes. And coyotes. And even bears, she thought, although she'd yet to see one. Indeed, the most intrusive of all the pests in the Adirondacks were the tourists who flocked here in droves during the summer months, many of whom got lost in the woods while hiking the nearby trails, and some of whom actually knocked on their door, asking to please use the bathroom. When Ellen answered their knock, she'd politely decline and send them on their way. If Stuart answered, being the soft touch he was, he sometimes let them in.

"Did you say something?" Stuart asked now.

"What? Oh, no. Just thinking out loud, I guess."

"About what?"

"Just wondering how long this storm is going to last." Ellen didn't want to get into a discussion about Ben and his latest wife, a topic that inevitably digressed into a debate about their failings as parents. Yes, it was true that one son was a doctor and the other a lawyer, so clearly they must have done something right. But just as clearly, they'd done something equally wrong. Ellen had wasted far too many hours trying to figure it out. Children didn't come with a list of instructions, she remembered reading, and the fact was that she and Stuart had done the best job they knew how.

But it was also true that she and Stuart had always existed in their own little cocoon, never really needing anyone but each other. And that had always been something of a sore spot as far as their sons were concerned. Still, that didn't explain why neither of them was able to sustain a relationship. If their parents' marriage of almost half a century hadn't provided them with a solid enough example, Ellen didn't know what would. Besides, what's done is done, she thought. It was too late to change anything now.

Wasn't it?

Ellen cut across the living room toward the kitchen and removed the black cordless phone from its carriage. "I'm calling Ben," she told her husband before he could ask.

He nodded, as if this was no surprise, and continued working on the fire. The comforting aroma of burning cedar quickly filled the large rectangular space that was living room, dining room, and bright, modern kitchen combined. At the back of the cottage were three bedrooms and a bathroom. The beds in the two guest bedrooms had never been slept in, although the McQuakers had promised to drive up this weekend, a visit Ellen was greatly looking forward to.

She punched in her younger son's phone number and waited as it rang once, twice, three times before being picked up.

"Hello?" a woman's voice answered, her strong accent overpowering the simple word.

"Katarina, hi," Ellen said cheerily. "This is . . ."

"Who is speaking?" Katarina interrupted.

"It's Ellen. Ben's mother."

"I'm sorry. Connection is very bad. I must ask you call back later."

It took Ellen a few seconds to realize that Katarina had hung up on her. "I think we were disconnected," she told Stuart, trying to think positively and deciding to call Todd instead. But there was no longer a dial tone. "Oh. I think the phone's gone dead."

"Really? Let me see." Stuart pushed himself to his feet and walked toward his wife, his right arm extended.

Ellen tried not to bristle as she handed her husband the phone. She knew he didn't mean to imply that he didn't believe her, or that she was somehow at fault for the phone going dead, but still, she found it irritating that he felt the need to check.

"Well?" she said.

"It's dead all right." He handed the phone back to her.

"Will the computer be dead, too?"

"No. The battery should still be working. You can give it a try, if you want."

"No," Ellen said, the urge to speak to either of her sons having passed. "The lights will probably go next."

Stuart grunted his agreement. "Feel like a glass of wine?"

Ellen smiled. "Yes, that's exactly what I feel like."

Stuart walked around the burgundy-and-blue-striped sofa toward the wine cabinet on the far wall. His hand was reaching for a bottle of Sauvignon Blanc when they heard a loud banging.

"What's that?" Ellen asked as the banging took on greater urgency, filling the room. "Is that the door?"

Stuart took several tentative steps toward the sound.

"Don't answer it," Ellen warned.

"Hello!" they heard a voice call out. "Hello! Please! Is anybody there?"

"It sounds like a child," Stuart whispered.

"What would a child be doing out in this weather?" Ellen asked as Stuart reached for the doorknob. "Don't answer it," she said again.

"Don't be ridiculous," Stuart chastised, pulling open the door.

A girl was standing on the other side, the storm swirling around her, water cascading off the raised hood of the plastic raincoat she was wearing. The rain was dripping with such force into her eyes and nose that it was impossible to make out her features, except that she was young. Not a child exactly, Ellen thought. Not an adult either. Probably in her mid-teens.

"Oh, whew," the girl said, flinging herself inside the cottage without waiting to be asked, and shaking the water from her hands and hair, like a large, shaggy dog. "I was afraid nobody was home."

"What in God's name are you doing out in this mess?" Stuart asked, shutting the door on the outside storm, the wind howling in protest.

"I had a fight with my boyfriend." The girl's large, dark eyes flitted about the room.

"Your boyfriend?" Ellen looked toward the door. "Where is he?"

"Probably still in the damn tent. He's so stubborn. Refused to go to a motel, even when it started coming down in buckets. Not me. I said I was going to find somewhere warm. Except, of course, I got lost, just like he said I would, and I've been wandering around in circles for the past hour. Then I saw the lights from your cottage. I'm so glad you were home. I'm absolutely frozen."

"Oh, you poor thing. Let me make you some hot tea," Ellen said, biting down on her tongue to keep from adding, "You poor, *stupid* thing!" Who picks a fight with her boyfriend on a night like this? Who takes off in the dark, in a storm, to go running through the woods in thunder and lightning? Who does things like that?

Teenage girls, she thought in the next breath, answering her own question.

Ellen walked quickly to the kitchen sink and filled the kettle with water. "This should only take a few minutes." She glanced back over her shoulder at the young girl. Little Red Riding Hood, she thought, as the girl stood dripping onto the beige rug, her eyes casually absorbing and assessing her surroundings.

"Here, let me hang that up," Stuart offered, and the girl quickly removed her raincoat, revealing a slender body dressed in a white T-shirt and a pair of denim shorts. A large canvas bag was draped around her shoulder.

Ellen noted the girl's long legs, full breasts, and large eyes, which continued scanning the room. Her eyes are definitely her best feature, Ellen thought, noting that the rest of the girl's face was relatively nondescript, her nose long, her mouth small. Of course it was hard to look your best when you were dripping wet. Ellen decided she was being overly critical, something both sons had occasionally accused her of being. She resolved to be friendlier. "I'll get you a towel." She walked to the bathroom, returning with a fluffy white bath towel.

The girl was already curled up on the sofa, her bare feet propped under her thighs, her wet sandals on the floor in front of her, her canvas bag beside them. Stuart was sitting in the navy velvet armchair across from her, kind eyes radiating grandfatherly concern. He's always been the nicer one of us, Ellen thought, realizing how much she'd relied on him to smooth over her sharper edges during their fifty years together.

"This is a beautiful cottage," the girl said, uncoiling her feet and taking the towel from Ellen's outstretched hands. "You've really done a nice job with it. I love the fireplace." She began rubbing the ends of her long hair with the towel. "Thank you."

Ellen tried not to notice that dirt from the girl's feet was staining her sofa and that she wasn't wearing a bra under her flimsy white T-shirt. I'm just a jealous old woman, she admonished herself, remembering when she used to have full, firm breasts like the ones now casually on display. "I'm Ellen Laufer," she said, forcing the introduction from her mouth. Maybe if she'd been nicer to Katarina, friendlier to all her sons' wives, she'd have more of a relationship with her grandchildren today, she couldn't help thinking. "This is my husband, Stuart."

"Call me Nikki." The girl smiled and continued towel-drying her hair. "With two k's. I like that name. Don't you? You don't happen to have a hair dryer, do you?"

"No. Sorry," Ellen lied, ignoring the questioning look from Stuart. It's one thing to give the girl a towel and a cup of tea, her eyes told him silently, but enough is enough. And what did she mean by "Call me Nikki"? Was that her name or not?

"You mean that curl's natural?" Nikki asked. "It's gorgeous."

"Thank you." Ellen touched the blond hair she'd spent half an hour fussing over with a curling iron this morning and immediately felt guilty. I should have let her use my hair dryer, she thought. What's the matter with me?

"Is that water almost boiled?" Nikki asked.

"Oh. Yes, I believe it is." Ellen walked back to the kitchen. The girl certainly isn't shy about asking for what she wants, she thought, removing a mug from the pine cupboard and searching through another cupboard for some tea bags. She wondered how long they were going to have to play host to this girl, who couldn't be more than sixteen. Where was her mother, for God's sake? What had she been thinking, letting her daughter go off camping in the Adirondack Mountains with a young man who clearly didn't have enough sense to come in out of the rain? "Which would you prefer, English Breakfast or Red Rose? I have both."

"Do you have herbal?" Nikki asked.

"Actually, yes. Cranberry and peach. It's my favorite."

The girl shrugged. "Okay."

Ellen dropped the tea bag into the mug of boiling water, thinking that her mother would be horrified. How many times had she told her that the proper way to make tea was to let it steep in the kettle for at least five minutes? Oh, well. Her mother had been dead for almost twenty years, she thought again, and times changed.

Twenty years, Ellen repeated silently, the thought seeping into her skin, like tea in boiling water. Could it really be so long?

"What's taking that tea so long?" Stuart was asking, returning Ellen abruptly to the present tense. "The poor girl's teeth are starting to chatter."

"Can I have milk with that?" Nikki asked.

"With herbal? I really don't think it's necessary . . ."

"I prefer it with milk. Skim, if you have it."

"I'm afraid we only have two-percent."

"Oh." Another shrug. "Okay. And four teaspoons of sugar."

Ellen dutifully added the 2 percent milk and four spoonfuls of sugar to the already sweet herbal tea, then walked back into the main room and handed the sturdy blue mug to Nikki. "Careful. It's hot." She sat down in the burgundy-and-beige overstuffed chair next to her husband and watched the girl lift the mug gingerly to her lips. "I can't imagine what it tastes like. I don't know how you can stand it so sweet."

"That's what my grandmother always says." Nikki took a sip, and then another.

"Your grandmother sounds like a very wise woman."

"She's a witch," Nikki said. Then, "Do you have any cookies or anything?"

What do you mean, she's a witch? Ellen wanted to ask.

"I'm sure we do." Stuart jumped to his feet before Ellen could voice this thought out loud.

"I'm sorry to be such a pest," Nikki said, "but I haven't had anything to eat since lunch, and I'm starving."

"Well, then, I think we can do better than a cookie," Stuart said. "We still have some sandwich meat in the fridge, don't we, Ellen?"

"I think we do," Ellen said, although what she was thinking was, That meat was for our lunch tomorrow. Now I'll have to drive into Bolton Landing tomorrow morning to get some more. Assuming this damn rain stops by then. And how long is this girl going to be here anyway, this girl who speaks so disrespectfully of her elders? Yes, I know we can't very well send her back into that storm, she answered Stuart, although he hadn't spoken. But what if it rains all night? What if it doesn't let up for days? "Maybe you should try calling your parents," Ellen suggested to Nikki. Surely the girl had a cell phone in her canvas bag.

"What for?"

"To tell them you're safe. To let them know where you are, tell them where they can come and get you," she added, trying not to put too noticeable an emphasis on this last point.

Nikki shook her head. "Nah. I'll be all right."

"We have roast beef and a little bit of smoked turkey," Stuart said, his head buried deep inside the fridge.

"I'm kind of like a vegetarian," Nikki told him.

Ellen had to sit on her hands to keep from grabbing the ungrateful girl around the throat.

"How does a grilled cheese sandwich sound?" Stuart asked pleasantly, although the slight twitch at his temples indicated he was losing patience with their unexpected guest as well.

"Sounds good," Nikki said. "I guess you don't get a lot of visitors."

"Not a lot," Ellen agreed. "We're a little off the beaten track."

"You're telling me! You don't get scared, living out here all by yourselves?"

"There are some cottages not too far down the way," Stuart said.

"Far enough. Where's your TV?" Nikki asked suddenly, her eyes once again scanning the large room.

"We've never watched a lot of TV," Ellen told her. Probably another reason the grandchildren showed no inclination to visit.

"We have a radio," Stuart offered as he removed a chunk of cheddar cheese from the fridge and retrieved two slices of bread from the bread box on the counter, then began buttering both sides of the bread. "And we can watch shows on the computer, if we really want."

"I couldn't live without a TV. I'd get so bored," Nikki said. "So, you guys have a gun?"

"Why on earth would we have a gun?" Stuart asked.

"You know, for protection."

"Why would we need protection?" Ellen asked.

"You obviously haven't heard about those people who got murdered last week in the Berkshires," Nikki said matter-of-factly.

The butter knife slipped from Stuart's hand. It ricocheted

off the counter before dropping to the floor, where it bounced along the wide wooden planks before disappearing underneath the stove. "What people?" he and Ellen asked together, their voices overlapping.

"This old couple in the Berkshires," Nikki said. "They lived alone, miles from anyone, just like you guys. Somebody butchered them."

Ellen realized she was holding her breath.

"Hacked them to pieces," Nikki continued. "It was pretty nasty. Police said their place looked like a slaughterhouse. Blood everywhere. It was in all the papers. You didn't read about it?"

"No," Ellen said, glancing at her husband with eyes that said, Get this girl out of my house *now*!

"Terrible thing. Apparently, whoever did it, they almost cut the poor guy's head right off. Here, you want to read about it?" She grabbed her canvas bag from the floor and fished inside it, retrieving a piece of neatly folded newspaper. She unfolded it carefully and handed it to Ellen.

Ellen glanced at the lurid headline, ELDERLY COUPLE SLAUGHTERED IN REMOTE CABIN, and the accompanying grainy, black-and-white photograph of two body bags lying on stretchers, surrounded by grim-faced police. "Why would you be carrying something like this around?" she asked.

Nikki shrugged. "How's that sandwich coming along, Stuart? You need some help?" She pushed herself off the sofa and walked into the kitchen.

What's going on here? Ellen wondered, trying not to overreact. "I think we should call your parents," she heard herself say, barely recognizing the tentativeness in her voice.

"Can't. I'm not getting any reception on my cell, and your phone's dead."

There was a second's silence.

"How do you know our phone is dead?" Ellen asked.

Nikki smiled sweetly. "Oh. Because my boyfriend cut the wires." Then she marched purposefully to the front door and opened it.

A young man filled the doorway. As if on cue, a streak of lightning slashed across the sky, highlighting the coldness in his eyes, the cruel twist of his lips, and the polished blade of the machete in his hand.

"Hi, babe," Nikki said with a giggle as the young man burst inside the cottage. "Meet tomorrow's press clippings."

Stuart lunged toward the drawer containing an assortment of kitchen knives, but despite years of regular exercise, he was easily overpowered by the merciless young man, whose machete ripped across Stuart's wrinkled neck in one fluid, almost graceful, motion. "Ellen," Ellen heard her husband whimper, the word gurgling from his open throat as he collapsed to the floor, the young man on top of him, slashing at his limp form repeatedly, Stuart's once-vibrant eyes rolling dully toward the ceiling.

"Stuart!" Ellen screamed, spinning around in helpless circles, knowing there was nowhere for her to run. She felt the girl at her back, hostile hands in her hair, pulling her head back, exposing her jugular to the executioner's blade. She felt something slash across her throat, watched in horror as a whoosh of blood shot from her body in an impressively wide arc.

Fifty years together, she was thinking. Such a long time. And then suddenly, without warning, it's over. *This is way too violent to last very long,* she thought, recalling her husband's earlier words regarding the storm.

She fell to her knees, saying a silent goodbye to her sons as she watched the room turn upside down. The last thing she saw before one last thrust of the knife closed her eyes once and for all was the warm and loving face of her mother.

ONE

"**B**RIANNE," VALERIE CALLED FROM the foot of the stairs, "how are you doing up there?"

No answer.

"Brianne," she called a second time. "It's almost eleven o'clock. Your father will be here any minute."

Still no answer. Not that Val was surprised. Her daughter rarely answered until at least her third try.

"Brianne," she dutifully obliged, "how are you coming along with the packing?"

The sound of a door opening, agitated footsteps in the upstairs hallway, a blur of shoulder-length brown hair and long, lean legs, the shock of a lacy black thong and matching push-up bra alternating with layers of bare skin, the sight of a pair of balled fists resting with familiar impatience on slender hips. "I'd be coming along fine if you'd stop interrupting me." Brianne's voice tumbled down the green-carpeted steps, almost knocking Valerie over with the force of their casual disdain.

"You're not even dressed," Valerie sputtered. "Your father . . ."

". . . will be late," her daughter said with the kind of rude certainty that only sixteen-year-old girls seemed to possess. "He's always late."

"It's a long drive," Valerie argued. "He said he wanted to get there before dinner."

But Brianne had already disappeared from the top of the stairs. Seconds later, Valerie heard her daughter's bedroom door slam shut. "She's not even dressed," she whispered to the eggshell-colored walls. Which meant she probably hadn't started packing, either. "Great. That's great." Which meant she'd have to entertain her soon-to-be ex-husband and his new fiancée until their daughter was ready. Which just might work to her advantage, she thought, since lately Evan had been hinting that things weren't going all that well with darling Jennifer, and that he might have made the biggest mistake of his life in letting Valerie go.

It wouldn't be the first time he'd made that particular mistake, Val thought, walking to the front door of her modern glass and brick Park Slope home and opening it, looking up and down the fashionable Brooklyn street for signs of Evan's approaching car. He'd left her once before, running off with one of her bridesmaids just days before their wedding. Six weeks later he was back, full of abject apologies, and begging her to give him another chance. The girl meant nothing to him, he'd sworn up and down. It was just a case of raw nerves and cold feet. "I'll never be that stupid again," he'd said.

Except, of course, he was.

"You're all the woman I'll ever need," he'd told her.

Except, of course, she wasn't.

In their eighteen years together, Val suspected at least a dozen affairs. She'd turned a blind eye to all of them, somehow managing to convince herself that he was telling the truth whenever he called to say he'd be working late, or that an urgent meeting had forced him to cancel their scheduled lunch. She'd even insisted it was no big deal to concerned friends when they told her they'd seen Evan at a popular Manhattan restaurant, nuzzling the neck of a young brunette. You know Evan, she'd say with a confident laugh. He's just a big flirt. It doesn't mean anything.

She'd said it so many times, she'd almost come to believe it.

Almost.

And then she'd come home one afternoon, tired and depressed after a day of dealing with her mother, who stubbornly continued to resist dealing with her drinking problem, to find Evan in bed with the young woman he'd recently hired to design a new ad campaign for his string of trendy boutique hotels, the girl's toned and shapely legs lifted high into the air above his broad shoulders, both of them totally oblivious to everything but their own impressive gymnastics, and her blind eye was forced wide open once and for all.

Even then, it had been his choice to leave.

I should hate him, Val thought.

And yet, the awful, unforgivable truth was that she didn't hate him. The awful, even more unforgivable truth was that she still loved him, that she was still praying he'd come to his senses, as he had after running off only days before their wedding, and come back to her.

What's wrong with me?

It's my own damn fault, she'd chastised herself now. I knew

what he was like when I married him. I knew from the first minute I laid eyes on him in the lobby of that small chalet in Switzerland, tanned and fit and holding court in front of a roaring fire, surrounded by adoring ski bunnies, that he was trouble. Exactly the kind of man she'd spent her entire twenty-one years up to that point trying to avoid, a man of grand gestures and small cruelties, as charming as he was unsubtle. She knew the type well, having been raised by just such a man.

"It doesn't mean anything," she'd told her friends, the same words her mother had said to her.

Well, maybe it didn't mean anything to men like her father, men like Evan, Val understood, but it meant the world to the women who loved them.

And, ultimately, where did all that fortitude and forbearance leave them?

It left them nowhere.

They got dumped anyway.

Her friends had breathed a collective sigh of relief at Evan's departure. "He's a moron," her closest friend, Melissa, had pronounced. "He doesn't deserve you," their mutual friend, James, had agreed. "Believe me, you're better off."

Her mother had been too drunk to say anything.

Val could still picture the stricken look on her mother's face after her father had announced he was leaving her for one of his much younger conquests. "It doesn't mean anything. He'll be back," her mother had assured Valerie and her younger sister, Allison. But he never did come back, eventually marrying again and fathering two more children, both girls, daughters to replace the ones he'd so easily abandoned. Meanwhile Val's mother had gradually morphed from a bright, engaging woman into a joyless and bitter old crone whose main source of comfort was a bottle. Is that what Val wanted for Brianne?

"Brianne, do you need some help?" Val called out now, shutting the front door on the oppressive July heat and returning to the foot of the stairs.

Evan was giving her pretty much everything she asked for in the divorce—the house, the white Lexus SUV, substantial alimony, more than generous child support. Within days of moving out of their large home in Brooklyn, he'd settled into Jennifer's small condo in Manhattan, seemingly none the worse for wear.

I should hate him, Val thought again.

Except that you don't stop loving someone you've loved almost half your life just because they treat you badly, she'd discovered, regardless of whether or not you should. Still, it wasn't fair that a woman celebrating her fortieth birthday would be pining over a man who'd openly betrayed her, as if she were a lovesick teenager crying for the one who got away.

Although he wasn't just any man. He was her husband of almost two decades, her husband for another month at least, until their divorce was final, despite the fact he was already engaged to somebody else. He was the love of her life, a man she'd traversed the globe with repeatedly, helicopter skiing with him in the Swiss Alps, white-water rafting with him in Colorado, trekking with him to the top of Mount Kilimanjaro. "The only woman who can keep up with me," he'd said . . . how many times?

"The only woman I've ever really loved."

It had been while they were hiking in the Adirondacks that she had suddenly dropped to her knees and surprised them both by proposing. "What the hell," he'd proclaimed with a laugh. "It'll be an adventure."

An adventure it had certainly been, Val thought now, trying—and failing—not to succumb to nostalgia. Those first few years before Brianne was born had been such a heady rush that it had been relatively easy to overlook Evan's wandering eye, to tell herself that she was imagining things, and when that proved impossible, to hold herself at least partly responsible for his actions, to urge herself to try harder, be more desirable, more available, more . . . all the things she obviously wasn't, all the while reminding herself that nothing mattered except that she was the one he really loved, and that no matter how far or how often he strayed, he would always come back to her.

Evan wasn't her father.

She wasn't her mother.

Yet Val had been devastated to realize that she'd fallen into the same trap as her mother after all, which made her all the more determined to react differently, to not give up, and to fight for her man with every ounce of her being. She hadn't even allowed her pregnancy to slow her down, indulging Evan's combined love of travel and danger by continuing to chase him down the steepest slopes and up the highest peaks. She'd missed her daughter's first birthday so that she could accompany him to the Himalayas, justifying the trip by rationalizing that her husband came first, that a year-old child couldn't differentiate one day from the next, and that they'd celebrate Brianne's birthday when they got home. She even wrote an article about their trip that was subsequently published in the travel section of the *New York Times*.

It was the beginning of an unexpected, and unexpectedly successful, career, a career that came to an abrupt and equally unexpected halt the day Val returned home early from a trying day of dealing with her mother to find Evan in bed dealing with the comely Jennifer.

It's my fault, Val told herself at the time. I got careless, complacent. As the years had progressed and Brianne had grown from infant to toddler to little girl who needed her mother, Val had become more and more loath to leave her. The threat of danger no longer held the same appeal it once had. She was a mother now. She had responsibilities. She even had a career. It wasn't just about her anymore.

Except it had never really been about her. It had been about Evan.

Always about Evan. Even now.

How did that happen?

Val wasn't some stupid little girl. She wasn't a complainer or a crybaby. She was very much in control of every aspect of her life, except one—Evan. And maybe her mother. Okay, so, two aspects of her life. Make that three, she decided now, thinking of Brianne. "Brianne," she shouted up the stairs in a renewed effort to silence the voices in her head, "get a move on."

The phone rang.

Hopefully my mother calling to wish me a happy birthday, Valerie thought, cutting across the front foyer to the stainless-steel kitchen at the back of the house. Was it possible she'd actually remembered? Val shook her head. More likely, she was calling to ask whether Val could drop off a few bottles of Merlot on her way into Manhattan.

The sun had temporarily managed to break through the heavy rain clouds that had been hovering over the area for the better part of the week and was shining through the two-story-high window that took up the kitchen's entire west wall. Val hoped the rain had finally ended. The Adirondacks were undeniably beautiful, but camping wasn't a whole lot of fun in the rain, and unlike Val, Brianne was a reluctant camper at best.

"Why do I have to go on this stupid camping trip anyway?" she'd been whining for weeks. "I'd much rather go into the city with you and your friends, go shopping, see some shows . . ."

"I'd like that, too, sweetheart," Val had said truthfully. It was so rare that Brianne expressed an interest in doing anything with her these days. She was at the age where she considered her mother a necessary nuisance at best, an outright pain in the butt at worst, and it seemed they hardly spent any time together anymore. What time they *did* spend together was filled with pointless arguments that went nowhere and exhausting confrontations that left Val despairing over who this strange and willful creature was and what she'd done with her daughter. Brianne was growing up and away from her so fast that it would have been nice having her along this weekend to celebrate her birthday. They could have used the time to get reacquainted.

"I still don't understand," Brianne was complaining again now, "why I have to go on this dumb trip."

"Because your father wants you to go camping with him and . . ."

". . . the slut?" Brianne asked with a smile, watching for her mother's reaction. "Don't look so shocked. That's what *you* call her."

Val made a silent promise to stop referring to Jennifer in this way. At least when her daughter was within earshot. "Hello," she said now, picking up the phone, on the alert for the telltale slur in her mother's response.

"Hey, you," Evan said instead, the same way he'd been greeting her voice on the phone for almost two decades. Casual, yet intimate. Intimate, yet casual.

Their marriage, in a nutshell.

"Hey," Val echoed, afraid to say more. She pictured her soon-to-be ex-husband sitting behind the wheel of his new black Jaguar, his soft, dark hair falling into his light blue eyes, his full lips curled into an easy smile, one hand on the wheel, the other hand sliding under Jennifer's skirt. "Is there a problem?" she asked, banishing the image.

He laughed. "Am I that transparent?"

It's part of your charm, Val thought, but didn't say. Instead she said, "You're running late."

"About half an hour."

Val immediately doubled his estimate. Half an hour, Evantime, meant at least an hour on anybody else's clock. "Okay. I'll tell Brianne."

"Tell her a problem came up that . . ."

". . . has to be dealt with," Val finished for him, having learned the script by heart years ago.

"I'll be there as soon as I can."

"I'll tell her."

"It'll be strange," he added, his voice trailing off to a whisper.

"What will?"

A sigh. Then, "Being there without you. Not celebrating your birthday together."

Val said nothing. How could she speak when he'd knocked the wind right out of her?

"Val?"

"I'll tell Brianne you'll be here in half an hour." Val hung up the phone before either of them could say another word. What was he trying to tell her?

"What are you doing?" Brianne asked suddenly.

Val spun around. Her daughter was standing in front of her, still wearing only her underwear.

"Is everything all right?" Brianne continued. "Did something happen to Grandma?"

"What? Why on earth would you think that?"

"Because something's obviously wrong. You've been standing there for the last ten minutes with your hand on the phone, not moving."

"I have not."

"Yes, you have. I've been watching you."

Val was about to argue when she glanced at her watch and realized her daughter was right. What did it mean? That Evan now had the power to make time stand still? "Your grandmother's fine."

Brianne shrugged. "So, who called?"

"Your father. He's . . ."

"Not your problem anymore," Brianne reminded her.

"He's running late," Val continued, ignoring her daughter's interruption.

"Let me guess. A problem came up . . ."

". . . that had to be dealt with," mother and daughter said together, then laughed, something they did less and less these days. With each other anyway.

"He'll be here in half an hour," Val offered.

"Yeah, right."

"You should get dressed, just in case."

The doorbell rang. Val's head shot toward the sound. Were James and Melissa actually here already? Could it possibly be Evan? She glanced at her reflection in the black glass of the oven. I should have washed my hair, she thought. I should have put on some makeup.

"You look fine," Brianne said, as if reading her mother's thoughts. "Besides, it's only Sasha."

"Who?"

"Sasha," Brianne repeated, walking out of the kitchen toward the front door, her round bottom a perfect circle sliced into two wondrously high halves.

Just shoot me now, Val thought, following after her. "Who's Sasha?"

"My friend who works at Lululemon. You met her a few weeks ago. Honestly, Mom. You never remember any of my friends."

Val was about to protest when she realized Brianne was right. She couldn't keep track of her daughter's friends, who seemed to change as often as her moods. One day Kelly was her best friend; the next day it was Tanya, then Paulette, then Stacey. And now this Sasha person who worked at Lululemon. Val vaguely remembered a pretty girl with waist-length blond hair waiting on them a few weeks ago when they went shopping in Manhattan for exercise clothes. What was she doing here now? "What's she doing here now?" Val heard herself ask.

"Returning my BlackBerry."

"What's she doing with your BlackBerry?"

"I left it at the store the other day."

"What were you doing in Manhattan?"

"Just trying on some stuff."

"And you left your BlackBerry? Do you know how expensive those things are? You can't be so careless."

"What's the big deal? I left it; Sasha found it. And she very nicely volunteered to bring it over on her way to work." Brianne pulled open the front door, effectively silencing further discussion.

The first thing Val thought when she saw Sasha was that the girl was both prettier and older than she remembered. She was wearing a lime-green T-shirt and a pair of black workout pants that emphasized her considerable curves. At least eighteen, maybe even closer to twenty, Val estimated. Why would she want to be friends with someone who'd just turned sixteen?

"Come on in," Brianne said, ushering her inside. "Wow. Is that your car?" She motioned toward the bright orange 1964 Mustang that was parked so far from the curb it looked as if it had been abandoned in the middle of the road.

"Isn't it great?"

"It's totally great. I love the color."

"Maybe you should park it a little closer to the curb," Val suggested.

"It's fine where it is," Brianne said. Then, with an exaggerated sigh, "You remember my mother."

"Hi, Valerie," Sasha said with a toss of her long blond hair.

Val had to bite down on her lower lip to keep from saying, "I prefer to be called Mrs. Rowe, thank you." She reminded herself that she wouldn't be Mrs. Rowe for much longer, followed by an even more disconcerting thought: Who *would* she be? "Hello, Sasha. Nice to see you again."

"How are you enjoying those outfits you bought? Aren't they the greatest?"

"Yes, they're . . ."

But Sasha had already returned her full attention to Brianne. "Would you just get a load of you," she was saying. "What a great little body you have."

"No," Brianne demurred. "I have to lose five pounds."

"What?" Val said.

"Not to mention I'm getting my nose done."

"You're not doing anything to that nose," Val said with more vehemence than she'd intended. How many times had Melissa cautioned it was best to let such pronouncements slide?

"It's too long. It doesn't go with my face." Brianne motioned to Sasha to follow her up the stairs.

"There is absolutely nothing wrong with your nose!" Val shouted after them.

"It's too long and too wide. I'm getting it fixed," Brianne insisted without turning around.

Val stood motionless at the bottom of the stairs, listening to Brianne's bedroom door close and fighting the urge to burst into tears. Who was putting these stupid ideas in her daughter's head?

Probably the same woman with whom her daughter was going to be spending the next three days, camping in the Adirondacks.

Well, not camping exactly. The Lodge at Shadow Creek was hardly anybody's idea of roughing it. Val sighed, remembering the times she and Evan had stayed there, the morning she'd unexpectedly dropped to her knees and asked for happily ever after.

"It'll be strange," Evan had said earlier, "being there without you. Not celebrating your birthday together."

What was he really saying? That he wished he could go back and undo the things he'd done? That all Val had to do was say the word and he'd tell sweet, slutty Jennifer he was sorry but her time was up? That he loved his wife after all? That she was the only woman he'd ever really loved? That he couldn't imagine going to Shadow Creek without her? That he didn't want to go anywhere without her ever again? That all he wanted was to come back home?

"Yeah, right," Val said, borrowing her daughter's favorite phrase. Then, "God, you're pitiful." Still, she decided as she headed up the stairs, it wouldn't hurt to put on a little makeup and comb her hair before Evan arrived.

TWO

"YOUR MOM'S FUNNY," SASHA was saying as Brianne closed her bedroom door.

"Yeah, a real bundle of laughs." Brianne bounced down on her unmade, queen-size bed, next to her empty overnight bag, causing her flowered comforter to billow up around her, like a parachute.

"This is a neat room." Sasha glanced appreciatively around the large, lavender-and-white bedroom, equipped with the latest in modern technology: a computer on a modern stainless-steel and glass desk that stood in front of the window, a high-definition TV that was mounted on the wall. "Well, maybe *neat* isn't exactly the right word." She laughed, her eyes skirting the pale mauve carpeting that was almost completely covered with discarded clothing, neglected shoes, and the latest celebrity and fashion magazines. Sasha scooped a well-worn copy of *To Kill a Mockingbird* off the floor, opened it, then laughed. "I see somebody owes the school library some serious change."

Damn, Brianne thought. She'd meant to return that book before the end of the school year but had never quite gotten around to it.

"Have you even read it?"

"I saw the movie on TV a while back," Brianne offered, sheepishly.

"That Gregory Peck was pretty hot."

"Kind of old."

Sasha's voice turned sly. "I thought you liked older guys."

Brianne felt her face grow warm and tried to brush away an unwanted blush from her cheeks with the back of her hand. Blushing was for silly young girls. Which she most decidedly was not. Not anymore.

"And speaking of older guys, your dad's really hot," Sasha said, absently checking herself out in the mirror on the wall opposite the bed as she lifted a framed photograph of Brianne's father from the top of the hand-painted dresser.

"I guess."

"Did I tell you he came into the store again the other day?"

"Did he? Cool. I told him you had some great new stuff he should check out."

"He's really fit."

"He works out a lot."

"It shows." Sasha returned the picture to the dresser and picked up a small bottle of Prada perfume. "What's with him and the girlfriend?"

"Fiancée," Brianne corrected.

"Whatever. She was kind of clingy. Hanging all over him, as if to say, 'Back off, bitches. He's mine.' You know the type. She was all 'What do you think of this outfit, honey?' and 'What color do you like better, sweetie-pie?' Pretty nauseating."

"She calls him sweetie-pie?" Brianne fought off the sudden urge to gag.

Sasha shrugged, returning her attention to her reflection and smiling in silent approval. She sniffed at the bottle of perfume, then opened it, dabbing a few drops behind each ear without asking. "Hmm. This smells yummy. Expensive?"

"Probably." Brianne hoped she didn't sound as guilty as she felt. It was her mother's perfume. She'd borrowed it without asking the other night and hadn't gotten around to putting it back.

"Sooo?" Sasha asked, stretching the word out for several syllables. She swiveled around to face Brianne. "We didn't get a chance to talk when you were in the store, and I didn't drive all the way to Brooklyn just to deliver this." She tossed Brianne's BlackBerry toward her. "I'm waiting . . ."

Brianne quickly checked her BlackBerry for messages, smiling to see there were at least ten missed calls. All from him. "What is it you want to know?"

"Everything," Sasha said with a laugh. "Every last little thing."

"Well, actually," Brianne said, giggling along with her, "his thing isn't all that little."

Sasha shrieked with delight. "You tramp. Tell me."

"Brianne," her mother's voice suddenly rang out, bursting through the closed door of her room and ricocheting off the walls. "How's that packing coming along?"

"Oh, for God's sake." Brianne's eyes rolled across a framed poster of a semi-naked Lady Gaga on the wall behind her bed. "Almost done," she called out, carelessly tossing a few sweatshirts into her overnight bag. "I can't wait to move out," she said, knowing this wasn't really true.

"Don't blame you," Sasha said. "I've been more or less on my own since I was fifteen. My parents said I was incorrigible, whatever that means. Sent me to live with my grandparents. In Kansas, of all fucking places. It was so awful, I can't tell you. It was like I was in the army. I ran away at least half a dozen times. But then they threatened to put me in a group home if I didn't 'straighten up and fly right.' Yes, people actually talk that way in Kansas. Anyway," she continued, tossing her blond hair from one shoulder to the other, "I stuck it out until my eighteenth birthday, got my high school diploma, and then ran away for good. Came to New York. Made some friends. Slept on a lot of floors. Found a job, saved my money, got my own place. It's pretty much a hole in the wall, but hey, at least I don't have Mommy Dearest trying to tell me how to live my life."

"You're so lucky." Brianne glanced toward the door, her body bracing for the sound of her mother's footsteps in the hall. What was with her anyway? Did she go out of her way to embarrass her in front of her friends? Although it could be worse, Brianne thought, picturing her grandmother stumbling drunkenly around her small apartment. "She's just paranoid I won't be ready on time and she'll be stuck having to entertain my father."

"I'd be more than happy to entertain him," Sasha volunteered with a laugh.

"Grab a number. The line forms on the right."

"Maybe he just hasn't met the right woman."

"Oh, he found her," Brianne said, the sudden wistfulness in her voice catching her by surprise. "He just didn't keep her."

Sasha's large green eyes opened wide. "Are we talking about your mother now?"

"Oh, God. Let's not." Brianne groaned. "I thought you wanted to hear about the other night."

"You thought absolutely right. So, spill. How was it? Was he any good?"

"He was . . ." Brianne said, disguising an involuntary wince with a loud laugh, ". . . the best."

"Really? Because sometimes when they're that cute, they think all they have to do is lie there and let you do all the work."

"Trust me. He didn't just lie there."

"Okay, so, details, details. How big was it? Did he know how to use it? How long could he go? Did he go down on you first?"

Oh, God, Brianne thought. She hadn't expected this kind of grilling. How much did she trust Sasha? How much could she tell her? She looked toward the door, suddenly hoping for the sound of her mother's voice. Nothing. Naturally, she thought. Always lurking, but never there when you actually needed her. Which wasn't really the truth, she thought in the next breath, irritated nonetheless.

"So, did you give him a blow job?" Sasha prodded.

Brianne felt a sudden surge of pride. "He said it was the best one he'd ever had."

Sasha shook her head dismissively. "They all say that."

Do they? Brianne wondered, wishing she had Sasha's experience.

"What else did he say? Did he tell you he loved you?"

"No." The truth was that after it was over, he hadn't said much at all.

"So where'd you do it? Not here!"

"No. Are you kidding? My mom would have a fit if she knew I was dating anyone like that."

"Well, you're not exactly *dating*," Sasha said, emphasis on the final word. "Oh, God, look at you," she squealed. "You're turning all shades of red. Definitely not your color. I'm sorry. Did I hurt your feelings? I didn't mean to."

"You didn't."

"I was just kidding. You know that. I'm sure he really likes you."

"Has he said anything?" Brianne asked. After all, it had been Sasha who'd introduced them.

"No. I haven't seen him in weeks." Sasha plopped down on Brianne's bed. "So, go on. Tell me. Where'd you go?"

"His place."

"You dirty girl. What'd you tell your mom?"

"That I was spending the night with this friend from school."

"And she believed you?"

"Why wouldn't she?"

"Maybe because you were lying?" Sasha asked in return.

"I can be pretty convincing."

"I bet you can. I bet you're just full of surprises."

"Maybe." Another surge of unexpected pride.

"It's always the ones who look so innocent who are the ones you have to watch out for."

"Mothers are easy to fool," Brianne said.

"Not mine," Sasha countered. "She always saw right through me. My grandmother, too. 'Who do you think you're kidding?' she used to say. Then she'd shake her finger in my face. Made me want to bite it off. I thought grandmothers were supposed to be nice. You know, bake you cookies and spoil you with presents."

"My grandmother's an alcoholic," Brianne said.

Sasha absorbed this latest tidbit without comment. "So, how many times did you do it?"

Brianne felt a frown tugging at her lips. She really didn't want to talk about this anymore. "I kind of lost count. Five . . . six, maybe."

"Six times? Are you kidding me? Who can go six times?"

"Maybe it was only four," Brianne quickly backtracked.

Sasha laughed. "Stop kidding around. How many times? Seriously."

"Three," Brianne lied, pretending to be picking some lint off the comforter, hoping Sasha hadn't inherited her mother's and grandmother's talent for ferreting out falsehoods. "It was three times."

"Wow. Still pretty impressive. Aren't you sore?"

"A little." Actually a lot, Brianne thought, although it had only been twice, and the first time was so quick, she wasn't sure it really counted.

"Are you going to see him again?"

"Of course."

"When?"

"Hopefully this weekend."

"I thought you were going hiking in the Adirondacks this weekend with Daddy."

"That's the plan."

"And plans have a way of changing," Sasha stated more than asked.

"Especially where my father is concerned," Brianne conceded. The phone beside her bed rang. Brianne reached over and picked it up before it could ring a second time. "Hello?"

"Hi," the voice said. Low. Deep. Dangerous.

Like he was, Brianne thought. "Hi," she said, feeling her heartbeat quicken and lowering her voice to a whisper.

"Is it him?" Sasha asked, her eyes wide with excitement.

Brianne nodded, wishing now that Sasha hadn't come over.

"How are you?" he asked. "I've been texting you like crazy . . ."

"I left my BlackBerry at Lululemon. Sasha just brought it back. She's here now."

"Good old Sasha. Tell her, 'hi.'"

"He says 'hi,'" Brianne said, dutifully.

"Hi, yourself, stud."

"What'd she say?"

"She said 'hi,'" Brianne told him, leaving off the last word and pushing herself off the bed. She crossed to the window, staring down at Sasha's bright orange Mustang. A silver sports car suddenly turned the corner onto the street and came to a stop halfway down the block. Brianne leaned her forehead against the glass, trying to make out the person behind the wheel.

"How are you doing?" he asked.

"Good."

"You're sure?"

"Yes."

"Thinking about the other night?"

"Yes."

"It was pretty intense."

"Yes."

"So, are we on for this weekend?" he asked.

It was at that moment Brianne heard a click on the line and realized someone had picked up the extension. "Just a minute," she warned. "Hello? Hello? Mom? Is that you?"

"Sorry," Val answered immediately. "I thought it might be your grandmother."

"I've got to go. Text me later," Brianne said, hanging up the phone in a panic. How long had her mother been listening? How much had she heard? "Shit."

Sasha was instantly on her feet. "Your mother was listening in on the extension? Shit."

"What did I say? What did I say?"

"Nothing," Sasha told her. "I swear. *Good. Yes. Yes. Yes.* Honestly. It was very frustrating. You'd make a great secret agent."

"Shit," Brianne said again, hearing her mother's footsteps approaching her bedroom door.

"Brianne," her mother said, knocking gently. "Can I come in?" She opened the door before Brianne had time to object.

"I'm sorry. I really didn't mean to eavesdrop," her mother apologized immediately. "I . . ."

". . . thought it was Grandma. It's okay."

"Who was it?"

"Just some guy I know from school."

"I thought I heard him say something about the weekend . . . My God, would you look at this room," Val exclaimed. "How can you bring anybody in here? It's a mess. And you haven't finished packing. You're still in your underwear." She looked helplessly around the room, her eyes moving from the bed to the floor to the dresser. "Is that my perfume?"

"I'm going to be late for work," Sasha interjected quickly, already halfway to the door. "Don't worry. I can find my own way out. Be sure to call me as soon as you get back. Bye, Valerie. Nice seeing you again." She blew Brianne a kiss, then left the room.

"Aren't you embarrassed to bring friends up here?" Val was asking as Brianne watched from the window while Sasha climbed into the front seat of her orange Mustang and sped past the silver sports car idling down the street.

"They don't care about stuff like that."

"There are clothes all over the floor. This nice blouse," Val said, bending down to scoop it up. "The one you *had* to have. The one you begged me to buy. And these shoes . . ."

"Okay, okay, I get it. I'm a slob. I'll clean it up."

"And these jeans. These three-hundred-dollar designer jeans."

"I was going to pack those."

"And this T-shirt . . ." Val stopped suddenly, turned the T-shirt over in her hands, the color quickly draining from her cheeks. "My God, what happened to this shirt?"

"What are you talking about? Nothing happened."

"What is this? Is this blood?"

Brianne tried grabbing the once white T-shirt from her mother's hands. "Of course not. Don't be ridiculous."

"It looks like blood," her mother said, sniffing at the large stains. "My God, what did you do? Did you fall? Did you cut yourself?"

"No." Brianne spun around. "See? No cuts. No bruises. I'm fine. Don't be crazy. It's not blood."

"Then what is it?"

"I don't know. I must have brushed up against something. Wet paint, maybe."

"Brianne . . ."

"Did you know you have a visitor?" Brianne looked back out the window, hoping to distract her mother.

"What? Who?" Valerie approached the window, stared down at the street below.

Brianne used the moment to snatch the T-shirt from her mother's hands. How could she have been so stupid to leave it lying around? First her BlackBerry. Now this. Her mother was right. She couldn't afford to be so careless. "The silver sports car. Halfway down the street." She watched her mother's shoulders slump. "Is that who I think it is?"

"Shit."

"What are we going to do?"

"*You* are going to get dressed and then finish . . . *start* . . . packing," Valerie said, checking the mirror over the dresser to make sure she'd put her lipstick on straight. "I'm going to find out what the hell is going on."

THREE

THIS DAY IS GOING downhill faster than a skier in Aspen, Valerie was thinking as she ran down her front steps toward the street, the July heat instantly closing around her. Damn this humidity, she thought, taking a slow, painful breath as she approached the car door and knocked on the window.

The driver peered over at Val from behind the glass, then smiled. The smile was one of trepidation rather than joy, more "Oh, God, what happens now?" than "It's so nice to see you." Perfectly normal under the circumstances, Val thought. Although nothing was really normal about these circumstances.

"You don't have to wait out here," she said without any preamble as the window slowly lowered.

"That's all right," came the soft reply. "I have the air-conditioning on."

"Good way to run down the battery."

"Really, I'm fine. Thank you."

"I take it Evan asked you to meet him here," Val stated.

"He said he was running a bit late and it would save time if I could just meet him at your place."

Val nodded. "Well, then. You might as well come inside. It might be a while."

"I'm sure he'll be here any minute."

Val gave the young woman a look that said, Are you kidding me?

Her soon-to-be ex-husband's new fiancée sighed deeply. The sigh said, You're probably right. "You really don't have to do this."

"I know," Val agreed. Why *am* I doing this? she asked herself as Jennifer opened the car door, long bare legs extending into the open air, siren-red toenails peeking out from the open toes of her ridiculously high platform sandals. The last time I saw those legs they were wrapped around my husband's neck, Val thought. "I believe you know the way," she couldn't resist adding as she extended her right arm toward the glass and stone house down the street.

Val wiped the sweat from her upper lip with the backs of her fingers, noting that in spite of the heat and humidity, Jennifer looked as fresh and as lovely in her yellow T-shirt and white shorts as the proverbial daisy. She found herself studying her replacement as the young woman walked ahead. Why can't I walk like that? she wondered, ruing that she'd never mastered the art of the subtle wiggle. Or the subtle anything, she conceded.

"You don't just walk," her friend Melissa had once told her. "You *stride*."

"I think 'lope' is a better description," her friend James had quickly corrected.

"I lope?"

"Like a newborn colt," James said.

"I walk like a horse?"

"It's very charming," Melissa had assured her.

Charming. Yeah, right, Val thought now, already regretting her act of impetuous altruism as she watched Jennifer gracefully ascend the half-dozen concrete steps to her front door. How does she even move in those sky-high platforms? she wondered, picturing Jennifer tripping over a large boulder in the Adirondacks and tumbling into Shadow Creek. The image made her smile, and then frown. So much for altruism, she thought.

Jennifer opened the front door, then stepped inside the air-conditioned house, stopping just inside the gray-and-gold-flecked marble foyer.

Val motioned toward the living room to her left. "Make yourself at home," she said, getting more than a slight degree of satisfaction when she saw Jennifer wince.

"Maybe I should wait outside," Jennifer said, not moving.

"Don't be silly. I'm not going to bite you."

Jennifer nodded, although she looked far from convinced.

"Would you like some iced tea?"

"No, thank you."

"You're sure? I'm going to have some."

"Why are you being so nice to me?" Jennifer asked.

Val shrugged. Why *was* she being so nice? "It's just a cold glass of tea. Take it or leave it."

"Well, okay. Iced tea sounds great. If you're sure it's no trouble."

"No trouble at all." Val led the wary young woman into her recently refurnished living room, directing her toward the new purple velvet sofa in front of the leaded front window. "As you can see, I've made some changes since your last visit." Her tone was casual, even friendly. Val could see that Jennifer didn't know whether to relax or run for the hills. Well, what do you know? she thought. Maybe watching Jennifer squirm was the real reason she'd invited the young woman into her home. This might actually be fun, she decided. "Be right back."

Brianne was waiting for her in the kitchen. "What are you doing?" she asked.

"Getting our guest some iced tea."

"Are you crazy?"

"Probably. Are you packed?"

Brianne's shoulders slumped even as her eyes rolled toward the ceiling. "What are you trying to do? Win points with Dad?"

"Don't be ridiculous." Is that what I'm doing? Val wondered.

"I'm not the one who's being ridiculous," Brianne said before stomping out of the room.

"And get dressed," Val called after her. Now where was I? she asked silently. "Ah, yes. Getting the lovely Jennifer some iced tea."

Jennifer was indeed lovely, Val was forced to admit. Not slutty at all. She was tall and slender, with large breasts, slim hips, and an enviably narrow waist. Her dark blond hair fell to her shoulders in a series of expensively layered waves around her heart-shaped face. Her eyes were big and blue, her cheekbones high and pronounced, her lips seductively full. And her legs went on forever.

Right to the ceiling, Val thought, once more picturing those legs on either side of her husband's head.

"Shit," she whispered, banishing the image while trying to avoid her own reflection in the dark glass of her microwave oven. I used to look like that. At least a little, she amended, as she removed two glasses from a nearby cupboard and filled them with iced tea. At five feet, seven inches, she was relatively tall, although probably two inches shorter than Jennifer, and she'd always been slim, although she had maybe ten pounds on the younger woman, who had the added advantage of being ten years her junior. They shared roughly the same hair color, although Val's was darker and had more curl. Nor were her eyes as big or as blue. And her mouth failed to form the same naturally seductive pout when at rest. Val's lips were thinner, more ordinary. "Shit," she said again, slightly louder this time. She tucked her green-and-white-striped blouse into her white capris and kicked off her strictly utilitarian white flats, revealing unadorned toenails in need of a trim. No siren-red nail polish for her. She couldn't even remember the last time she'd had a pedicure.

That was about to change. Melissa had suggested the possibility of a spa day as a way of capping off their three-day birthday sojourn in the city. Val had initially balked at the idea of spending an entire day being massaged, pampered, and painted when she could be out running around Madison Avenue, traipsing from the MoMA to the Met, trying to squeeze in just one more gallery, one more interesting shop. She'd never been someone who enjoyed sitting still.

"The only woman who can keep up with me," Evan had said, sounding both pleased and proud.

And yet he'd left her for a young woman who clearly had no problems with sitting still no matter where she was, be it in a sports car idling on the street or on the new purple velvet sofa of her fiancé's soon-to-be former wife.

Impressive in its own right, Val decided, returning to the living room with a glass of iced tea in each hand. "I forgot to ask whether you wanted sugar."

"No, thanks. I don't take sugar."

"Sweet enough, are you?"

Another wince from Jennifer that made Val smile. She handed Jennifer the glass of iced tea, then sat down in one of two beige linen tub chairs in front of the sofa.

"I like what you've done with the room," Jennifer offered, taking a sip of her tea and allowing her gaze to flit aimlessly about, careful to avoid looking directly at Val.

"I'm so glad you approve," Val said before she could stop herself. Then, "Sorry. That just slipped out."

"It's all right. I don't blame you for hating me."

"I don't hate you." Val was surprised to realize this was true.

"We honestly never meant to hurt you," Jennifer offered weakly, focusing her attention on the multicolored swirls of the silk and wool rug that covered the hardwood floor.

"It just never occurred to you that having sex with my husband in my very own bed, which I've also replaced, by the way, might hurt my feelings," Val stated, not about to let Jennifer off the hook with something as mundane as a simple apology, especially one as blatantly insincere as this one.

Maybe she really *did* hate her.

Jennifer's gaze shifted guiltily to her lap. She sipped at her tea, said nothing.

"Sorry," Val said again, thinking that one insincere apology deserved another. "This is awkward enough. I shouldn't have said that."

"No, you're right. What we did was thoughtless."

It was Val's turn to fall silent. "Okay, then," she said after a pause of several seconds. "Moving right along . . . Those might not be the best shoes for hiking." She pointed toward Jennifer's feet.

Jennifer laughed, perhaps a bit too loudly. "Oh, I have running shoes in my suitcase. And Evan bought me a pair of hiking boots." She stopped, cleared her throat, took another sip of iced tea.

Val flinched at the sound of her husband's name on the other woman's lips. "Is this your first trip to the Adirondacks?"

"Believe it or not, it is, yes."

"Oh, I believe it."

"I've never really been into hiking. Or any sports, for that matter. Except for tennis. I'm pretty good at tennis."

Val nodded. What was Evan doing with this girl? she wondered. He hated tennis. It was the one sport he couldn't abide. "Tennis is for cowards," he used to say.

"Evan was never much of a tennis player," Val said now. "He's more into extreme sports."

"Tell me about it," Jennifer said with a laugh, clearly relieved they'd found something to agree on. "He scares the hell out of me sometimes. The risks he takes. Bungee jumping, mountain climbing, helicopter skiing. Well . . . you know."

"Yes, I do."

"You like those things, too, I understand."

"Yes, I do," Val said again. Or, at least, I *did,* she added silently.

"I just can't imagine jumping out of a helicopter and skiing down the side of a mountain."

Is she joking? Val wondered. "Well, you don't actually jump out of the helicopter with your skis on," she clarified.

"You don't?"

"No. The helicopter drops you off at the top of the mountain, and then you ski down."

"Oh, that's great. I'm so relieved," Jennifer said, without a trace of self-consciousness. "I mean, it's still scary, but not quite so bad. Obviously I'm not a skier."

"Obviously."

"I don't like being cold."

"Perfectly reasonable."

"I don't like anything where I'm not in control of my feet."

Val immediately pictured Jennifer's feet squirming high above her husband's head.

"I broke my wrist twice ice-skating when I was a kid," Jennifer babbled nervously. "Roller-skating is just as bad. I dislocated my shoulder the first time I tried it. And just the thought of water-skiing makes me a nervous wreck. I'm not much of a swimmer."

Again Val pictured Jennifer tumbling over a rock formation and falling into Shadow Creek.

Going down once . . . twice . . . "It sounds like you should stick to tennis," she said before Jennifer could take her final bow.

"I think you're right. And Evan's been taking lessons."

"He has?"

"He's picked it up very quickly."

"He picks most things up very quickly," Val said with a smile. She could tell by the slight widening of Jennifer's eyes and the smile that froze on her lips that the poor woman didn't know quite how to take this latest barb. "I understand you met my husband through work," Val continued sweetly, as if she were interviewing a potential nanny.

"I didn't know he was married when we met," Jennifer explained quickly.

"The gold band on his left hand wasn't enough of a clue?"

"He wasn't wearing one."

"Really?" Had Evan made a practice of removing his wedding ring before he got to the office?

Jennifer nodded. "We'd been working on a campaign for his new hotel . . ."

"*When luxury beckons . . .*" Val said, remembering an early mock-up of the brochure.

"Yes. I believe that was one of the slogans we discarded."

"Among other things."

Jennifer took another sip of her iced tea, then quickly lowered the glass to her lap, as if she were beginning to suspect it contained poison.

"Go on," Val prompted. She'd never actually heard the story before, in all its inglorious detail.

"We'd been working late," Jennifer obliged her by continuing, "and Evan suggested we break for dinner."

"And you were hungry." It was Val's turn to study the carpet at her feet.

"Over dinner he told me he was very attracted to me and that it might be a problem with us working so closely together. I told him I was attracted to him, too, so what problem could there be? That's when he told me he was married. He said he wanted everything to be honest and aboveboard."

"Except where I was concerned, of course," Val qualified.

"Maybe we shouldn't be talking about this," Jennifer demurred, looking anxiously over her shoulder toward the front window, obviously praying for the sight of Evan's Jaguar.

"Maybe not," Val agreed. Interesting as the story was, she already knew how it ended.

And it wasn't with "They all lived happily ever after."

At least, as far as she was concerned.

Except . . .

"It'll be strange," Evan had said earlier. "Being there without you."

"Someone's pulling into your driveway," Jennifer said now.

Val jumped to her feet. "Evan?"

"No. Two people. A man and a woman."

Melissa and James, Val realized, marching from the living room. She should have called them, told them Evan was going to be late. "Hi," she said, opening the front door to her two best and—if she was being honest—*only* friends. She'd pretty much given up on the idea of girlfriends after Evan had run off with one of her bridesmaids. But then, Melissa had never posed any kind of threat, and James . . . well, James was *James*.

"You ready to party, birthday girl?" Melissa asked, her natural exuberance filling the small foyer. Melissa was forty-six but seemed curiously both older and younger than her years, an old soul brimming with childlike enthusiasm. She stood only five feet, two inches and weighed all of ninety-five pounds, but she was a powerhouse, full of energy and good humor. She wore her straight black hair in a blunt cut to her chin, with thick bangs that completely covered her forehead and extended over the tops of her oversized black square-framed glasses. Her small eyes were equally dark; her lips were never without their trademark coral lipstick. When the travel agency she'd founded and operated for fifteen years had fallen on hard times, she hadn't wasted any time on tears. She'd simply closed up shop and started a new business, turning her long-standing hobby of collecting vintage costume jewelry into a booming business. Her pieces were often showcased in the pages of *Vogue* and other fashion magazines and were regularly photographed gracing the emaciated bodies of celebrities and socialites on both coasts.

It was this no-nonsense, no-holds-barred approach to life that had drawn Val to her. Melissa was also an inveterate gatherer, amassing enviable collections of everything from antique tin toys to Depression-era glass dishes. Her house in Westchester was filled to bursting with once-popular china dolls, old cameras, and ancient, cast-iron piggy banks. She also collected husbands, having been married and divorced three times and widowed once. Ever since her last "and best" husband had succumbed to cancer three years earlier, Melissa had sworn to wear nothing but black.

"You only wear black anyway," James had pointed out.

Curiously, for a woman who'd never had any children of her own, Melissa was surprisingly maternal, another quality that had no doubt attracted Val, who still ached for the protective embrace of her mother's arms, for the healing kiss that made everything "all better."

James, on the other hand, was the proverbial Peter Pan, the little boy who never grew up. He favored creamy pastels and had never been married. "Even if I weren't gay, I wouldn't get married," he'd insisted many times over the years. James was the same height as Valerie and the same weight as Melissa, or so he claimed. He lived on coffee, fruit, and raw fish. His hair was a shock of carrot-orange spikes, although admittedly there weren't as many spikes as there used to be. A former dancer who'd been a staple in Broadway musicals ever since he turned eighteen, he'd retired when he broke his ankle at the age of thirty-five. For the last several years, he'd been working for Melissa, scouting for great vintage brooches, bracelets, and necklaces at various antique and collectible shows up and down the east coast.

Val had met Melissa when she and Evan used her travel agency to book a trip to the Grand Canyon about a dozen years earlier. She'd met James through Melissa, who'd grown up on the same street as James and used to babysit him when he was a child. Val credited the two of them with getting her through the last year with her sanity largely intact.

"What's wrong?" James asked as soon as he saw Val's face.

"Nothing."

"Let me guess," Melissa said, already walking toward the living room. "Evan's running a bit late. Oh, my God," she said, stopping in the doorway, staring at the young woman sitting in the middle of the purple velvet couch. "Tell me that's not who I think it is." Her jeweled fingers quickly covered her coral-colored lips.

"Is that 'the Slut'?" James whispered, resting his chin on Val's shoulder in order to muffle the sound of his words.

"Don't call her that," Brianne said, approaching the trio from behind and pushing past them into the living room.

Val was relieved, both for her daughter's sudden appearance and the fact she was wearing clothes.

"Hi, Jen," Brianne said, joining the young woman on the sofa.

Jennifer's relief was so palpable, she looked as if she might burst into tears. "Your dad's running a little late."

"So I gather. Love your shoes."

"Thank you. Those jeans are fabulous."

Val found her jaw tightening at the easy camaraderie that existed between her daughter and her husband's fiancée. We used to have that, she thought, feeling Brianne slip even farther from her reach. "These are my friends, Melissa and James," she said, forcing the words from her mouth. "This is Jennifer, Evan's . . ."

"We know," James said. "Those are fabulous shoes. Louboutins?"

"Yes," Jennifer said. "I'm impressed."

"James is a shoe freak." Brianne laughed. "You're such a cliché," she told him, managing to make the barb sound endearing.

"Right back at you," James said.

The phone rang.

"That's probably my mother," Val said, quickly excusing herself from the room.

"Mom says you have tickets for *Wicked* tomorrow night," she heard Brianne say on her way to the kitchen. "Haven't you already seen it, like, thirteen times?"

"Eighteen," James was saying as Val picked up the phone. "I'm going for lucky number twenty-one."

"A total cliché." Brianne's laugh filled the house.

"Hello?" Val said.

"Hey, you," said Evan.

Two minutes later, Val returned to the living room. "Brace yourself, everyone," she said. "There's been a change of plans."

FOUR

"ARE WE THERE YET?" Brianne asked from the front passenger seat of Val's crowded SUV some three and a half hours later.

"Still a ways to go," Val said.

"How much longer?"

"At least an hour. Maybe more."

"Shit." Brianne pulled her BlackBerry out of her oversized leather purse.

"Who are you texting now?" her mother asked.

"Sasha."

"You just saw her."

"So?"

Val gripped the steering wheel, watching her knuckles grow white. This wasn't going quite the way she'd expected when she'd agreed—against her better judgment—to act as chauf-feur for her daughter and her husband's fiancée, then somehow managed to cajole Melissa and James into postponing their trip into Manhattan in order to drive to the Adirondacks and the Inn at Shadow Creek.

First of all, she'd forgotten what a long trip it was—five hours of twisting and congested highway—and while it was true she'd driven up here dozens of times and probably knew the way blindfolded, all previous trips had been with Evan, and he'd always insisted on doing the lion's share of the driving.

Second, while it was also true that Jennifer's car was too small to hold Evan's daughter, his fiancée, and their combined luggage, they could have simply postponed their trip until Evan's business was completed, as Jennifer had suggested repeatedly. It hadn't really been necessary for Val to put her own plans on hold to accommodate her soon-to-be ex. So why had she?

The answer was sitting in the seat beside her, pointedly ignoring her.

Silly me, Val acknowledged, reluctantly dismissing her erst-while fantasies of mother-daughter bonding. Brianne had said barely two words to her since they'd left Brooklyn, spending almost all her time on that damn BlackBerry. Had Val really thought she might be able to mitigate Jennifer's influence on her daughter, at least a little, by going head-to-head with her? *She may be younger and prettier, but I'm smarter and a much better driver.* Was she seeking to remind the other woman that even though she might have taken her place in Evan's heart, this would never be the case with his only child? *I'm still Bri-anne's mother. No one can take that away from me.*

"I still can't believe we're doing this," James remarked from

the backseat, glancing out his side window at the passing pan-
orama of woodlands, meadows, and streams, as the car continued along Route 9N toward Prospect Mountain.

"What are you complaining about now?" Melissa asked from
the other side of the car. "Can't you just enjoy the scenery?"

"The only scenery I like is on a Broadway stage."

"So picture Julie Andrews coming up over that ridge singing 'The hills are alive . . .'"

"Please . . . that was in the movie. It was Mary Martin who
originated the role on Broadway. Julie, sweet though she may
be, doesn't compare to Mary."

"That had to be, what, fifty years ago?" Melissa reminded
him. "You weren't even born then."

"So what? My grandmother attended the premiere, and she
told me it was spectacular."

"It's spectacular here, too, if you'd give it a chance," Val
interrupted, again glancing over at Brianne. "Nature at its most
breathtaking."

"I hate nature," James said. "It makes me nervous."

Brianne laughed.

So, she *is* listening, Val thought.

"You laugh, but there's something very unnatural about it,"
James said. Now everybody laughed.

Everyone except Jennifer.

What does she think of all this? Val wondered, deciding that
the poor woman probably didn't know what hit her. She looks
as if she's about to burst into tears, Val thought, almost feeling
sorry for her. Maybe that was the real reason she'd agreed to act
as chauffeur—to stick it to her husband's young lover.

It couldn't have escaped Jennifer's radar that it was Val
whom Evan had called, and not her, that he hadn't even bothered to check with her first, and that he'd left it to Val to spring

the change in plans on her as a fait accompli. What must she be thinking?

"Look at that gorgeous waterfall," Melissa suddenly exclaimed. "You don't get that in Manhattan."

"And poison ivy and mosquitoes. You don't get those in Manhattan, either," James said.

"Oh, my God. Is that a real deer?" Brianne asked with surprising enthusiasm, pointing one out at the side of the road.

Val resisted the impulse to reach over and hug her daughter.

"Yuck," James said. "Deer ticks. Hello? Lyme disease, anyone? Please tell me this isn't happening."

My sentiments exactly, thought Jennifer from her cramped position in the backseat between James and Melissa. She was still trying to figure out how what had originally been intended as a weekend getaway with her fiancé and his daughter, designed for the express purpose of bringing them closer together, had turned into an alarming free-for-all involving her fiancé's about-to-be ex-wife and her two decidedly weird friends.

It doesn't bode well, she thought in her father's voice.

"It doesn't bode well," he'd told her this morning when she'd dropped by his apartment in Queens to tell him she was going away for a three-day weekend with her fiancé and his daughter.

She never should have told her father that Evan was still legally married, although she really hadn't given the matter serious thought. She certainly hadn't been expecting a response. They'd been sitting in the hot, musty stillness of his run-down, third-floor apartment for what felt like hours but was likely closer to fifteen minutes at most. Her father disliked both noise and light, so the one-bedroom apartment was dark and the air conditioner that was jammed into a small front window turned off, despite the oppressive summer heat. Jennifer had insisted on opening a window, but the results were negligible. There was no breeze, no relief. Her father didn't seem to notice or care. If he did, he didn't let on. He hadn't spoken more than a dozen sentences since her arrival.

"Cameron and Andrew got a new car," he'd said, offering up his dry cheek to be kissed, his own lips remaining stubbornly closed.

"So I hear. Have you seen it?"

Her father returned to the shabby, rust-colored wing chair in the corner of the living room, across from the small TV that was always on and tuned to Fox News. His white shirt was spotted with old food stains, as was his maroon-colored tie. Her father always insisted on wearing a tie. As a child, Jennifer had sometimes wondered if he wore one to bed. Even after he'd been forced to retire from his job as manager for a canned goods supply company, he'd continued to wear a tie every day. At first it made him look dignified. Now it made him look pathetic.

Jennifer noted that the fly of his heavy wool trousers was only halfway done up. She didn't want to contemplate the cause of the dark stains to either side of the zipper.

The question went unanswered, her father's attention captured by the televised image of two body bags being removed from a remote cabin in the woods, surrounded by a cadre of solemn-faced police officers. "A few new details emerging on those grisly murders in the Berkshires," an accompanying voice announced, with no small degree of enthusiasm.

Jennifer walked over to the television and lowered the volume. Her father stared vacantly into space, said nothing.

"Cameron and Andrew got a new car," he remarked a few minutes later.

"Good for them. I don't suppose they've stopped by to take you for a ride in that new car, have they?"

"Cameron's very busy."

"Really? Doing what?" Having her hair straightened? Having her teeth whitened? Shopping for her fall wardrobe? Jennifer thought, but refrained from saying. "Did you have breakfast, Dad? Do you want some coffee or some toast?"

Her father shook his head. "Cameron and Andrew got a new car," he said moments later.

"Well, since you asked," Jennifer said, walking toward the window and gulping at the stale air, staring down at the old-fashioned, black wrought-iron fences lining the front yards of the small houses across the street, "my job is going great. I got a promotion and a new title. I'm now officially an account supervisor, which means I'll be getting a raise. Not a big one, mind you. But still, every bit helps. I know," she said before her father could interrupt. "Cameron and Andrew got a new car."

Her father smiled, his first smile since she'd come over.

"So did I, incidentally. That little silver number about two doors down. See?" She pointed toward it. Her father made no move to get out of his chair. "Evan knows this guy who owns a dealership. He got me this really great deal. Anyway," Jennifer continued when her father failed to respond, "I just stopped by to tell you that I'm going away for a few days. To the Adirondacks with Evan and his daughter. Dad, have you heard anything I've said?"

Her father stared at her blankly.

"I said I'm going to the Adirondacks with Evan and his daughter."

"The Adirondacks, of course."

"Evan is my fiancé. You remember I told you about Evan?"

"Cameron has a lovely diamond ring," he added, pointedly glancing at the empty third finger of Jennifer's left hand.

"Yes, she does." And a lovely wedding band and a lovely husband and two lovely children and an even lovelier nanny to look after them because we all know how busy lovely Cameron is. "I'm sure Evan will get me a ring after his divorce is final."

"His divorce?"

"It'll be final next month."

"He has a wife?"

"Not anymore. He left her . . ."

"For you?"

It was Jennifer's turn to say nothing.

Now her father looked angry. He began to shake his head and tap his feet on the scratched hardwood floor, a sure sign he was becoming agitated. "It doesn't bode well," he said, beginning to rock back and forth in his chair. "If he cheated on his wife, he'll cheat on you. I'm a man. I know."

Except what did her father know anymore? Jennifer wondered now. Early onset Alzheimer's had robbed him of most of his faculties, and in those increasingly rare moments when he was lucid these days, his thoughts were always focused on Cameron.

Her sister. His firstborn.

His clear favorite.

Even though she rarely visited. Even though it was Jennifer who'd borne the brunt of looking after him since their mother had died two years earlier.

"I don't know if I can just drop everything and drive into Queens just because you've decided to go on a 'dirty week-end,'" Cameron had said on the phone the other night.

"It's hardly a 'dirty weekend.' Evan's daughter will be with us."

"Whatever."

"Look, it's only for three days."

"Right. Dad will be fine for three days."

"Not if he forgets to eat."

"He won't forget to eat."

"He forgets everything else."

"You're being very dramatic," Cameron had proclaimed as Jennifer pictured her older sister tucking her newly straightened blond hair behind her right ear.

"And you're being very selfish," Jennifer shot back.

"I'm not the one who's being selfish here."

"What? You're saying *I'm* being selfish?"

"I don't know. Which one of us is married with two children under the age of four? Which one of us has a great job in the city and drives a new sports car?"

"It's two years old, I'm just leasing it, and Evan is friends with the man who owns the dealership."

"Which reminds me, which one of us was selfish enough to go after a married man with absolutely no thought to his existing family?"

"Whoa. That was really a low blow."

"I'm just saying . . ."

"And I'm just asking . . ."

"I know what you're asking. You don't have to say it again."

"And?"

"I'll phone him every day."

"Not good enough."

"I don't understand why not."

"And I don't understand the problem," Jennifer said, trying not to sound as exasperated as she felt. Why did everything always have to be such a big deal? Why couldn't at least one thing in her life be easy?

"It's just hard for me," Cameron said after a lengthy pause during which Jennifer wondered if she'd hung up.

"What is?"

"Seeing him like this."

"What—you think I like it?"

"I think you're just better at dealing with it," Cameron said, paying her the first compliment Jennifer could ever remember getting from her sister. "I guess I'm just more sensitive than you are," she added, immediately taking it back.

"Okay, listen. We're going around in circles," Jennifer said. "The fact is that I'm going away for three days and our father will be alone. It's hot; he refuses to use the air conditioner; he may or may not remember to eat. Somebody has to check in on him. In person."

"Fine. I'll see what I can do."

"Fine," Jennifer conceded, deciding it was the best she could hope for.

Fine, she thought now, banning further thoughts of her sister from her mind with a shake of her head.

"Careful with that," James warned, brushing several strands of Jennifer's hair away from his face with a dramatic flick of his hand. "That hair's a lethal weapon."

"Sorry."

"And speaking of lethal," James said, lowering his voice to achieve proper dramatic effect, "can you turn the radio up a bit?"

"More details with regard to the shocking murders in the Berkshires last week," a male voice was announcing.

"Those poor people," Melissa said. "Can you imagine getting to be almost ninety, only to be murdered?"

"Police are refusing to confirm that one of the weapons used to slay Marie and William Carteris was the same weapon used to kill another elderly couple, Arlene and Frank Wall, in their cottage in Plainfield the previous week. They also insist there is nothing to connect these murders to that of Brian Grierson, a hiker whose dismembered torso was discovered in a shallow grave several miles from the Walls' cottage a few days later," the announcer continued.

"Hello? Is anybody hearing this?" James asked. "Mountains, murders, dismemberment. What are we doing here, people?"

"This is the Adirondacks, not the Berkshires," Val reminded him with a chuckle.

"Same difference."

"Different states."

"*Neighboring* states," James pointed out. "Look. The murders all took place in isolated spots in the middle of nowhere, that's all I'm saying."

"The Lodge at Shadow Creek is hardly the middle of nowhere," Jennifer said, irritation clinging to each word. What am I doing with these people? she wondered again. Why did I agree to spend almost five hours in a car with Evan's ex-wife and her crazy friends, having to listen to talk about murder and dismemberment? Why didn't I just say no?

But even as she was asking herself these questions, she'd already conceded the answer.

She was here for the same reason Valerie was.

Different women, same rationale.

The rationale even had a name.

It was Evan.

"If he cheated on his wife," she heard her father say, "he'll cheat on you."

With his soon-to-be former wife?

Was Valerie still harboring hopes of getting back together with Evan?

Was Evan encouraging those hopes?

And if so, why?

"For God's sake, Brianne," Val said, interrupting Jennifer's thoughts. "Who are you texting now?"

"Nobody." Brianne made an exaggerated show of returning her BlackBerry to her purse. "I'm going to sleep," she announced to the rest of the car's inhabitants. "Wake me up when we get there."

Great, Val thought, letting go of whatever hopes remained for some quality time with her daughter.

"And try to keep the hysteria to a minimum," Brianne added, with a glance over her shoulder at James.

In response, James burst into song. " 'The hills are alive,' " he sang out, Val and Melissa quickly joining in.

I'm in hell, Jennifer thought sullenly, as they continued along Route 9 toward Prospect Mountain.

FIVE

AS SOON AS SHE closed her eyes, she saw the blood. The sheer volume of it had surprised her, along with the way it had literally shot from its source in one great, exuberant whoosh. Also a surprise was its rich, bright red color. Her lips creased into a small, almost imperceptible smile. She always expected the blood to be browner, duller, less vibrant.

Vibrant, she repeated silently, chewing on the word as if it were gum. Exuberant.

Funny words to describe death.

When she was younger and she used to cut herself with a razor, she remembered watching with fascination as the rivulets of blood streamed down her thighs and calves, relief quickly overtaking the initial pain of her self-inflicted wounds.

"Doesn't it hurt?" her friend Molly had once asked.

"No. It feels wonderful," she'd confided with a deep, satisfied sigh, about to continue, to tell her friend that every slice into her flesh was like scratching an overwhelming itch, that each cut brought with it its own heady rush, like a narcotic, temporarily freeing her soul, releasing the demons lurking just beneath the surface of her skin. She'd stopped only because of the look of growing horror on Molly's face. Her friend was incapable of understanding what she felt, she'd realized in that moment. It was pointless to try to explain.

"Does your mother know?" Molly had asked on another occasion.

"Of course not."

"But there are marks all over your legs."

"She doesn't notice."

"What if she does?"

"I'll tell her I fell into a bunch of bushes."

"What if she doesn't believe you?"

"That's her problem."

"I think you should stop," Molly cautioned before switching to another—safer—topic.

And she did stop, although not because of Molly's misguided concern or any fear that her mother might find out. She quit for the same reason she quit most of the things she'd once enjoyed—books, hobbies, friends. She got bored.

Besides, she'd found something else that was even better at releasing her inner demons.

She'd met a boy.

A boy who not only understood, but supported and encouraged her darker impulses. Her "uniqueness," as he liked to say.

The smile widened on her lips. You don't call someone his age a boy, she decided, even though she wasn't sure exactly how old he was. Somewhere between twenty and thirty. He was vague about specifics. "What does it matter?" he'd ask. "Age is just a number. It's irrelevant." He stopped short of saying, "You're as young as you feel," for which she was grateful. It was something she remembered her grandmother saying with irritating frequency.

He was similarly vague about his name. "Call me Ishmael," he'd said on one occasion, laughing with her at the reference to *Moby Dick,* a book they'd both loathed in high school. At other times he called himself Jonah or Moses or Elijah. He loved biblical names. Once he'd even told her to call him Jesus, but the name had proved to be something of a deterrent when it came to having sex, so he'd quickly abandoned it. Lately he'd turned to more mundane monikers—Brad, Steve, Michael. "I refuse to be contained by the boundaries imposed on me by others. I am whoever I want to be," he said, encouraging her to follow suit. "You are your own creation."

And so one day she created Catherine, and in the days after that, Veronica, Clementine, Joanne.

By far and away, her favorite so far was Nikki. Nikki, with two *k*'s.

It was Nikki who had the most fun.

"Call me Nikki," she'd instructed that silly woman at the cottage on the edge of Shadow Creek. Stupid woman, she thought now. Selfish, too. Wouldn't even let me use her hair dryer when there was one right under her bathroom sink. She'd stumbled on it when she went to take a shower. The thought turned her smile into a frown. It had taken the better part of thirty minutes to wash away that stupid woman's blood. It had gotten on everything—her clothes, her hair, even her teeth.

"Did you get any in your mouth?" Kenny had asked with obvious worry. He'd been calling himself Kenny for several weeks now. The name was good luck, he'd said, although he couldn't say why. "Wouldn't want you picking up any strange viruses."

"I didn't get any in my mouth," she told him, so touched by his concern for her welfare that she could barely breathe. Nobody had ever worried about her like that before. Nobody had ever been so protective. Nobody had ever made her feel so special, so loved. She would do anything not to disappoint him.

Anything.

They'd made themselves dinner with the leftovers in the fridge, helped themselves to two bottles of wine, then had sex repeatedly in their victims' too-soft bed, listening as the still-torrential rain pummeled the roof over their heads.

"That's one hell of a storm," Kenny said.

"Good thing we're inside," she agreed.

"Safe and snug as two bugs in a rug."

"I can't believe they don't have a TV."

"Cheap bastards," Kenny said.

"You should have seen their faces when I told them you'd cut the wires." She laughed. "When they realized something wasn't right, that they were going to die . . . That was the best part."

"Sorry I missed it."

"Next time you'll be there," she said. "So you won't miss anything."

"Thinking about what's best for me, are you?"

"Always," she said.

And it was true. Ever since they'd been introduced—"Call me Jason," he'd said—she'd thought of little else.

"Honestly," her mother had remarked. "I don't know what's gotten into you lately. It's like you're on another planet."

It wasn't even that he was all that good-looking. Rather, he was what her grandmother used to describe as "interesting."

His features were somewhat coarse—his nose wide, his lips full, his eyes an unremarkable shade of brown. Still, there was something about him that commanded attention. Maybe it was the way he stood, the insolent tilt of his shoulders, the subtle forward thrust of his slender hips, the manner in which his thumbs hooked into the side pockets of his too-tight jeans, the way his eyes appeared paradoxically vacant and knowing at the same time.

The way he looked into her eyes, and then past them, as if he could see right through them into the furthest recesses of her soul, effortlessly settling into the darkest corner of all.

Her secret place.

"We don't keep secrets," he'd told her. "Not from each other." Which was when he told her about his parents' multiple marriages, how he'd taken a knife to stepmother number two after a particularly nasty argument and been placed in an adult psychiatric hospital for the better part of a year, how he'd slept in a ward with psychotics and schizophrenics, all much older than his eleven years, and how he'd been raped by one of the attendants, a middle-aged man with graying hair and a potbelly, whose breath smelled of black licorice, how even now the slightest whiff of black licorice made him retch.

He told her that while he was in the hospital, his mother had married some old guy from Texas and left New York without so much as a word of goodbye, and how he'd been released into the not-so-welcoming arms of stepmother number three, who had two children of her own and who was forever calling them by each other's names. "That's when I realized how unimportant such things were," he told her. "Call me Daniel, call me Frank, call me Ishmael. It doesn't matter what you call me. It's not who I am."

I love you, she'd thought, whoever you are.

"I am everyone," he'd continued, unprompted. "I am everyone and I am no one. I am whoever I choose to be. Who are you?" he'd challenged, staring deep into her eyes, his hand reaching out to caress her cheek. His touch sent spasms of electricity throughout her body, causing her knees to wobble and her hands to shake.

"I don't know," she whispered, completely in his thrall. "I don't know who I am."

"You are whoever you choose to be," he intoned solemnly.

"Whoever I choose to be," she agreed.

Which was when she'd told him about her grandparents.

"My mother used to take me over to their house every Saturday night when I was a little girl," she began, "so that they could babysit me while she and my father went out. My grandparents had these friends they used to play bridge with, the Farellis. Mr. Farelli was pretty good-looking for an old guy, but his wife was really overweight and unattractive. She had this big mole on her upper lip and there were always a couple of hairs sticking out of it. Not a pretty sight, let me tell you. Anyway," she continued with a laugh, "one Saturday night when I was about five or six, I was at my grandparents' house, in the guest room, in bed, trying to sleep, and listening to my grandparents and the Farellis hollering at each other, which they always did when they played bridge. I actually grew up thinking that screaming was part of the game." She laughed again. "So Mrs. Farelli gets all upset at something my grandfather says, and she comes into the guest room to cool off. And she sits down on the side of the sofa bed—I'm not even sure she realized I was there—and she's yakking away to herself, and I'm, like, captivated by that ugly mole on her upper lip, which is moving back and forth as she's talking, with these hairs wagging at me like tails, and I suddenly reach up and grab one of them. Pulled the damn thing right out. Took half the mole with it. And Mrs. Farelli starts screeching and carrying on, like I'd deliberately tried to maim her or something. I mean, I'm a kid, right? What do I know? What's she doing in my room anyway? And then suddenly everybody's in the room, and what's left of that damn mole starts bleeding like there's no tomorrow, and I'm watching this blood dripping down her lips into her mouth, which is wide open because she's still screaming, and I'm, like, fascinated by it. I can't take my eyes off it. And now everybody's yelling. 'What's the matter with you? Are you stupid? How could you do such a terrible thing?' And I say, 'But it looks better now. It was ugly.' And my grandmother says, 'Who do you think you are, dummy, to decide what's ugly and what isn't?' And then she yanks me out of bed and turns me over her knee and spanks me, hard, right in front of everybody. And then she calls my parents and makes them come over and get me, says there's something very wrong with me, and they were really mad because I ruined their evening, right? And that was the last time I ever stayed overnight at my grandparents' house."

"So, who do you think you are, dummy?" Kenny repeated with a laugh.

"Please don't call me that," she said, the word stinging even more than usual, coming from his lips. "I'm not stupid."

"No, you're not. What are you?" he challenged.

"I'm whatever I want to be."

"What else?"

"I'm *whoever* I want to be," she said with growing conviction.

"And who is that?"

She gave the question a moment's consideration. "I've always liked the name Catherine."

"Then Catherine you shall be."

And then, the following week, "Call me Veronica."

"As in *Betty and* . . ."

"I'm definitely not a Betty."

"That's for damn sure."

And then soon after that, "I love the name Nikki. With two *k*'s."

"Then Nikki, with two *k*'s, it is."

"Call me Nikki," she'd said to that stupid Ellen Laufer. Opening her door to a total stranger in the middle of the night. In the middle of a storm. How ridiculous was that?

No more ridiculous than living out in the middle of nowhere, she thought, answering her own question. No more ridiculous than not having a TV.

It was like her grandfather had once said: some people were just too stupid to live.

"What was it like when you tried to kill your stepmother?" she'd asked Kenny one day. They were sitting on the double bed in the sparsely furnished room he was renting. "I mean, did you actually get to cut her?"

"Nah. I was too little. She was too fast for me. I just chased her around the kitchen with a steak knife. Freaked her right out."

"I bet."

"It was fun."

"I bet," she said again. Then, "I used to cut myself."

"I know."

"You do?"

"Those scars on your legs." He touched her thighs, his fingers tracing a series of thin lines on top of her jeans. "Do you still do it?"

She shook her head. "I stopped."

"Why?"

She shrugged.

"Would you start again—if I asked you to?"

"Yes," she said without missing a beat. Didn't he know that she would do anything for him?

"I want you to do it now," he said. "I want you to show me how you cut yourself."

She quickly wriggled out of her jeans and kicked them to the floor. "I need a razor."

Kenny pushed himself off the bed and walked purposefully into the bathroom, returning with a razor and a towel.

"Watch," she said.

His eyes followed her hand as she lowered the razor blade to her bare skin, drawing a line along the flesh of her inner thigh, as easily as if she were taking a pen to paper. It took a second for the wound to open and the blood to appear, another second for the pain to register, then disappear into pleasure. Her lips parted; her jaw slackened; her head rolled back. She felt the familiar rush, as if someone had just stuck a needle full of heroin into her veins.

And suddenly his head was between her legs, and he was licking the blood from her thighs, and moaning along with her. "I want you to cut me," he whispered.

"No. I can't hurt you."

"You won't. Here," he said, prying the razor from her fingers and removing his jeans, flinging them to the floor beside hers. "Show me. Guide my hands." He'd placed the palm of her hand over the back of his and waited. And when she pressed the blade into his skin, when she ran it along his flesh, he'd shuddered, then pulled her to him and kissed her, deeply, tenderly.

She'd never felt so much love.

A few days later, he suggested they find someone else to cut.

"Stepmother number one has an old aunt and uncle who live in the outskirts of Plainfield," he said, his enthusiasm increasing as his idea expanded. "Arlene and Frank Wall. They always had a soft spot for me."

"Their name is Wall?"

"As in 'brick.' "

She laughed, trying to remember if she'd ever been so happy. She would do anything to hold on to this man, to this feeling. Anything and everything. Anything he wanted. Everything he asked.

"Anyway, they have this cottage in the woods, almost as old as they are, and they've gotta be almost eighty by now. No kids. No neighbors. Just the two of them. Nobody'd even miss them."

"Are you serious?" she asked.

"Yeah. Are you scared?"

"No. Are you?"

"Hell, no. I'm excited. A couple of old farts. They've been around long enough. We'd be doing the world a favor by getting rid of them."

"We're going to kill them?"

"Well, dummy, we can't very well cut them up and just leave them there to tell everyone, can we?"

She felt her heart sink. Why had she asked him such a stupid question? She'd let him down. She'd disappointed him. If she wasn't careful, he'd leave her, find someone smarter, someone who didn't ask such dumb questions. And what would happen to her then? Who would she be without him? She'd be no one. Like she was before they met. "Please don't call me that."

"I'm sorry," he apologized immediately, and her heart swelled with gratitude. "I won't do it again. Promise."

And so she'd told her mother she was going to be spending the weekend with a girlfriend, and she and Kenny had driven up to Plainfield and the cottage of Arlene and Frank Wall.

"Yes?" Arlene asked, squinting through the screen door at the smiling young couple on her doorstep.

"Auntie Arlene?" Kenny said. "Don't you recognize me?"

"Matthew?" she asked. "My God, is that you? It's been years. Look how big and tall you've grown. What are you doing here?" She opened the door. "Frank," she called toward the living room, "you'll never guess who's here." She looked from the young man she knew as Matthew to the girl standing beside him.

"This is my friend, Nikki."

"Very nice to meet you, Nikki."

It was the last thing she said before Kenny drove his large knife deep into her chest, Nikki quickly following his example with a knife of her own. Frank had proved harder to kill. It took three thrusts to bring him to his knees and a vicious stab to his neck to silence his moaning once and for all.

Afterward, they'd raided the refrigerator and made love in Frank and Arlene's bed. "Smells like old people," she'd said before drifting off to sleep.

The next morning, they ate breakfast, the butchered bodies of Frank and Arlene Wall lying at their feet, their blood covering the knotted pine floor like a layer of fresh paint. Then they took whatever money they could find, disconnected the new wide-screen TV, and carried it out to Kenny's old Chevrolet.

"Do you need a hand with that?" someone asked suddenly, scaring them both, so that they almost dropped the TV to the ground. "Sorry," the young man apologized immediately. He was about Kenny's age, wearing a black baseball cap, a white

T-shirt, black Spandex shorts, and white running shoes, all bearing the familiar Nike swoosh. "Didn't mean to scare you. Name's Brian."

"Appreciate the help, Brian," Kenny said, waiting to kill him until after the TV had been safely loaded into the backseat of his car. "Can't leave any witnesses," he said with a shrug.

They'd carried him back into the cottage and hacked off his arms and legs, then his head, because Kenny had seen someone do that on TV and thought it would be neat to try. "Off with his head!" she'd giggled, watching her lover with something approaching awe. It took hours, even with her help, and they were exhausted when they were done. So they showered and took a short nap before burying Brian's torso in a shallow grave a few miles down the road, then scattering the rest of him in various locations along the route home. They also stopped at a flea market where Kenny purchased an old machete that had caught his eye. "You never know," he'd said. "It could come in handy."

It had indeed come in handy the following week in the Berkshires, where they'd made mincemeat out of William and Marie Carteris, although he'd used it sparingly. "Till I get the hang of it," he'd said. Which he had by the time they paid a visit to the Adirondacks and the cottage of Ellen and Stuart Laufer.

Good times, she thought now, looking forward to their next adventure. To all their future adventures. Nothing mattered as long as they were together.

"I'm ready whenever you are," he'd told her.

I'm ready, she thought now, opening her eyes.

SIX

"WELL, YOU CERTAINLY HAD a good sleep," Val was saying as Brianne sat up in her seat and looked around.

"Are we there yet?"

"We're here."

"This is it?" Brianne stared toward the unassuming wood and stone structure in the middle of a hub of giant pine trees. "I thought you said this place was supposed to be so luxurious."

When luxury beckons, Val thought, stealing a glance over her shoulder at Jennifer, and knowing by the expression on her face that the younger woman was thinking the same thing. "It's quite lovely inside," she assured her daughter as Brianne reached inside her purse for her BlackBerry. "Who on earth are you texting now?"

Brianne pushed open her car door and stepped onto the semicircular driveway in front of the lodge, ignoring her mother's question as her fingers furiously worked the miniature keypad.

A young man approached. The name tag on his crisp white shirt identified him as Wesley. He was thin and somewhat gangly, his arms seemingly too long for the rest of him. "Welcome to the Lodge at Shadow Creek," he said, his voice surprisingly robust, as the others began climbing from the car. Melissa and James exited together from either side of the SUV, Melissa's short legs sliding toward the ground, the dark eyes behind her large black glasses casually absorbing her surroundings while James made an exaggerated show of stretching and then bending from the waist until his elbows touched his toes.

"I'm super flexible," James told Wesley with a sly grin.

"Down, boy," Val whispered, staring at her daughter, still texting away. "There are children present."

"I'm not a child," Brianne said without so much as a glance in their direction.

Jennifer was the last to leave the car, hanging back as if to underscore her trepidation, then pushing one bare leg out after the other, as if she were riding an invisible bicycle. This was followed by the firm breasts that impressively filled out her sunny yellow T-shirt and the formidable rush of thick blond hair that temporarily hid her face from view.

Wesley watched her exit, his mouth dropping open just enough to be noticeable, from the side of the car. "Check-in is right through those doors," he managed, indicating the row of massive glass doors directly behind him. "Can I help you with your luggage?"

Val quickly directed him to the back of the SUV. "Just the top two," she said, opening the trunk. "Oh, and that overnight bag. That's it," she confirmed as Wesley began unloading the bags. "The rest stay where they are."

"How long will you be staying with us?" Wesley inquired, his eyes drifting back to Jennifer.

"We're not all staying," Val told him. "It's only my daughter and . . ."

". . . the Slut," James whispered out of the side of his mouth, his hand serving as a muffler, so that the words emerged as more of a sigh.

". . . *her*." Val nodded toward Jennifer. "They'll be staying for three nights. The rest of us will be leaving after we grab something to eat."

"You're staying for dinner?" Jennifer's voice echoed the look of horror on her face.

"I've been driving for almost five hours," Val reminded her.

"Of course. I didn't mean to imply . . ."

"I could use a bit of a break."

"No, I understand perfectly."

"We're happy to eat at another table, if you'd prefer."

"Stop it, Mother," Brianne said, tossing her BlackBerry back into her bag as she approached. "Martyrdom doesn't suit you."

"I'm not trying to be a martyr. I'm just trying to make things easier for everybody."

"By giving Jennifer a hard time?"

"How was I giving her a hard time?" It annoyed Val that her daughter was taking Jennifer's side, and although she tried to hide it, the brittleness of her tone betrayed her.

"I think we're all a little tired here," Melissa interrupted as the familiar chimes of Brianne's BlackBerry rang out, signaling the arrival of another text message.

"Is that your father?" Val asked. But Brianne was already moving away from her, her thumbs poised and ready for action.

"Lovely," Val said, heading toward the front doors of the lodge, the others following dutifully behind. "Brianne!" she called out.

Brianne responded with a dismissive wave of her hand.

"Don't worry. She knows where to find us," Melissa said as they entered the front lobby.

"I don't know who she's so busy texting."

"You know how it is when you get a new boyfriend," Jennifer said absently.

"What new boyfriend?" Val stopped so abruptly that Jennifer walked right into her.

"I'm so sorry," Jennifer apologized immediately, although she wasn't sure whether she was more sorry for stomping all over Val's bare toes or for revealing that Brianne had a new boyfriend her mother clearly knew nothing about.

"Brianne has a new boyfriend?" Val asked accusingly. Both women understood that what she was really asking was *Why do you know about this and I don't? Why would Brianne confide in you and not me? Isn't it enough you stole my husband? Do you have to steal my daughter, too? Why are you here? Why do you even exist?*

"I don't know," Jennifer qualified quickly. "I just assumed it must be a boy . . . But I don't know for sure. It was just a guess," she added, unconvincingly.

"Isn't this place magnificent?" Melissa asked loudly, turning around in a slow circle, her arms extended at her sides, as if trying to draw the whole scene to her. "Just look at that ceiling. It must be fifty feet high."

Melissa's exaggerated enthusiasm forced everyone's eyes toward the wide wooden planks of the ceiling. It was indeed magnificent, Val agreed silently, trying not to picture Jennifer's shapely legs stretching toward it.

"And that fabulous stone fireplace," Melissa continued. "And these carpets . . ."

"And that crystal chandelier," Jennifer added, grateful for Melissa's intervention.

"And that concierge," James said, lowering his chin and staring toward the young man behind the concierge desk. "Just look at those lips."

"I'm getting my lips done," Brianne suddenly announced, joining the small group in the middle of the lobby.

"What do you mean, you're getting them done?" James asked.

"They're too thin. I'm getting them done."

"Over my dead body," Val said.

"Val . . ." Melissa warned.

"A friend of mine had her lips done," Jennifer said. "She had these beautiful lips, kind of like yours, Bri, and then she had them done. Now she looks all swollen, like somebody punched her in the mouth."

"I don't want to do anything drastic," Brianne demurred quickly. "Just a little bit of plumping. Here." She indicated a spot to the side of her upper lip. "And maybe here."

"That's what she said, but once you do anything to your lips, you never look natural again."

Val waited for Brianne to protest, but all she said was "You really think my lips are beautiful?"

"Are you kidding? They're gorgeous."

"Thanks," Brianne said.

Great, Val thought, torn between hugging Jennifer and wrestling her to the wide stone floor. "I tell her the same thing," she whispered to Melissa. "She doesn't listen to me."

"When was the last time you listened to *your* mother?" Melissa whispered back.

Probably around the same age, Val thought, then decided it had actually been the other way around. Her mother had stopped listening to *her*. Val pictured her mother lying in her bed, a half-empty bottle of red wine balanced precariously on the pillow beside her head. First her father had checked out, then her mother, her abandonment of her children somehow made worse by the fact she was still there. At least, physically.

She probably doesn't even remember it's my birthday this weekend, Val thought, trying not to feel too sorry for herself and deciding she might as well call her mother to remind her. No point in standing on ceremony. Maybe she'd even invite her mother to join them for dinner on Sunday night.

"Can I help you?" a young woman was asking from behind the polished wood of the long reception counter. Her name tag identified her as Tori.

"You certainly can." Val's voice was louder than she'd intended. The young woman took an immediate step back. "We have a room booked for the next three nights. The name is Rowe."

Tori entered the name into her computer. "Mr. and Mrs. Evan Rowe and daughter?" She looked from Val to Jennifer to Brianne to Melissa to James, as if trying to decide who was who.

"I'll take it from here," Jennifer said as Val stiffened. She felt Melissa's gentle hand on her arm, urging her to stay calm. "I'm Mrs. Rowe," Jennifer said, somewhat prematurely, Val thought. Their divorce wasn't final yet. There was still time for Evan to change his mind.

"Is this your first time staying at the lodge, Mrs. Rowe?" Tori asked.

"Yes," Jennifer answered. "It's Brianne's first time, too."

"Well, I'm sure you'll enjoy your stay with us." Tori's smile managed to include the entire group. "We have everything. A fabulous spa and an Olympic-size pool, plus there's boating and hiking and all sorts of interesting excursions you can sign up for. I'll just need your signature on this form, if you will, Mrs. Rowe, and if I could have an imprint of your credit card . . ."

"Certainly." Val watched Jennifer sign the registration form with a pronounced flourish, then hand over the credit card Evan was undoubtedly paying for.

"You're in room 313 on the third floor of the west wing." Tori stuffed three keycards into a small envelope and handed it to Jennifer. "Nonsmoking, two queen-size beds."

"What? No. We're supposed to have a suite."

"That *is* our standard suite," Tori explained. "A living room and a bedroom with two queen-size beds. It's really very lovely."

"Not to mention, kind of kinky," James whispered. "Dad, teenage daughter, hot new fiancée."

Val winced, not sure if she was reacting to the image or to James's referencing of Jennifer as "hot."

"You don't have any suites with two bedrooms?" Jennifer persisted. "Maybe two adjoining rooms . . ."

"I'm afraid we're fully booked. We might be able to find a cot . . ."

"I'm not sleeping on any cot," Brianne said quickly.

Jennifer took a deep breath, forced her lips into a reassuring smile. "We'll let your father work this out when he gets here. Room 313, you said?"

"Just go down that hall and turn right," Tori said quickly. "The elevators are on the left. Your luggage will be brought up shortly. And if there's anything else we can do for you, please don't hesitate to let us know."

"Are there any messages?" Val asked, reasserting her presence.

Tori checked her computer. "No. Nothing."

"Hopefully that means he's on his way," Jennifer said, leading the way. "I'm sure Bri and I can manage by ourselves from here on in," she said as Val pressed the call button for the elevator.

"I was hoping I could use your bathroom," Val said, bristling at the easy shortening of her daughter's name as she motioned toward James and Melissa. "I'm sure we'd all appreciate it if we could freshen up a bit before we eat."

"Of course," Jennifer said, suspecting that Val just wanted to check out the room, since there were bathrooms off the lobby they could have used. But she was too tired to argue about it.

The elevator door opened and a young girl marched purposefully into the hall, head down, long, straight hair falling into her face. Val had to jump out of her way to avoid being trampled.

"I believe the word you're looking for is 'Excuse me,'" James called after her.

"That's two words," Melissa corrected, as the girl raised the middle finger of her left hand high into the air and continued on her way without looking back.

"Did she just give me the finger?" James asked.

"And a most emphatic finger it was," Melissa said, turning back to Val. "Are you all right?"

"Yeah. Guess she's in a hurry. Oh, for Pete's sake," she said as her daughter received yet another text. "Would you put that thing away."

"What if it's Dad?" came Brianne's response as they stepped inside the elevator.

"Is it?" Val and Jennifer asked together.

Brianne rolled her eyes and said nothing. They rode in silence to the third floor, accompanied only by the clicking of

Brianne's thumbs as she typed in her response. She was still typing when they exited the elevator and headed down the long ivory corridor to their room.

Jennifer removed one of the keycards from its envelope and inserted it into the slot by the door as Brianne returned her BlackBerry to her purse. The door refused to open, even after several tries. "What's the matter with this stupid thing?"

"Why don't you let me do that?" Val took the card from Jennifer's hand and gently pushed it into the slot. The green light immediately flashed, allowing the door to open.

"Wow," James exclaimed as they stepped over the threshold. "Not bad."

Val felt the gentle pressure of Melissa's hand on her arm as they entered the suite. "Breathe," Melissa whispered.

Taking one deep breath, and then another, Val looked around the suite's sun-filled living room, with its impossibly high ceiling and beautiful gold-and-ivory-striped wallpaper. They'd redecorated since her last visit, updating and upgrading. Just like Evan, she thought, catching a glimpse of her tired-looking reflection in the ornately framed mirror hanging above the overstuffed beige velvet sofa. A brass-legged glass coffee table stood in front of the sofa and two floral-patterned wing chairs sat to either side of the gas fireplace on the opposite wall. A series of photographs of local wildlife graced the walls at regular intervals. A bottle of champagne sat chilling in an ice bucket on the round glass table in front of the large picture window overlooking Shadow Creek. Val wondered if the champagne was Evan's idea or a gift from the hotel.

I could certainly do with a little alcoholic refreshment right about now, she thought in her mother's voice, as she followed her daughter past the beige-marbled bathroom into the ivory-and-gold bedroom. Here the floral pattern of the living room chairs was repeated in both the curtains and the bedspreads of the two queen-size beds. Watercolor renderings of the surrounding landscape had replaced the photographs of local fauna. A gold canopy was draped across the headboards of both beds, matching the gold upholstery of the chair in front of the exquisitely carved mahogany desk next to the window.

"My God, is that an antique Chippendale?" Melissa asked, temporarily abandoning Val's side to check it out.

"Don't you have to use the bathroom?" Brianne reminded her mother.

"Right."

"So, who's going to sleep with who?" Val heard Brianne ask as she was leaving the room.

The question remained unanswered as Val closed the bathroom door.

Val was washing her hands when she remembered her earlier decision to call her mother. The poor woman had no doubt been trying to reach her all day to wish her a happy birthday, she thought, pulling her cell phone out of her purse and trying to find a connection. She was probably worried sick. "Yeah, right," Val thought in Brianne's voice, tossing her cell phone back into her purse when no connection could be found. When was the last time her mother had remembered her birthday? When was the last time she'd worried about anything other than where her next drink was coming from? "Would it be okay if I use your phone?" she said when she returned to the bedroom. "My cell phone isn't getting any reception and I really should call my mother."

"Now?" Brianne asked. "What for?"

"Just to check that she's okay."

"You mean sober."

Val approached the phone by the side of the bed farther

from the window, studied the instructions for placing an out-side call, and punched in her mother's number. "We'll give you some privacy," she heard Melissa say as her mother's line rang once, twice, three times, four . . .

"My turn in the bathroom," James was saying as they left the room.

The phone was picked up in the middle of its eighth ring, although no one said hello. "Mom? Are you there?"

"Allison?" her mother asked.

"No, Mom, it's Valerie."

"Valerie, dear. You're sounding more and more like your sister every day. How are you?"

Val wondered when was the last time her mother had actually spoken to Allison, who'd relocated to Florida two years earlier in a largely futile effort to reconnect with their father. "I'm fine. You?"

"Just fine, darling. Although you caught me at a rather inopportune moment. I was just about to step into the bath."

Val bit down on her lower lip. Her mother was always either just stepping into or out of the bath. It meant she was either about to pass out or pour herself another drink. "I just wanted to let you know that I'll be in Manhattan for the weekend. I was going to call earlier but . . . something came up." She waited several seconds for her mother to ask what. "Anyway, I'll be at the Plaza," she continued when no such question was forthcoming. "In case you need to reach me."

No curiosity as to why she might be staying at the Plaza for the weekend. Just silence.

"It's a fortieth-birthday present from James and Melissa," Val offered.

Another long pause. Then, "I was planning to phone you later . . ."

"I'm sure you were."

"You didn't think I'd forget my daughter's fortieth birthday, did you?"

"I was hoping not."

"So, have a great day, darling," she said after an uncomfortably long pause. "I really have to go now. My bath is getting cold."

Val nodded into the receiver.

"If you're talking to your sister, be sure to give her my love."

"I'll do that." Val doubted that Allison would remember her birthday, either, or call her even if she did. She couldn't remember the last time they'd exchanged such mundane pleasantries. And it had been years since she'd spoken to her father.

If I have a birthday, and my family doesn't remember it, she asked herself now, do I even exist?

"Bye, darling."

"Maybe we could have dinner on Sunday," Val began. But the line was already dead.

Brianne appeared in the doorway between the two rooms. "How drunk was she this time?"

Val lowered the receiver to its carriage. "Please don't talk that way about your grandmother."

"Why not? It's the truth."

"It's not that simple."

"Yeah," Brianne said. "It is."

"Are you all right?" Jennifer asked from beside Brianne.

"Of course I'm all right. Why wouldn't I be?" Val jumped to her feet. The last thing she needed at this particular moment was Jennifer's sympathy. What she needed was a drink. Hell, it worked for her mother. She marched into the living room. "So, is everybody hungry?"

"I think I'll wait to eat until Evan gets here," Jennifer said.

"I'll wait with Jennifer," Brianne said before anyone asked.

"Your father might not be here for hours," Val reminded her as James and Melissa walked toward the door.

"That's fine. It's too early to eat anyway."

"Suit yourself." Val was just stepping into the hall when the phone rang, its surprisingly shrill sound bouncing off the walls like steel balls in a pinball machine.

"Hello? Evan? Thank God," she heard Jennifer say. "We got here about fifteen minutes ago. Where are you? Are you on your . . . What?"

Val waited outside the door for the inevitable.

"No, please don't tell me that. Not till tomorrow?" Jennifer said.

"Surprise, surprise," Val muttered.

"That's just great," Brianne said.

"I'm really sorry," Val imagined Evan saying, "but this whole deal is exploding in my face. There's no way I can leave now."

"But how can they be threatening to renege?" Jennifer was asking. "The deal is in danger of falling apart," she explained to Brianne in the next breath. "They have to work through the night. Hopefully they'll have everything sorted out by morning . . ."

"Believe me, I'm as upset as you are about this," Val could almost hear Evan continue. "I'm doing my best to get out of here as fast as I can."

"Of course you are," Jennifer told him. "I understand. And you'll be able to leave first thing in the morning?" Jennifer's voice was wobbly with the threat of tears. "Yes, I know you'll try your best. I'm just disappointed, that's all. I really *do* understand. What? Um . . . yes, I think she's still here. Okay, sure. Just a minute. I'll check. Val?" she called out. "Are you still there?"

Val quickly reentered the room.

Jennifer was standing beside the sofa. She held the phone toward her without saying a word.

"Hello?" Val said softly into the receiver.

"Hey, you," came Evan's automatic response.

Val listened as Evan explained the situation again, then added, "I just wanted to thank you again for all you've done."

"No need."

"Look. Why don't you stay the night? You must be exhausted. Don't argue," he said as she was about to. "This way, you and your friends can get a good night's sleep before heading back. You don't want to have an accident, and I don't want to be responsible for anything bad happening to you."

Too late for that, Val thought.

"You can enjoy the spa, go shopping, anything you want—my treat."

"I can't . . ."

"In all likelihood, I won't get there till tomorrow afternoon," he continued, as if she hadn't spoken. "Please stay. Consider it part of your birthday gift," he added enticingly.

What's the other part? Val wondered, trying to decipher what, if anything, Evan was really saying.

"I'll think about it." She handed the phone back to Jennifer.

"What's happening?" Brianne asked.

I wish I knew, Val thought. What she said was "Let's say we go have some dinner."

SEVEN

THE GOOD-LOOKING YOUNG COUPLE seated at the table next to them in the hotel's casual yet elegant dining room had been arguing almost from the moment they sat down. "You're being obstinate," the man was saying, with a perceptible stiffening of his square jaw.

"You're being ridiculous," the woman quickly countered, tugging at her diamond-studded eternity band and pushing her auburn hair away from her flushed cheeks.

"Don't tell me I'm being ridiculous."

"Then don't tell me I'm being obstinate."

"Newlyweds," the waiter whispered to Val as he poured her a third glass of wine.

Val watched the deep red liquid fill her glass. What am I doing? she wondered. Because of her mother's unfortunate proclivities, she'd never permitted herself more than one glass of wine, never allowed herself the luxury of being even vaguely tipsy. But, hey, these were special circumstances, she decided, signaling the waiter to keep pouring. It was her fortieth birthday in a couple of days and no one in her family seemed to give a damn. Her mother was too drunk, her father too involved with his other family, her sister too estranged, her daughter too self-absorbed. Only her soon-to-be ex-husband, the love of her life, who was only weeks away from no longer being part of that life, had even mentioned it.

Consider it part of your birthday gift, he'd said.

What did he mean?

Thank God for James and Melissa, she thought, banishing thoughts of Evan and smiling at her two best friends. Not only had they remembered her birthday, but they'd unselfishly put their own celebratory plans on hold in order to accommodate her. And for what? For this?

The unhappy group was now seated at a round table next to the window overlooking Shadow Creek, Lake George in the distance below, tension hanging over their heads like a shroud. It was still light out, darkness perhaps an hour away. Night fell much more abruptly in the mountains than in the city, Val knew, wishing now that she'd followed Jennifer's example and showered before coming downstairs. At least she should have changed her clothes for dinner. Not that she would have been any competition for the always lovely Jennifer, in her fashionably rumpled white linen slacks and crisp, red-and-white candy-striped shirt.

What competition? Val wondered, gulping at her wine. The contest was over. Jennifer had already won.

"Hey, Mom. Go easy on that stuff, okay?"

"Is something wrong with your salmon?" Val asked in

return. Brianne had been pushing at her food the entire meal without eating much of anything.

"I'm not very hungry."

"Would you like to try some of my veal? It's wonderful."

"It's a baby calf. I think it's disgusting."

"No, actually, it's delicious." Val chewed with exaggerated enthusiasm while stealing a glance at everyone else's plates. Both James and Jennifer had ordered the sushi-grade tuna, while Melissa was finishing up her bowl of pasta primavera. Even the bickering newlyweds at the next table had agreed on fish. Am I the only meat-eater left on the planet? she wondered.

"I pretty much stopped eating meat when I was eleven," Jennifer said, as if Val had asked the question out loud. "My mother had to prepare two different meals every night for dinner."

Brianne gave her mother a look that said, You see. It's not such a big deal.

Just add it to my ever-lengthening list of failings, Val thought, feeling the room spin. She thought she recognized the young woman who'd plowed into her earlier, then given her the finger, sitting several tables away, engrossed in earnest conversation with the young man sitting across from her, although she couldn't be sure it was her. Hell, she wasn't sure of anything anymore.

"Everything—and I do mean *everything*—was a big deal to my mother," James was saying. "She hated cooking with a passion. Although, surprisingly, she loved to bake chocolate cake. And I have to admit, it's still the best chocolate cake I've ever tasted."

"My mother's idea of cooking was to open a can," Melissa said, not to be outdone. "I was twenty-one before I realized there was such a thing as fresh vegetables."

"I've been thinking of becoming a vegetarian," Brianne said.

Who *is* this girl? Val wondered, staring hard at her daughter and watching as her face divided into two blurry halves. What has she done with Brianne?

Brianne's BlackBerry signaled yet another text message coming through.

"Don't answer that," Val warned.

"What?"

"Answer it and it goes in the garbage."

"What's *your* problem?"

You're my problem, Val wanted to shout. You and that piece of eye candy sitting next to you. Not to mention, my mother's a drunk who didn't remember my birthday, your father is bombarding me with mixed messages, the room is doing cartwheels, and I think there's a distinct possibility I'm going to throw up. What she said was "I just think it's rude to text at the dinner table, that's all."

"So, I'll go into the lobby." Brianne was already halfway out of her chair.

"You'll do no such thing. Sit down. Now."

"Oh, for crap's sake." Brianne plopped back down in her chair, pursing her lips into an unattractive pout. "When are you guys leaving anyway?"

"Something tells me your mom's not in any condition to drive," Melissa said softly.

"So you or James can drive," Brianne volunteered for them.

"Sorry, kiddo. I'm way too tired to drive back to New York tonight," Melissa said.

James nodded his agreement. "Looks like we'll be spending the night here, pumpkin."

"What? No. I'll be fine in an hour," Val protested.

"You won't be fine," James said.

"You're not driving," Melissa told her.

Brianne glared at her mother. "You did this on purpose."

Val wondered if Brianne was right. Had she deliberately had too much to drink so that they'd have no choice but to take Evan up on his offer and spend the night? Or was she more upset about her mother forgetting her birthday than she'd allowed herself to consciously admit? She leaned back in her seat, fighting her growing dizziness.

"I told you about this trip months ago," she heard the man at the next table say, and for a minute she thought he might be talking to her.

"No, David, you didn't," his new wife insisted. "This is the first I'm hearing about any trip."

"Because you don't listen."

"Don't tell me I don't listen."

"If you listened, you would have heard me say I was going fishing with Scott and Peter over the Labor Day weekend."

"But I already told my parents we'd be coming to the cottage over Labor Day."

"You can still go."

"Alone?"

"Your sisters will be there."

"Yeah—with their husbands. And kids."

"So you'll have a nice visit."

"Thanks a lot. Those kids are a pain in the ass."

"Which is exactly why I'm going fishing."

"You're not going fishing."

"Yes, I *am* going fishing."

Am not; Am, too, Val recited silently.

"Don't be ridiculous, David."

"Don't be a bitch, Alicia."

And we're off, Val thought, hearing the imaginary bell that signaled the start of round two.

"Don't call me names."

"Sorry. Your name isn't Alicia?"

"Don't be a wise-ass. You called me a bitch."

"No, I didn't. I said, don't *be* a bitch. There's a difference."

"The hell there is. I'm not talking to you again until you apologize."

"For what?"

"For being an asshole."

"Now who's calling who names?"

"Just calling them as I see them. *Asshole*." With that, Alicia jumped to her feet, threw her apricot-colored napkin down on the white linen tablecloth, and stomped out of the dining room.

Is anybody in this room having a good time? Val wondered, finishing off what was left in her glass.

"Sorry about that," David mouthed sheepishly in Jennifer's direction.

As if I don't even exist, Val thought, checking for her reflection in the curve of her coffee spoon.

"Anybody for dessert?" James asked.

"WHAT DO YOU mean, you don't have any rooms?" Val swallowed, trying to contain the hysteria she heard creeping into her voice. Behind her, Jennifer stiffened.

"I'm very sorry," the young woman behind the reception counter apologized quickly. She had big brown eyes and a sweet little half smile that made it hard for Val to be angry with her. Her name tag identified her as Kathy. "But we're filled up right through the end of Labor Day."

"Well, that's just wonderful. What are we supposed to do now?" Val said to no one in particular.

"I can try some of the other hotels in the area, if you'd like," Kathy offered at the same time, immediately reaching for the phone.

"Please." Val turned toward the others, watching the lobby tilt to the right. "There appears to be a slight glitch."

"This happened to me once when I was in Italy," James said. "I'd made reservations at this fabulous little hotel just outside of Florence a full year ahead of time. Only when we got there, they told us they had no record of my reservation and we'd have to go elsewhere. I was so mad, I haven't been back to Italy since."

"You're making that up," Melissa said.

"Well, yes," James admitted. "It just seemed like the right time for a supportive anecdote."

Val sighed with sudden, overwhelming fatigue. She'd been hoping for a long, hot bath and maybe even a massage. She certainly didn't feel like driving around searching for a place to stay the night. Not that she was in any condition to drive. Had Brianne been right? Had she done this on purpose?

What purpose?

"I'm sorry," Kathy announced a few minutes later. "I'm not having any luck. It looks as if every hotel in the area is fully booked."

Brianne groaned.

"There might be something by Fort Ticonderoga . . ."

"I definitely don't like the sound of that," James said.

Val shook her head. Fort Ticonderoga was at least an hour's drive away.

"I've tried everywhere . . ."

"Could you try one more time?" Jennifer pleaded.

"Sorry, sweetheart," Val apologized to her daughter when further entreaties failed to turn up any vacancies, "but it's looking as if . . ."

"Don't say it," Brianne said.

"We might have to share a room," she said anyway.

"I don't believe this," Jennifer muttered.

"Look. It could be worse," James said. "There are two queen-size beds plus a living room sofa."

"We are not all sleeping together," Brianne said loudly. "No way. No way."

"I think it might be time for another anecdote," Melissa said to James.

"There must be another solution," Jennifer said.

"I guess we could sleep in the car," Val offered.

"Yeah, right," Brianne scoffed.

"Okay," Jennifer said, hugging Brianne to her side. "It's a suite after all. And it's just for one night. It's not the end of the world."

James smiled. "Don't be too sure."

"WELL, THIS SHOULD be interesting," Melissa said, eyeing the two queen-sized beds. "What do we do—draw straws?"

"This is getting kinkier by the moment," said James.

"James, you take the couch," Val heard Jennifer say, as she focused on the sofa's cushions in an effort to stop it from swaying. She was desperate to lie down and wasn't sure how much longer she could remain standing. "Melissa and Val can take the bed over there. Brianne, you can share with me."

"Sounds like a plan," Brianne said, unpacking her toiletries and heading toward the bathroom.

"Don't be long. There are four other people waiting," Melissa called after her.

"And no texting," Val added.

Their answer was the sound of a door slamming shut, followed by the sudden torrent of bath water escaping the faucets.

"Looks like it's going to be a long night," Melissa said.

Val watched Jennifer pull a pretty pink negligee out of her suitcase. No way am I getting undressed in front of that woman, she thought, approaching her own canvas bag at the foot of the bed, the bellboy having recently brought their luggage up to the room. No way am I climbing into my ratty old nightshirt while she's here. *No way, no way, no way,* she thought in Brianne's voice.

Jennifer looked similarly confused, sitting down at the end of her bed and clutching her nightgown to her chest.

No need to be shy, Val thought. It's not as if I haven't seen you naked.

James flipped on the television. "Oh, no. Look," he said as smiling pictures of Arlene and Frank Wall, their arms encircling each other's waists, quickly filled the wide screen across from the beds.

"Speculation is increasing that the murders of Frank and Arlene Wall might indeed be connected to that of slain hiker Brian Grierson," the announcer was saying as the picture of the Walls was replaced by a photograph of a gap-toothed young man with wavy brown hair and a bulging backpack slung over his slender shoulders.

James sank down at the foot of the second bed, Val and Melissa joining him on either side.

"Police are still refusing to confirm that the two incidents are related, although sources tell us that DNA recovered from the bodies seems to have come from the same source. And while officials continue to deny that the murders of Marie and William Carteris are connected to those of either Brian Grierson or Frank and Arlene Wall, what they can't deny are the disturbing similarities: all the victims were stabbed and hacked to death; the Carterises and the Walls were both elderly couples who lived in relatively isolated locales; and while Brian Grierson doesn't fit the profile of the other victims, his stabbed and dismembered body was found not far from the Walls' cottage, leading investigators to consider that he might have inadvertently stumbled upon the killer. Or killers," the announcer continued solemnly, "as sources tell us the police are now reasonably certain that more than one person was involved in the brutal slayings."

"Lovely." James clicked off the TV and pushed himself off the end of the bed. "Sleep tight, everybody," he said as he left the room. "Pleasant dreams."

EIGHT

JENNIFER WAS STARING AT the digital clock on the table between the two beds, the bold, blood-red numbers staring back at her, as if daring her to challenge them: 12:35, they announced. More than half an hour after midnight. Less than fifteen minutes since the last time she'd checked.

She flipped onto her right side, facing the window and trying to get comfortable, despairing that she'd ever fall asleep. It wasn't looking good, she decided, feeling Brianne flopping around beside her like a fish out of water. Did the girl never stop moving? She was tempted to grab Brianne's leg to keep it from twitching, or her fingers to keep them from tapping. She'd never shared a bed with such a restless sleeper before. Brianne was rarely still for more than a few seconds at a time, pulling her sheets this way and that, extending them over her head one minute only to kick them to her feet the next. And what made it even worse was that those few instances of relative calm lulled you into a false sense of security, allowing you to relax and even start to drift off when wham!—she was at it again. As if the girl had a built-in sensor. As if she was doing it on purpose.

No, Jennifer thought, deciding to be generous. Brianne wasn't like Val. She wasn't mean-spirited. She wasn't bossy and proprietary. She didn't have an agenda. She was just a teenager. And teenagers were notoriously restless sleepers. Weren't they? Jennifer shrugged. She could barely remember her teenage years, having stumbled through half of them in pretty much of a fog after her mother's breast cancer diagnosis.

Jennifer was barely fourteen, her own breasts just starting to fill out and attract male attention, when her mother underwent a double mastectomy. This procedure was followed by numerous rounds of chemo, the chemo accompanied by nausea, fatigue, and the loss of her beautiful hair. Then there were the radiation treatments, which scorched her mother's skin and robbed her of whatever energy and dignity she had left. "Hopefully we got all of it," the doctor had said.

And miraculously the various treatments did seem to work. After five years of holding its breath, the family had breathed a collective sigh of relief when the doctor pronounced Jennifer's mother "cancer-free."

And then suddenly it was back. Unprompted, unexpected, unwelcome. Her mother had endured more chemo, more radiation, more surgeries, as the cancer spread its poison like a slow leak, ultimately infiltrating her lungs, her liver, her pancreas, her spine, her bones, and finally even her brain. Inoperable. Unresponsive. Terminal.

Over those last seven years, Jennifer had watched her

mother disappear a little bit at a time, her once-happy family vanishing along with her: Jennifer into her work and a series of casual affairs; Cameron into an ever-deepening well of self-absorption; her father into an ever-thickening haze.

She pictured her father, alone in his stuffy apartment in Queens, a mere shell of the man he once was, with not even fond memories to sustain him. Sometimes death could be a blessing, she decided, thinking that as grisly as the awful murders they'd been hearing about were, perhaps being murdered—quickly and with ruthless efficiency—was preferable to the slow, agonizing death by cancer her mother had endured, or her father's equally slow and agonizing deterioration.

What the hell is the matter with me? Jennifer thought in the next instant, wondering where such dark thoughts were coming from. She flipped back onto her right side, propping herself up on her elbow and peering through the darkness at the sleeping figures in the next bed, watching the steady rise and fall of Val's shoulders. What are you doing here? How did this happen?

"Is something wrong?" Brianne asked groggily beside her.

"No, honey. Sorry if I disturbed you. Go back to sleep."

Jennifer fell back against her pillows, praying for unconsciousness to overtake her. Is that what those poor people prayed for while they were being butchered? she wondered. Did they fight for their lives or did they hope only for a swift end to their pain? Did they think about their families or did their panic preclude any thoughts at all? Did they believe in an afterlife and if they did, did that belief provide them with any comfort?

Jennifer didn't believe in an afterlife, although she'd tried. When her mother was first diagnosed, she'd prayed often. Prayed for the doctors to be wrong, prayed for scientists to discover a cure, prayed for her mother to get better, or ultimately to live out what little time she had left in relative peace and comfort. But if there was a God, He hadn't been paying attention. Or maybe He just didn't have time to answer all the prayers He undoubtedly received on a daily basis from the families of the sick and the dying. Whatever the reason, her prayers had gone unheeded, and the day her mother died, Jennifer had stopped praying altogether.

And then she'd stopped believing.

It was easier that way. There were fewer expectations, and fewer expectations meant fewer disappointments.

"If there *is* a God," she remembered telling her sister, "He doesn't affect my life one way or the other."

"God's gonna get you for that one," Cameron had said with a laugh.

Now Jennifer was sharing a bed with her fiancé's daughter, listening to the soft whistle of his soon-to-be ex-wife's gentle snores, and wondering if this was God's revenge. For not believing. For not honoring His commandments. For having an affair with a married man.

It doesn't bode well, she heard her father say.

"Shut up, Daddy," she thought, not realizing she'd spoken the words out loud until she felt movement and opened her eyes to see Brianne's face looming only inches above hers.

"Did you just tell me to shut up?" Brianne asked, her breath warm and smelling of spearmint mouthwash.

"No. Of course not."

"It sounded like you said 'shut up.'"

"No."

"Ssh," Val admonished from the other bed. "There are people trying to sleep over here."

"I thought you *were* asleep," Brianne said.

"I've been trying to."

"You've been snoring loud enough."

"I have not."

"Yes, you have. Hasn't she?" Brianne asked Jennifer.

"It's really not a big deal," Jennifer said.

"That's so generous of you," Val said.

"For God's sake, Mom. She was being supportive."

"I don't need her support."

"Can we all please settle down?" Melissa asked groggily from beside Val.

"What's going on in there?" James called from the next room. "Am I missing something?"

"Isn't anybody asleep?" Brianne wailed.

"I do not snore," Val insisted.

"Then why did Dad always say that your snoring kept him awake half the night?"

"I don't know," Val said, biting off each word, "but I guess it's a good thing he doesn't have to worry about that anymore." With that, she flipped over with such force that both beds shook.

THEN WHY DID Dad always say that your snoring kept him awake half the night?

The question twisted through Val's brain like a tornado. Damn it, she thought. Yes, Evan had occasionally complained about her snoring, but so what? Snoring was hardly one of the seven deadly sins.

Val suddenly found herself trying to recall exactly what those seven sins were. Pride, she thought. Gluttony. Anger.

I've certainly been guilty of each of those on more than one occasion, she thought.

What else?

Lust.

Ah, yes, she thought, recalling the last time she and Evan had made love. She hadn't slept with a man since. Hadn't had so much as an urge. Talk about sins. Although that was more of a shame than a sin, actually.

Envy.

Okay, yeah, all right. You got me. I'm envious all right.

Sloth.

Probably guilty of that as well.

What else? *Pride, gluttony, anger, lust, envy, sloth.* That's six. What's the seventh? "Melissa," she whispered into the back of her friend's black silk pajamas. "Melissa, are you asleep?"

She felt Melissa wiggle around to face her, her head joining Val's underneath the covers. "Did you say something?"

"What are the seven deadly sins?"

Even under the covers and in the dark, Val could make out the look of disbelief on her friend's face. "Are you kidding me?"

"I can only think of six."

"Pride," Melissa said sleepily. "And anger."

"Got those. Also envy, lust, gluttony, and sloth."

"I hear whispering," James called from the next room.

Melissa whipped the covers off her head and sat up. "We're trying to remember the seven deadly sins."

"I don't believe this," said Brianne from the next bed, underlining her displeasure with a prolonged groan.

"Lust," said James quickly. "Anger. Gluttony. Envy."

"Pride and sloth," Val and Melissa said together, their voices overlapping.

"What's sloth?" Brianne asked.

"We can't think of the seventh sin," Melissa said.

A moment of quiet, then, "Covetousness," Jennifer said quietly from beside Brianne.

"Of course," James said. "As in 'Thou shall not covet thy neighbor's . . .'" He stopped abruptly.

How appropriate for you to know that one, Val thought.

"What's next?" Brianne asked. "Twenty questions? Charades?"

"I love charades," James said.

"Can we all just get some sleep?" Brianne begged. "Please?"

"Sorry, darling. Good night, everybody."

"Good night," Melissa said.

"Good night," echoed Jennifer.

James laughed. "This is just like *The Waltons*."

"Who are the Waltons?" Brianne asked. Then quickly, "Never mind. Don't tell me. Just please, everybody—get some sleep."

BRIANNE'S THUMBS WORKED furiously beneath the sheets. *I can't believe it,* she typed angrily into her BlackBerry. *They're still up.* She flipped onto her side. This way she'd be able to see when Jennifer came out of the bathroom. *Try 2 b patient a little while longer,* she continued typing. *I'll b there as soon as I can.*

It was after one o'clock in the morning. Why wasn't anyone asleep yet? Why did everyone seem intent on drawing out their misery by staying awake as long as humanly possible?

Almost as if they knew.

Except how could they?

And what was with all that nonsense about the seven deadly sins? They must have made those up, Brianne decided. She could think of far worse sins than any of the ones they'd mentioned. Anger and envy? Big deal. If they were considered deadly sins, the entire population was going to burn in Hell. And covetousness? Wasn't *committing* an act far worse than just *wanting* to do it? And what was the matter with pride? Pride in your work, your appearance, your accomplishments? Wasn't that supposed to be a good thing?

As for gluttony, well, okay, there were definitely too many fat people in the world, but was being a glutton really as bad as being a thief or a child molester?

What about assault? Rape? Torture?

And in what kind of warped universe did sloth trump murder? Guess murder isn't deadly enough, Brianne thought with a smile as Jennifer returned from the bathroom.

"My turn," Brianne said, climbing out of bed as Jennifer crawled back in. At least in the bathroom she'd be able to text in peace. Besides, it was getting hot lying in bed with her clothes on underneath her pajamas.

Once in the bathroom, she locked the door, turned on the taps, and tore off her pj's. Holding her breath to keep from being overwhelmed by the thick cloud of Jennifer's perfume, she sat down on the edge of the tub and began texting. *Sorry about this, babe. These morons seem intent on ruining my life. I promise I'll make it up to u. Tonite will be the best ever. Don't start without me.*

Minutes later, there was a knock on the bathroom door. "Brianne," her mother whispered, "are you all right?"

Brianne bristled with annoyance. "I'm fine, Mom."

Silence, then, "You're not texting in there, are you?"

Brianne immediately buried her BlackBerry underneath her arm. "Go back to bed, Mom." Brianne waited until she was sure her mother was no longer standing outside the door, then entered one last text: *2 dangerous 2 text anymore tonite. Hopefully everyone will conk out soon. Then the fun begins.*

She climbed back into her pajamas, flushed the toilet, turned off the water in the taps, and left the room.

"Are you all right, pumpkin?" James asked as she tiptoed past the sofa on which he was sprawled.

"Fine." Damn it. Wasn't anybody asleep?

Another hour elapsed before Brianne was satisfied everyone was finally unconscious. Both her mother and Melissa were snoring in gentle unison, and Jennifer hadn't moved so much as a muscle in twenty minutes. Pushing herself slowly and gingerly out of bed, Brianne tiptoed toward the living room. She saw James lying on his stomach, one foot reaching for the floor, his head to the wall, eyes closed, mouth open, seemingly dead to the world.

Brianne quickly removed her pajamas, like a snake shedding its skin, stuffing them into her canvas bag along with one of the keycards she'd swiped from the top of the desk. Hopefully she'd be back before anyone even realized she'd been gone. And if someone did wake up and see she wasn't there, she would simply claim that the earlier ruckus had left her too wound up to sleep and, not wishing to disturb anyone further, she'd gone out for a walk.

That's me, she thought as she opened the door and stepped into the hall. Always thinking of others.

HE WAS SITTING by himself on a chaise beside the deserted swimming pool when she spotted him.

"Hi," she said, approaching slowly, looking back over her shoulder to ascertain whether anyone else was watching.

He looked up at her, sad eyes radiating confusion.

"Can't sleep?" she asked.

He nodded. "One of those nights."

"For me, too. Do you mind if I join you?"

"Lots of empty chairs," he said.

Not encouraging exactly, but not discouraging either, she thought. "I saw you earlier. In the dining room. David, right?"

He cocked his head to one side. Like a quizzical puppy, she thought. She'd never been a fan of puppies.

"I heard your wife call you David," she said, answering his silent question.

"Among other choice epithets."

"Yes. She seemed pretty upset."

"Sorry about that."

"You don't have to apologize."

He smiled. "You are . . . ?"

She gave him her sweetest, most beguiling smile. "Nicole," she said softly. "But you can call me Nikki."

NINE

"OKAY, SLEEPYHEAD. TIME TO wake up."

Brianne groaned and flipped over onto her stomach, pulling the covers up over her head in protest.

"Come on, sweetheart. We're starving. It's almost nine o'clock. Everybody's been waiting for you."

Brianne said nothing. Nine o'clock meant she'd been asleep barely four hours. She was exhausted. Every part of her was sore. All she wanted to do was sleep and dream about last night. Maybe if she refused to answer, her mother would go away and leave her alone.

"They stop serving breakfast at ten o'clock," Val said instead.

"I can't believe you feel like eating anything."

"I'm feeling much better this morning. Besides, we can't very well go hiking on an empty stomach."

"Hiking?" Brianne reluctantly poked her head out from beneath the sheets, squinting into the bright sunlight that was pouring into the room from the bedside window. Who had opened the drapes? What was her mother talking about? "You gotta be kidding me."

"It's no joke," Melissa said from somewhere across the room. "Your mother has decided to take us all hiking. We're going shopping for proper clothes right after we eat."

"Oh, happy day," said James.

"Forget it. I'm not going anywhere."

"We'll talk about it at breakfast," Val said.

"*You* talk about it at breakfast."

"Come on, Brianne . . ." Val began pulling at Brianne's sheets. "It'll be fun."

"Who are you—the camp counselor from Hell?" Brianne pushed herself up onto her elbows. Through eyes that were still half closed, she saw her mother and her friends, freshly scrubbed and dressed. She craned her neck for the sight of her father's fiancée. Surely Jennifer hadn't agreed to participate in any such insanity. "Where's Jennifer?"

"She went to the gym," James said. "You should have seen her in her cute little pink outfit from Lululemon."

"Said we should just do our own thing and not worry about her," Melissa said.

"Sounds like a plan." Brianne flopped back down, dragging the covers back over her head.

Val immediately pulled them down again.

"God, were you this bossy with Dad?" Brianne said. "No wonder . . ."

"Okay, that's enough," Val said, knowing exactly where this

little sentence was going. "Let's get something straight right now, shall we? Your father didn't leave because I was bossy." *Did he?* "And he didn't leave because I snore." *Did he?* "He left because he's an idiot!"

There was a collective intake of breath, Val's gasp the loudest of all. Had she really just called Evan an idiot? She'd never done so before, never even allowed herself the luxury of thinking it.

"Way to go, girlfriend," said James, as Melissa nodded vigorously.

"This weekend was not my idea," she continued softly. "But your father won't be here till later, and I thought we could use the time for . . ."

"For what? Some mother-daughter bonding?"

Was she really that transparent? Val wondered. More like pitiful, she thought. "Would that be so awful? I remember when we used to enjoy each other's company."

Brianne said nothing, which Val chose to interpret favorably. "Now, get your cute little behind out of bed, and meet us in the dining room for breakfast in twenty minutes. Brianne? Did you hear me?"

Brianne's response was a loud groan.

"Good. Then we'll look forward to seeing you in the dining room in twenty minutes." With that, Val swiveled around on her heels and marched from the room, Melissa and James scurrying to catch up.

"Well done," Brianne heard Melissa say as the door to their room opened and closed.

"Bravo," seconded James.

"Yeah, right," Brianne whispered. Then she flopped back down on her pillow and disappeared under the sheets.

*   *   *

"DO YOU THINK she'll show up?" James was asking as they stepped out of the elevator into the main lobby.

"Probably not," Val conceded.

"So, what happens then?"

"Damned if I know."

Passing by the reception desk on their way to the dining room, Val recognized the young woman who'd been arguing with her new husband at dinner the night before. She was wearing denim shorts and a sloppy gray sweatshirt. Val estimated her age as late twenties, and noted she didn't look any happier this morning than she had last night. Obviously David hadn't apologized.

"I'm telling you something has happened to him," Val heard her saying to the receptionist. "He went out last night around two o'clock and he never came back."

"If you'll give me a minute, Mrs. Gowan, I'll get the manager."

"Looks as if our resident asshole went fishing earlier than originally planned," Val muttered to her companions, steering them toward the dining room.

"Excuse me," a voice called from behind them.

Val turned back to see the young woman hurrying toward them. The closer she got, the more swollen her face appeared, the red rimming her eyes matching the quarter-size blotches that stained her skin like large freckles. Her auburn hair was pulled off her face into a ponytail and secured at the sides by two large bobby pins, clearly a matter of convenience over style.

"Excuse me," she said again. "I'm so sorry to bother you but . . ."

"Yes?" Val asked.

"My name is Alicia Gowan. I think my husband and I were sitting at the table next to yours last night at dinner."

Val pretended to mull this over. "Oh, yes. I think that's right."

"Have you seen him? My husband? Since then, I mean?"

"No, I'm afraid we haven't." Val looked toward James and Melissa for confirmation.

"No," Melissa concurred.

"Is there a problem?" asked James.

"We had a fight." Fresh tears filled Alicia Gowan's eyes and fell down her cheeks. "Not even a fight, really. Just a stupid argument. Well, I'm sure you heard it . . ."

"No," Val, Melissa, and James all said together, perhaps a beat too quickly.

"I told him I wouldn't talk to him again until he apologized. Stupid, right? I mean, what good is an apology when someone isn't sorry?"

Val nodded, deciding to say nothing. There is nothing I can say to this woman that will make her feel any better, she thought.

"Anyway," the woman continued, unprompted, "he was really angry, said I'd embarrassed him in front of the whole dining room, and that started another argument, and he stormed out. That was around two o'clock this morning. And I waited for him to come back, but he didn't, and I guess I fell asleep because suddenly it was morning, and he still wasn't back. So I waited and waited. And then I thought maybe he went back to the city. But his car keys are still here, and I checked the parking lot, and our car is right where we left it. I even looked in the backseat, in case he slept there." She shook her head. "So then I thought, Well, maybe he hitched a ride back to New

York. But I know David. He would never do that. He wouldn't just leave and not tell me, no matter how angry he was. And he's not answering his cell. And the concierge hasn't seen him. The receptionist hasn't seen him. None of the waiters has seen him. *You* haven't seen him," she said, as if this were the ultimate proof that her husband was truly missing.

"I'm sure he'll turn up," Val said, although she was sure of no such thing.

"Maybe he went to another motel," Melissa offered.

Val thought this was highly unlikely since they both knew there were no vacancies in the vicinity.

"Or maybe he just curled up in a chair somewhere on the grounds and fell asleep," James said.

"You're right," Alicia said. "I'm probably overreacting. But if you should happen to see him . . ."

"We'll chew him out good and tell him to get his ass back to you pronto," James said.

Alicia tried to smile, but her lips were quivering too much to stay still.

"I'm sure he'll turn up," Val said again, although she was no surer this time than she'd been the last time she'd said it.

"Mrs. Gowan?" a soothing voice asked.

Everyone turned toward the sound.

The manager, a round little man named Edward Cotton, stood before them, a sympathetic smile on his reassuringly bland face. "I understand there's a problem?"

"My husband didn't come back to the room last night," Alicia began immediately.

"Perhaps we should discuss this in my office."

"Keep us posted," Val said as the manager led the distraught woman away.

*   *   *

THE PARK RANGERS were in the lobby interviewing Alicia Gowan when Val and her friends returned from breakfast.

"Looks like he still hasn't shown up," Melissa commented.

"Do you think maybe a bear got him?" James whispered as they walked past.

"I think it's more likely that a *bar* got him," Melissa said. "He probably drank himself into a stupor and is somewhere sleeping it off."

Val tried—and failed—not to picture her mother sprawled unconscious in the alley behind her apartment building. She made a silent vow never to take another drink.

"Ten bucks says Sleeping Beauty's still asleep," James said as they entered their suite.

Jennifer was sitting on the living room sofa, rifling through the latest issue of *New York* magazine. She was still dressed in her pretty pink exercise outfit, and her long blond hair was pulled into a high ponytail and secured by a pink scrunchie.

How is it possible to look so glamorous after exercising? Val wondered. "Where's Brianne?"

"I assumed she was with you."

"How long have you been here?"

"About ten minutes."

"She probably went downstairs for breakfast," Melissa said.

"We must have just missed her," said James.

Jennifer put down her magazine. "Why don't I see if I can find her?" She was clearly eager to put as much distance between her and the others as possible.

"I'd appreciate that. Thank you," Val said as Jennifer left the room.

A few minutes later, a series of familiar chimes filled the air. Val followed the sound into the bedroom, her hand rifling under the sheets of Brianne's bed and emerging seconds later with her daughter's BlackBerry. "Honestly, sometimes I think she'd lose her head if it weren't attached . . ." She glanced at the incoming message.

Last night was something else, she read. *Can't wait to do it again.* What the hell did that mean?

"Is it from Evan?" James asked from the doorway.

"No. There's no name. Just a number."

The door to the suite suddenly opened and Brianne burst into the bedroom as if someone were chasing her, stopping abruptly when she saw her BlackBerry in her mother's hands.

"Forget something?" Val asked.

"Give me that," Brianne said. "It's mine."

"Last night was something else," Val recited from memory. *"Can't wait to do it again?"*

"You have no right to read my messages."

"What does it mean, *last night was something else?*"

"It doesn't mean anything. Sasha went to this club I told her about. Obviously she had a good time. What's the big deal?"

"Sasha?"

"Yes, Sasha. She who works at Lululemon and drives an orange Mustang." Brianne reached for her BlackBerry. Val quickly moved it behind her back. "What are you doing? Give it to me."

"Why? You don't take very good care of it."

"It's your fault I forgot it," Brianne countered. "You made me rush."

Val shook her head. "Okay, fine. It's my fault. But there's been enough texting for one trip. The BlackBerry stays with me until your father gets here."

"Oh, for crap's sake. Why don't you just chill? Have another drink, Grandma," she said with an audible sneer.

"Okay, Brianne. I think that's quite enough."

"You want to know what *I* think?" Brianne snapped. "I think Dad got out just in time."

Val wasn't sure of the precise order of the events that followed. She felt both arms moving at once, one hand hurling the BlackBerry toward the far wall just as Jennifer walked back into the room, the other hand connecting solidly with Brianne's cheek. "She's not in the dining room," Jennifer was saying as the BlackBerry flew past her ear, missing her by inches.

And then everybody was screaming.

TEN

"OKAY, SO HOW WOULD you describe this if you were writing about it for the *New York Times*?" James asked as the three friends made their way along the steep, forested ridges of Prospect Mountain.

Val stopped on a large flat rock overlooking the valley, adjusting the wide-brimmed Tilley hat she'd purchased at the hotel gift shop earlier that morning. "I'd probably say something like 'The spectacular view includes the thirty-two-mile-long expanse of crystal-clean, sparkling blue waters of Lake George some two-thousand-plus feet below, along with mile after mile of fragrant evergreens and an assortment of broadleaf trees that shoot from the sides of the surrounding mountains like fireworks.' "

James removed his own new hat, waving it up and down in

front of his face as if it were a fan. "Took the words right out of my mouth."

"It really *is* spectacular." Melissa's eyes scanned the horizon from underneath the rim of her black baseball cap, with its *Welcome to the Adirondacks* logo emblazoned in red across it. "Although I'm surprised it's so hot."

"That's what you get for wearing a black T-shirt," Val said. "You know black holds the heat. How are the shoes?" Val had taken her friends to one of the hotel's many shops to buy suitable clothes and shoes for their hike around Prospect Mountain, charging their various purchases to the room. It was, she'd decided, the least Evan could do after the horrific scene with their daughter earlier this morning.

"The shoes are great," Melissa said. "It's my feet that are killing me."

"My calves are starting to cramp," James complained.

"You're a dancer," Val reminded him. "Shouldn't you be used to exercise?"

"I'm used to dancing, not climbing. And I'm retired, remember? The only exercise I get these days is searching out fine pieces of vintage costume jewelry."

Melissa concurred. "There's not a lot of climbing in costume jewelry."

"So tell us more about the fascinating world of flora," James urged, squatting on a large piece of rough stone and trying to make himself comfortable.

"You just want to sit down."

"True enough. So shoot me. These legs need a break."

"Mine, too," Melissa said. "How about we take a five-minute recess?"

"We've been up here for almost two hours. That's enough

wilderness for this queer city boy. How about we just head back to the lodge? That's where all the fun stuff is happening."

"I think I've had enough fun for a while," Val said.

"Ah, but you were magnificent. Wasn't she, Melissa?" James asked. "The way that BlackBerry went flying across the room . . ."

"Almost decapitating poor Jennifer," Melissa said wistfully.

". . . who screamed almost as loud as Brianne."

"Nobody screams as loud as Brianne," Val said, trying to block out the memory of those awful sounds. "I can't believe I actually slapped her."

"She had it coming," Melissa said. "I almost slapped her myself."

"She hates me."

"She's sixteen," Melissa reminded her. "She's supposed to hate you."

"I shouldn't have left her alone. I should have insisted she come with us."

"Which would have made this hike even more fun," James said.

"Besides, she's not alone," Melissa reminded her. "She's with Jennifer."

"Great. Her new best friend. And when did we stop calling her 'the Slut'?"

"Sorry about that. Would you rather she hated her?"

"Better her than me."

"Then you have to lay off the sarcasm and start killing her with kindness," Melissa said. "That's what I did with mother-in-law number two."

Val regarded her friend quizzically, waiting for her to continue.

Melissa quickly obliged. "She was this old battle-axe. Hated me from the word *go*. Made my life a living hell. At first I fought back, but it only seemed to excite her. Like it was a contest, who could get in the most zingers in the shortest amount of time. Then one day I just decided I wasn't going to play that game anymore. Instead I was going to be the sweetest, nicest daughter-in-law a mother-in-law could possibly want. I was going to smother the old witch with compassion. And I did. Two months later, she had a heart attack and died. It was great." Melissa's smile filled the entire lower half of her face.

"You're just saying that to make me feel good."

"Is it working?"

"Yes." Val laughed. "God, when did I become such an awful person?"

"You've always been awful," James said.

"He's right," Melissa agreed. "You have."

"Thanks, guys. I feel much better now."

"Any time."

"So, tell us more about wherever the hell it is we are so we can get the hell out of here." James gestured toward the valley below. "You've got five minutes."

Okay, Val thought, trying to recall enough geographical details of the area to take her mind off what had happened in the hotel room. "The Adirondack Park is the largest park in the continental United States," she began, thinking of the times she and Evan had hiked through these very woods. "It's shaped like a giant oval and is bigger than Yellowstone, Yosemite, Glacier, and the Grand Canyon combined. Six million acres, if you can imagine it. It's actually larger than many of the neighboring states. A virtual tapestry of meadows, lakes, streams, woodlands, mountain peaks, and tiny villages."

"A virtual tapestry," James repeated. "That's rather good."

"If memory serves me, there are over five thousand public and private campsites in Lake George alone," Val continued, poring through the invisible file cabinets in her brain where such bits of information were stored. She and Evan had been to at least half a dozen. Val knew these woods as well as she knew the streets of the city.

"And at least that many deer flies," Melissa said, swatting several of the pesky insects away from her face and neck.

"Okay, I've definitely had enough splendor in the grass for now," James said. "Time to drive back to the lodge and lounge around some civilized concrete and chlorine. I think I'll even let Evan treat me to that sweet little bathing suit I saw in the gift shop this morning, the one with the leaping dolphins."

"Oh, come on, guys. You don't really want to go back yet . . ."

"Yes, we really do," James said. "Don't we, Melissa?"

Melissa nodded. "What's that expression, *too much of a good thing*?"

Can you ever really have too much of a good thing? Val wondered, deciding not to protest. Her friends had been good-enough sports, postponing their own plans in order to accompany her to the mountains, agreeing to go hiking in order to get her away from Jennifer and Brianne long enough for everyone to calm down, supporting her when she acted like a jerk, which seemed to be most of the time lately, all the while trying to keep her spirits up and her sanity intact.

Too late for that, Val thought. "Okay, let's head back."

Which was when they heard the sound of rustling in the nearby trees.

"Please tell me that's not a bear," James said.

"If it is," Val cautioned, "just stand very still and then start backing away slowly. Whatever you do, don't run."

"Are you joking? Is she joking?" James asked Melissa.

"And don't climb a tree. Bears are great climbers."

The rustling drew nearer.

"This is not happening," said James, shouting out in fear as the leaves parted.

A young man suddenly appeared before them. Tall, muscular, smooth-skinned. He was wearing a checkered shirt and khaki pants and his long, dark hair was pulled into a ponytail at the base of his neck. "Oh," he said, seemingly as startled as they were. "Sorry. I didn't realize anyone else was here."

"They thought you were a bear," James said.

The boy laughed. "Only when I'm hungry."

Val found herself staring at the dimples that creased the young man's cheeks. I know those dimples, she thought, trying to figure out how that was possible. Is he a friend of Brianne's? she wondered. He looked older than Brianne, but maybe they'd gone to the same school, or maybe even acted together in a school play. "Do I know you?" she asked, peering deep into his hazel eyes.

The boy returned her gaze with equal intensity. "No, I don't think so."

"I think you might know my daughter. Brianne. Brianne Rowe?"

He shook his head. "No. The name doesn't ring a bell."

"She goes to Erasmus High in Brooklyn."

"I'm from Connecticut."

Connecticut? Val didn't know anybody who lived in Connecticut. "Sorry. It's just that you look so familiar to me."

"Hayden," a distant voice called out. "Where the hell are you?"

"Up here, Dad," the boy called over the sound of branches being parted and sticks being trampled underfoot.

Seconds later, another figure emerged from the dense foliage. He was breathing heavily and his forehead glistened with the sweat of his recent exertions. "You gotta slow down, partner. Your old man's not as young as he used to be. Hello," he said upon seeing the others.

I don't believe it, Val thought. What are the chances? "Gary?" she asked. "Gary Parker?"

"I'm sorry." The man squinted through the sunlight. "Do I know you?"

Val whipped off her Tilley hat, giving a quick fluff to the matted hair beneath. "It's Valerie. Valerie Marcus. Or, at least, it used to be Marcus. I went to Lincoln High. We were on the swim team together."

"Oh, my God," said Gary Parker. "It's been . . . how long?"

"Must be twenty-five years."

"Valerie Marcus," he repeated with a shake of his head. "My God, how *are* you?"

"I'm fine. I can't believe how much your son looks like you did at his age."

"I can't believe you remember."

Neither can I, Val thought. Even though they'd been on the swim team together and had been in several of the same classes, they'd spoken maybe half a dozen sentences to each other during their entire tenure at Lincoln High. In fact, Gary Parker had probably said more to her in the last minute than he had their entire senior year. "These are my friends, James and Melissa."

"Nice to meet you both," Gary said, a sentiment that was quickly echoed by Melissa and James. "And I take it you've met my son, Hayden."

"They thought I was a bear."

"An understandable mistake." Gary affectionately tugged on his son's ponytail before returning his attention to Val, his hazel eyes twinkling mischievously. "So, you come here often?"

Val smiled. "Actually, I do. Or rather, I *did*. It's been a few years. You?"

"Every chance I get. Magnificent, isn't it?"

"Yes, it is. Your son was saying you live in Connecticut."

"For almost twenty years now. I moved there right after I graduated from college."

"Full athletic scholarship to Duke, if I recall correctly," Val said.

"That's one impressive memory you've got."

"Thank you, but I've never been sure if that's a blessing or a curse."

"Probably a bit of both."

"Probably," Val agreed. "So, what made you decide on Connecticut?"

"I met a girl."

"Of course." Something else she remembered: Gary had never had any trouble attracting female companionship. She noted that sometime in the last few sentences, Melissa and James had wandered a discreet distance away and were currently engaging Gary's son in some idle chitchat.

"We were both majoring in business. Ruthie's father was a stock trader, had his own brokerage firm in Connecticut. We got married, I joined the family firm, we had a son and then a daughter. And then, I'm sorry to say, a rather nasty divorce." He lowered his voice. "That was five years ago. I left the firm but stayed in Connecticut to be near the kids."

"So what business are you in now?" Val said, not the question she really wanted to ask. The question she really wanted to ask: Why the nasty divorce? To be immediately followed by: How nasty exactly?

"Same business," Gary said, answering the only question voiced out loud. "More understanding boss this time around: me."

Val agreed. "It's nice to be your own boss."

"So, what about you? Married? Divorced? Children? Career?"

"All of the above," Val said. "Married. Divorced. Or almost, anyway. One daughter. One lapsed career."

"What career? How lapsed?"

"I did some travel writing for the *New York Times* and a few other publications."

"Yeah? Why'd you stop? I bet you were really good at it."

"Why would you say that?"

"Because you were good at everything you did."

"Why would you say that?" she asked again, fighting back the unexpected urge to burst into tears.

"Because you were fearless."

"I was?" More like terrified, she thought.

"Are you kidding? I remember you at swim meets. You were this skinny little thing, all arms and legs; you hadn't really filled out yet." He stopped, coughed self-consciously into his hand. "But you were always so gung-ho. Your butterfly stroke was unconventional, to say the least. You had way more enthusiasm than technique. And yet you won every damn race you entered."

Val smiled. It had been at her mother's instigation that she'd first started swimming. Her mother still kept a shoe box full of her medals in one of her closets, although she'd probably forgotten where.

"And track and field, the same thing. You were quite the competitor."

"Not so much anymore," Val said, thinking of Jennifer.

"But still pretty athletic, I see."

"I guess. You?"

"Not really. I ski a bit. Cross-country mostly. I bet it's downhill for you or nothing."

Yes, it's been all downhill, Val thought. "I used to go heli-skiing, believe it or not."

I just can't imagine jumping out of a helicopter and skiing down the side of a mountain, she heard Jennifer say, followed soon after by *I don't like anything where I'm not in control of my feet.* What did Evan see in this girl?

"Oh, I believe it." Gary shook his head in admiration. "Fearless."

"Well, maybe I used to be."

"Divorce can really do a number on your head," Gary said. "Don't worry. Your courage will come back."

Val glanced toward her friends, catching a look of restless impatience on the face of Gary's son. "I think Hayden's anxious to get going," she said.

"Ah, youth," Gary said with a smile. "Always thinking that the next stop will be better than where they are now."

"Should we tell him it only gets worse?"

"And spoil the fun of watching him find out for himself?" Gary wiped a fresh outbreak of perspiration from his forehead. "This getting older is for the birds."

"You'd think we could at least get better-looking," Val said.

Gary laughed. "You have."

It was Val's turn to laugh. "Well, I don't think that's true, but thank you anyway. It was nice of you to say so."

"I never say anything I don't mean."

"That can't be good." Val extended her hand. "Well, good-bye, Gary Parker. It was really nice running into you again."

He held on to her hand for several long seconds. She felt an unexpected charge. "You, too."

Hayden approached, trailed by Melissa and James. "Dad, we should get going or there won't be any tents left."

Gary explained. "I let him talk me into going camping tonight."

"Camping?" James asked with a perceptible shudder. "As in sitting around a campfire and sleeping on the ground?"

"Not your cup of tea?"

"James likes his creature comforts," Melissa said.

"As opposed to creatures that crawl," James explained.

They all laughed.

"We're staying at the Lodge. Down by Shadow Creek," James volunteered. "That's about as primitive as I like to get."

"Great place," Gary said. "Well, enjoy your stay. Maybe we'll run into each other again sometime."

"Take care," Val said.

"Dad . . . ," Hayden beckoned.

"Remember," Gary whispered to Val. "Fearless." He waved goodbye to the others, then turned and followed after his son.

"Well, isn't he the hunk?" James said. "In that rugged, diamond-in-the-rough kind of way. Don't you think, Val?"

"I think I'm ready to go back," she said in response.

"You notice she didn't answer my question," James said.

"Yes, I noticed that," said Melissa.

"Are you guys coming or what?"

"Lead the way," Melissa and James said together.

ELEVEN

THEY RETURNED FROM THE lofty summit of Prospect Mountain in time for lunch, having decided on the drive back to the lodge to leave for Manhattan as soon as they'd had a bite to eat. Eat first, load the car, bid adieu to Brianne and Jennifer, they'd agreed. Then hightail it out of there. Val couldn't bear the thought of any more confrontations. She'd had all the mother-daughter bonding she could take.

"I'll check for messages." Val's eyes swept across the lobby as she approached the reception desk. The park rangers were no longer in evidence. Alicia Gowan's wayward husband had no doubt been discovered sleeping off his misery in a hidden clump of manicured grass somewhere on the premises. *And the beat goes on,* Val sang to herself, smiling at the toothy receptionist with the modified beehive hairdo who was standing ramrod straight behind the counter. "Hello, Alexandra," she said, reading the young woman's name tag on the lapel of her crisp navy jacket. "I'm Mrs. Rowe. In room 313. Are there any messages for me?"

Alexandra looked vaguely confused as she consulted her computer. "No. Nothing since the other Mrs. Rowe checked about an hour ago."

Val felt her fists clench at her sides. There's still only one Mrs. Rowe, she fought the urge to say. At least for the time being. "Thank you." She stopped, turned away, turned quickly back. "Tell me, did they find David Gowan?"

Alexandra glanced nervously over her shoulder, as if she'd been cautioned not to say anything to anyone. "They're still searching the grounds," she whispered. "So far there's been no sign of him. Personally, I think he flew the coop."

"And Mrs. Gowan?"

Alexandra shrugged. "I haven't seen her since this morning. She was pretty upset. I understand her parents are on their way here from Maine."

Val nodded. "Well, hopefully he'll turn up before they get here." Although he may wish he hadn't, she thought. "If any calls come in for me in the next hour, could you please have them transferred to the dining room?"

"Certainly."

"Any news?" Melissa asked as the hostess was leading them to a table by the window.

"Nothing. You'd think Evan would have called by now."

"Because he's so considerate and reliable?" Melissa asked sweetly as the waitress handed them each an open, oversized menu.

"Let me see," James said. "I think considerate and reliable

Evan would like me to have this shockingly expensive lobster salad and a glass of Chardonnay."

"Considerate, reliable, and *generous*," said Melissa, ordering the same thing.

Val smiled at her friends. "Make that three," she told the waitress.

"BRIANNE?" VAL CALLED as they entered the suite approximately one hour later. "Brianne, honey . . ."

"Save your 'honeys,'" James said. "It doesn't look as if anyone's home."

"They're probably at the pool." Melissa glanced into the bathroom as Val checked the bedroom.

"Might as well start packing up." Val began gathering her things together, wondering if they should skip the formal goodbyes and just leave a note. So much for "fearless," she thought, hearing the door to the suite open. "Brianne?" she called, walking back into the living room.

"Just me," Jennifer said, removing her large floppy hat and cover-up, then shaking her long blond hair free. It fell in perfect waves around her toned shoulders.

Naturally, Val thought, trying not to notice the diamond stud that pierced Jennifer's navel between the tiny halves of her pink bikini. Had Evan bought her that diamond? Did it qualify as an engagement ring? "Where's Brianne?" she asked.

Jennifer shrugged. "She's not here?"

Here we go again, Val thought.

"She said she'd had enough sun and was going back to the room to wash her hair," Jennifer explained without prompting.

"How long ago was that?"

Jennifer checked her watch. "About half an hour. Maybe forty minutes. We had lunch at the pool, then she said she was going up to the room to wash her hair."

"And you just let her go?"

"What was I supposed to do, Val? Tell her she couldn't wash her hair?"

"You could have come back with her."

"Why would I do that?"

"Because she was your responsibility."

"She's sixteen years old, Val. She doesn't need a chaperone to watch her wash her hair."

"Except she didn't wash her hair, did she?"

"I don't know. Maybe she finished washing it and went out again."

Val poked her head into the impossibly tidy bathroom, its fresh white towels folded neatly on the heated racks. There was no lingering shampoo scent or trace of humidity. "No one's been in this room since housekeeping was here this morning."

Jennifer looked toward Melissa and James. *Help me,* her eyes pleaded.

"Shit," Val muttered. Then again, louder. "Shit."

"What's the big deal?" Jennifer kicked off her espadrilles. "I'm not sure I understand what you're so upset about."

"My daughter is missing."

"She's not missing," Jennifer insisted. "She's just not here."

"Then where is she?"

"I don't know. I *do* know you're overreacting. Again."

Val sank into the nearest chair, a fresh headache hovering. "Look. You're not a parent. I don't expect you to understand."

"I understand you shouldn't have hit her. I understand why she might not want to be here when you got back."

"Yes, you're a veritable pillar of understanding," Val snapped.

"Val," Melissa cautioned between lips that didn't move, her fingers fluttering in front of her mouth. "Kindness," she whispered. "You're killing her with kindness, remember?"

Val took a deep breath, feeling an enormous wave of guilt wash over her. "Did she say anything to you . . . about . . . what happened?"

Jennifer shook her head. "No. But for what it's worth, I told her I think she owes you an apology."

Val scoffed. "Why would you do that?"

"Beats me." Jennifer shrugged. "I also think it wouldn't hurt if you apologized to her."

"Excuse me?"

"Kindness," Melissa whispered between tightly clenched teeth.

"Look. If you're really worried, why don't you just try her on her cell?" Jennifer asked.

Val reached into her pocket, removed Brianne's battered BlackBerry, and held it up. "Because I confiscated the damn thing. Remember?"

"So you did," Jennifer said. "Okay, I'm out of suggestions. If it's all the same to everybody, I'm going to take a shower before Evan gets here."

"He called?" Val tried not to sound too surprised.

"Well, no. Not yet. But I'm sure he will any time now."

"Right."

"I know what you're thinking," Jennifer said defensively. "But you really don't know him as well as you think you do."

"Right. Because I was only married to him for eighteen years and you've been fucking him for . . . how many months has it been exactly?"

"Why don't we go downstairs and see if we can find Brianne?" Melissa said quickly, pushing Val in the direction of the door.

"Yes," said Jennifer icily. "Why don't you?"

"I'll check the pool," James offered as they stepped into the hall.

"I'll check the shops," said Melissa.

"I'll check the grounds," Val said.

"And I'll see all you lovely folks later." With that, Jennifer kicked the door shut.

VAL HAD BEEN sitting on one of two overstuffed green leather sofas in front of the enormous stone fireplace across from the reception desk in the lobby for half an hour when she saw him. He was wearing neat black trousers and a purple-and-white-checkered shirt, looking more like an actual diamond than the diamond-in-the-rough James had earlier pronounced him to be. Although no less rugged, Val thought, her breath catching in her lungs as she watched him approach. "Gary," she said, jumping to her feet, surprised by the unexpectedly visceral intensity of her reaction. For two decades, she'd had eyes for only one man—Evan. Despite his many infidelities, she'd remained hopelessly faithful. And there'd been no one since he left. What's wrong with me? she thought. "What are you doing here?" she said.

"Didn't think you'd see me again quite so soon?"

"No, I sure didn't. What are you doing here?"

"It seems I'm asking you out to dinner."

"What?"

"If your friends can spare you for an evening, that is."

"What?" Val said again.

"Or they're free to join us, if you'd prefer."

"I don't understand."

"It's really not all that difficult. You're not one of those women who don't eat, are you?"

"How did you find me?" Val asked, ignoring the question she assumed was rhetorical.

"Your friend, James, mentioned you were staying here."

Val nodded, remembering. She looked behind him. "Your son . . . ?"

". . . is back at the campsite. He met some guys and it looks like they're gonna be doing their own thing tonight, so I thought I'd take a chance you might be free . . ."

"I can't."

"Oh. All right. I . . ."

"My daughter seems to have vanished."

"What?"

"We've searched everywhere. I've been sitting here for half an hour," Val explained, tears filling her eyes, "waiting for her to walk through those doors."

Gary guided her back toward the sofa, sitting down beside her. "Okay. Start at the beginning."

Val quickly explained the situation, telling him all about Jennifer and the fight she'd had with Brianne that morning.

"Wait a minute," Gary said. "You're telling me you're all staying in the same room?"

Val clarified. "It's a suite."

He nodded, as if trying to picture the scene. "Still . . ."

"You think she just needed a little space?" Val asked hopefully. She'd been trying to convince herself of that for the last two hours.

"You have to admit it's a rather unusual situation."

"Yes, it is. And normally, I might not make such a big deal out of everything. I mean, we had this fight." Val lowered her voice to an embarrassed whisper. "*I hit her.* Naturally, she's angry. Hell, she's furious. So, yes. She doesn't want to be around me right now. She's made that very clear. Jennifer's the beautiful princess and I'm the Wicked Witch. I get it. But enough is enough. It'll be dark in a few hours, and I've been sitting here imagining all the awful things that could happen to her, and thinking that one person has already disappeared . . ."

Gary interrupted. "What? Somebody else has disappeared?"

Again, Val explained the situation, noting the bemused look that crept into Gary's soft hazel eyes. "Yes, I know I'm being ridiculous, that David Gowan probably just went home, and that he's not answering his phone because he wants to teach his wife a lesson. At least that's what the park rangers think."

"You've spoken to the park rangers?"

"No. I spoke to the hotel manager about an hour ago. The poor man practically begged me not to get the rangers involved again."

"I don't think that's his call to make."

"He doesn't want to start a panic. And I understand his concerns, I really do. I don't want to cry wolf. I just want my daughter to come back." Val watched the front door open and a teenage girl walk through.

"Is that her?" Gary asked.

The girl drew closer, her long hair swaying back and forth across her shoulders as she walked. She was wearing a white, off-the-shoulder peasant blouse and a pair of fraying denim shorts, their long threads trailing down her tanned thighs. Val recognized her as the girl who'd almost mowed her down the night before, punctuating that affront with a raised middle finger.

"No." Her shoulders slumped forward in disappointment.

The girl smiled at Gary as she walked by.

Val's cell phone began ringing. She grabbed it from her pocket and flipped it open, raising it to her ear, hearing it crackle. "Hello?"

"Just me," Melissa said over the static. "I take it you haven't seen her?" At Val's urging, Melissa and James had returned to their room, in case Brianne called.

"No," Val said. "I take it she hasn't phoned?"

"No."

Val sensed a "but" in her friend's voice. "But . . . ?"

"Evan did."

"Thank God. Is he on his way?"

"Apparently he's been delayed again," Melissa said. "It looks as if he won't be able to make it until tomorrow."

"Did Jennifer tell him about Brianne?"

"No. She said that he had enough to deal with at the moment, and that there was no need to worry him unnecessarily."

"No, we'd never want to do that."

"He promised to be here before noon, even if it means he has to get up at the crack of dawn. Poor baby," Melissa said, managing to make the two words sound like an expletive. "Do you want James and me to come down and keep you company?" The cell's reception was getting weaker. Melissa's voice on the line kept going in and out.

"No. It's okay. Gary's here."

"Who?"

"Gary Parker. You met him this morning."

"Diamond-in-the-rough Gary? Gary Parker's with her," Val heard Melissa tell James over the increasing static.

"Please tell me she's finally going to get laid," came James's immediate response.

"I'm thinking of calling the park rangers if Brianne's not back in the next ten minutes," Val said.

"If Brianne's not back in ten minutes, Val's going to call the park rangers," Melissa repeated to James.

"What? No. That's ridiculous," Val heard Jennifer cry before the line went dead in her hands.

Val returned her cell phone to her pocket. "Apparently my husband's girlfriend doesn't think that's a very good idea," she told Gary.

"Screw her."

"Thank you, but I think my husband's doing a pretty good job of that already."

Gary laughed.

"Sorry. I don't mean to sound bitter."

"Sounds pretty normal to me. What can I do to help?"

"You're doing it. Thank you." A few minutes later, Val was on her feet. "Okay, that's it. I've waited long enough." Gary was at her side as she cut across the lobby toward the manager's office.

"Wait," a familiar voice called after them.

Val spun around to see Jennifer rushing toward her, long blond hair bouncing around her attractively flushed face, Melissa and James following close behind.

"Where are you going?" Jennifer demanded of Val. "What are you doing?"

"Look, Jennifer," Val said, resisting the impulse to grab the other woman by the throat and hurl her into the fireplace. "I know you think I'm crazy, but I have every right to be concerned. Brianne is *my* daughter, not yours, and she's been gone for too long."

"Brianne is fine."

"I really don't have time for this."

"Make time," Jennifer said adamantly.

Val stared into Jennifer's cool blue eyes. "What are you trying to say?"

Jennifer took a deep breath, exhaling it in one long rush. "I'm saying that Brianne is perfectly okay. I'm saying that I know where she is." She looked to the ceiling, as if asking a higher power for help. "I'm saying that you'd better sit down."

TWELVE

S HE'S NOT GOING TO like this, Jennifer was thinking as she sat down on the sofa opposite Val. She's not going to like this one bit. She already hates me, not without reason, and this is going to push her off the deep end, dragging me along with her. I'll be lucky to get out of here alive.

How did I get into this mess anyway? she asked herself, nervously smoothing out the wrinkles in the beige linen pants she'd changed into after her shower. A torrent of hot water had brought a much-needed few minutes of peace and then it was right back into the maelstrom. She'd barely had time to finish blow-drying her hair before the Dynamic Duo had returned, mercifully without their revered leader.

Jennifer steeled herself to look at Evan's soon-to-be ex-wife, who, as usual, was glaring back at her with a combination of curiosity and contempt. Jennifer adjusted the heart-shaped topaz necklace Evan had recently bought her; she was careful not to snag it on the beige silk blouse he'd also selected. She wondered what a man as stylish as Evan would make of the loose khaki shorts and garish orange T-shirt Val had purchased this morning to go hiking. Not to mention the orange-and-white argyle socks folded over the top of her new boots. God—those socks.

"So?" Val asked impatiently. "Where is she?"

"Brianne is fine."

"So you've said, but I didn't ask you *how* she is. I asked you *where* she is."

"What difference does it make, as long as she's okay?" Jennifer knew she was only delaying the explosion that was sure to follow.

"Don't make me have to kill you," Val said.

The man beside her laughed. Who the hell is he? Jennifer wondered.

Melissa, sitting to Val's right, mumbled something out of the side of her mouth—a word that sounded, strangely enough, like "kindness"—while James perched at the far end of the sofa, leaning forward expectantly. Four against one, Jennifer thought, not liking her odds. If only Evan were here to even things out. Although if Evan *were* here, none of this would be happening.

Damn you anyway, Evan Rowe, Jennifer thought. It was Evan who'd made all the arrangements, who'd persuaded her this little excursion would go a long way toward cementing her budding relationship with his daughter. How many times had he told her he couldn't wait to share one of his favorite places on earth with her?

What he'd failed to mention was that all his previous visits to Shadow Creek had been with Val and that it was one of her favorite places as well. Or that she might end up sleeping in the next bed! Although, to be fair, nobody could have predicted *that*.

And who was this other guy who'd turned up out of nowhere? Jennifer glanced over at him. He was a big man, handsome in a just-past-his-prime, rough-hewn kind of way. What was he doing here? Had Val already notified the authorities? Was he a park ranger? Or was he something else altogether? *Please tell me she's finally going to get laid,* she'd heard James squeal. Was it possible that this man and Val were romantically involved?

From your mouth to God's ear, Jennifer prayed silently, repeating one of her mother's favorite expressions. Is that all it would take to make a believer out of me again? she wondered with a shake of her head. For Valerie to find herself another man?

Certainly it would go a long way toward clearing her own conscience. *Yes, I might have stolen another woman's husband,* she could tell her sister, *but look at how much happier Val is now.* Which would mean that she could stop looking over her shoulder, knowing the ghost of Valerie was lurking somewhere in the shadows, just waiting for her to slip up and make a mistake. She wouldn't have to be constantly checking her rearview mirror for Val's condescending gaze. Evan could stop feeling guilty; he could stop worrying about how she was doing; he could stop feeling responsible for her; he could stop mentioning her name at least three times a day.

Does he even realize how much he talks about her? Jennifer wondered.

So, yes, it would be wonderful indeed if Val actually had another man in her life.

'Tis a consummation devoutly to be wished, she recited silently, recalling the line from *Hamlet.* Funny thing to be remembering now, she thought, turning the word *consummation* over on her tongue, thinking back to the afternoon that Val had returned home earlier than expected and found her in bed with Evan, her legs wrapped around his broad shoulders.

Evan had been too distracted by his own pleasure to hear the front door open and his wife's footsteps on the stairs. For a second, she'd considered alerting him—what if it was Brianne?—but then she'd remembered that Brianne was in rehearsals for a school play and wouldn't be home until much later. So it must be Valerie, she'd deduced correctly, turning her head to one side and opening her eyes an imperceptible sliver, bracing herself for fireworks as her lover's wife appeared in the doorway.

But instead of an explosion, there'd been only silence. Val had backed away from the door without so much as a word. "I think I might have heard someone come in," Jennifer whispered when they were done. "Maybe you should check."

"No," Evan said moments later, returning to the bed. "There's no one."

The next few weeks had brought only more silence. Jennifer had begun to suspect she might have imagined the whole thing. "What kind of woman walks in on her husband making love to another woman and doesn't say anything?" she'd asked Cameron.

"The kind of woman who loves her husband and doesn't want to lose him," her sister had answered.

It doesn't bode well, she heard her father say.

"Okay, that's it," Val said now, jumping to her feet. "I'm calling the park rangers."

"She's with her boyfriend," Jennifer said quickly.

Val immediately sat back down. "What?"

"She's with her boyfriend," Jennifer repeated, understanding that Val had heard her fine the first time, but that she needed to hear the words again for the message to sink in.

"What are you talking about?" Val's initial shock was quickly giving way to anger.

Jennifer noted that Melissa, James, and this other person, whoever he was, were all leaning forward, waiting for her to continue. "His name is Tyler Currington."

"Tyler Currington? Never heard of him."

"They've been going out for about a month."

"A month?"

"Take it easy," Melissa cautioned Val.

"Look. I really don't know a whole lot."

"And yet you know so much more than I do," Val said, interrupting.

"Apparently she met him through her friend who works at Lululemon."

"Sasha?"

"Sasha. Yes, that's right. Anyway, this girl Sasha introduced them, and they hit it off, and they've been, you know, seeing each other."

"When?"

"Pretty much every chance they get."

"Why is this the first I'm hearing about it?"

Jennifer knew the question Valerie was really asking was *Why do you know about this and I don't?* "Because she was afraid you wouldn't approve."

"Why wouldn't I approve?"

"Because he's a little older than Brianne."

"How much older?"

"I'm not sure."

"Take a guess," Val said, her voice flat.

Jennifer breathed deeply, exhaled slowly. "Four, maybe five years."

A brief pause, a narrowing of Val's eyes, then, "You're telling me my sixteen-year-old daughter is dating a twenty-one-year-old man?"

"I don't know for sure he's twenty-one."

"But you *do* know Brianne is only sixteen," Val said, accusingly. "What does Evan say about this?"

"He doesn't," Jennifer said.

Val pounced, like a dog on a bone. "What do you mean, he doesn't? Are you saying he doesn't know about this?"

"He knows she has a boyfriend."

"But he doesn't know how old he is?"

"I don't know. I don't know what Brianne's told him."

"What have *you* told him?" Val asked, clearly not about to let go of that bone.

Jennifer hesitated. Oh, hell, she decided. What was it her father used to say? *In for a penny, in for a pound*? "I haven't told him anything."

"You haven't told him *anything*?" Val repeated.

"That's right."

"So let me make sure I understand this. You didn't tell your fiancé that his sixteen-year-old daughter is dating a twenty-one-year-old man?"

"No, I didn't."

"Do you mind my asking *why the hell not*?"

"Because I didn't think it was my place."

"Interesting," Val said. "You never worried about that when you were screwing my husband."

Jennifer decided to ignore Val's latest dig. What could she say in her own defense, after all? It was true. "Brianne told me about Tyler in confidence," she said, despising the quiver she heard in her voice. *Don't you dare cry,* she thought, noting that several people in the lobby had slowed their steps and were lingering nearby, listening. "I didn't want to betray that confidence," she said quietly.

"I see. So you pick and choose your betrayals. Is that right?"

Jennifer fought to retain her composure. "If you wouldn't mind lowering your voice. Not everyone in the Adirondacks needs to hear our conversation."

Both Jennifer and Val glanced toward the bystanders, most of whom quickly dispersed. Only one person held her ground, the teenage girl who'd given them the finger the night before. The girl smiled at Jennifer, as if to tell her she understood and supported her position.

Jennifer returned her attention to Val. "Look. I know you hate me, but—"

"I don't hate you," Val said quickly. Then, "Well, no, maybe I *do* hate you, but that's beside the point."

"Exactly what *is* the point?"

"The point is that a sixteen-year-old girl has no business dating a twenty-one-year-old man. And you should know that. And you should have told me. At the very least, you should have told Evan. He's going to be furious when he hears about this."

"Which should make you very happy."

"You think anything about this situation makes me happy?" Val demanded.

"I think you're blowing this whole thing way out of proportion. That's what I think. A five-year age difference is not the end of the world."

"It is when you're sixteen. God, I can't believe I have to tell you this."

"You don't have to tell me anything. Just like I'm not obligated to tell *you* anything," Jennifer continued, angry now, as much as embarrassed. "I know you don't understand this, but I'm in a bit of an awkward position here—"

Val interrupted. "I thought you liked awkward positions."

Jennifer shook her head, knowing they were both picturing her legs wrapped around Evan's shoulders. "I really can't see the point of discussing this any further."

"The point is determining where Brianne is now," the man sitting next to Valerie said simply.

"Who *are* you?" Jennifer asked.

"That's none of your business," Val said.

"Are you a park ranger?" Jennifer asked Gary directly.

"No," Gary said. "Just an old friend of Val's."

Great, Jennifer thought, wondering what he meant by "old friend." "Is your name some kind of state secret?"

The man smiled, attractive dimples creasing the afternoon stubble of his cheeks. "The name's Gary."

"Well, I'm sure that under normal circumstances, it would be a pleasure to meet you, Gary."

Val interrupted. "Are you going to tell me where my daughter is or not?"

"I don't know where she is, exactly."

"Then tell me where she is *approximately*."

"She's somewhere in the area. That's all I know."

Val made a sound halfway between a sigh and a scream. "You're saying you have no idea?"

"I'm saying they made arrangements to meet in the parking lot."

"When did they make these arrangements?"

"I don't know. I assume that's what she was so busy texting him about."

"You knew she was texting him?"

"I *assumed* it was him." Jennifer watched Val trying to digest this latest tidbit.

"So when did they meet up?" Val pushed her hair away from her forehead, her hand noticeably shaking.

She really *does* want to kill me, Jennifer thought. "She texted him right after you guys left this morning."

"How could she? I had her BlackBerry."

"She used mine."

Val nodded, as if to say, *Of course she did*. "So she's been with this man pretty much the whole day."

"Twenty-one is hardly a man," Jennifer protested. "He's still really just a kid."

"I see. You've met him, have you?"

"Well, no. I haven't."

"Is he in college? Does he have a job? Where does he live? Does he do drugs? Has he spent time in prison?"

"Okay, okay, I get the point."

"Do you know anything about him, other than that his name is Tyler Currington, which, frankly, doesn't even sound like a real name to me?"

"I know Brianne is crazy about him."

"Well, then, I guess that makes everything all right."

They fell silent for several long seconds.

"So what do we do now?" James asked.

"What *can* we do?" Val said, looking toward the front entrance, everyone's eyes trailing after her. "We wait."

ABOUT AN HOUR later, Val watched in horror as the front doors opened and two uniformed park rangers—both tall and clean-shaven—strode through, a noticeably disheveled-looking Brianne and her equally unkempt, shaggy-haired companion in tow. Val was immediately on her feet, rushing toward them, her friends right behind.

Jennifer hung back, noting that the boy's black T-shirt, festooned with a skull-and-crossbone motif, was tucked half in, half out, of his low-slung skinny jeans. Shit, she thought, reluctantly following after them. Couldn't Brianne have picked someone a little more presentable?

"What's going on?" Val was asking, her voice vibrating with barely controlled hysteria. "Brianne, are you all right?"

"You know this young lady?" the younger of the park rangers asked as Jennifer spotted the hotel manager hurrying across the lobby toward them.

"She's my daughter. Brianne, sweetheart, are you okay?"

"I'm afraid we found your daughter and her companion in a rather compromising position in some woods around Bolton Landing."

"What?"

Shit, thought Jennifer again, her heart sinking. We're all in for it now.

"A cottager reported spotting the two of them going at it in a clearing when she was taking her five-year-old twins for a walk. Needless to say, she wasn't too happy about it."

"What do you mean, going at it? You're saying they were making out?"

"I'm saying it was a bit more than that."

"How much more?"

The older of the two men explained the situation as tactfully as he could. Still, he left no doubt as to what he was saying: Brianne and her companion had been discovered naked, having sex in a public area.

"I can't believe this." Val's face reflected both her shock and her dismay. Her heart was pounding so fast she was afraid she might faint. "You were having sex in a public place? You were naked?"

"Maybe you could say it a little louder," Brianne said defiantly. "I think there might be someone in Florida who didn't hear you."

"How could you do something like that? What the hell were you thinking? Brianne. Answer me."

Brianne pursed her lips and looked toward Jennifer.

Shit, Jennifer thought. Now for sure I'm a dead woman.

"Don't look at her," Val snapped. "Look at me."

"Why?" Brianne spun around to face her mother. "So you can hit me again?"

Val took a step back, almost as if she'd been slapped herself.

She looks so utterly defeated I almost feel sorry for her, Jennifer thought, realizing that they'd attracted the attention of virtually everyone in the lobby.

"I'm so sorry," Val apologized to the rangers, although it wasn't clear if she was apologizing for her daughter's behavior or her own.

"Look. It's not the first time something like this has happened," the ranger said, continuing, "and it won't be the last. We're not interested in making trouble for these young people or in pressing charges . . ."

"Thank you so much," Val muttered, tears rolling down her cheeks.

"But if it happens again . . ."

"It won't," Val said quickly.

There was some further discussion, and then the rangers left.

"Assholes," Tyler Currington muttered under his breath.

"*You,*" Val shot back, "don't say another word."

"Excuse me, Mrs. Rowe," the manager said as they were preparing to leave the lobby. Both Val and Jennifer turned toward him. "We need to talk," he said.

THIRTEEN

B RIANNE STARED AT HER mother, trying to picture what she'd look like dead. Maybe with a knife through her heart or her throat slit from ear to ear. Like those people in the Berkshires, she thought, immediately pushing such disquieting thoughts from her mind. Yes, she was furious with her mother. Yes, she wished she'd go away and leave her alone. Yes, sometimes she even wished she'd drop off the face of the earth. But did she really want her dead?

She stole another glance in her mother's direction, studying her in quiet conversation with some old high school classmate she'd supposedly happened upon while hiking. Gary Something-or-other. Had their running into each other really been nothing but a happy coincidence or had they been planning to meet up all along?

Like mother, like daughter, Brianne thought, gathering her long hair into a loose ponytail at the base of her neck with her hand, then releasing it, letting her hair spread like a fan across the tops of her shoulders. No, she decided. More like *father,* like daughter. He was the go-to person for secret assignations and clandestine affairs. Her mother couldn't keep a secret if she tried. She simply wasn't devious enough to have set all this up in advance. She was much too honest. Much too *obvious.*

And besides, she was still pining for her wayward husband. It was painfully clear she still loved him, and that she was still hoping he'd see the error of his ways and come back home. So what difference did it really make if her meeting with Gary Whoever-he-was had been planned or not? The man probably wouldn't be around for long. All her father had to do was cock his little finger and her mother would go running. He was her drug of choice, not alcohol.

What a disaster this weekend was turning into. Nothing was turning out the way it was supposed to.

When her father had first floated the idea for this weekend getaway, she'd balked. No way was she spending three days and nights in the mountains with the twit who'd broken up her family. No way was she about to make nice with the sweet-faced slut who'd caused her mother so much grief.

Except that Jennifer had turned out to be neither a twit nor a slut. She was actually pretty cool. Not at all bossy or judgmental. She seemed genuinely interested in Brianne's opinions and, unlike her mother, she actually listened to what she had to say. Sometimes Jennifer even asked *her* for advice. When was the last time her mother had done that?

If anything, her mother had grown increasingly withdrawn, impatient, even dismissive, in recent months. Maybe because the divorce was almost final. Maybe because she was turning

forty. Maybe because *her* mother was a hopeless drunk. Whatever the reason, she was certainly no picnic to be around these
days. Brianne had eventually warmed to the idea of escaping
her mother's watchful eye, even welcomed it.

Tyler had welcomed the news as well. "Can't you see?" he'd
asked when she told him about the planned excursion. "It's
perfect."

His plan was simple. He'd follow them to the lodge, stay in a
nearby motel, or even sleep in his car, if necessary. They'd fake
a chance meeting and then she would persuade her father to
allow Tyler to join them. She doubted that would be a problem.
For all his seeming sophistication, Evan Rowe had always been
surprisingly easy to manipulate.

Unfortunately, he was just as unreliable.

So she hadn't been particularly surprised or disappointed
when he'd called to say he'd be late. She'd been expecting as
much. She'd even warned Tyler to count on at least a two-hour
delay, but Tyler, as cocksure as ever, had left at the appointed
hour anyway. "Might as well get up there a little early and
scout out the territory," he'd said with a laugh.

And then her father had announced he'd been further
detained. And then her mother had agreed to act as chauf-
feur . . .

And then . . . And then . . .

Brianne glanced at her mother, feeling the sting of her slap
as if it were fresh.

"Are you okay?" her mother mouthed, catching her look.

Brianne turned away without answering.

As it turned out, their fight had been a blessing in disguise,
providing her with a legitimate excuse to get away from the
group. Her mother had gone off hiking with her friends in an
effort to cool down, and it hadn't been very difficult to con-

vince Jennifer to let her meet up with Tyler for a few hours.

And what a mistake that had turned out to be. She never should have let Tyler convince her to make love in such an open area. Yes, it had sounded kind of exciting, and no, she hadn't wanted to come across as a prude, but come on, what *had* she been thinking? What had happened to her common sense, her better judgment? Had she been trying so hard to impress some boy that she'd allowed his words to get the better of her own best instincts?

She'd heard them before she saw them: two giants in what she first assumed were police uniforms sneaking up on them, ordering them to stop what they were doing, to get dressed and come with them.

Do you realize this is a public place? Don't you know there are children in the area? Do you know what you're doing is against the law? Followed by *What's your name? Where are you from? Where are you staying? How old are you?*

Thank God they'd turned out to be park rangers, and not actual cops. Instead of arresting them, they'd merely lectured them nonstop during the drive back to the lodge. Brianne had been hoping for a quiet entrance, but of course, that was not to be. Her mother had been waiting for her in the lobby, Jennifer having betrayed her confidence and spilled the beans about Tyler.

You really can't count on anyone these days, Brianne thought, recalling the hotel manager's words: *We can't afford to have this kind of scene in our lobby. We cater to an exclusive clientele who don't appreciate inappropriate behavior from our guests. Normally we would never allow five people to stay in one room, and we only intended it to be for the one night, in any event. I'm sorry but I'm afraid I'm going to have to ask you to vacate the premises as soon as possible.*

"That's it. We're going home," her mother had immediately announced.

"I'm going with Tyler," Brianne said, knowing she was pushing her luck, but figuring, what the hell?

"You're not going anywhere with Tyler. Tyler is leaving immediately," her mother informed them in no uncertain terms, "unless Tyler wants to find himself facing a charge of statutory rape."

"What?" The self-satisfied smirk Tyler had been wearing instantly disappeared from his tanned face.

"Did my daughter tell you she's only sixteen years old?"

"What?" Tyler said again.

"Goodbye, Tyler," her mother said.

"I'll call you later," Brianne whispered to him out of the side of her mouth as he hurried from the lobby.

Which was when Gary had suggested they spend the night at the campground where he and his dorky son were staying. "It's been a pretty tense afternoon," he'd said. "I don't think any one of you wants to spend five hours trapped in a car together. You can rent a couple of tents, we'll barbecue hot dogs . . ."

Brianne interrupted. "I don't eat meat."

"Then don't eat," her mother had snapped, promptly taking Gary up on his offer.

"I think I'll pass," said Jennifer.

"Suit yourself," Val said. "Good luck finding a place to stay."

"Shit," said Jennifer, her eyes registering defeat.

And so here they were—together again—at Starbright Campsites, just a few miles of twisting road down from the Lodge at Shadow Creek, on the banks of Lake George. They'd rented what turned out to be the last three available tents, two large and one small. Brianne had categorically refused to share a tent with either her mother or Jennifer, and so it was finally agreed that Melissa and Val would share one tent and James would bunk down with Brianne. Jennifer would occupy the third and smallest of the tents alone.

"Why can't I have that tent?" Brianne had demanded, not really surprised when nobody answered.

That's what happens when you get old, she thought. You not only lose your looks, you lose your sense of humor.

Better to die young, she thought.

So what was she supposed to do now?

Brianne's gaze shifted across the campsite to where her father's girlfriend was sitting off by herself, pretending to be engrossed in a book. Except that her flashlight was pointed aimlessly at the ground instead of on the page, and the moon, while almost full, was mostly hidden by trees and would hardly have provided enough light to read by. Despite all the stars, it was still spooky dark out, Brianne thought, shivering as she hugged her knees to her chest, pretending her arms were Tyler's.

What the hell was she doing sitting on the hard, cold ground in front of an enormous bonfire, surrounded by canvas tents of various shapes and sizes, in the company of a bunch of tree-hugging strangers she hoped never to see again as long as she lived? How had this happened?

Brianne knew that he was still in the area, probably close by, waiting for her to contact him. All she had to do was get to a phone. Not quite as easy as it sounded, she thought, knowing that despite her mother's seeming interest in all things Gary, she was watching her like a hawk.

She knew her mother was angry. She also knew she felt guilty about hitting her earlier, that she might even blame herself for her daughter's subsequent behavior. Maybe if I hadn't slapped her, Brianne imagined her mother thinking, I wouldn't have driven her into that boy's arms. This whole thing is *my* fault, she could almost hear her mother saying.

So why not play on that guilt? Why not let her mother take the blame?

Slowly Brianne pushed herself to her feet, her legs more than a little shaky as she tried to balance her red three-inch heels on the bumpy ground. Not exactly appropriate footwear for a campsite, she knew, but Tyler liked her in heels, and she hadn't been about to give her mother the satisfaction of changing into more sensible footwear. "These are fine," she'd insisted when her mother suggested she might like to change into a pair of sneakers. She'd also ignored her mother's suggestion to swap her white shorts for a pair of jeans, the result being that she was both uncomfortable and cold.

"Can I talk to you?" she said to her mother now.

Val immediately pushed herself to her feet, leaving Gary's side to follow Brianne to a more private space farther down the way.

"I want to apologize," Brianne began.

"All right." Her mother folded her hands across her chest. "I'm listening."

Not exactly the response Brianne had been expecting. She'd already decided that her mother would interrupt her apology with one of her own: *No, sweetheart, I'm the one who should be apologizing to you.*

"I'm sorry about what happened with Tyler."

"You should be."

Huh?

"I was just so upset about the fight we had this morning," Brianne continued. "You've never hit me before."

Silence.

Feel free to interrupt at any time, Brianne thought. "Aren't you sorry you hit me?" she asked when no such interruptions were forthcoming.

"Frankly," her mother said, "I'm not sure."

What?

"I *was* sorry. Now . . ."

"Now what?"

"Now, to be honest, I don't know."

"But what happened with Tyler would never have happened if you hadn't hit me."

A long pause.

"I see," her mother said.

Finally, Brianne thought, continuing. "Not that anything actually happened. With Tyler and me, I mean," she lied. "Nothing happened."

"Nothing happened," her mother repeated.

Brianne offered her mother her most winsome smile. "I know what those park rangers *thought* they saw . . ."

"You were found pretty much naked," her mother reminded her, her voice cold.

"Yes, but it wasn't how it looked."

"I see," her mother said again, although it was becoming less and less clear that she did.

"Anyway, I'm sorry you misunderstood . . ."

"I misunderstood?"

"Tyler's a really nice boy, Mom. You'd like him."

"I doubt that. And he's a man, Brianne," her mother corrected. "Not a boy."

"He's only a few years older than me," Brianne argued. "It's not that big a deal. Dad's older than you."

"I didn't start dating him when I was sixteen. Besides, this isn't about your father and me."

"You're right," Brianne said quickly. What was the matter

with her mother? Why was she making this so difficult? "Anyway, I just wanted to say I'm sorry."

"Okay."

Again Brianne waited for her mother to offer her own apology. Again, none came.

"Is there anything else?" her mother asked.

"Can I have my BlackBerry back?"

Her mother rolled her eyes toward the star-filled sky. "Not a chance."

"I just want to see if Tyler's all right."

"So this whole apology was just a ruse to get your phone back," her mother said.

"No, of course not."

But her mother was already walking back toward the center of the campsite.

"I'm not finished," Brianne called after her.

"Oh, yes, you are."

"We need to talk about this."

"Don't worry. We'll talk plenty when we get back to the city."

Shit, Brianne thought, her eyes catching sight of Jennifer watching from the distance. Brianne took a step toward her.

Don't even think about it, Jennifer's expression warned, stopping Brianne in her tracks.

Turning, she caught her heel on a small mound of earth and collapsed to the ground. "Ow," she cried, looking to see if her mother had seen what happened. It would serve her right if I broke my ankle, she thought, knowing she'd merely given it a slight twist. She sat for a few seconds, rocking back and forth in exaggerated discomfort, cradling her ankle, waiting for her mother to come running back, to take her in her arms and console her, tell her everything was going to be all right, but she didn't. "Shit," Brianne muttered, letting go of her foot and rubbing her bare arms with her hands.

"Are you okay?" a voice asked from somewhere above her head.

Brianne looked up. "I'm fine," she told the young man as he knelt to crouch beside her.

"It's Hayden," he said. "We were introduced before."

"I know who you are."

"Did you hurt yourself?"

"Not really."

"Those probably aren't the best shoes to wear camping."

"No kidding."

"You need some help getting up?"

"Who says I want to get up?"

"Oh. Okay. Sorry I bothered you." He pushed himself back to his full height.

"No, wait. I'm sorry. You were just being nice, and I'm being a bitch."

Hayden immediately crouched back down, his ponytail settling across his left shoulder.

"What happened to your friends?" she asked.

"They decided to drive into Bolton Landing."

"How come you didn't go with them?"

"Thought I'd get to bed early. My dad and I are planning to go up to Mount Marcy tomorrow, do some serious hiking."

God, he really *is* a dork, Brianne thought. Tall, not bad-looking. But a dork nonetheless.

And just maybe a dork with a cell phone?

"So, you really like this sort of thing?" she asked.

"Love it. The mountains, the lake, the fresh air." He took a long, deep breath as if to underline his point. "What's not to like?"

"Oh, I don't know. Maybe the mountains, the lake, the fresh air?"

He laughed.

"I guess I'm just not much of a camper."

"So I gather from the shoes."

"You don't like my shoes?" She offered another of her most winsome smiles, hoping it would work better on him than it had on her mother.

"No, your shoes are great." He looked toward the ground to hide his obvious embarrassment.

Oh, this is just too easy, she thought. "So, you want to show me the lake?"

His eyes shot to hers. "Sure. It's just down that way." He motioned with his right hand while the left one helped pull her to her feet.

"You wouldn't happen to have a cell phone on you, would you?" she asked when they were safely out of earshot.

"Sure," he said. "Why?"

"In case we get lost."

"Don't worry. You're safe with me."

Brianne glanced back toward her mother, who was talking to Gary and hadn't noticed them leaving. She smiled, reaching for Hayden's hand. "I'm not worried," she said.

FOURTEEN

S O, TELL ME EVERYTHING about your divorce," Val said.
Gary laughed.

"I'm serious. I want to know all the gory details." What the
hell? Val figured. He lives in Connecticut. I'll probably never
see him again. Might as well make the evening as entertaining
as possible. "You said it was nasty."

"And nasty it was."

"Why is that? And please don't tell me it's none of my business. I already know that."

Gary laughed again, a full-throated sound that chopped
through the still night air like an axe through wood. "The lady
wants all the nasty details."

Val nodded, catching a hint of blush in Gary's rugged
cheeks. Although maybe it was only the light from the fire,

she thought, hoping the flames were bathing her complexion in a similarly flattering glow. "I assume there was a third party involved."

"At least three parties that I know of," Gary said.

"Your wife had affairs?"

"You sound surprised."

"Just that it's usually . . ."

". . . the husband who's unfaithful?" Gary glanced toward Jennifer. "Was that your experience?"

"We're talking about you now, remember?"

"Ah, yes. Well, where was I?"

"Your wife's affairs."

"The first one was with her personal trainer. The second one was with a stay-at-home dad who lived down the street."

"You never suspected anything?"

"Not a thing. You?"

"I never suspected," Val said. *I knew,* she added silently.

"I actually thought we were very happy. We never fought. In fact, we hardly ever disagreed. Our sex life was good; our social life was active. Too active, as it turned out. At least on her part."

"I'm sorry."

"The truth is that I probably never would have found out about any of my wife's affairs if her sister hadn't spilled the beans."

"Your wife's sister told you?"

"She was pretty angry."

"Why would she be angry?"

"Because my wife's third affair was with her sister's husband."

"Seriously?"

"I think this is where things start getting nasty," Gary said.

Val thought of her own sister, Allison, three years her junior. They'd never been particularly close, but sisters were sisters, for heaven's sake. There were some lines you didn't cross. Even Evan would balk at having an affair with her sister. Wouldn't he? "Did your wife ever say why she picked her sister's husband?"

"Because he was there?" Gary asked in return.

"It's a pretty hostile thing to do. Her sister must have been devastated."

"She was."

"Are they still together?"

"No. Breakups all around."

"And is your ex seeing anyone now?"

"My son tells me that she's currently involved with one of my former partners."

Val absorbed this latest tidbit. Clearly the former Mrs. Parker liked to keep her affairs close to home. Val wondered if she'd also brought them *into* her home, as Evan had done. "And how do you feel about that?"

"Part of me feels sorry for the poor bastard. The other part thinks it serves him right. Never did like the guy."

"And what does Hayden think of all this?" Val looked around the campfire for Gary's son, but didn't see him.

"He was pretty shaken up by the divorce. Didn't see it coming." Gary shrugged. "But then, neither did I."

"Does he know . . . ?"

"About his mother and his uncle? I don't think so. At least *I* didn't tell him. But kids have a way of ferreting out things you don't want them to know."

Val nodded her agreement. "He seems pretty well-adjusted," she offered.

"Maybe. It's kind of hard to tell with Hayden. He's quiet,

tends to keep things bottled up inside. I'm still waiting for the eruption."

There was a second's silence, as if he were, in fact, waiting for some kind of explosion. The bonfire obliged with a few desultory crackles, like gunfire.

"What are we doing to our kids?" Val asked.

"No worse than what our parents did to us," Gary answered matter-of-factly. "Somehow we all manage to survive."

"Do we?"

Another silence. More snap, crackle, and pop from the burning, sweet-smelling wood. Val noticed that James and Melissa had joined a small group of campers who were roasting marshmallows over the open fire, James leading them in a surprisingly melodious rendition of "My Favorite Things." She strained to see whether Brianne was among them.

"So, how long ago did all this take place?" Val asked, deciding that her daughter would probably rather be dead than participate in a campfire sing-along. She felt a sudden chill and leaned over to hug her knees to her chest.

"About four years ago, I guess. Sometimes it feels like yesterday. Other times, it's like it happened a lifetime ago. Someone else's life," he added. "You're shivering. Are you cold?"

"A little."

"We could move closer to the fire."

"No, it's okay. You haven't met anyone else?"

"Actually, I just met a very lovely woman."

"Oh."

"Well, actually I knew her from before."

"Oh?"

"It turns out we went to high school together."

Val smiled. "You did?"

"Yeah. She was this feisty little thing. I always had a bit of a crush on her."

"You did?" Val repeated.

"Well, no," Gary admitted. "But I was just this big, dumb lug. What did I know?"

Val laughed.

"I think I might have a crush on her now," Gary said.

Val laughed. Which was when he suddenly leaned forward and kissed her. And she just as suddenly leaned in and kissed him right back. And it felt good. Hell, it felt great. She'd almost forgotten how good kissing a man could feel.

This is crazy. What am I doing? she thought in the next breath, trying desperately to push such thoughts from her head, to not think anything at all, to exist simply in the moment. Except she couldn't. What if Jennifer was watching? Or worse, Brianne? Hadn't she just berated her daughter for having sex in a public place? What kind of example was she setting? She twisted her head suddenly to one side, looking for her daughter. The result was that Gary's lips slid across her cheek and ended up buried in the side of her hair.

He laughed, his breath tickling her neck. "That was interesting."

"Sorry."

"Something wrong?"

"This probably isn't a good idea."

"Okay," he said easily, pulling away.

"It's just that . . ."

"No explanation necessary."

"Not that it wasn't very nice, or that I didn't enjoy it. It was and . . . I did . . . very much."

"In that case, maybe we could do it again sometime."

"When?" The word popped out of Val's mouth, catching them both off guard.

"How about later?" he suggested, eyes twinkling. "After everyone's asleep."

Val nodded. "That might work." What was she saying? Was she really planning a midnight tryst with a man she hardly knew, regardless of their past connection?

She took a deep breath, her eyes skirting the edge of the campsite. Melissa and James were still singing, Jennifer was still pretending to be engrossed in her book, Brianne was still nowhere to be seen. "I don't see my daughter anywhere. Do you?"

Gary craned his head to look through the crowd. "Maybe she went back to her tent."

"I should check."

Gary was instantly on his feet, extending a helping hand in Val's direction. They walked quickly toward the assembled tents. "Brianne?" Val called as they approached the far end of the campsite. She bent down to peer into the first of the three tents they'd reserved, already knowing Brianne wouldn't be inside.

Nor was her daughter in the second or third tent they checked.

"Where the hell is she?" Val pushed herself up on her toes and stared through the darkness.

"Maybe she's with my son."

"What makes you say that?"

"Just a hunch. I saw them talking earlier, and I haven't seen either of them since."

"You really think they might be together?"

"It's a possibility."

What would Brianne be doing with Hayden? Val wondered. "Does Hayden have a cell phone?" she asked, the answer suddenly very clear.

"Sure."

"I'll kill her," Val said.

Gary laughed. "As I'm sure you've discovered, cell phone reception in these mountains is sketchy at best. Chances are she won't be able to get through to anyone. And you don't have to worry about Hayden. He's a good kid. He'll make sure she doesn't get into any trouble."

Val decided Gary was right. Even if Tyler *was* still in the area, there was zero chance of him reconnecting with her daughter tonight. There was no reason for her to worry or to let her daughter spoil what was shaping up to be a very interesting evening. "I'm still gonna kill her."

She watched Gary's lips curl into a seductive grin, teasing her with unspoken possibilities. *You were the moment,* Val thought sadly, recalling the lyrics of a song she loved. *And the moment is gone.*

Except the moment wasn't gone. The moment was standing right in front of her.

Fearless, Gary had called her.

But being fearless wasn't the same thing as having actual courage. And, in truth, she wasn't fearless. She never had been. The truth was she'd been running scared all her life, afraid she wasn't worthy of love because those closest to her had all abandoned her, first her father, then her mother, then her sister. Evan was merely the latest in a long line.

She wondered when she'd come to define herself only as an adjunct to others—her mother's daughter, Brianne's mother, Evan's wife. When had she, all too willingly, it now seemed, surrendered her once-considerable power? Where at one time had existed a thriving core, there now existed a kind of wilderness, a confusing and overgrown landscape she'd been stumbling blindly across for years. Somewhere in the middle of that wilderness, she understood, was the girl she'd lost, the girl she, herself, had abandoned.

And while her husband's womanizing had been at least partly responsible for the slow and steady erosion of both her pride and self-esteem, she couldn't place all the blame on Evan. Nor could she blame everything on her father's desertion or her mother's drinking. She was forty years old, for God's sake. Wasn't it time she grew up and accepted responsibility for her own actions? How much more time was she going to waste?

Val looked deep into Gary's eyes, knowing that tomorrow they would undoubtedly go their separate ways, she back to Brooklyn, he to Connecticut. And while the distance between the two places was hardly insurmountable, it was far enough. Oh, he'd probably promise to stay in touch, but in all likelihood, after a few e-mails, their contact would cease. Soon she'd be little more than a curious addendum to his high school memories. *You'll never guess who I ran into a few weeks back. You remember Valerie Marcus? Feisty little thing. Couldn't do the butterfly stroke to save her life. Not a bad kisser, however.*

Might as well give him more to remember me by than that, Val thought now, moving closer. All right, so he wasn't Evan. But at this moment, he had one distinct advantage over her errant husband—he was here.

This time *she* was the one to initiate the kiss. "Come on," she whispered in the next instant, backing out of his arms and pulling him toward her tent.

He hesitated. "Now?"

"You have a problem with now?"

A growing smile filled his face. "As fearless as ever," he said with an admiring shake of his head.

"As fearless as ever," she agreed.

*   *   *

"VAL! VAL, OVER here!" James was calling as she and Gary returned to the center of the campsite approximately half an hour later. James beckoned them toward the bonfire with broad waves of his skinny arms. "Come sit down. We're about to do 'Everything's Coming Up Roses.'"

"He's in his element," Melissa said.

"Who knew camping was this much fun?" James asked rhetorically.

"Have either of you seen Brianne?" Val was dismayed to discover her daughter wasn't back yet, and already second-guessing her impromptu dalliance with Gary. Probably not the smartest thing I could have done, she was thinking, before deciding quite the opposite was true. Making love to Gary was the smartest thing she'd done in years.

Melissa shook her head as James squinted through the darkness toward Jennifer. "Maybe *she* knows where she is."

Val walked briskly toward her husband's fiancée. "Have you seen Brianne?" she asked as the young woman reluctantly looked up from her book, her finger ostensibly marking the spot at which she'd been interrupted.

"Last I saw she was with that boy . . . your son, I believe." Jennifer acknowledged Gary with a nod, her eyes openly quizzical.

Does she suspect anything? Val wondered. Had she seen their earlier kiss, watched them wander off together, counting off the minutes until they'd returned? Was she planning to tell Evan about her suspicions? How would he react? Would he be jealous? Was that why she'd virtually thrown herself at a man she hadn't seen since she was a teenager?

Or were her motives even more pathetic than that? Had she given herself to Gary simply because he'd been nice to her? Because she liked the way he looked at her? Because he obviously found her desirable? Was that all it took? "Did you see where they went?" she asked, over the barrage of silent questions.

"No. But she can't have gone far. I wouldn't worry."

"You never do."

"I think Val would just feel better knowing where her daughter is," Gary said, as if sensing trouble ahead.

"I think she should give it a rest." Jennifer returned to her book.

Val spun around on her heels, stomping back toward the bonfire.

"Sorry," she said as Gary struggled to catch up to her. "It was either leave immediately or strangle her on the spot."

"I think you showed remarkable restraint. For what it's worth, I probably would have strangled her back at the lodge."

"You say the sweetest things."

Gary laughed.

Val glanced back at Jennifer. "She's very beautiful. Don't you think?"

He shrugged. "I think you're prettier."

It was Val's turn to laugh. "You just think I'm easy."

"I think you're fabulous."

Val smiled, understanding that her appeal to Gary was based on a total misconception. He thinks I'm someone I'm not. He thinks I'm fearless when, in fact, I'm scared to death. Although maybe not quite as scared as I was half an hour ago.

"Val . . . Gary," James called, his voice echoing through the darkness as he patted the ground beside him. "Come on back. We've decided to tell ghost stories. I'm first."

"You've created a monster," Melissa said as Val approached.

"I'll go see if I can find Hayden," Gary offered.

"I'll come with you."

"No. You'll stay here and play with your friends. Let me deal with this."

Val nodded a heartfelt thank-you.

"What's going on?" Melissa asked as Val squeezed in beside her.

"We think Brianne might be with his son . . ."

"I'm not talking about Brianne. I'm talking about you and that twinkle in your eye."

Val protested. "Don't be silly. There's no twinkle."

"There's a definite twinkle."

"You're crazy."

"Val and Gary sitting in a tree," James sang softly under his breath. "K-i-s-s-i-n-g."

"You saw that?"

"I think pretty much everyone saw it," Melissa acknowledged.

"Including Jennifer?"

"Definitely including Jennifer."

"I thought her eyes were going to pop right out of her head," James said.

"Shit."

"And then, of course, the two of you disappeared," he added, "for . . . how long was it exactly?"

"Thirty-three minutes," Melissa said.

"You counted?"

"Of course we counted. What are friends for?"

"Would you believe me if I told you we were just looking for Brianne?" Val asked.

"Of course we would."

"Absolutely," said James. Then, after a slight pause, "So, how'd it go? The search, I mean."

Val smiled. For thirty-three minutes she had actually managed to forget about Brianne, to forget about Jennifer, to forget about her mother, to forget about Evan. "It was great," she said, unable to contain her delight any longer. "Best. Search. Ever."

Melissa let out a whoop of joy. "Amen to that. It's about time."

"Amen," said James, giving Val's knee an appreciative squeeze.

"Amen," Val repeated, discovering she liked the sound of the word, and settling back into the crook of Melissa's arm as James took a deep breath and began his ghost story. "It's called 'The Hook,'" he announced to the assembled gathering of mostly middle-aged faces, the younger campers having pretty much disappeared during the *Sound of Music* medley.

"Oh, God," Melissa wailed. "Not that old chestnut. I haven't heard that one since I was ten years old."

James took a deep breath, continuing undeterred. "All day long the news was full of reports that a lunatic had escaped from a nearby asylum," he began, lowering his voice to a conspiratorial whisper. "They called him the Hook Man because he'd lost one arm in a freak accident and had replaced it with a hook, a hook he now used to kill and dismember innocent men, women, and children." James looked around the campfire, eyes sparkling. "There was this girl. We'll call her Sienna."

"Sienna?" Val and Melissa asked together.

"I'm updating," James explained. "Anyway, Sienna was sixteen and she didn't give a hoot about the Hook Man or all the people he'd butchered. She cared only about what she was going to wear on her date that night with Bryce, the captain of the football team."

"Bryce?"

James rolled his eyes. "Anyway, she finally selected a low-cut Tory Burch blouse, a pair of stone-washed skinny jeans from Dolce and Gabbana, and a fabulous pair of Manolo Blahnik leopard-print, five-inch heels."

"Nice touch," Melissa said.

James smiled, looking very pleased as he continued his story. "Bryce came to pick up Sienna in his silver Porsche. He drove to a secluded Lovers' Lane where he parked and they started making out. Suddenly, they heard a scratching on the car door. 'What's that?' asked Sienna, pulling out of Bryce's arms and looking around. 'I didn't hear anything,' Bryce insisted. 'It must be your imagination.' The song on the car radio was suddenly interrupted by a warning that the Hook Man might be in the area. 'Take me home right now,' Sienna ordered as the car started rocking menacingly back and forth, like someone was shaking it. Bryce immediately threw the car into gear and tore out of Lovers' Lane, tires screeching. When they got to Sienna's house, Sienna jumped out of the car. Then she stood there, screaming. 'What is it?' Bryce asked, quickly joining her by the passenger door. And then he saw it. Hanging from the door's handle was a bloody hook!" James sat back, soaking up the applause that followed.

Val suppressed an involuntary shudder, not because of the story, which was silly at best, and unsatisfying at worst. She was thinking that James's story bore an uncomfortable resemblance to the recent murders in the Berkshires. Her eyes scanned the campsite, looking for any sign of Brianne. There's nothing to worry about, she assured herself again. No need to feel spooked. There was no monster lurking in the dense bushes, waiting to hack her daughter to pieces. Besides, in a confrontation between the Hook Man and Brianne, she'd bet money on her daughter every time.

The Hook Man didn't stand a chance.

FIFTEEN

J UST HOW FAR IS this stupid lake anyway?" Brianne asked
Hayden, not even trying to mask her impatience. They'd
been walking around in circles for what felt like hours, she was
being eaten alive by mosquitoes, and her once-beautiful Jimmy
Choos, the open-toed, red stilettos she'd successfully snagged
after waiting in line for hours in front of H&M with hundreds
of other like-minded young women jostling to be the first in the
doors when the store opened and the designer's new line of reasonably priced footwear was introduced, were being pummeled
into oblivion by the rugged terrain, their once-soft leather now
bearing the scars of disrespectful twigs, their slender four-and-
a-half-inch heels overwhelmed by ugly, fat clumps of mud. Not
to mention, she'd already gone over on her right ankle again
twice and it was starting to throb. She should have changed

into her sneakers when her mother had suggested it, along with jeans and a sweatshirt. The white shorts and sleeveless T-shirt she was wearing had been fine when the sun was still out, but the temperature had dropped about twenty degrees in the last hour alone. She should have listened to her mother.

Except then her mother would have won.

Won what? Brianne wondered now, slapping a mosquito away from her left ear and ducking to avoid being slapped in the face by the wayward branch of a tree.

She stopped to rub her sore ankle as Hayden disappeared around a bend in the trail. Damn it, this was all her mother's fault. "Great," she said, peering through the darkness after him, seeing nothing. Where were they anyway? He kept saying that the lake was just around the next tree, but it never was. Where was he taking her?

Everything is turning to rat shit, Brianne thought, fighting back tears. She was supposed to be spending this time with Tyler, and instead here she was in the middle of nowhere, wasting half the night with the dorky son of one of her mother's former classmates. And not only did his cell phone not work—his phone plan didn't include texting. *Who doesn't have texting?*

"We might get better reception down at the lake," he'd assured her after she'd tried, and failed, to get a signal soon after leaving the campsite.

Except there didn't seem to be any lake. There were just trees and bugs, and then surprise—more trees and more bugs. "Damn it," she cursed, wondering if her mother was behind this little excursion, if she'd cooked up this whole scheme to teach her some kind of lesson—"Just go over and ask her if she'd like to go for a walk, casually mention you have a cell phone," Brianne could almost hear her mother suggesting to Hayden. "Then take her on a nice long walk to nowhere."

Except that *I'm* the one who suggested the walk, she realized. *I'm* the one who asked Hayden if he had a cell phone. He'd just been making pleasant conversation, offering her a sympathetic shoulder to cry on. Of course, her mother might have decided that this was the best way to play her, knowing the way her mind worked.

Except she *doesn't* know how my mind works, Brianne thought defiantly. She thinks she knows me, but she doesn't. She has no idea what I'm feeling. She doesn't know me at all. Sometimes Brianne wondered if her mother had ever been young.

Brianne heard a sudden rustling, the snapping of wood, and glanced warily over her shoulder. Hadn't James mentioned the possibility of bears?

"Brianne?" Hayden's voice shook the leaves of the surrounding trees. "Brianne, where the hell are you?"

"Back here!" she shouted, her words ricocheting off a nearby cluster of rocks.

"Why'd you stop?" he asked, his face suddenly popping into view.

"Are there bears around here?" she asked, ignoring his question.

Hayden shrugged. "I don't think you have to worry about bears."

What did that mean? Was he implying there was something else she should be worrying about? "Where's the lake?" she asked, as if he might have moved it.

"Just around the next bend."

"You've been saying that for the past hour."

Hayden checked his watch, then laughed. "We've been walking less than fifteen minutes."

"You're kidding."

"No." He held out his arm to show her the Swiss Army watch dangling from his slender wrist. "See for yourself, if you don't believe me."

"I believe you," she said, although truthfully, she wasn't entirely convinced. "It just feels like we've been walking forever."

Hayden glanced pointedly toward her feet, but said nothing. He didn't have to.

"You sure your phone will get better reception at the lake?"

"No," he admitted. "Look. We can go back, if you'd like."

After coming all this way? Brianne thought. After ruining my new shoes? "No. We've come this far. We might as well see if we can get your stupid phone to work."

"Who are you trying to call anyway?"

Brianne frowned as they resumed walking. "Like you don't know."

"I don't."

"Your dad didn't tell you?"

"Was he supposed to?"

Brianne came to an abrupt stop. "You're seriously trying to tell me that your dad didn't say anything to you about what happened this afternoon?"

Hayden shrugged. "Just that there was some mix-up at the lodge about your room and that you guys would be spending the night at the campground."

"That's all he said?"

"I take it he left something out."

"I don't want to talk about it." She pushed her way in front of him, picking up her pace.

And then suddenly, the lake was right there in front of them, the smooth surface of its clear water sparkling in the moonlight, like a picture on a glossy postcard.

Hayden smiled. "Beautiful, isn't it?"

Brianne silently acknowledged that it was. "If you like that sort of thing."

"You don't?"

"Never really thought about it."

"I would have thought you liked to swim." He picked up a pebble, gracefully flicking it into the lake. It skipped across the water's glassy surface, creating a series of expanding ripples, like cracks in a mirror.

Brianne watched the ripples round out and expand, only to disappear before they reached the shore. "Why would you think that?"

"Wasn't your mother on the swim team with my dad at school?"

"Just because my mother likes to swim doesn't mean I do. Do you like everything your father does?"

"I was just trying to make conversation."

"No need. Can I try your phone again?"

Hayden reached into the pocket of his jeans and handed her his cell without further comment.

"Damn it," Brianne said when she still couldn't find a signal. "What's the matter with this stupid thing?" She began pacing along the edge of the lake, shaking the small phone as if it were a container of salt. "Where'd you get this dinosaur anyway? It's like from the Dark Ages."

"Hey. Careful. You'll break it."

"I think it's already broken."

"Sometimes it takes a few minutes."

"Shit."

"What's with the urgency?" Hayden asked.

"None of your business." Brianne felt her shoulders slump.

Could this night get any worse? "Promise you won't tell my mother?"

"Tell her what? Why would I tell her anything?"

Brianne's prolonged sigh combined equal portions of fatigue and defeat. "I'm trying to reach my boyfriend."

Hayden nodded, as if he understood. "A boyfriend your mother doesn't like?"

"She hates him."

"Why?"

"Because she thinks he's too old for me." And maybe because some nosy park rangers caught us without our clothes on in the middle of a public place in the middle of the afternoon, she added silently.

"How old *is* he?"

"Not *that* old." Brianne decided it was probably best to avoid particulars. She tried the phone again. Still nothing.

"We could walk some more. Shadow Creek is just up that way a bit." Hayden pointed off in the distance.

"You're joking, right?" Brianne handed him back his phone as she sank to the ground, feeling the earth's dampness immediately seep through her shorts. Hell, my shoes are already ruined, she thought. Might as well destroy the rest of my wardrobe. It was obvious she wouldn't be meeting up with Tyler again tonight. Seconds later, Hayden was sitting on the ground beside her, although he was careful to keep a respectful distance between them. "Don't get any ideas," she said anyway.

"What?"

Brianne couldn't tell from Hayden's tone whether he was more shocked or repulsed by her suggestion. What's his problem? she wondered. "So, you have a girlfriend?"

He shook his head.

"Boyfriend?" She was being deliberately provocative and was disappointed that the surrounding darkness prevented her from fully appreciating his reaction.

"You think I'm gay?"

"Are you?"

"No. Why would you think that?"

"It's no big deal if you are, you know."

"I'm not."

"My mother's friend James is gay."

"Yeah, I kinda figured that."

"Subtlety isn't exactly his strong suit. I keep scolding him for being such a stereotype, but he says he was raised by an eccentric single mother to be a dancer on Broadway, so what did I expect?" She laughed.

"Seems like a nice enough guy."

"Nice enough for what?"

"What's that supposed to mean?" Hayden asked.

"Nothing. Why are you so touchy all of a sudden?"

"I'm not touchy."

Brianne shrugged. "Whatever."

"What's with the woman in black?" Hayden asked after several seconds of silence, his voice strained.

"Melissa. She always wears black. It's kind of her trademark. She's pretty cool, actually."

"So, it's only your mother you don't like," Hayden said.

The casual observation made Brianne bristle. "What are you talking about? I love my mother."

"You *love* her. You just don't *like* her."

"What are you talking about?" Brianne asked again.

"Now who's being touchy?"

"I'm not being touchy."

"It's okay. I don't like my mother much, either."

"You don't? Why?"

"She's a slut," he said simply.

"Whoa! Did you just call your mother a slut?"

"Yeah, I guess I did. It kind of popped out. Sorry."

"No, don't apologize." Brianne laughed.

"You think it's funny my mother's a slut?"

"No. Of course not. It's just that that's what my mother calls Jennifer. My father's fiancée. The one . . ."

"With the legs," Hayden said.

Okay, so he's not gay, Brianne thought. Still, there was clearly more to Hayden than she'd originally suspected. He might be a dork, but he was an angry dork. A dork with mommy issues. Which made him marginally more interesting. "So, tell me why you think your mother's a slut."

"Because she cheated on my dad with half the planet. Don't say anything," he added quickly. "My dad thinks I don't know."

"How did you find out?"

"One of my friends saw her coming out of a motel one night with some guy who wasn't my dad. He told me."

"I once saw my father making out with Jennifer in his car. Like they were two horny teenagers. Pretty disgusting."

Hayden nodded. "Looks like we have something in common."

"Did she really sleep with half the planet?" Brianne asked, not appreciating the inference that she could have anything in common with someone so obviously uncool. She thought of her father, wondering how many other affairs he'd had. She knew Jennifer wasn't his first.

There was the time she'd walked past his study and heard him whispering into the phone, followed by a quick goodbye and a too-bright smile when he saw her, and there was that other time, a few years ago, when she'd dropped in on him at work only to find his office door locked and his new assistant away from her desk. She'd been about to leave when she heard muffled noises—giggles, sighs, low murmurs—coming from inside his office, and so she'd approached cautiously, putting her ear to the frosted glass of the door, then knocking gently. "Daddy," she'd called out, growing bolder when she heard someone moving around inside. "Daddy, are you there?" It had taken a few minutes for the door to open and his new assistant, one Miss Jacqueline Gum, to emerge, slightly flushed and clearly flustered. "Why, hi there, Brianne," Jacqueline Gum had said. "How are you today?" Her father had quickly waved her inside, smiling that too-bright smile. "Well, isn't this an unexpected pleasure?" The next time Brianne had paid her father a visit she discovered Miss Gum was no longer in his employ. "How come none of your assistants lasts very long?" she'd asked him. He'd only laughed and shaken his head, as if to say, Beats me.

"I heard my dad talking to his lawyer on the phone," Hayden was saying, answering the question she'd already forgotten she'd asked. "He told the lawyer there were three guys that he knew of, including—get this—my uncle."

"No shit." Wow, Brianne thought. This guy has to be seriously messed up.

"Since the divorce there have been at least four more that I'm aware of," he continued, unprompted. "She's been dating this one guy now for about six months. Looks like he could be a keeper."

"How do you feel about that?"

He laughed. "You sound like my therapist."

"You see a shrink?"

"I did for a while. My dad thought it was a good idea. To help me deal with the divorce . . ."

"How long did you go for?"

"A few years." He shrugged. "It was no big deal," he said. But his eyes said otherwise.

"Your dad seems like a pretty smart guy."

"He's great. Salt of the earth, as my grandfather used to say."

"Salt of the earth?" Brianne repeated. "What does that mean?"

"It's just an expression."

"Can I try your phone again?"

Hayden handed her back his cell phone. Brianne once again tried, and failed, to find a signal.

"Damn it," she said.

"We might have more luck if we move around." Hayden pushed himself to his feet. "Here. Let me try."

Brianne watched him punch in a few numbers as he edged closer to the water. "Anything?"

Hayden began pacing back and forth along the shoreline. "No. Hey, you want to know where the expression 'It's raining cats and dogs' comes from?"

"No," Brianne said. God, he really *was* a dork.

"Way back in the 1500s," he told her anyway, "houses had thatched roofs which, as you know, are made of thick straw, piled really high, with no wood underneath. Since that was the only place for animals to get warm—because, of course, they didn't have central heating in those days—all the cats and dogs and small animals, like rodents and stuff, lived in the roof. And when it rained, the roof became slippery and sometimes the animals would slip and fall down from the roof. Hence the saying . . ."

"'It's raining cats and dogs.'" Brianne managed a weak smile. Poor guy is pathetic, she thought. "Okay, I've had enough." She clambered to her feet. "Let's go back."

"Wait," Hayden said suddenly. "I think I may have something."

Brianne was immediately beside him, snatching the phone from his hand. "It's really faint," she said, distancing herself from him as she entered the numbers for Tyler's cell. "It's ringing. Hello? Hello? Tyler? Damn it," she said, as static took over the line, forcing her to move back toward Hayden. "Tyler? Can you hear me? I don't know if he can hear me," she whined.

"Brianne?" a faint voice answered.

"Tyler, Tyler, thank God. Where are you?" His response was inaudible. "Never mind. Listen, we're at Starbright Campsites near Lake George. What time is it?" she hissed toward Hayden.

He checked his watch. "Almost nine o'clock."

"I'll meet you at the front entrance to the campground at midnight," she said, not sure whether Tyler was even still on the line. "Did you hear me? Tyler?" Again, static filled the airwaves. And then, nothing. "Damn it. It's dead. I don't know for sure if he heard me."

"You really think that's a good idea?"

"Do I think *what* is a good idea?"

"Meeting your boyfriend. Your mom'll be pissed."

"My mom will be sound asleep."

"Yeah, right."

"Unless you're planning on telling her . . ."

"No, of course not."

"'Cause then I'd have to come back and kill you," Brianne said without smiling. "You know that, don't you?"

"You're one scary chick," Hayden said.

Brianne laughed, feeling better about tonight already. It was almost nine o'clock. Everyone was exhausted. In another hour, they'd very likely be asleep, including James, with whom she'd be sharing a tent. She'd plead a weak bladder, make hourly trips to the john, so that in the unlikely event James woke up, she'd have an excuse ready. It would be easy. Like taking candy from a baby, she thought, wondering if Hayden could tell her where *that* expression came from. "Let's go," she said, eager now to get back to the camp.

Which was when they heard the rustle of leaves and the cracking of twigs and knew they weren't alone. Someone had been watching them. Someone had overheard their entire conversation.

A bear? Her mother? Brianne held her breath, not sure which option she preferred.

"Excuse me. I didn't mean to frighten you," a voice said, as a man stepped out of the shadows.

It took Brianne only a few seconds to recognize the familiar uniform of the park rangers: the crisp beige shirt, the tin badge, the holstered gun. "You've got to be kidding me," she said with an audible groan.

"You two mind telling me your names?" the ranger asked.

"Why should we?" Brianne challenged.

"Hayden Parker," Hayden answered, speaking over her, his back automatically straightening, his shoulders stiffening, as if he'd been instructed to stand at attention. "This is Brianne Rowe. We're staying at Starbright Campsites."

"Henry Voight. Pleased to meet you," the ranger said with a sheepish grin. "Look, believe it or not, I was once as young as you are, and I'm truly sorry to have to do this, but I'm afraid I have to insist you get back there. It's really not a good idea for you to be out here alone at this hour. It's dark, there are animals—"

"We were just about to head back," Brianne interrupted,

thinking that, in the dark, the ranger didn't look much older than Hayden. And he was much cuter, she couldn't help but note.

"Then please allow me to escort you," he said.

"No, really, that's not necessary."

The ranger's smile hardened with authority. The smile said it wasn't up to her. "It would be my pleasure."

Brianne gritted her teeth. She knew from experience there was no point in arguing.

SIXTEEN

J ENNIFER TURNED OFF HER tiny flashlight and closed the
book she'd spent all evening pretending to read, wondering if she'd fooled anyone. She shook her head, deciding she
was no different than the others. They'd all spent the night
pretending: Melissa and James acting as if they were having
a grand old time singing show tunes and sharing ghost stories
around the campfire when they'd undoubtedly rather be in
Manhattan, sharing a luxury suite at the Plaza; Brianne playing the role of obedient daughter while, all the while, her eyes
were hurling invisible daggers at her mother; Val going off with
some guy she'd known from high school when it was painfully
obvious to anyone with half a brain that she was still hung up
on her soon-to-be ex-husband. Not to mention that ridiculous
kiss. In clear view of everyone. What was that all about? Was

Val challenging her to report it to Evan? Did she really think it might make him jealous? Did she really think he'd care?

Would he? Jennifer wondered, trying to erase all such thoughts from her mind.

Go ahead, make a fool of yourself, she told Val silently, glancing toward the campfire through downcast eyes to where Val was now not so comfortably lodged between her two friends. I'm not going to be the one who reports your adolescent maneuverings to Evan. What you do is of no concern to me. Or him.

Hopefully he got the message she'd left for him after they were forced to vacate their suite, telling him where they'd be and asking him to contact her through the campground office, since her cell phone was pretty much useless out here. So far, nothing. Jennifer glanced in the direction of the entrance to the camp, praying to see Evan striding purposefully toward her, a big smile on his handsome face, his arms open wide to embrace her, but all she saw was Val in animated conversation with Melissa and James. Go ahead—pretend to ignore me, she thought. Pretend you aren't acutely aware of my every move. Pretend you aren't enjoying my discomfort. Pretend you're not loving every fucking minute of this whole awful, ridiculous sideshow of a weekend.

Jennifer's eyes dropped toward the ground. They were no better than the unruly children they'd watched running around the campfire earlier in the night, waving long sticks and shouting, "Bang! Bang! You're dead!" as they pretended to mow one another down with machine guns. She'd breathed a deep sigh of relief when their parents had finally, mercifully, sent them off to sleep, although one little girl continued to cry out, at regular intervals, for her mother.

Sudden tears swam into Jennifer's line of vision, catching her off guard. Do we ever stop needing our mothers? she found herself wondering, watching as an image of her once-vibrant mother filled the dark sky, only to start breaking up and disintegrating in the cool air, shrinking and caving in on itself, her cheeks hollowing out, her eyes retreating inward, as if seeing only pain.

Amazing, she thought, how in the end, it all came down to mothers.

Do we ever stop missing them? Do we ever stop crying out for them, however silently? Do we ever outgrow our desire to crawl inside their arms and press our head against their breasts and wallow in the singular comfort of their unconditional love?

Do we ever grow up? Do we ever even graduate from high school? she thought with a chuckle. How fitting that Gary should turn up on this, of all weekends. She pretended to be yawning as she pushed some hair away from her eyes while secretly stealing another glance at Val.

She'd been plagued by Valeries all her life. While she might have been routinely selected head cheerleader and regularly voted Most Beautiful, it was the Valeries of this world who generally triumphed in the end. They somehow managed to get the grades and the guys without alienating anyone. They were just pretty enough to attract attention, but not so attractive as to be considered a serious threat. They were smart, but smart enough to keep it under the radar. They were the girls nobody begrudged being voted Prom Queen and Most Likely to Succeed, not because anyone thought they were particularly worthy of such honors but because they seemed the least dangerous choice.

But you *are* dangerous, aren't you? Jennifer thought now, as

Val's eyes reached through the darkness toward hers, grabbing them and refusing to let go. Your confidence is your weapon of choice, and you wield it without mercy.

Jennifer felt herself melting under the intensity of Val's gaze, and she looked away, pushing herself to her feet and taking off with no clear idea of where she was headed. She felt Val's eyes following her. "Careful," she heard somebody say as she tripped over her feet, righting herself before her knees hit the ground, then continuing to stumble toward the far end of the camp. "Too much to drink," she heard someone mutter with disapproval.

A sudden impulse seized her—the urge to run, as far and as fast as she could. Run from the campsite, from the mountains, from all the Valeries of this world. I give up! she imagined shouting back at them as she fled. You win. I'm tired of trying to compete. I'm tired of never measuring up. I'm tired of being the object of your scorn, of pretending to be who you think I am, tired of pretending to be who you *want* me to be.

"I'm just plain tired," she said out loud, coming to an abrupt halt in front of the row of portable toilets at the far end of the camp.

"So, go to bed," a voice said from out of the darkness.

Jennifer spun around. "Brianne?" she asked, watching the girl emerge from behind a line of dense trees, followed immediately by two young men. One of them was Hayden. She didn't recognize the other. "Where have you been? Your mother's about to call in the troops. *Again.*"

"Too late. They're already here." Brianne motioned toward the uniformed stranger. "This is Henry," she said, introducing the park ranger. "Henry, meet Jennifer."

"A pleasure." Henry extended his hand, his eyes swallowing her in one appreciative glance.

Jennifer noted his handshake was surprisingly gentle,

although his gaze was direct and penetrating. "Is there a problem?" she asked guardedly, thinking she should have run away when she had the chance.

"No problem," he said. "I just thought it was a little late and a little dark for these two to be off in the woods alone."

"If you're asking if I was caught with my pants down, *again*," Brianne said, repeating both the word and the emphasis, "the answer is no."

Jennifer tried not to look either shocked or annoyed, although in truth she was a bit of both. "You should probably go reassure your mother."

"Honestly," Brianne said with an exaggerated roll of her eyes, "you'd think I was two years old." She turned toward the park ranger. "So, you want to come meet Mommy?"

"No, thank you. I think my job here is done."

"Coward," said Brianne over her shoulder as she turned and walked away.

"Love the shoes," Henry called after her.

Brianne extended one bare arm above her head and waved without looking back.

"Nice meeting you," Hayden said, offering his hand to the ranger.

"Easy, there," Henry said as Hayden pumped his hand enthusiastically. "That's quite the grip you've got."

"Sorry. I didn't mean . . ."

"That's all right. A strong handshake is usually a good indicator you have nothing to hide."

Hayden looked vaguely puzzled by the remark. "Okay, yeah, well . . . I don't . . . have anything to hide, that is."

"You're sure of that?" the ranger teased.

Now Hayden looked startled, as if he'd been caught with his hand in the cookie jar.

"Hey, man, just kidding," the ranger assured him.

Hayden began quickly backing away.

What was that all about? Jennifer wondered, watching Henry as he watched Hayden disappear from sight. In profile, the park ranger seemed older than he did face-on, his nose wider, his jawline squarer, more pronounced. Probably about my age, she decided, thinking he looked exhausted, maybe even as tired as she felt. "It's a little late to be patrolling, isn't it?"

"Normally, yes. But we were asked to put in a little overtime."

"Any particular reason?"

A look of concern flashed through the ranger's eyes.

"Not that you're obligated to tell me anything," Jennifer immediately qualified.

"No, it's okay." He paused, clearly debating with himself whether to continue. "A man's been reported missing," he said after another pause of several seconds.

"You mean David Gowan?"

Henry looked surprised. "Yes. You know him? Have you seen him?"

"No," Jennifer said quickly. "Just that we were all staying at the lodge last night, and this morning, we heard he'd disappeared. You still haven't found him?"

"Not yet," Henry admitted. "But if he's somewhere in these woods, he'll turn up sooner or later. Although probably not tonight." He checked his watch. "I was actually just about to pack it in when I ran across Brianne and Hayden. And, just to set your mind at ease, they *were* fully dressed."

Jennifer smiled wearily. "Not really my concern."

Now it was Henry's turn to smile. He shifted his weight from one foot to the other, seemingly in no hurry to leave. "Do you mind my asking what your relationship *is* to Brianne? Not that you're obliged to tell me anything," he added, with a sly smile. "I mean, I'm not asking in any official capacity or anything. It's just that . . . God, you're beautiful," he said in the next breath. "Sorry to sound like such a dolt. I'm sure you hear that all the time."

Jennifer lowered her eyes and tried not to smile. It was true. She was used to this reaction from men. Still, after the last twenty-four hours, it felt nice to be acknowledged in a positive way. "Believe me, it's not something you get tired of hearing. In fact, thank you. I think I needed that."

"Entirely my pleasure. Anytime."

"Brianne is my fiancé's daughter," Jennifer explained, deciding she'd better put the park ranger out of his misery before he got his hopes up too high. If Henry *was* entertaining any thoughts of cuddling around the campfire, it would be in everyone's best interests to put those thoughts to rest as soon as possible.

He nodded understanding. "I had a feeling you might say something like that." He stared idly in the direction of the center of the camp, his brow furrowing in obvious confusion. "And yet, didn't I hear you say that Brianne's mother is here, too?"

"Aha! The plot thickens. Yes, Brianne's mother is indeed here, too."

"You got a sort of *Big Love* thing going on?" Henry was referring to the once-popular TV show about a man with several wives.

Jennifer laughed out loud. "No, I'm afraid there's not a lot of love going on around here, big or otherwise."

"Sounds even more interesting."

"It isn't, really."

"But it *is* none of my business."

"It wasn't supposed to turn out this way," Jennifer surprised

herself by saying, then surprised herself even more by continuing, unprompted, the words gushing from her mouth as if from
a broken water main. "This was supposed to be a nice long
weekend getaway for me, my fiancé, and his daughter, a chance
for us to spend some quality time together, to get to know each
other better, you know . . . to *bond,* and all that crap. But then,
Evan got delayed—this deal he's been working on started falling apart—and he had to stay behind, and so his wife—his
soon-to-be *ex*-wife—decided she'd play Mighty Mouse and
save the day, in spite of the fact she was supposed to be spending the weekend in Manhattan with her two weirdo friends,
the Wicked Witch of the West and Toto. And so we all drove
up here," she continued, unable to stop now even if Henry had
stuffed a gag in her mouth, "and what do you know? The ever-
agreeable, gruesome threesome decide to spend the night, and
we all end up sharing a room—don't ask," she warned, before
barreling on, "and then Evan calls and says he's been further
delayed, and Val decides to go hiking, and I'm doing my best to
be invisible and stay out of everyone's way, because I think this
is probably the safest course of action, but then Brianne takes
off with her boyfriend, and a couple of park rangers find them
naked in the woods . . ."

Henry tried—and failed—to suppress a smile. "Yes, I
believe I heard some gossip about that. I didn't realize Brianne
and Hayden were the couple in question."

"Hayden isn't her boyfriend. It was actually Brianne and
Tyler . . . It doesn't matter . . . What matters is we got kicked
out of the lodge. And then some guy Val used to know in high
school, who happens to be Hayden's father, shows up out of
nowhere, and he comes up with the bright idea that we should
all spend the night here in this godforsaken place. So here
we are, in the middle of Hell's Campfire, swatting mosquitoes

and freezing our butts off. And I'm beginning to think David Gowan had the right idea after all. I can't believe I just told you all that," she said, then promptly burst into tears.

In the next second, she was in Henry's strong arms, her face buried in the stiff cotton of his shirt. "I'm sorry," she said, pulling back, although not entirely out of his reach. "I'm getting your nice shirt all wet." She rubbed at the now damp fabric, stretched taut against the impressive muscles of Henry's chest. Somebody's been overdoing the workouts, she thought, thinking he was about to burst his buttons.

"No problem," Henry said, his voice somewhat huskier than before.

"You must think I'm crazy."

"Just a little."

"I honestly don't know how I get myself into these situations."

"Doesn't sound like you had a whole lot of control over any of it."

"You're being very generous."

He looked toward the ground, pausing several seconds before he spoke. "You don't have to stay here, you know."

"Unfortunately, yes, I do." Jennifer hated the whine she heard in her voice as she felt fresh tears beginning to form. "All the hotels in the area are filled up."

"I have a place," Henry offered. "It's not much, but it has the benefit of being nearby. It even has a guest room. No funny stuff, you have my word as a park ranger."

"Oh. No, no, I couldn't. I mean, that's very kind of you, and everything. I appreciate the offer. I really do. But I . . . I just . . . I couldn't." Jennifer took another step back, her hands falling limply to her sides.

"I understand." Henry quickly reached into the pocket

of his crisp black pants and pulled out a small notepad and a ballpoint pen. "Look. I'm gonna give you my phone number," he said, scribbling it down and tearing off the page, "and you can call me if you change your mind. It's a special phone they give us that operates by satellite, so you won't have any trouble reaching me, and you can call anytime. Doesn't matter how late it is. Don't worry about waking me up. You understand? If you can't sleep or you just want to talk some more or . . . anything at all. You call me. Okay?"

Jennifer slipped the piece of paper into the back pocket of her jeans. "Okay."

"You're sure you're all right?"

"I'm fine."

"You gonna stay fine, if I go?" It was almost as if he was seeking her permission to leave, now that it was clear she wasn't going with him.

"Don't worry," a voice said, a slender figure with a shock of orange spiky hair emerging from behind one of the portable toilets and slinking toward them. "Toto will take good care of her."

Shit, Jennifer thought as James stepped under the spotlight of an overhanging light. "How long have you been hiding behind there?"

"I wasn't hiding. I was simply waiting for my cue." James extended his hand toward Henry. "Officer Krupke, I presume?"

Henry declined James's hand, his face registering his confusion. "I'm sorry?"

"My God. Don't tell me you've actually never seen *West Side Story*? Please say it isn't so."

"And you are?" Impatience with the interloper edged concern for Jennifer from Henry's voice.

"James Milford, also apparently known as Toto. Stereotypical gay friend of Melissa Atkins, aka the Wicked Witch of the West, and Valerie Rowe, also known as the Wife of Evan. *Still Wife,* we like to call her." He glanced pointedly at Jennifer. "The aforementioned Gruesome Threesome. And I see you've already met Jennifer, known affectionately in some quarters as the . . ."

"Okay, I think that's quite enough nicknames for one night," Melissa interrupted forcefully, breaking into the center of the group.

"My God," Jennifer wailed. "Are you all out there?"

"Believe it or not, we saw you leave and got concerned when you didn't come back. Silly us."

"Look, I'm sorry if you were offended by what I said," Jennifer began.

"But just to be clear, not sorry you said it?" James asked.

"I was upset. Surely you can understand that."

"Why? Being gay doesn't mean I'm especially sensitive."

"He actually isn't sensitive at all," Melissa said.

"Thank you," said James.

"In fact, he's quite obtuse."

"Oh, you're just saying that."

"Is this supposed to be funny?" Henry's patience was clearly at an end. "I mean, what the hell is this?"

"It's okay," Jennifer said. "It's my fault. I deserve it."

"It's not your fault," Henry argued.

"Yes, it is. It's all her fault," James insisted. "Anyway, I have to pee. So, if you'll excuse me . . ." He disappeared into the nearest porta-potty.

"This night just keeps getting better and better," Melissa said.

"I think I'm going to bed now," Jennifer said.

"I think that's a great idea." Melissa turned toward Henry.

"Thank you for all your trouble. I'm sure we can handle things from here."

"Thank you, Henry," Jennifer said before he could protest.

"You'll call me if you need me?"

Jennifer patted the side pocket of her jeans. "I have your number," she said.

SEVENTEEN

"ARE YOU KIDDING ME? She called you the Wicked Witch of the West?" Val was torn between being offended for her friend and laughing out loud.

"She tried to explain she was only referencing my proclivity for black, but I told her I wasn't buying it."

"She actually said she was 'referencing your proclivity for black'?" Val asked, astonished. "Those were her words?"

"No, of course not. Those are *my* words. I was paraphrasing. But I think you're missing the point here."

"And she really called James 'Toto'?"

"I thought his eyes were going to pop out of his head. You should have seen him. You should have *heard* him. *The dog?* he kept saying. *She thinks I'm the damn dog? Everyone with half a brain can see I'm Dorothy, for God's sake.* Then he started clicking his heels together and chanting, *There's no place like home. There's no place like home.* It was more than worth the price of admission."

This time Val did laugh. "You're really being very good sports about all this. I owe you both, big-time."

"Please, you don't owe us a thing. I think this might be the best trip we've ever taken."

Val glanced around the claustrophobic, heavy canvas walls of the tent she and Melissa were sharing, picturing the high-ceilinged, Wedgwood-blue baroque interior of the suite they were missing out on at the Plaza. My kingdom for a down-filled mattress, she thought, trying to get comfortable inside the sleeping bag the campground had provided for each of them, wondering how she'd ever enjoyed crawling inside a thin layer of flannel and feeling the uneven contours of the earth underneath her back. "Do you think they ever wash these things?" she wondered out loud, sniffing at the brown lining, catching a brief reminder of Gary's scent, and wondering if Melissa could smell it, too.

"Don't ask me," Melissa said. "You're the camper in the group. I thought you'd be in your element."

"Times have changed, I guess."

"They always do. Anyway, it's not all that awful."

"You're just saying that."

"Yes, I am. But you have to play the hand you're given."

"What if I want to trade in a few of my cards?"

"Then you'll have to go play with somebody else. I'm too tired for extended metaphors. Anyway," Melissa said, groaning as she turned over in her sleeping bag, "I'm going to close my eyes now and dream about what goodies tomorrow has in store for us."

"Oh, God. I shudder to think."

"Don't shudder. Sleep."

"Melissa?"

"Hmm?"

"Where'd you ever find black pajamas?"

Melissa answered with her signature chuckle, a sound that Val had always considered the audible equivalent of a corkscrew, and said nothing. Seconds later, her gentle snoring filled the tent.

"Good night," Val whispered, watching her words dissolve in the cool mountain air and closing her eyes, although she doubted she'd get any sleep tonight. There was too much on her mind. First, of course, was Brianne and that stupid boy—correction, *man*—Tyler. Thank God her daughter was safe and Hayden's cell phone hadn't been able to connect to the outside world. Then there was Jennifer and that consistently smug little expression on her smug little face, not to mention those stupid legs that went on forever. Women like Jennifer had always made her feel clumsy and inferior, bringing back painful memories of the awkwardness she'd felt throughout her high school years. And speaking of high school, who could forget Gary and their unexpected, not to mention unexpectedly wonderful, romp in the sack, or sleeping bag, as the case may be? An involuntary groan escaped her lips as she pictured the two of them rolling around the tent's cramped interior. She bit down on her bottom lip to keep from groaning again, still feeling him inside her. Dear God, what had she been thinking? Had she lost her mind entirely? Why now, of all times? In this, of all places? Under these, of all circumstances?

Other men had come on to her in the immediate aftermath of Evan's desertion, and she'd had no trouble turning down any of them. In truth, she hadn't even been vaguely tempted, so shattered was she by Evan's decision to leave her. So why succumb now—hell, she hadn't succumbed, she'd *instigated*—just when Evan had started dropping some none-too-subtle hints that he wanted to come back?

Was that what *she* wanted? she wondered, the surprising thought causing her eyes to open wide. Was a lifetime of lies and self-doubt really preferable to a lifetime of loneliness and regret? And were those her only options?

And while on the subject of errant husbands, where exactly was David Gowan and would they ever find out what happened to him?

So there was definitely a lot to think about, Val decided, flipping over onto her back and surrendering to the certainty that this was going to be one very long night indeed.

In the next instant, she was fast asleep.

"ARE YOU KIDDING me?" Brianne asked, trying not to laugh at the theatrically pained expression contorting James's already exaggerated features. "She called you Toto?"

"The *dog*," he said, pulling a gray sweatshirt over his orange hair. "The fucking dog."

"Can't she see you're so much more Dorothy?" Brianne asked.

"Exactly. Bless you, my child. At least *somebody* understands me."

"Oh, God. You are *such* a cliché," Brianne said, as she'd said many times before. She reached over to give him a big hug.

"Right back at you." James lifted the sleeping bag above his head. "Just look at this stupid thing. What's one supposed to do with it exactly?"

"One is supposed to climb inside it."

"Oh, please. God only knows how many people have been in it already."

"Funny, I've heard people say the same thing about you."

James gasped, his fingers fluttering about his face in mock outrage. "You filthy girl. I'm going to report you to your mother."

Brianne giggled at her own naughtiness. Despite her sour demeanor and loudly proclaimed abhorrence for how this extended weekend was playing out, she was actually starting to enjoy herself. Maybe because she knew it was about to come to an end. She checked her watch. Almost ten o'clock. Just two more hours. And then *The Great Escape,* she thought dramatically. "I have to go to the bathroom," she announced, deciding it was time for another trip to the john.

"Again?"

"I have a small bladder."

"Since when?"

"Since I was a baby. Hasn't my mother told you about how, when I was little, I had to go to the bathroom, like every ten minutes, and how I couldn't be bothered, so I'd just pee in my pants?"

"Charming."

Brianne continued, unabashed. "Apparently I peed in my pants until I was seven years old. My mother decided there was no point in making us both crazy by turning it into a big deal—she said she figured I'd be potty-trained by the time I was ready to walk down the aisle—so she'd just send me off to school with a bag full of clothes to change into."

"So tolerant and understanding. No wonder you hate her."

"Who says I hate her?"

"You don't?"

"Of course not. She's my mother. I love her."

"Then why are you so mean to her?"

"I'm not mean to her."

"Are too," James said.

"Am not," Brianne insisted.

They both laughed.

"You're such a cliché."

"Ditto."

"I have to go to the bathroom," Brianne announced again.

"I'll go with you."

"What? Why?"

"Why?" James repeated.

"You went the last time I did," Brianne said.

"Maybe you're not the only one with a small bladder."

"Does that mean you're going to go to the bathroom every time I do?"

"It might."

"That's just ridiculous. Don't you trust me?"

"Of course I don't trust you." He sounded amazed she would even ask the question. Somehow, Brianne thought, he even managed to make his distrust sound endearing. "But it's also dark out there, there are wild animals hovering, and I would think you'd be glad for the company."

"Then you would think wrong."

"I could protect you against anything . . . untoward," James said.

"Untoward?"

"Unexpected. Unwanted. Unfavorable. Unfortunate."

"Unbelievable," Brianne said with a shake of her head.

"I know kung fu."

"You do?"

"Yes. I had to learn it for a musical I did some years back.

High Jinks and High Kicks, it was called. Unfortunately, it closed in previews. Too bad. I was really very good at it."

"You're going to high-kick a bear?" Brianne asked.

"I'll do whatever it takes to protect you."

"What if I don't need protecting?"

"Everyone needs protecting."

"No," Brianne argued. "What everyone needs is sleep. Now, climb inside that bag. I'll be right back."

"Is there some reason you don't want me to accompany you?"

"Like what?"

"I don't know. You tell me."

"You think I'm going to sneak off and meet my boyfriend?" Brianne asked, growing bored with the conversation and beginning to get the uncomfortable feeling that this evening might not go exactly as planned.

"Are you?"

"How could I? Tyler doesn't even know where I am."

"Your mother's right about him, you know," James said.

"What do you mean? How could she be right about him when she doesn't even know him? And neither do you."

"I know he's too old for you."

"Maybe I'm more mature than you think."

"You peed your pants until you were seven," he reminded her.

"I told you that in confidence," Brianne said, bristling. "Now you're using it against me?"

"I'm sorry. I was just trying to be clever."

"Well, you aren't clever. You aren't clever at all. Maybe Jennifer is right. Maybe you're just . . . *Toto*." Brianne angrily pushed her way out of the sleeping bag that was gathered in folds around her waist, then opened the front flap in the tent and breathed in a big gulp of night air. "When did you become so, so . . . uncool?" she said, spitting the words back at him as she crawled outside.

Seconds later, she was stomping toward the portable toilets at the far end of the camp.

She didn't have to turn around to know that James was right behind her.

JENNIFER HEARD BRIANNE and James arguing in the tent next to hers and wondered if she should do anything to intervene. I think you've said quite enough, a little voice told her, advising her to stay where she was. The angry words grew louder, then came to a sudden halt. The ensuing seconds of silence were immediately followed by two sets of footsteps clomping past her tent toward the far end of the camp. She burrowed deeper into her sleeping bag and shivered, even though she'd put on an extra sweater. She wondered what Evan was doing, if his meetings had finally ended, and if he'd been successful, if he was at this very moment lying in their bed, missing her as much as she was missing him.

Or maybe it was Val he was missing, she wondered, too tired to push the troublesome thought away.

Truthfully, it wouldn't come as all that big a shock to learn he still had feelings for his wife. He'd pretty much admitted as much already. "Of course I still have feelings for her," he'd told her one night after too many drinks had made her both bold and stupid enough to ask. "We were together a long time. I wasn't always the best husband," he'd added, almost wistfully.

You were a lousy husband, Jennifer thought now, although she'd been quick to put all the blame on Val at the time.

It doesn't bode well, she heard her father say.

Go away, Daddy, she thought. This tent isn't big enough for all of us.

Except he was already before her, food stains dotting his wrinkled clothes, his thinning hair uncombed and in need of a wash, visible scabs forming on his too-pink scalp, staring accusingly in her direction. She wondered if Cameron had bothered checking in on him, and if she had, if she'd stayed more than a few minutes. Had her sister made sure he'd had something to eat? Had she taken him for a drive in her new car? Or had she just sat with him and commiserated about his younger daughter's selfishness?

Shit, Jennifer thought, hearing Brianne and James return to their tent and thinking she should probably go out there and apologize to James again. None of this was his fault after all. But then, absolutely nothing about this weekend was the way it was supposed to be.

Was it possible Val actually enjoyed this type of thing? Or had she just gone along with it because it was something Evan enjoyed? And wouldn't she be doing exactly that, if Evan were here?

Except he wasn't here, Jennifer thought, sparing herself the danger of further self-examination. If Evan were here, everything would be completely different. None of this would be happening.

Damn it, she thought, feeling the walls of the tent closing in on her as her father's disapproving gaze fell across her face like a suffocating pillow. It doesn't bode well.

AN HOUR LATER, emboldened by the sound of James's steady breathing, Brianne climbed out of her sleeping bag and crept through the front flap of the tent.

"Hi," Jennifer's voice greeted her as she emerged.

"Oh, my God!" exclaimed Brianne, dropping to her knees, her heart beating so fast it threatened to burst from her chest. What the hell was Jennifer doing out here at this hour? Now what was she supposed to do?

"Sorry. Did I frighten you?"

"What do you think?" Brianne asked, her brain going, *Shit, shit, shit, shit!* "What are you doing out here?"

"I couldn't sleep. The tent's very claustrophobic, don't you find?"

Brianne shrugged. She'd never had a problem with tight spaces.

"I don't like anywhere where I can't stand up," Jennifer said, continuing. "I'm pretty good in places where I don't have to crouch. Like elevators. I don't have a problem with elevators. I even got stuck in one once. In New York. Between the thirty-second and thirty-third floor of William Morris Endeavor on Avenue of the Americas. You know the building?" she asked, plowing right on before Brianne could answer, tell Jennifer that not only did she not know the building, but that she wasn't the least bit interested in either it or Jennifer's story. "Well, I had a meeting there one day. It was just after the merger, and they were thinking of launching a campaign . . . anyway, it doesn't matter."

It certainly doesn't, Brianne thought.

"And so I'm in this elevator with about half a dozen other people, and everything's fine. Three people get off. A few others get on. And suddenly the damn thing lurches and comes to a stop. And there we are . . . stuck. Four of us. In this old elevator. And we're there for almost an hour. And this one guy is freaking out. I mean, he's sweating and hollering and carrying on. 'Let me out of here. Let me out of here.' And we manage to get him calmed down, but it's hot in there, because it's summer, and the air-conditioning isn't working now, either, and the other people in the elevator are starting to get a little upset. And I'm fine. I'm absolutely fine."

"Amazing," Brianne deadpanned.

Jennifer nodded her agreement. "And yet, put me somewhere where I can't stand up, like a cave or something. Or like this stupid tent," she said, slapping at it with her hand, her voice trailing off. "I didn't realize tents were so confining. Did you?"

"It's a tent," Brianne said, as if this were explanation enough.

"I saw this movie once. It was about some girl who was being held prisoner in an underground cave, and in order to escape, she had to crawl through this long tunnel. And every so often, she'd come to a little space where she could just manage to sit up, but that was all, she couldn't stand up straight, and then she'd have to start crawling some more, and I just freaked. I had to leave the theater. Just shoot me now, I said to myself."

With pleasure, Brianne thought, glancing at her watch. In twenty more minutes, it would be midnight.

"Or like in the days of the Roman Empire . . ."

"Whoa!" Brianne said, stopping her. "I get it. You don't like places where you can't stand up."

"When my mother was sick," Jennifer said, either oblivious to Brianne's indifference or ignoring it, "she had to have an MRI. You know what that is?"

Brianne nodded. She'd seen enough reruns of *ER* and *House* to be able to operate the damn machines herself.

"Well, my mother had to have one. And, you know, they put you through this tube . . ."

"I know."

"And there she was, lying on that skinny table, about to be swallowed up by that awful thing, and I'd think . . ."

". . . Just shoot me," Brianne said.

"I'd think, she must be so scared." Tears suddenly spilled from Jennifer's eyes and down her cheeks. "Being so trapped, being so helpless, knowing she was going to die, knowing there was nothing she could do about it."

Brianne sat very still for several more seconds, wondering what the hell she was supposed to do now. She had less than twenty minutes to meet Tyler at the camp's entrance and here she was, stuck with Little Miss Doom and Gloom. "Well, as much as I've enjoyed our little talk," she said, reaching back and reopening the flap to her tent, "I think I'm gonna try to get some sleep now."

"I'm sorry. Weren't you on your way to the johns?"

"Lost the urge." Brianne was already halfway back inside the tent. "It's getting pretty chilly out here. Don't you think you should at least try to get some sleep?"

"Don't think I can."

"I think you should try. Maybe if you closed your eyes, you'd forget about your phobias."

Jennifer didn't move. "I read somewhere that all phobias are really just a fear of death."

"Sounds logical." Brianne crawled back inside her tent and into her sleeping bag, then lay in the dark with her eyes wide open. Just shoot me, she thought.

EIGHTEEN

THE GIRL SAT UP in the too-soft bed and looked toward the window. Okay, so where is he? she wondered, checking the clock on the end table beside the bed, and noting that it was almost 2 A.M. She was starting to worry. He should have been back by now. How long did it take to dispose of a body?

Her mind raced through the night's events: the lateness of his arrival; the look of relief on his face when he saw that she wasn't mad—"I got interrupted," was all the explanation he'd offered; the unfamiliar clothes he was wearing, and how he'd kept them on even as he was pulling off her jeans and pushing his way into her, first on a blanket of cold, damp leaves, then back here in the Laufers' cottage, in their unwitting hosts' too-soft bed. Lovingly, she retraced the bloody imprint his hand had left on her breast and smiled at the memory of the taste of fresh blood on his lips.

Whose blood? she'd wondered. But she hadn't asked.

He'd killed again, she knew that for certain, and she felt a stab of jealousy that she hadn't been there with him, a flash of anger that he hadn't waited for her, but she also knew better than to call him on it or question him. He didn't like to be questioned.

There was a reason for everything. He'd tell her all about it when the time was right. "Later," was all he'd said to the question mark in her eyes. That single word—overflowing with promise and intrigue—had excited her all the more. And then, after he'd taken her a third time—this time from behind, riding her as if she were a bucking bronco—he'd announced that he had to go out again.

"I'll go with you," she'd said immediately.

"No. Stay here," he'd told her. "I have some cleaning up to do. You hate that. I'll be back soon."

So where was he? What was taking him so long? Had something happened to him?

She climbed out of bed, pushing the uncomfortable thought from her mind. She would simply not entertain such a horrifying possibility. If anything *had* happened to him, if he'd been captured by the police or, God forbid, injured in any way, she didn't know what she would do. She loved him so much, she simply wouldn't want to live without him. "There is no me without you," she said out loud. Catherine . . . Veronica . . . Nikki—they would all cease to exist.

Did he feel the same way about her?

She wasn't sure.

Which was when she was seized by another uncomfortable thought: that he might be with someone else.

The very idea of him with another girl made her feel sick to her stomach and she flipped on the overhead light to wipe out the image, watching the bedroom come into sharp focus. "Ugh," she said, her eyes skipping across the yellowing lace doily on top of the dark oak dresser, then continuing over to the matching lace curtains draping the large, rectangular window. Old people's stuff. Although she'd rather enjoyed the Percodan she'd found in their medicine cabinet, she thought, popping another one into her mouth in an effort to still her growing anxiety.

On top of the doily sat an ornate, silver-framed photograph of the people she'd helped slaughter. The Laufers smiled back at her pleasantly, innocent to the fate that awaited them at her hands, as she lifted their picture closer to her eyes. Why is it that all old people look alike? she found herself wondering, without pity or remorse. Interchangeable faces. Interchangeable lives.

Interchangeable deaths, she added, smiling at her cleverness.

She thought of the other couples they'd murdered. There'd been nothing remotely exceptional about any of their victims, except the exceptionally violent manner of their deaths.

Yet even under such spectacular circumstances, they'd proved remarkably alike, all dying with the same horrified looks in their pale, watery eyes—as if they couldn't believe that after having managed to survive this long, this was to be their fate, as if the simple fact of having lived such long, boring, and utterly inconsequential lives entitled them to slip into death's peaceful embrace with a minimum of fuss and pain.

"Surprise!" the girl shouted gleefully, popping yet another Percodan into her mouth as if it were candy, and letting the photograph slip from her hands to the floor. She began pulling open the dresser drawers, her hands rummaging thoughtlessly through their contents. The top drawer contained a bunch of ugly rhinestone brooches and gaudy beaded necklaces, the middle one an assortment of delicate undergarments and night-gowns. "Don't think you'll be needing any of these things any-more," she said, retrieving a pale pink silk camisole that fell from the drawer and caught on her big toe. She picked it up and held it against her naked breasts. She went to the closet, examining her image in the full-length mirror hanging on the inside of the door. "Why, Grandma, what big tits you have!" She tossed the garment up into the air and watched it float gently back toward the floor, like a parachute. "What other stuff have you got in here?" She rifled through the clothes hanging neatly on the row of dark green plastic hangers. In quick succession she tried on a lilac-colored shift, a royal blue cashmere sweater, and a pair of white Capri pants, all at least several sizes too big for her, and all of which she left lying on the floor. "You're not the only one who gets to play dress-up," she said, thinking of Kenny and wondering what he was doing at this precise moment, once again praying he was all right, and hoping there was a good reason he'd chosen to exclude her from his latest kill.

"Please don't let him be with anyone else," she whispered, hearing the fear in her voice bounce off the walls. Could that be where he was now? Back at the lodge, where they'd treated themselves to several celebratory dinners, auditioning her replacement?

The thought made her double over, and she fought back the urge to gag. No one had ever made her feel so wanted, so valued, so loved. Surely he would never betray her. And yet, there were times when she caught him checking out other girls, which had made her feel so inadequate. Sometimes she doubted her ability to hold his interest, times she was afraid he would leave her for someone prettier, smarter, more adventurous.

Still, hadn't she done everything he'd asked of her, and more? Hadn't she performed each assigned task to his satisfaction, even the cleanup part she despised? Hadn't she been instrumental in not only finding their latest victim, but in leading him directly to the slaughterhouse?

"Hi," she heard herself say, sighing with the memory. She watched herself approach him as he sat off by himself at the far end of the lodge's Olympic-sized swimming pool, its shiny blue chlorine shimmering in the moonlight. "Can't sleep?"

"One of those nights."

"For me, too. Do you mind if I join you?"

The look that said he was intrigued. "Lots of empty chairs."

"I saw you earlier. In the dining room. David, right? I heard your wife call you David."

"Among other choice epithets."

"Yes. She seemed pretty upset."

"Sorry about that."

"You don't have to apologize."

"You are . . . ?"

"Nicole. But you can call me Nikki."

"Pretty name."

"Thank you. I've always liked the name David."

He'd shrugged, although she could tell he was flattered. Men are such suckers for a few kind words, she remembered thinking. "Pretty common name," he said.

"Maybe. But it's a strong one. And very handsome, I think. You wear it well," she added for good measure, repeating a line she remembered hearing on one of those Lifetime TV movies.

David chuckled, and for a second she feared she might have gone too far, that her boldness might send him running for cover. He was on his honeymoon, after all. But after fidgeting for several seconds, he settled back in his chair, not ready to go anywhere. "Aren't you going to ask me what the fight was about?"

"No need."

He arched one eyebrow.

"I pretty much heard the whole thing."

He laughed, and she looked around, wary that the sound might have attracted attention. But there was no one watching, or even close by.

"For what it's worth, I think you were right."

"I appreciate that." Then, "Isn't it a little late for you to be up?"

"How old do you think I am?" she asked in return.

"I don't know. Sixteen, seventeen."

"I'm twenty."

"No way."

"All right. You got me. Nineteen and a half."

"You look younger."

"You want to see my ID?"

A smile, colored with a hint of relief. "Don't think that will be necessary."

"I think you should be able to go fishing," she told him, "if that's what you want."

"What I want doesn't seem to matter much."

"It should."

"It's not even that important. Just that I made these plans weeks ago, and I told her about them. Really, I did."

"And I really don't see the problem. You want to go fishing; she wants to spend time with her family. Why can't you both have what you want?"

"My sentiments exactly."

"Maybe she'll come around."

"Maybe hell will freeze over." He made a sound halfway between a laugh and a snort, and she tried to imagine the sound he'd make as she was sliding a long knife between his ribs. "I shouldn't have called her a bitch," he said.

"She shouldn't have called you an asshole," she reminded him, giving her imaginary knife a nasty twist.

"Maybe that's what I am." The tone in David's voice begged her to disagree.

She obliged him. "You're not an asshole."

"You don't know me very well."

"I don't know you at all. But I have good instincts."

"And your instincts are telling you . . . what exactly?"

"That you're a pretty decent guy. That you don't deserve to be yelled at and embarrassed in public."

David stiffened with the memory. "You know what my instincts are telling me right now?"

She held her breath, looking up at him through strategically lowered eyes.

"That I should probably get out of here before I do something really stupid."

"Like what?" she asked provocatively.

He paused, clearly debating with his conscience over what to do next. Then he leaned over and kissed her. "Shit," he said in the next breath. "I really *am* an asshole. I'm on my fucking honeymoon, for God's sake." He pushed himself to his feet. "I'm sorry. I really need to get back upstairs."

"Of course. This is all my fault."

"No. Of course it's not your fault. You were just being nice."

"I'm not," she said. "Nice, that is."

He smiled and turned to leave.

"Can I ask you a favor?" she asked.

He turned back.

"Forget it. It's too much to ask."

"What is it?"

A moment's hesitation. Then, "It's just that I'm not actually staying at the lodge. I just came here for dinner. I'm staying at a friend's cottage. Just up the road a bit. And I was wondering . . . if you wouldn't mind walking me home. It's so dark and everything. I promise it won't take more than a few minutes. You've already kissed me good night," she added softly, playing on his guilt.

It was his turn to hesitate. "Sure. What the hell? What's another couple of minutes? It's the least I can do."

And the last, she thought now, picturing them as they walked beside the creek that ran behind the lodge and up the winding dirt road. "We're almost there," she'd said several times. Then, after more than ten minutes had passed, "Sorry. I didn't realize it was so far." And when the cottage finally popped into view, "If you could just wait till I'm safely inside . . ." And finally, "Would you mind coming in for a minute? Just till I get the lights on."

The knife was in his back almost as soon as his foot crossed the threshold. He'd grunted and lurched forward, the air rushing from his lungs as he spun around, the initial confusion in his face giving way to the recognition of what was happening, and then to fury. He lunged at her, his hands reaching for her throat even as his legs were collapsing under him.

"Jack be nimble, Jack be quick," she'd teased, ducking out of his reach, watching his fingernails scratch impotently at the air.

And then they were both on him with their knives and machete, joyously severing muscle from bone and skin from cartilage until their clothes were soaked with the sweat of their exertions and David lay beneath a blanket of blood, virtually unrecognizable. "Hope you're enjoying your fucking honeymoon as much as we are," she'd laughed as they'd had sex beside his torn and tattered corpse. Then, suddenly starving, they'd made themselves sandwiches, polishing off the late-night snack with another bottle of expensive Bordeaux from the Laufers' collection, while discussing the pros and cons of younger versus older prey.

They'd agreed that both young and old presented their own series of risks and rewards. The young ones were stronger and reacted faster, making them more of a challenge. And yet, they simply weren't as much fun or as deeply satisfying as killing old folks, she thought.

Still, what was that famous saying? *Variety is the spice of life.*

And death, she thought now, smiling as she remembered returning to the lodge the next morning, the place buzzing with the news of David's disappearance. Later, after going back to the cottage, she saw that the floor had been washed down and David's body removed, although she spotted tiny bits of his flesh still clinging to the floor, like stubborn specks of dust.

She tugged a floral-print cotton dress off one of the hangers and pulled it over her head, grabbing a big rhinestone bow off the dresser and pinning it to the ample folds between her breasts before leaving the bedroom. "Peekaboo, I see you," she said, spying a splatter of blood on the far wall of the living room. "I'm bored," she announced moments later, suddenly aware of the scent of stale blood emanating from the still damp and probably permanent stain on the beige rug.

The trouble with killing was that it was addictive. Like dope, she thought, searching through the cushions of the sofa for the baggie full of freshly rolled joints she'd left lying around earlier. "There you are, you little devil," she said with a laugh, pulling the fattest one out with her teeth and walking into the kitchen to light it with one of the front burners of the stove. She inhaled deeply, swallowing most of the smoke before blowing out a succession of perfectly round circles with the little that remained. Her grandfather had taught her that trick, albeit with conventional cigarettes, around the time he stopped bouncing her on his knee and started slipping his hand down her pants.

Or maybe he hadn't done that at all, she thought. Maybe her grandmother was right, and she was just a stupid little girl who'd made the whole thing up. "There's something wrong with that child," she'd overheard her grandmother whispering to her mother one night. "I think she needs professional help."

"Liar, liar, pants on fire," she sang out now, smoke rings rising, like miniature halos, around her head. "Honest to God," she yelled in the next instant, spinning around in frustrated circles, "how can people not have a TV?" They should have brought that one with them that they'd stolen from the Berkshires, instead of pawning it. Although who knew they'd pick the one cottage in the area without a television set? "Who doesn't own a TV, for fuck's sake?"

"We have a radio," she remembered Stuart Laufer saying.

"Yeah, right. Hooray for that." She puffed furiously on the joint, smoking it down halfway, then grinding the lit end into the kitchen counter, watching a small brown circle form in the laminate as a pleasant buzz settled at the base of her neck, like a warm scarf. Her mother would have a fit if she saw her now, she thought with a smile, wondering absently what her mother was doing at this precise moment, if she even knew she was gone, if the woman had any idea where she was or what she'd been up to these last weeks?

If not, she'd hear about it soon enough.

"I'm getting bored again," she said to the walls, her voice a singsong as she debated relighting the joint, smoking it all the way down. Kenny would be angry with her for not waiting till he got back. He'd say she was selfish. But what the hell? He was selfish, too, showing up late, then going off by himself again, killing without her. Not to mention that she'd caught him ogling that waitress's ass at the lodge the other night when he didn't think she was looking. He'd even hinted that maybe one day they could try a three-way, she recalled, a thought she'd managed to suppress until now.

What did that mean? That he didn't love her anymore?

Again, she felt tiny bubbles of panic spreading through her bloodstream. She had to stop thinking such thoughts. Of course Kenny loved her. It was the marijuana that was making her paranoid. And the Percodan. They were fogging her brain and filling her head with crazy ideas. She had to find something else to occupy her mind, she thought, suddenly remembering Stuart's computer. Maybe she could find something to watch on that.

"Okay, let's see what we have here," she said, retrieving the laptop from the kitchen counter and carrying it over to the couch. She sat down cross-legged with it on her lap, turned it on, and waited until the machine booted up and the screen turned several pretty shades of blue. She quickly punched in the appropriate keys. "Let's see what kind of mail you guys get," she said, hoping she wouldn't need a password. "Thatta girl, Ellen," she said, as a frighteningly enthusiastic voice announced cheerfully, *You've got mail*. "No silly passwords for you. Probably wouldn't remember it anyway." She giggled as she noted only three messages in the inbox. "Not very popular, are you? And one of them is from Saks. They're having a sale this weekend, which it looks like you're going to miss. What a shame. Summer merchandise is thirty percent off on selected items and as much as fifty percent on others. That's quite the deal. Especially since I noticed your closet is looking a little sparse." She glanced down at the floral-print dress she was wearing. "I think you could have used a few new things." She deleted the message and opened up the next one, feeling the buzz at the base of her neck rising to fill her head.

Hi, Ellen, she read, the words floating across the screen on a wave of Percodan. *Just wanted to let you know that Wayne and I got back from Paris yesterday—you can check out our photos at franandwaynemcquaker.com—and it was wonderful, as always. It really is the most beautiful city in the world. Of course Wayne's back was giving him trouble and I had a terrible cold for the first part of the trip. And we had such awful turbulence on the plane ride home that my ears got completely plugged. Frankly, it still feels as if someone is standing behind me with their fingers in my ears. Most irritating. Anyway, I'll tell you all about everything this weekend. Wayne and I are so looking forward to our visit. It's been way too long. Love, Fran.*

"Franandwaynemcquaker.com," the girl said, feeling their surname sticking to her tongue. *"McQuaker . . . McQuaker,"* she spit out, as if trying to dislodge it. She sank back against the pillows, her mind trying to focus through the haze that was rapidly enveloping her. What did good old Fran McQuaker mean, *I'll tell you all about everything this weekend?* "Wayne and I are so looking forward to our visit," she repeated aloud, the words not quite registering, their meaning elusive.

She noted that the message was dated this afternoon. "Looks like we might be having company," she said as her eyes closed. She'd have to tell Kenny some potential victims were on their way. Although he wasn't calling himself Kenny anymore, she reminded herself, trying—and failing—to remember the new name he'd come up with.

Probably should have gone easier on the weed, she thought, laughing as she opened the third and final e-mail. Not to mention the Percodan. "Might as well have a look at what's behind door number three."

Hello, Mother, the message began.

The girl edged forward in her seat, the previous e-mail already forgotten. Now this could be interesting, she thought.

Katarina just told me she thought you might have phoned the other day. It was a bad connection and she was in the middle of doing something and couldn't talk. She sends her apologies. So how's everything up there in Shadow Creek? (The name still gives me the shivers, by the way.) Everything is good here in sunny, unshadowy California. Willow and Mason are enjoying camp and Katarina has started taking acting lessons, hoping to land an agent. My law practice is doing well and my golf game's even better. Shot a 78 the other day. Handicap getting closer to single digits. (That's a good thing.) I'm afraid it doesn't look good for coming out east in the fall. September is such a busy time, what with my practice—we're contemplating merging with another firm—and the kids going back to school, and casting season in full swing. Why'd you have to get married in September anyway? Maybe you could think about coming out here for a few days next spring. There's a great new restaurant just down the way from us and we could celebrate your fiftieth there. Make that fiftieth and a half. Pretty impressive. Anyway, think about it. Say hi to Dad for me. Bye for now, Ben.

"Well, now, aren't you the loving son?" she thought, feeling strangely angry on Ellen's behalf. "Can't make it home for your parents' anniversary, but hey, you shot a seventy-eight. Good to know somebody has his priorities straight." She yawned, stretching her arms high above her head. "How to respond, how to respond. Let's see," she said, hunching forward over the computer. "*Dear Ben. Dear, dear Ben. My darling son. Ben, you sack of shit . . .*" She grinned, the grin stretching across the entire lower half of her face. "No, I think I can do better than that."

Dear Ben, she typed slowly with her thumbs. *Don't worry about not being able to come to our fiftieth anniversary party this fall. Your father and I have decided to get a divorce. Love, Mother.*

She pressed Send, then collapsed in a fresh fit of giggles.

That was when she heard the noise outside. She jumped to her feet, letting the computer slide off her lap and fall to the floor. "Hello?" She edged cautiously toward the front door. "Is somebody there?"

Her question was answered by a loud knocking.

She ran into the kitchen, grabbing a large knife from the counter, her head suddenly very clear. "Who is it?" she asked, her ear to the door.

"Sorry to bother you, Mrs. Laufer," came the immediate reply. "It's Henry Voight. I'm with the park rangers."

The girl hid the knife behind her back as she opened the door to the handsome young man in uniform. "My grandmother's asleep," she began.

"I'm really sorry to be bothering you so late," he began. "I didn't realize the Laufers had visitors. I've been patrolling the area and I saw your lights were on or I never would have knocked. I just wanted to make sure everything is okay."

"That's so sweet," she told him. "You must be freezing. Why don't you come in? I'll make you some lovely peach and cranberry tea." She was smiling as she ushered him inside, closing the door after him.

NINETEEN

AT PRECISELY TWO O'CLOCK in the morning Val awoke from an unpleasant dream, the details of which were already evaporating by the time her eyes were fully open. Something to do with being chased by a hooded giant with a hook where his hand should have been. Great, she thought, as a familiar tug on her bladder pushed the last fragments of the dream from her mind.

She sat up, realizing she had to pee and wondering if she could hold out until it got light out. Another twinge told her there was no way she'd be able to make it through the night and she might as well make the trip now rather than lie here uncomfortably for hours, only to have to succumb to nature's call eventually anyway. If she got up now, at least she had a chance of falling back to sleep. "Melissa," she whispered, wriggling free of her sleeping bag and hoping her friend was awake enough to accompany her. "Melissa, are you up?" But Melissa was sleeping soundly and even a rough push on her shoulder failed to rouse her. "I have to pee," she told her anyway.

An eerie stillness had settled over the campground, like a thick fog. Except for the myriad of insects wildly circling the lights that shone from the high posts at strategic intervals throughout the camp, nothing moved. Rain was definitely in the air. Whatever possessed me to make this trip? she wondered for the hundredth time, the unanswered question pursuing her to the area where two dozen porta-potties stood like sentries, surrounded on three sides by tall pines and spruce trees. As soon as it gets light, she decided, I'm getting the hell out. I never should have come. What in God's name was I thinking?

She picked the closest portable and opened its door, her eyes automatically scanning the dark interior for unwanted spiders or snakes. "And wouldn't that just be the icing on the cake," she said, quickly lowering her jeans and hovering above the plastic seat.

Which was when she heard something moving around outside.

Damn it, she thought, holding her breath and waiting.

For a few seconds, there was nothing. Val was beginning to think it had been her imagination, along with her bladder, working overtime. Which was when she heard the noise again. The telltale crackling of branches, the muffled shuffling of feet drawing nearer. An animal? she wondered as the door handle began to jiggle, causing the entire structure to shake.

Someone—or some *thing*—was trying to open the door.

The Hook Man, she thought, and might have laughed had she not screamed instead.

"Sorry," a familiar voice said immediately. "I didn't realize anyone was in there."

"Jennifer?"

"Valerie?"

"You scared the shit out of me."

"Well, at least you're in the right place."

Seconds later, Val emerged from the john, still shaking, although this time more in anger than fear. "Was that supposed to be funny?"

"Sorry," Jennifer apologized again, barely managing to suppress a grin. "Did you think you were going to find a bloody hook hanging from the door handle?"

"Don't be ridiculous," Val said testily. Damn that James and his stupid story anyway.

"Sorry," Jennifer said a third time, sidestepping Val and disappearing into the next portable.

How is it possible that anyone can look so damn good in the middle of the night, in the middle of nowhere? Val found herself wondering. The young woman was wearing no makeup, but even under the harsh overhead lights her complexion was still flawless, her hair artfully tousled. Even when she was all dressed up for a night on the town, Val had never looked that effortlessly put together. She always looked as if she just needed another ten minutes.

Which was what Evan had always claimed to love about her: that careless confidence, as he'd once called it. Well, she was still acting as carelessly as ever, but what the hell had happened to her confidence?

You were fearless, Gary had said earlier. But maybe *reckless* was the better word. *Proceeding with a potentially dangerous course of action without thought to its consequences.* She'd certainly been guilty of that lately. How else to explain what she was doing here?

The door to Jennifer's portable opened and Jennifer emerged, luminous blue eyes widening at the sight of Valerie still standing there. "You didn't have to wait for me," she said, appearing genuinely touched. "That was very sweet of you."

Val was about to contradict her, tell her the truth, that she hadn't been consciously waiting for her at all, that she'd simply been lost in thought, then decided against it. Hell, if Jennifer wanted to think she was sweet, in spite of all evidence to the contrary, she was too exhausted to argue. "Not a big deal," she said instead, starting back toward their tents.

"I owe you another apology." Jennifer hurried to catch up to her. "For the mean things I said earlier."

Val continued walking.

"I was tired and cranky and upset."

Val offered no response.

"I was feeling very sorry for myself."

Val stopped, swiveling on her heels toward the other woman. "There's no need to keep apologizing."

"No. I owe you that much, at least."

Yes, it's definitely the least you owe me, Val thought. What she said was "It's okay. I understand."

Jennifer's blue eyes opened even wider than before. "You do?"

"Believe it or not, yes, I do," Val surprised herself by saying, even more startled to realize she was telling the truth. "You'd been looking forward to the weekend. You thought you were going to be spending three days with the man you love and his daughter in a luxurious spa hotel, not camping out in the woods with his disgruntled ex-wife and her two somewhat less than conventional friends. I get it. I really do. Enough said."

Jennifer's lips trembled, as if she might burst into tears. "Thank you."

Val brushed the other woman's gratitude aside with a tired wave of her hand. Forgiveness was more exhausting than she'd imagined. "And you don't have to worry. I'll be out of your perfect hair in the morning." She resumed walking.

Jennifer was immediately back at Val's side. "I'm sorry about what happened before with Brianne."

"Enough with the apologies."

"I should have told you about Tyler."

"You didn't want to betray her confidence. I get it."

"I just really wanted her to like me."

Val sighed, once more stopping in her tracks. "She does."

"Thank you," Jennifer said again. "I know this must be very hard for you."

"I don't need your sympathy."

"I'm sorry."

"Please. I think you've apologized more than enough for one night. Let's give it a rest."

They returned to the center of the camp, Val debating whether or not to continue on to Gary's tent as soon as Jennifer went inside hers, but Jennifer sank to the ground in front of her tent instead, hugging her knees to her chest.

"You're not going inside?"

Jennifer shook her head. "I don't like it in there."

Val glanced toward the voluminous dark clouds that were gathering around the moon like a hostile gang of delinquents, preventing its light from escaping. "Looks like it's going to rain. You'll get drenched."

Jennifer looked up at the sky, then back at her tent, and didn't move. "I'm kind of claustrophobic."

"Oh." Val paused, not sure what else she could say. "I thought you just didn't like anything where you weren't in control of your feet." She recalled the conversation they'd had the day before. Was there anything this girl wasn't afraid of?

"I guess I must seem pretty pathetic to you."

"No more pathetic than I probably seem to you."

"I don't think you're pathetic."

"I don't think you are, either."

A brief moment of silence, then, "Can somebody else join this little lovefest?" James emerged from his tent. "Or are dogs not welcome at the table?"

"I'm really so sorry about that," Jennifer said as Val groaned.

"Please tell her to stop apologizing."

"Stop apologizing," James said dutifully, lowering himself to the ground. "So, what's going on here? Are we bonding?"

"Jennifer is claustrophobic."

"Really? I read somewhere that all phobias are actually a fear of death."

"I read the same thing," Jennifer said brightly, clearly thrilled they'd found some common ground.

"And just what are you afraid of, James?" Val asked.

James thought for a few seconds before answering. "Teenage girls."

Val laughed, glancing over her shoulder toward his tent. "Speaking of which, how's my daughter doing?"

"Sleeping like a log. Hasn't moved a muscle all night. Or at least, hasn't moved since she stopped getting up to go to the bathroom every two seconds."

Val felt a dull headache starting to gnaw at her temples. She closed her eyes, trying to block out the thoughts she felt forming.

"Something wrong?" James asked.

"Do you mind if I go in there to check on her?" Val was already moving toward James's tent.

James was immediately behind her. "Why do I have this sudden, horrible feeling in my gut?"

Val opened the flap of the tent James was sharing with Brianne, her eyes struggling to adjust to the cocoon-like darkness. She was able to make out James's empty sleeping bag on the ground by her feet, and then Brianne's sleeping bag against the tent's canvas wall. From this angle, it looked as if Brianne were indeed sound asleep inside it. The sleeping bag was curled into a semi-fetal position and the hood of Brianne's sweatshirt was protruding from its top. Still, there was something that wasn't quite right. Val edged closer, straining to hear the sound of Brianne's breathing.

It's too quiet, she realized, her hand reaching toward the sleeping bag, gently touching the rounded curve of its side, feeling for her daughter's hip, her back, her legs. "Shit," she exclaimed loudly, pulling back the top of the bag to reveal the empty sweatshirt beneath, the rest of the clothes from Brianne's overnight case stuffed into the bottom half of the sleeping bag. "Shit. Shit. Shit."

"That little skunk!" James exclaimed.

"Don't tell me," Jennifer said as Val and James reemerged into the chilly air. "She's not there?"

"Do you know where she is?" Val asked accusingly.

"No. I swear. I would tell you."

"Oh, Val," James said. "I'm so sorry. I watched her like a hawk for hours. I went with her to the john, I can't tell you how many times. I thought she'd finally fallen asleep. And then I guess I must have dozed off . . ."

"It's not your fault. She's not your responsibility. I should have kept watch."

"There's no way you could have foreseen she'd do something like this."

"She and Tyler must have cooked up this whole thing . . ."

"You think they're together?" Jennifer asked.

"Where else would she be?" Val wasn't sure which scenario she preferred—that her daughter was with Tyler or that she was out wandering the woods at night on her own. In the dark. In the rain, she thought, feeling a few drops land on her shoulders. "Great."

"Maybe she's with your friend's son," Jennifer said. "Hayden, right? I mean, they were together earlier. Maybe she's with him."

"You think so?" Val found herself desperately wanting to believe this was a possibility.

"What's going on out here?" Melissa asked sleepily, poking her head out of her tent.

"Brianne's missing," Jennifer said.

"Again?" Melissa pushed herself into the open just as Val took off, running toward the other side of the campsite.

She ran blindly, suddenly unable to remember exactly where Gary's tent was located. In the dark, one section of the campground looked pretty much like all the others, and the tents were essentially variations on the same theme. "Where are you, Gary?" she whispered loudly into the darkness.

"Come out, come out, wherever you are," James stage-whispered behind her.

"Which tent do you think is his?"

"I think it was over that way," Melissa offered, joining them, Jennifer right behind her. "There, that one."

"You're sure?"

"Maybe."

Val drew closer. "Gary?" she called out, first softly, and then more forcefully, her lips pressing against the tent's stiff canvas. "Gary?"

No answer.

"Damn it."

"It's starting to rain," Jennifer said.

"Thank you for that weather update," Melissa said.

"It's not my fault it's raining."

"Gary?" Val called again, silencing them. "Gary, are you in there?"

"Could you yahoos keep it down out there?" someone called out. "There are people here trying to sleep."

"Sorry." Val heard a loud sob escape her lips. "Damn it." The last thing she needed to do was start crying.

"Val?" Gary emerged from his tent about ten yards down the way.

Val rushed toward him. "Oh, thank God."

"What's the matter?"

"We can't find Brianne."

"What?"

"We thought she might be with Hayden."

"Hayden's asleep."

"You're sure?"

Gary quickly returned to his tent. He was back seconds later, shaking his head, his eyes reflecting his concern. "He's gone."

"Which means they're probably together," Jennifer said. "That's good, isn't it? At least it means she's not with Tyler."

"I don't know what it means," Val said. "Hayden didn't say anything to you about meeting up with Brianne?"

"No. Not a word. We talked about our plans for tomorrow, said good night, went to sleep. I didn't hear another thing until two minutes ago when I heard you calling my name."

"Maybe he went to the bathroom," Melissa said.

"I'll go check," James volunteered.

"I'll come with you." Jennifer quickly followed after him.

"I'll check our tents again," Melissa offered.

"I can't believe this is happening," Val said.

"If she's with Hayden, then we know she's safe," Gary assured her.

"Do we?"

"Could you shut up out there?" someone yelled.

"Quiet!" another voice shouted in response.

Melissa was back almost immediately, followed in the next few seconds by Jennifer and James. Val knew by the expressions on their faces that they hadn't found either Hayden or Brianne. "We should spread out," she said, "each take a different direction . . ."

"Look," Gary interjected, his voice calm and steady. "It's not going to do anyone any good if we all go running off half-cocked and get ourselves lost in the process. It's dark and it's starting to rain. There's no way we're going to find them until it gets light." He touched Val's arm reassuringly. "Hayden is an experienced camper. If he's with Brianne, he'll make sure they find their way back here. I guarantee it."

"And if he's not with Brianne?"

"Where else would he be?"

"We should notify the park rangers," Val said.

"Agreed. But we can't do anything until morning, and I'm certain that by then it won't be necessary."

"Maybe we don't have to wait until morning," Jennifer said.

"You have a better idea?" Val asked.

Jennifer reached into the pocket of her jeans and pulled out the slip of paper on which Henry Voight had written his phone number. "I know somebody we can call."

TWENTY

BRIANNE FELT SEVERAL DROPS of rain on her shoulder and glared up at the sky. "Thank you. That's just what I need."

"What's your problem now?" her companion asked, stumbling through the dark woods until he reached her side.

"It's starting to rain, in case you hadn't noticed."

"And I guess that's my fault, too."

"It probably is."

"Of course," the young man conceded. "Everything is my fault."

"No arguments from me on that score." Brianne began spinning around in helpless circles. "Damn it! Where the hell are we?"

"You think I know?"

"I thought you knew everything, big shot."

"Look. I don't know why you're so angry at me. I'm the one who said we should stay in the car."

"I'm sorry, but are you referring to the car you drove into the fucking ditch?"

"It was pitch black. You were yelling at me. I didn't see the damn thing."

"You didn't see it because you were too damn drunk to see anything."

"I wasn't that drunk."

"Drunk enough to be half an hour late, drunk enough to start throwing punches, drunk enough to get stuck in a fucking ditch!" Brianne stomped away, her heels drilling tiny holes in the wet earth as twigs from overhanging branches slapped the side of her face and poked at her ear. "Ow. Damn it."

"I had, like, six beers," her companion insisted, following after her.

"More like sixteen. You reeked. You still reek. Shit—you smell just like my grandmother."

"What?"

"I said you smell like my grandmother, tough guy. God, I can't believe what a mess you've made of everything."

"So why'd you get in the car with me?"

"Because you fucking grabbed my arm and pushed me inside. You practically kidnapped me." Brianne stopped so suddenly that her companion walked right into her, stomping all over her toes. "Ow. Watch where you're going."

"Take it easy. It was an accident."

"Yes, you're very good at those. Why'd you have to drink so much anyway? You knew you'd be meeting me."

"I was in a bar when I got your call. What was I supposed to do until midnight?"

"I don't know. Play darts? Listen to music? Have a soft drink instead of getting plastered?"

"I'm starting to think I didn't get plastered enough."

"Don't think. It's not your strong suit."

Tyler Currington brushed several raindrops from the tip of his nose. "Geez, Brianne. When did you turn into such a bitch?"

"I don't know, Tyler. Maybe around the same time you turned into fucking Muhammad Ali."

"Muham . . . what? What are you talking about?"

"I'm talking about the fact you could have killed that boy."

"What? No way. I hardly touched him."

"You knocked him out."

"It was a lucky punch."

"Not so lucky for him."

"He's fine," Tyler insisted. "Besides, I did it for you."

"For me?"

"You were the one yelling at him to back off."

"I just wanted him to go back to the campground."

"Where he probably is right now. Telling everybody what happened."

"I doubt that, since you left him unconscious by the side of the road," Brianne reminded him. "What if something happens to him?"

"Nothing's going to happen to him."

"You don't know that. Damn it. I have to get back there." With that, she took off again, running blindly in the dark.

"Where the hell do you think you're going?"

"To find the main road."

"Then you're going the wrong way."

"I am not."

"I think you are."

"Okay, big shot. Which way do you think it is?"

Tyler squinted through the dark, his right hand lifting into the air, his index finger poised and ready to point. "That way. No, wait. Maybe that way. I don't know," he admitted in defeat seconds later. "I'm all turned around."

"Great. So, what are you suggesting? That we stay here all night?"

"I don't know."

"You don't know much, that's for sure." She resumed walking.

"Would you at least slow down?"

"I don't want to slow down. I want to go home."

"You're gonna walk all the way back to Brooklyn? In those shoes?"

Brianne wasn't sure if Tyler was serious or trying to make a joke, but she had no patience for him either way. She was tired and wet and angry, although she wasn't sure if she was angrier with him or with herself. She never should have arranged to meet him. She should have listened to her mother. At the very least, she should have listened to Hayden's entreaties to return to the campground. He'd been looking out for her and she'd repaid him by leaving him unconscious and alone by the side of the road. If anything happened to him, it would be all her fault. I want my mother, she thought, and had to swallow several times in order to keep from saying the words out loud.

"Everything would be okay if we'd stayed in the car," Tyler was muttering from somewhere behind her. "At the very least we wouldn't be out in the middle of nowhere, in the rain, getting soaked to the skin. We could have crawled into the backseat, fucked ourselves silly all night, which I kind of thought was the plan . . ."

"Yeah, like you were in any condition to do anything."

"Hey. Tyler Currington always rises to the occasion."

"Please. Spare me." Brianne's stomach lurched at the thought of the two of them rolling around in the backseat of his car. To think she'd once actually found him appealing. So appealing she'd actually surrendered her virginity to him. She groaned at the memory of trying to wipe up the resulting blood with her T-shirt, the one her mother had found on the floor of her bedroom.

What is this? her mother had asked suspiciously, holding the stained shirt up to the light. *Is this blood?*

I'm sorry, Mommy, she said silently, trying to push her mother from her thoughts. "Damn it." Did she always have to be so . . . right?

"What's the matter now?"

"It's starting to rain harder, in case you hadn't noticed."

In the distance, thunder rumbled.

"You've got to be kidding me." Brianne checked the sky for lightning.

"I told you we should have stayed in the car."

"Thank you. That's very helpful. Do you want to say it again?"

"Why does it have to be so fucking dark?"

"I don't know. Maybe because it's night and we're in the middle of fucking nowhere?"

"Do you think you could lay off the sarcasm for a little while?" Tyler asked.

"I don't know," Brianne answered. "Think you could lay off the stupidity?"

"Okay. Here's a thought. Why don't you just shut up? Okay? How's that for a bright idea?"

"Dickhead." Brianne's eyes filled with tears, mingling with

the rain pelting her cheeks. Damn you anyway, Tyler Currington, she thought, forging ahead with absolutely no idea where she was going. And damn you, Sasha, for introducing us in the first place. And damn you, Daddy, for being late and fucking everything up. Again. As always. Damn everybody, she thought, the high heel of her shoe catching on the side of a stray log, sending her sprawling into a pile of leaves.

Tyler was immediately at her side. "Are you all right?"

Brianne brushed the dirt and wet leaves from her face and hands, then burst into tears, her already weak ankle starting to throb once again. "No, I'm not all right. I'm wet and I'm cold and I think I just broke my fucking ankle."

"Come on. You didn't break it."

"Oh, really? I'm sorry, when exactly did you get your medical degree?"

"It's probably just twisted. What did you expect in those stupid shoes?"

"They're not stupid," Brianne said. "You are."

"I'm not the one running through the woods in high heels. Come on. Stop crying, and try to stand up."

Brianne sniffed back her tears and reluctantly did as she was told, but the pain proved too intense and she sank back to the ground. "I can't. Oh, God. It's really starting to hurt."

Another rumble of thunder, like a distant explosion, shook the sky.

"Was that lightning I just saw?"

"I didn't see anything," Tyler said.

"I did. I saw lightning. Great. Now we'll probably get electrocuted."

"Nobody's getting electrocuted. Come on. Try again." He reached for her arm.

"Don't touch me, you jerk." She pulled the shoes from her feet, hurling them in his general direction for emphasis.

"What the?" Tyler ducked, then threw his hands up in the air in frustration. "Okay, fine. I give up. You don't want my help? You don't want anything to do with me? You want me to leave you alone? Fine by me. I won't help you. I'll leave you alone." He turned around and began stomping away.

"You're just going to leave me here?" Brianne shouted after him in disbelief.

Tyler spun back toward her, his face glistening with a combination of rain and fury. "What do you want from me, Brianne? Tell me. Whatever you want, I'll do it. Just tell me what you want."

I want my mother! "I want to get out of here."

"Then the first thing you have to do is stand up."

"Not till I know where we're going. We can't just keep wandering around in the dark all night in the middle of a storm."

Another flash of lightning, this one unmistakable, followed seconds later by a loud clap of thunder.

"Try your phone again," Brianne instructed.

Tyler pulled his phone out of his jacket pocket and began punching in numbers. "Not getting a damn thing."

"No!"

"Okay, look," Tyler said. "We passed a little clearing a while back. I think we'd be safer there. There aren't so many trees."

"I don't remember any clearing." Brianne struggled to stand up. "Shit. I can't put any weight on my ankle." She tried hopping, feeling the wet earth cold on the bottom of her bare foot, as twigs, like dozens of hypodermic needles, poked at her flesh. "This isn't going to work."

"All right. It looks like I'm gonna have to carry you."

"I don't think—"

"Good idea. Don't think," he said, lobbing her earlier words back at her. "It's not your strong suit." With that, he hoisted her into his arms, almost losing his balance in the process and staggering forward half a dozen steps before he was able to regain control of his footing.

"Don't you dare drop me," she warned.

"Don't tempt me." He carried her back in the direction from which they'd just come, trying to retrace their steps in the dark. "Damn it. I can't see a thing."

"Guess we should have left breadcrumbs."

"Breadcrumbs?" Rain dripped from the tip of Tyler's nose into his mouth, causing him to spit the word out.

"Your mother never read you the story of Hansel and Gretel?"

"She may have. I don't remember."

"You really don't remember the story of Hansel and Gretel?"

"I don't remember my mother."

"What do you mean, you don't remember her?" Brianne burrowed her face into his chest, trying to escape the worsening rain.

"She died when I was two."

"She did? You never told me that. What happened to her?"

"I don't think this is the best time to be having this discussion." Another bolt of lightning split the sky, followed almost immediately by another crack of thunder.

"The storm's getting closer," Brianne observed. "Where's that stupid clearing?"

"It should be around here somewhere."

"Great. That's very reassuring."

They continued on for another minute, the rain pelting them from all sides as the wind picked up its pace. "Okay, here we are," Tyler said after another minute, lowering her carefully to the ground and kneeling beside her.

Brianne brought her hand up to shield her eyes from the rain and looked warily around. "What do you mean, 'here we are'? We're nowhere."

"We're away from the trees, so there's less chance of us being struck by lightning."

"But we're gonna get soaked out here."

"We're already soaked."

"We're gonna catch pneumonia."

"Would you rather be struck by lightning?" Tyler sat down, removing his wet jacket and holding it above both their heads. "I had pneumonia once," he said. "It was no fun."

"And this is?"

Another flash of lightning, another rumble of thunder, one right on top of the other.

"That should be the worst of it," he said.

"So, how'd your mother die?" Brianne asked him after another minute had passed. Might as well make conversation, she was thinking. Anything to distract her from her predicament.

"Drug overdose."

"Really?"

He nodded, turned his head away.

Is he going to cry? Brianne wondered, beginning to regret having been so mean to him. "Accidental or on purpose?"

"They think it was an accident."

"What do you mean, they *think*? They don't know?"

"It was kind of hard to tell. She was into some pretty heavy stuff. Heroin, crack, junk like that."

"She was a drug addict?"

"And a prostitute."

Holy shit, Brianne thought. What the hell am I doing with this guy? "What about your dad?"

"Last I heard he was rotting away in some Texas jail."

"Wow. Talk about heavy stuff."

"I guess."

"Why didn't you tell me any of this before?" *Why didn't Sasha?*

"Would it have made a difference?"

"No." *Probably.* "Of course not." *Definitely.*

"We never really talked a whole lot," he reminded her.

"What did he do? Your father, I mean."

Tyler mumbled something unintelligible.

"What?"

"Serial killer," Tyler said. This time the words were crystal clear.

"What!"

A smile began creeping into the corners of Tyler's dark eyes.

"You're making all this up, aren't you, you sick piece of shit?"

Tyler laughed. "Sorry. Couldn't resist. You got to admit you had it coming."

"Is your mother even dead?"

"No. She was in great shape the last time I saw her."

"And your father?"

"Never even had a speeding ticket, as far as I know."

"How could you do that to me?"

"It stopped you bitching for a few minutes, didn't it?" He laughed again, slapping at the wet ground with the palm of his hand.

"This isn't funny. God, you are such an imbecile."

"You deserved it. Like I wouldn't know the story of Hansel and Gretel. Hah! You should have seen your face when I said my dad was a serial killer. That was worth this whole fucking night."

"You know what? I've had enough of you. Just get away from me, okay? Find a hole somewhere and crawl inside with the rest of the rats."

Tyler pushed himself to his feet. "Fine by me. I've had more than enough of you, too." He hesitated.

"Well, go on. What are you waiting for?"

"Don't worry. I'm going. Just don't start hollering at me to come back."

"I won't. Go on. Get out of here."

"You sound just like your mother. You know that?"

"Good. I'll take that as a compliment."

"I wouldn't. Your mother's a bitch."

"My mother is *not* a bitch. Don't you dare talk about my mother like that."

He shook his head, water dripping from his hair. "You're crazy."

"Just leave me alone."

"You're sure this is what you want?"

Brianne looked away, then back at Tyler. "I'm sorry. Are you still here?" She looked away again. When she looked back a moment later, he was gone.

WHAT THE HELL is the matter with me? Brianne wondered, hugging herself against the cold. What had she been thinking, sending Tyler away like that? She'd only made things worse: she was still lost in the woods, in the dark, in the middle of the night. Except now, she was all by herself. Well done. Okay, at least the rain had stopped. Although the mosquitoes were back in full force. Did they never sleep?

What time is it? she wondered, glancing at her watch but unable to read what it said. She estimated that Tyler had been gone about thirty minutes, so it had to be at least three, maybe even four o'clock in the morning by now. That meant it should be getting light in another few hours. Surely she could last till then. Unless an animal gets me, she thought suddenly, listening for suspicious sounds as she cast a glance over both shoulders. And if an animal doesn't kill me, my mother definitely will.

My poor mother, she found herself thinking. As if she hasn't enough on her plate to deal with. An alcoholic mother, turning the big 4-0, her soon-to-be ex-husband's recent engagement to a younger woman. Brianne knew that no matter what her mother said, she was still in love with her father, that she desperately wanted him back, and that her heart was breaking at the thought of him marrying someone else. She also knew, without having to be told, that her father was just using her mother, that he had no real intention of coming back, and that he was stringing her along, keeping her dangling in case things with Jennifer didn't work out. "Always have a fallback position," she remembered him saying once with regard to some deal he was working on. Her mother didn't deserve to be treated so cavalierly, she thought angrily. Not by him. Not by me, she added reluctantly. "I'm so sorry, Mom," she whispered into the darkness. "I love you. I love you more than anything in the world."

Her mother would be hysterical when she woke up and realized Brianne was missing. She'd call the park rangers, who would eventually find Tyler's car in the ditch; they'd organize a search party. Eventually they'd find her, tired and wet and hungry, nursing her broken ankle. There'd be tears and recriminations, and ultimately forgiveness. Her mother had never been able to stay angry at her for very long, although she'd probably take her BlackBerry away permanently, which wasn't the worst thing in the world. It had gotten her into more than enough trouble already. Truthfully, she didn't care if she never saw another cell phone device as long as she lived. Besides, her father would undoubtedly buy her a new one as a way of atoning for screwing up the weekend.

Brianne wrapped herself up in Tyler's jacket, grateful he'd either deliberately left it behind or more likely, simply forgotten to take it with him, and tried to find a comfortable spot on the ground on which to lie down. Maybe she'd even manage to fall asleep. Or maybe not, she thought, sitting back up almost immediately, aware of the sound of leaves shaking and wood snapping underfoot. "Hello? Is somebody there?" Her hand foraged through the leaves on the ground for a stick that could serve as a weapon, finding nothing but wet clumps of mud and a few useless twigs. "Hello? Who is it?"

Tyler was suddenly looming above her, like a giant bear. "Just call me Hansel."

Brianne gasped. How could he have gotten so close without her spotting him? "God, you scared me half to death, you jerk." Truthfully, she felt almost unbearably grateful to see him. "What are you doing back here? You get lost again?"

"Yeah," he admitted. "But I also found something. A road. Not the main one," he added quickly. "It's just a dirt road, but there looks to be a cottage or something at the far end of it."

"A cottage?" Brianne asked hopefully. Then, more skeptically, "Is it made of gingerbread?" She wasn't about to be fooled by one of his stupid stories again.

"I'm not making this up. I swear."

"You better not be."

"Look. You can believe me or not, but there's a road and a

cottage about a mile from here. I don't know if the place is occupied or not, but I think it's worth a shot."

"A mile? I can't walk a mile on this ankle."

"You don't have a choice." He grabbed her elbow and pulled her to her feet.

"You better not be kidding," she told him.

"Trust me," he said. "This is no joke."

TWENTY-ONE

W HAT TIME IS IT?" Val asked, feeling a fresh army of tears gathering strength behind her eyes.

"I'm too bleary-eyed to read my watch," James told her.

"Closing in on four o'clock," Melissa said, the words escaping her mouth on a yawn.

Val nodded. "Still no luck with that number?" she asked Jennifer.

"I'm not getting any reception at all," came the answer Val had been simultaneously dreading and expecting. Henry Voight might have a phone that operated by satellite, but she didn't. "I think we're going to have to wait until the office opens in the morning." She was referring to the Starbright office, which had a landline. It didn't open until seven. "But I'm sure Brianne will be back by then."

"I can't believe this is happening again."

"Three times a charm," said James.

Melissa suppressed another yawn. "I'm certain she was planning to be back before any of us realized she was gone."

"Listen, why don't you guys try to get a little sleep?" Val suggested. "There's no point in all of us being up the whole night."

"You sure you wouldn't mind?" Melissa asked.

"Positive."

"You'll shout if she comes back?" James said.

"They'll hear me in Canada."

They exchanged hugs, then Val watched her two friends disappear inside their tents.

"If you don't mind, I'd rather stay out here," Jennifer said.

Val nodded. The truth was that she didn't mind. The truth was she was actually quite appreciative of Jennifer's efforts on her behalf. The young woman had spent the better part of the last hour prowling the campground, trying to get through to Henry Voight's private line, albeit with no success.

"At least it stopped raining," Jennifer said.

Small comfort, Val thought, staring into the night, praying to see her daughter take shape in the darkness. But all she saw was the swaying of the tree limbs and all she heard was the whispering of the leaves. *Your daughter's in trouble,* the leaves told her. *Your daughter needs you.*

"Are you okay?" Jennifer asked after a silence of several minutes.

Val nodded. "I'm just scared. And angry. And disappointed. Which I guess pretty much sums up being the parent of a teen-ager."

Jennifer chuckled sadly. "Looks like I won't have to worry about that."

"You don't want kids of your own?" Val realized she was genuinely curious.

"I don't know. I always assumed I'd have a whole bunch," Jennifer confided. "But Evan . . ." She stopped abruptly. "Sorry." She hugged her knees, stared at the ground.

Val finished the sentence for her. "Evan doesn't want more kids."

"I can understand his reluctance," Jennifer said quickly. "I really can. He's older, and he's been there, done that."

"But *you* haven't."

"No, but . . . Well, we'll see. Maybe he'll change his mind."

Don't count on it, Val thought but didn't say out loud, sensing she didn't have to. Evan had always been very adamant about not wanting more children. "*I* like to be your baby," he'd told her every time she'd broached the subject.

"I probably wouldn't be a very good mother anyway," Jennifer said.

"What makes you say that?"

"I don't have a lot of patience."

"Really? You strike me as someone who has quite a lot of patience."

Jennifer laughed, although the sound was far from joyful. "Not according to my sister. She says I'm always on her about something."

"Well, sisters aren't necessarily our kindest judges."

"Do you have any?" Jennifer asked.

"One. Younger. Allison."

"Mine's older. Cameron."

"Are the two of you close?" Val thought she was asking the question as a way of passing the time, time she wouldn't have to spend worrying about Brianne, so she was surprised to discover she was actually interested in Jennifer's answer.

"No. We never were. I'm not sure why exactly. We're just so different, I guess. We always seem to piss each other off. What about you and Allison?"

"We used to be close when we were growing up. Things changed after my father left."

"Why did he leave?"

"Another woman," Val said with a wry smile. "Sound familiar?"

Jennifer stared at the ground. "My father has Alzheimer's," she said after a pause.

"I'm sorry." Again Val was surprised to realize that she was.

"So, I guess, in a way, he kind of left us, too."

Val nodded. "That must be very hard."

"It is."

"What about your mom?"

"She's dead. Yours?"

"She's working on it."

Jennifer's eyes connected with Val's through the darkness, although she said nothing.

"She drinks," Val explained without prompting. "A lot. Pretty much all the time, actually."

"Because of your dad?"

"Maybe in the beginning. But I think it's too easy to put all the blame on him. It's a disease. And she had choices. We all have choices."

Again, the women's eyes connected.

Which was when they heard the footsteps and saw the figure emerging from the shadows and lurching toward them.

"Hayden?" Val jumped to her feet and rushed toward him, catching him just before he collapsed in her arms. "My God, what happened to you?"

"Is he okay?" Jennifer asked.

"Go get Gary." Val heard the incipient hysteria in her voice, which pitched it several octaves higher than usual. Even in the dark she could see that Hayden's cheek was cut and bruised and that his clothes were soaked through and covered with mud. "What happened? Where's Brianne?"

"What's going on?" Melissa asked, emerging from her tent.

"Is Brianne back?" asked James, appearing at the same time.

"Can someone please get me some water?" Val asked, brushing flecks of stone and matted hair away from Hayden's face.

James immediately ducked back into his tent, returning seconds later with a bottle of mineral water. Val lifted it to the boy's lips, watching him intently as he tried to take a sip.

"Hayden, please, sweetheart, where is Brianne?" Val urged.

"Hayden! Hayden!" his father called as he scrambled toward them, tripping over his feet and almost falling. He collapsed to the ground, taking his son in his arms. "Are you all right? My God, what happened? Who did this to you?"

Hayden stared at his father for several seconds without speaking.

"Is Brianne all right?" Gary spun around. "Where is she?"

"We don't know. Hayden came back alone," Val told him. "Please, Hayden. Can you tell us where she is?"

"She's with that guy," Hayden finally managed to spit out.

"What guy? You mean Tyler?"

He nodded.

"Tell us what happened," Gary said as the others drew closer.

Hayden obliged, telling them of Brianne's attempts to reach Tyler when they were out for their walk. "The connection was bad and she wasn't sure if she'd gotten through to him. But I overheard her tell him to meet her at the camp's entrance at midnight. I didn't want her going out there alone—she doesn't have the best sense of direction—so I followed her. I know I should have said something to you," he told his father.

"What happened then?" Val asked. There was no point in discussing what could have or should have been. All that was important was what had actually taken place.

"He was really late, and I almost had her convinced to come back to the camp when he finally showed up. He'd obviously been drinking . . ."

"Oh, God."

"We got into an argument, and that's when he hit me."

"He hit you?"

"Next thing I knew, I was waking up by the side of the road."

"And Brianne?"

"Gone."

"They left you out there alone?" Jennifer asked.

"Oh, God," Val said to both father and son. "I'm so sorry."

"Wait. She's not back yet?" Hayden asked, the full reality of the situation starting to sink in.

"No. She didn't say anything to you at all about where they might be going?"

Hayden shook his head, gingerly at first, and then with more conviction. "I don't think they really had a plan."

"They probably found a place to park," Melissa said, "and then it started thundering and lightning, and they decided they'd better stay put and wait it out."

"The storm stopped an hour ago," Val reminded her.

"Maybe common sense prevailed and they're waiting till the moron sobers up before driving back," James offered.

"Common sense was never Brianne's strong suit," Val said. "Oh, God. What if they were in an accident? What if . . . ?"

"Let's not speculate," Gary advised.

"But what if . . . ?" *What if . . . what if . . . what if?*

"It's okay," Jennifer said, taking Val in her arms and holding her until she stopped shaking. "She's okay, Val. Brianne's a tough cookie. She's your daughter, isn't she? Wherever she is, whatever's happened, she's going to be fine."

"SHOULDN'T WE HAVE found the road by now?" Brianne asked, pushing another branch away from her face as she half hopped, half limped after Tyler.

"We've only been walking for ten minutes," Tyler reminded her.

Even with his back to her, she could read the expression on his face. And it wasn't pretty. He was fed up, and to be honest, she couldn't blame him. She was being a pain in the ass, and she knew it. The sound of her voice had become as irritating to her own ears as it undoubtedly was to his. But damn it, she was wet, she was cold, she was in considerable pain. And it was all his fault.

No, not just his fault, she amended immediately. Don't forget that this whole thing was your brilliant idea. And remember—nobody forced you to get into his car. How could she have allowed him to drive off, leaving Hayden unconscious by the side of the road? Please let him be all right, she prayed silently. Please let him have woken up and made his way back to the camp. Damn the consequences. All that mattered was that Hayden was okay. That they would all be okay.

"Surely we've gone a mile by now," she said after several more minutes.

"Are you kidding me? Maybe a quarter of a mile at best."

"What? Are you joking?"

"Believe me, I'm in no mood for jokes."

"We're not even halfway?"

"That's right."

"At this rate, we won't get there till morning."

"Maybe if you tried walking faster . . ."

"Maybe if you tried carrying me again . . ."

He glared at her over his shoulder.

"What? You think I'm too heavy?"

"Under the circumstances, Tinker Bell would be too heavy."

"You're saying you think I'm too fat?"

"That's not what I'm saying."

"Then what *are* you saying?"

"I'm saying you talk too much."

"Well, you drink too much," Brianne countered immediately.

"In case you hadn't noticed, I sobered up a long time ago."

"You're right. I didn't notice."

Tyler stopped, spun toward her. "You think you could give me a break? For just a couple of minutes? That's all I'm asking. It's not like I'm asking for a little gratitude or anything."

"Gratitude? You expect me to be grateful? For what, exactly?"

"For coming back, for starters. I didn't have to, you know."

"So why did you?"

"I don't know. I guess because I'm a dickhead. I believe that was the expression you used." He resumed walking.

"I'm sorry about that," she said quietly, not moving.

He stopped again, turned back toward her. "What did you say?"

"Nothing."

"Did I actually hear you apologize?"

"Only for calling you a dickhead."

"Of course."

"Not for anything else."

"Of course not."

"Everything else was your fault."

"Of course," he said again, a smile tugging at the corners of his lips. "Anyway, no biggie. What is it they say? 'Sticks and stones may break my bones, but words will never hurt me.'"

"I don't think that's true," Brianne said. "Words do hurt. Sometimes even worse than sticks and stones."

"Well, I've been called a lot worse things than dickhead."

"Yeah? Like what?"

He laughed. "Oh, no. No way I'm giving you any more ammunition. Come on." He reached for her hand.

To Brianne's surprise, she took it, and they proceeded at a snail's pace for another five minutes. "Are we there yet?" she asked, hoping to sound wistful, maybe even endearing. But what came out was more petulant than playful.

"Probably about halfway."

Brianne let go of Tyler's hand, sinking to the ground in defeat.

"What the hell are you doing now?"

"I can't go any farther. My ankle . . ."

"It hurts, I know. But you've got to at least try, Brianne."

"I've *been* trying. I *am* trying."

Tyler shook his head, any hint of a smile long gone. "Yeah. You're trying, all right."

"What's that supposed to mean?"

"Nothing. It doesn't mean a damn thing. Look. Can we just give it one more go?"

"No. I can't walk. There's no way I can manage another half a mile."

"So, what are you suggesting? That we just stay here and hope somebody stumbles across us?"

"No," Brianne said. What *was* she suggesting? Did she think her mother was going to magically find and rescue her?

"Then what? There aren't a lot of alternatives here, Brianne. Either you get up or I go on alone."

There followed a moment of silence. Then, "I can't get up. I just can't."

Tyler sank down to the wet ground beside her. "Okay, listen. Maybe it's not such a bad idea if I go on alone. I should be able to reach the road pretty fast from here on my own."

"Assuming you don't get lost," Brianne interrupted.

"Assuming I don't get lost," Tyler repeated. "Thank you for that vote of confidence, by the way."

"Any time."

"Anyway, hopefully somebody lives in that cottage and I won't scare them half to death by waking them up in the middle of the night . . ."

"And you'll tell them what happened . . ."

"And they'll call the authorities . . ."

"And then you'll come back for me."

"And then we'll come back for you," Tyler repeated.

"What if there's nobody home?"

"Then I'll break in, use the phone, get help . . ."

"What if you can't break in? What if there *is* no phone?"

"What if I run into the big bad wolf?" Tyler joked in response.

"This isn't funny, Tyler."

"Look. What's the worst that can happen? Nobody will be home; I won't be able to break in; I'll break in and they won't have a phone. Worst-case scenario: I'll have hiked there for nothing. So I turn around and come back."

"You promise? You won't just leave me here?"

"If I was going to do that, I wouldn't have come back the first time."

"Why did you? I've been such a bitch."

"I kind of had it coming, I guess."

"Yeah, you definitely had it coming."

He laughed. "I think I should quit while I'm ahead." He pushed himself up to his full height.

Immediately Brianne started having second thoughts. "I don't know. Maybe you should just stay here with me."

"It's your call," he told her. "But I can be there and back in less than half an hour."

"That fast?"

"Okay, maybe an hour, tops."

"Okay."

"Okay? As in . . . ?"

"Okay, as in, okay, go before I change my mind."

"Okay," he repeated, pushing himself back to his feet. "I'll be back soon."

"Hurry," she called after him, dismayed to realize she'd lost sight of him already. "Shit." I shouldn't have let him leave, she thought. "Tyler!" she called out. "Tyler, I changed my mind! Come back!"

But if he heard her, he gave no sign. Nor did he come back.

"Shit," Brianne said again, sitting absolutely still for what felt like an eternity but was probably closer to five minutes. Finally, exhausted by both the hour and her ordeal, she lay down, curling into a tight fetal ball and closing her eyes against the night, pretending she was wrapped in the safety of her mother's warm arms, and listening to the leftover drops of rain as they fell from the leaves rustling nearby.

Minutes later, her hand curling around a clump of wet earth, she fell asleep.

TWENTY-TWO

NIKKI WAS LYING IN bed, eyes closed but wide awake, reliving the night's events and listening to Kenny singing in the shower, when she heard the tapping at her window. At first, she dismissed the noise as the last dying remnants of the storm, helpless branches being buffeted by hostile winds and scratching at the glass in a doomed effort to find shelter. No shelter here, she thought, and smiled, luxuriating in the memory of the final, frantic efforts of their latest victims. Except in those cases, they'd been trying desperately to get out, not in. Still, the results had been the same. There'd been no escape. There'd been no mercy.

Nikki loved going over the details of each kill. They made her feel closer to Kenny, bound him to her forever. She loved reliving the strict sequence of events, careful not to leave anything out: the initial setup, or "meet-and-greet," as Kenny liked to call it; the pleasant, innocuous conversation that invariably followed; the slight wariness that began to creep into those conversations as they progressed, the wariness gradually giving way to fear, the fear melting into terror, as cruel reality replaced fairy tale and knives made short shrift of happily ever after.

Nikki had never liked fairy tales. The idea of a beautiful princess in a gossamer gown was nothing short of repulsive to her. She'd hated stupid, whiny Cinderella, much preferring her nasty stepsisters; she'd rooted for the Wicked Queen over that insipid Snow White, and loathed Sleeping Beauty, who waited a hundred years for her handsome prince to find and rescue her.

Nor had she ever had much faith in the Tooth Fairy, the Cookie Monster, or even Santa Claus, despite her parents' best efforts to convince her they were real. "Look what Santa brought you," she could still hear her mother squealing with almost manic enthusiasm each Christmas morning, waving the latest Barbie doll in her face. God, she'd hated those ridiculous dolls, with their outlandish outfits and huge plastic breasts. She'd pretended to be enthralled with them for a respectable period of time, then ripped off their designer clothes, hacked off their shiny blond hair, and ultimately pulled their stupid heads off altogether. "Oh, no. Look what happened to poor Barbie," her mother would inevitably wail, as if the doll's sorry condition were an act of God.

Luckily, her mother had an enormous capacity for ignoring the obvious.

Unlike her grandmother.

"Maybe you should take her to see someone," she'd overheard her grandmother whisper to her mother on more than one occasion, the tiresome refrain becoming more and more frequent the older she got. "There's something not quite right about her."

"Don't be silly. There's nothing wrong with her," her mother would protest.

"I don't know. That business with the mole . . ."

"Can you just forget about that stupid mole already? She was a child, for God's sake."

"And the awful things she made up about your father?"

"We've been through this—how many times? It was an unfortunate misunderstanding. The school fills their head with stuff about good touching and bad touching. She got confused, that's all."

"I'm telling you, she's not like other children. I can't put my finger on it. I just know there's something . . . missing."

"You're wrong," her mother said.

But Nikki knew her grandmother was right. And that she'd have to be increasingly diligent. She learned to study people's faces to gauge their reactions, and to mimic emotions that were obviously expected from her. Emotions other girls seemed to come by naturally. Emotions she simply didn't have.

She pretended to love her parents when what she really felt was indifference; she feigned interest in her playmates when, in fact, they bored her to tears; she made friends easily and discarded them with even greater alacrity, replacing them on a regular basis. What difference did it make? One person was as good as the rest. Everyone was interchangeable.

And when her grandfather died just days before her thirteenth birthday, and her mother canceled the party Nikki had been looking forward to for weeks, she'd buried her anger at her grandfather's thoughtlessness and even managed to squeeze out a few impressive tears at his funeral. "She must have loved him very much," she'd heard a mourner comment. And she'd smiled to herself. Well done, she'd thought.

Then she'd looked over to where her grandmother was standing, watching her from beside her grandfather's open casket, and the smile had frozen, then faded, from her face. But the damage was already done. Her grandmother had seen into her soul. She knew the truth.

There's something . . . missing.

And something *was* missing, Nikki thought now, turning over in bed. Until Kenny. Then everything had fallen into place.

Her grandfather had been the first dead person she'd ever seen. She remembered approaching his coffin with a deliberately solemn face, her hands shaking with what a casual observer would no doubt interpret as a mixture of trepidation and grief, but was actually excitement. She'd stared down at his pasty skin, heavily rouged cheeks, and thin lips that had been dusted with an unflattering, somber-colored lipstick, and thought he resembled nothing so much as one of those weird wax statues in Madame Tussaud's famed museums. His eyes were closed, and she'd had to fight the impulse to reach in and pry them open with her fingers. "Look at me, Grandpa," she'd wanted to shout, her gaze drifting toward his dark blue suit and unfashionably wide, red-and-navy-striped tie. She was disappointed to discover there was no visible indication of the heart attack that killed him, so she closed her eyes and tried to picture his heart ballooning up to ten times its normal size, then exploding like a hand grenade. She would have liked to see that, she thought. Paid money, in fact.

She'd leaned forward, pretending she was about to kiss him goodbye. Instead her lips slid across the cold gray flesh of his cheek to his ear. "Rot in hell," she'd whispered, thinking of her ruined birthday party.

She wondered if she'd still collect any presents from the so-called friends she'd invited, having hinted for weeks about the great new perfume from Juicy Couture and the dark green V-neck sweater she'd seen in the window of Forever 21. Probably all she'd get now were some boring old clothes from the Gap, her mother's favorite store, and a bunch of useless books from her grandmother. She doubted they'd even bother with a cake this year. Not that she cared about having a cake or disappointing her friends or even turning thirteen. What she enjoyed was being the center of attention, and now her stupid grandfather had gone and stolen her thunder.

Thunder, she repeated silently, thinking about tonight's sudden storm. While it had been no match for the storm that had been raging the night she and Kenny had first discovered this place, it had nonetheless been a pleasurable reminder of the mayhem they'd unleashed. She'd always loved storms, their moments of high drama—lightning flashing, thunder raging, winds howling. Sometimes she would go outside in the middle of a particularly violent storm and dare the lightning to strike her. She'd feel the rain slapping viciously at her face and experience a euphoria that was almost sexual, a release almost as intense as when she took a knife to her flesh.

Nothing fake about those feelings, that was for sure. Nothing missing then.

But her grandmother had been right about one thing—she wasn't like other people.

She was special.

Did Kenny still think so? she wondered, hearing his impromptu shower shudder to a halt. Kenny loved taking showers, sometimes as many as five in a single day, sometimes in the middle of the night, like tonight, when he was too wound up to sleep. He'd been talking again about their having a three-way. "Aren't I enough for you?" she'd asked plaintively.

" 'Course you are. Don't be silly. I just think it might be fun to experiment, that's all." He'd climbed out of bed, headed for the bathroom. Seconds later, she'd heard the shower running.

She was waiting for him to emerge from the bathroom when she heard the tapping at the window. Not branches against the glass, she realized suddenly, opening her eyes and turning her head toward the sound. More like the sound of someone knocking.

Was it possible?

"Kenny," she whispered toward the bathroom, pushing the covers back and climbing out of bed. "Kenny, I think someone's here."

The bathroom door opened and Kenny appeared, a ghostly apparition in a cloud of steam, a towel wrapped around his waist. He cocked his ear toward the window, listening as the tapping grew louder. "Busy night," he said with a smile. "Guess you better see who it is."

"What if it's the cops?"

"Then we deal with them."

Nikki grabbed Ellen's old, pale blue bathrobe from the foot of the bed to cover her nakedness. She walked to the window as Kenny retreated to the bathroom. Cautiously, she parted the lace curtains.

At first she didn't see him. Only gradually did a face emerge from the darkness, eyes first, opening wide with relief, then a mouth, as it broke into a huge, grateful grin.

Whoever he is, he's awfully happy to see me, Nikki thought, pushing open the window. The young man immediately hoisted himself up and inside. "It might have been easier to use the front door," Nikki said with a laugh, catching him as he fell into the room. *Come in, come in, said the spider to the fly,* she thought, not bothering to adjust her bathrobe, which had become dislodged, partially exposing one of her breasts.

"I'm just glad you're home," he exclaimed. "I'm sorry if I scared you."

She slowly brought the sides of her robe back together. "Do I look scared?"

He gave a nervous little laugh. "No," he conceded, eyes drifting back to the front of her robe.

He's tall and kind of cute, in a bedraggled sort of way, Nikki thought. A little on the skinny side, perhaps. Not much older than I am. Might as well have some fun, she thought, knowing Kenny was monitoring them and allowing the front of her robe to creep open again, giving the boy another peek at what was inside. He didn't look away.

"I'm Tyler. Tyler Currington."

"Nikki." She fluffed out her hair, causing her robe to gape open even more. "There's a country singer named Billy Currington. Are you related?"

"No. I don't think so."

"He sings about beer and stuff. I don't like most country music, but I like him."

"Cool," Tyler said. If he thought their conversation was odd, considering the circumstances, he gave no such indication. "Are your parents here?"

"No. I'm all alone."

"You're kidding."

She smiled, feeling even more powerful than when she'd risked being struck by lightning. It was a sensation she relished. "Tell me, what's a nice boy like you doing out on a night like this?" She found it amusing that he seemed to have completely forgotten the reason he was here.

A sheepish grin filled his face, his eyes never leaving the front of her robe. "It's a long story."

"I'm sure it's a good one."

He shrugged. "I drove my car into a ditch. We started walking, got caught in the storm."

Nikki glanced warily back toward the window. "We?"

"This girl I was with," he said, adding quickly, "Nobody special."

Nikki wondered if the girl in question would be surprised to hear this. "So where's this nobody special now?"

"In the woods. About half a mile from here. She twisted her ankle, so she couldn't walk."

"So you just left her there? In the woods? Alone?" A man after my own heart, she thought. This night just keeps getting better and better. She looked over Tyler's shoulder toward the bathroom, knowing Kenny was listening to every word. Was he excited by what he was watching? Maybe even a little jealous?

"It was her idea for me to go get help," Tyler explained. "If I could use your phone . . ."

"I'm so sorry. It's not working. The last storm we had knocked out the power, and nobody's been around yet to repair it."

"Oh," he said. But he didn't look too disappointed.

"Maybe I could help you."

"What do you mean?"

"I could help you carry her back here."

"Nah. You're too small."

"I'm stronger than you think."

"I bet you are."

They stared at each other for several seconds, neither one saying a word.

"So? What'll it be?" she asked finally. "You want to go back, rescue the damsel in distress?"

"To be honest, I don't think I could do it. I'm just too damn tired." His eyes scanned the room, stopping on the rumpled bed. "That looks really inviting."

"You're more than welcome to lie down."

"I am?"

"I'm sure your girlfriend will keep until morning."

"She's not my girlfriend. I told you, she's . . ."

". . . nobody special. Yeah, I remember." Nikki stretched her arms above her head, giving him another tantalizing flash of her breasts before lowering her arms and gathering the sides of her robe around her. "You're probably freezing in those wet clothes. Wouldn't you be more comfortable taking them off?"

The look on his face—somewhere between "Is she saying what I think she's saying?" and "Holy shit!"—told her he couldn't quite believe his good fortune. Here he'd spent the better part of the night lost in the woods in the pouring rain only to stumble across the mountain version of the farmer's daughter. Talk about getting lucky!

Silly boy, Nikki thought, reading his thoughts as clearly as if he'd spoken them out loud. Didn't anyone ever tell you that if something seems too good to be true, it usually is? Still, she could at least show him a good time before he died. And it would prove to Kenny how much she loved him, show him that she'd do anything, even give herself to another man, if it would make him happy. Maybe he'd even join in. Not exactly the three-way he'd been talking about, but hey, what's good for the goose . . .

At least that's what her grandmother always used to say. Of

course she doubted her grandmother had been talking about three-ways.

Besides, Kenny wouldn't have to wait too long. Tyler's girl-friend was less than a mile away. She and Kenny could tend to her after they were finished with Sir Galahad here. She'd do whatever he asked, whatever it took to hold on to him, she decided, moving closer to Tyler and tugging at the bottom of his T-shirt.

"I *am* kind of cold," he was saying.

"Of course you are. You're soaked right through. We wouldn't want you to die of pneumonia, now would we?"

Tyler's response was to pull his wet T-shirt up over his head and toss it to the floor.

He was more muscular than she'd suspected, with sculpted abs and impressively cut biceps. And he had surprisingly big hands. He could put up quite a fight. Maybe even give Kenny a bit of a challenge. Although muscles were no match for being caught naked and off guard.

In the next second, she was pulling down his zipper, not shocked to discover he wasn't wearing any underwear. He stepped quickly out of his jeans, kicking them impatiently aside. "Now you," he said.

Nikki threw open her robe and let it fall from her shoulders.

"Wow," Tyler said.

"You like?"

"I like very much." He pulled her toward the bed, his hands moving down to cup her buttocks.

"Bet you weren't expecting this when you knocked on my window."

"I gotta tell you, this is better than my wildest fantasies."

"Tell me what you like," Nikki said, climbing on top of him as they fell onto the mattress. "Tell me what you want me to do.

I'll do whatever you want." She began tracing a line from his chest to his groin with her tongue.

"You're doing it," he said hoarsely.

"What about this?" she asked, looking toward the bathroom as she took him inside her mouth, knowing Kenny was watching, transfixed.

"Are you kidding me?"

"Do you have a rubber?"

"What?"

"Gotta have a rubber."

"I have some in the pocket of my jeans," Tyler managed to croak out.

"Better get them."

"Right."

Nikki watched Kenny duck back into the bathroom as Tyler fumbled around in the dark for his jeans, standing up seconds later in triumph, a condom in his hand. He was returning to the bed when he stopped suddenly. "Do you smell something?"

Nikki sniffed lazily at the air. "Something probably crawled underneath the cottage to die."

"Kind of a grim thought."

"Things die." Nikki looked pointedly at Tyler's now flaccid penis.

"Don't worry," Tyler said, his eyes following her gaze. "I got distracted. I'm sure you can revive him."

"You know what I'd like?" Nikki asked as Tyler was about to climb back into bed.

"Name it," Tyler said eagerly.

"I'd like some tea."

"What? Tea? Now?"

"I have this great peach and cranberry tea. It's kind of an aphrodisiac."

"What's that?"

"Makes you horny. Lets you go all night."

"Really?"

"It's the best." Nikki pushed herself off the bed, leading Tyler by the hand out of the bedroom, and wondering if all men were this dumb. It was time to get this show on the road, she was thinking as they entered the main room. Tyler Currington was about as challenging as Little Bo Peep.

"The smell's even worse in here," Tyler said as Nikki walked purposefully toward the knives on the kitchen counter and Kenny emerged from the bedroom, blood-encrusted machete in hand. "And there's something sticky all over the carpet. God, what is it? Maybe you should put on a light."

Nikki flipped on the overhead switch, her low cackle slithering across the blood on the floor like a snake through high grass. "The better to see you with, my dear."

TWENTY-THREE

WHERE THE HELL IS everybody?" Val was pacing back and forth in front of the deserted campground office, a small, prefabricated cabin made of pine and glass. "It must be seven o'clock by now."

"Another five minutes," Melissa told her, checking her watch again.

"You'd think somebody would get here a little early. I mean, don't they have to get organized or anything?"

"Guess they're pretty organized already." James stared through the early morning fog at Jennifer, who was walking around the gravel parking lot in circles, still trying to get reception on her cell phone.

"I think I hear a car coming," Gary announced, looking toward the road.

Seconds later, a dark green van pulled up and a heavyset, middle-aged woman wearing a brown uniform and carrying a jumbo-sized cup of steaming hot coffee got out. Her name tag identified her as Carolyn Murray, Director. She didn't look happy when she saw them. "Is there a problem?" she asked warily, walking briskly toward the cabin.

Val glanced at Gary, afraid to let their eyes connect. Gary was as anxious as she was to contact the park rangers. Her daughter's boyfriend had knocked his son unconscious, then left him by the side of the road, in the middle of the night, in the middle of a violent storm. Understandably, he wanted charges filed against the young man. Val had been too afraid to ask whether he wanted those charges to include Brianne.

Val followed Carolyn Murray to the cabin's front door, trying to explain the situation as quickly and as best she could, the words somersaulting from her mouth in a twisted rush: her daughter had snuck out in the middle of the night to meet her boyfriend, the boyfriend had been drinking, he'd punched out Gary's son, left him unconscious by the side of the road, disappeared with her daughter in the middle of that terrible storm, her daughter hadn't returned to the camp, she was missing . . .

"Well, she's not exactly missing, is she?" Carolyn Murray interrupted, fumbling in her pants' pocket for her keys. "You just don't know where she is."

"Is there a difference?" Val felt Melissa's sudden grip on her arm, warning her to stay calm.

"I'm just saying, it's not as if she's been kidnapped, that's all. You said she snuck out to meet her boyfriend . . ."

". . . who'd been drinking . . ."

"He attacked my son," Gary interjected. They'd left Hayden at the tents to rest and watch for Brianne's return.

"I'm sorry, but are you suggesting that Starbright is in any way responsible for this?" Carolyn Murray asked.

"No, of course we're not suggesting . . ."

"We're just saying," Val began, her tongue sticking on the words. "We're just saying . . ." Dear God, what *were* they saying? "If we could just use your phone to call the park rangers . . ."

"Oh," Carolyn said, softening somewhat. "Certainly." She pushed her key into the front door lock, twisting it back and forth to no avail. "Damn this stupid thing," she cursed. "It's always doing this."

Could anything else possibly go wrong? Val wondered.

Jennifer suddenly screamed. "I did it! I got through. His phone is ringing. It's actually ring— Hello? Hello, Henry, is that you?"

Better late than never, Val thought, trying not to hear the expression's rarely voiced corollary whispering in her ear: *But better never than too late.*

"This is Jennifer. From last night. Wait, wait, you're cracking up . . . Hello?"

"Got it," Carolyn Murray exclaimed as the key suddenly turned in the lock and the cabin door fell open.

"Henry? Don't move. I'll call you right back on another line," Jennifer said, following the others into the cabin.

"You can use that phone over there." Carolyn pointed toward the wall, where an old-fashioned black telephone sat on a wobbly wooden coffee table between two worn turquoise-blue tub chairs. She walked behind the reception counter and took a long sip of her coffee, watching them intently while pretending to look over some papers. The expression on her face said she was still concerned about the campground's potential liability in the event of a lawsuit.

Jennifer punched in the numbers to Henry's line, numbers she now knew by heart. The phone was picked up immediately. "Henry, it's me again, Jennifer."

"Tell him Brianne is missing," Val instructed, glancing at Carolyn Murray through lowered eyes.

Jennifer nodded. "You know my friend's daughter," she began, stumbling only slightly on the word *friend*, "the girl you escorted back to the campsite last night. Right, that's the one."

"What's he saying?" Val asked.

Jennifer put her hand over the receiver. "He remembers who she is." She quickly filled Henry in on everything that had happened, conceding that Brianne had driven off with Tyler and might no longer even be in the area. "What kind of car was he driving?" she asked Val, repeating Henry's question.

"A black Honda," Gary answered before Val had a chance. "A Civic. Hayden said it was at least ten years old."

"Did he, by any chance, catch the license number?" Jennifer asked, echoing Henry's question word for word.

Gary shook his head.

Jennifer passed this information on to Henry. "Really? Right now? Okay. Okay, yeah. Thank you so much." She replaced the receiver in its carriage.

"What did he say?" Val asked. "What did he say?"

"He said he'll call ranger headquarters immediately and alert them that Brianne is missing, give them her general description, etc. He said we should go back to the campsite and wait in case she comes back on her own, and that they'll send some rangers out to interview us about Tyler and the car and everything. They'll probably put an APB out on the car, and in the meantime, he'll start looking around on his own, even though it's his day off. So, that's good. At least we've got the ball rolling."

Val nodded gratefully, feeling her knees start to wobble and give way. Gary caught her just as she was about to hit the floor. Suddenly she was surrounded.

"My God. Are you all right?" James.

"Can we get some water over here?" Melissa.

"What happened?" Jennifer. "Did she faint?"

"Not quite. Almost," Val said, trying to hold on to consciousness.

"Here's some water." Carolyn Murray elbowed her way into the middle of the tight group. "You all need to back off a bit, give the poor woman some air. You didn't hit your head or anything, did you?"

"No."

"You signed a waiver . . ." Carolyn reminded her.

"I'm not going to sue," Val said adamantly, taking a series of small sips from the glass of water. "I'm just a little wobbly."

"Understandably," Melissa said.

"We didn't get a lot of sleep last night," James explained.

"Think you can stand up?" Gary asked.

"I think so."

He helped Val to her feet. "Take your time."

"I'm so sorry," Val whispered, leaning into him and feeling his body stiffen, then pull away.

"I know."

"I feel so guilty."

"None of this is your fault, Val."

Val sighed. But you blame me anyway, she thought, understanding his anger, knowing she'd feel the same way if their situations were reversed. His son had been injured. Her daughter was, if not responsible, then at least involved. Gary had every right to be furious.

"Do you mind if I use the phone to call New York?" Jennifer was asking the camp director. "I'll call collect."

Carolyn nodded and shrugged simultaneously, her eyebrows lifting toward her forehead. "Go ahead."

Val knew that Jennifer was phoning Evan. She found it interesting that for a man who loved living on the edge, he was never actually there when everything started to collapse. She found herself wondering if this was more a matter of luck or cowardice.

"I keep getting his voice mail," Jennifer said, giving up in defeat after leaving messages on both Evan's private and work lines. "He promised yesterday he'd leave first thing this morning, so maybe that means he's on his way. I'll call the lodge again and leave another message for him there," she added, doing just that.

"You'll send the park rangers over to our tents as soon as they get here?" Val asked Carolyn.

"Count on it."

Count on it, Val repeated silently, savoring the sound of those three little words. There were fewer and fewer things one could count on these days, she was thinking as they left the office and began the trek back to the camp.

NIKKI WALKED INTO the living room from the bedroom, a fluffy white bath towel secured above her breasts, a smaller towel wrapped around her wet hair, like a turban. "Did I hear a phone ring when I was in the shower?"

"Listen to this," Kenny said, his voice resonating with excitement as he finished securing the top button of the shirt he'd taken off the body of the murdered park ranger. He gave the tin badge on his chest a reassuring pat.

"Tell me."

He relayed the details of his conversation with Jennifer. "I told her I'd notify my fellow officers immediately and start searching for Brianne personally, even though it's my day off."

"You're such a good guy."

"It should buy us a few hours anyway."

"You look so handsome in your new uniform."

"It's not too tight?"

"Just a little. But it suits you. You're making me horny all over again."

"Haven't you had enough?"

"Of you? Never."

"What about Tyler? Did you get enough of him?"

Nikki felt a wave of pride. Was that jealousy she was hearing in his voice? She waved a dismissive hand in front of her face. "He was nothing."

"You sure looked like you were enjoying yourself."

"I enjoyed knowing you were watching me."

"Like I'm going to enjoy knowing you're watching me," he told her, tucking the dead ranger's gun into its holster, "when I bring Brianne home."

Nikki felt a tightening in her chest, her previous resolve crumbling. She tried her best to sound casual. "Thought we were going to do her together."

"We will. After I get things warmed up a little first."

Nikki forced her lips into a smile, following after him. "Think she'll still be there?" She was desperately hoping the girl had somehow managed to find her way out of the woods.

"Where would she go?"

Nikki shrugged. "I like the name Brianne," she said, feigning indifference. "Maybe I'll start using it, after . . ."

"After?"

"After she doesn't need it anymore."

He smiled. "Then I better go find her. In the meantime, maybe you can do something about the smell in here. Tyler was right. It's getting pretty bad."

"What am I supposed to do?"

"I think I saw some air freshener in the bathroom."

"I hate those things. They make me gag."

"And while you're at it, maybe you can clean up some of this blood."

"What? Why? It's just gonna get bloodier. Isn't it?"

"Of course it is. But, in the meantime, we don't want Brianne thinking we keep a messy house," he said, with a wink. "How would that look?"

"Maybe we should just forget about her."

"What? No way."

"We're running out of time here, Kenny. Not to mention, we spent most of our money on those fancy dinners at the lodge. And how long's it gonna be before the real rangers start snooping around?" She smiled at the memory of him standing outside the cottage door, wearing the uniform of the park ranger he'd just murdered, the poor man having had the misfortune to cross his path while he was disposing of David Gowan's body parts.

"Don't you worry. We have plenty of time." He reached out to tug at the towel secured at her breasts. "Now I'm gonna go find our little lost babe in the woods. Maybe you could mix up a little of your special tea and Percodan combo to relax her. How's that sound?"

Sounds like a bad idea, she thought. "Sounds like a plan" was what she said. She'd learned there was no point arguing with him when his mind was made up, just as she was learning that if she wanted to keep him, she'd have to get used to the idea of other women. On the plus side, she reminded herself as he stepped into the early morning fog, once he was through with them, she'd get to cut them into hundreds of little pieces.

"Kenny," she called as he was about to disappear.

He stopped, turned back, his face partially obscured.

"Be careful."

"I will. Oh," he said, tapping the badge on his chest. "Remember, the name's Henry now."

"WHAT DO YOU think is taking them so long?" Val asked anxiously. She was pacing back and forth in front of a group of picnic tables located halfway between the site of last night's bonfire and their tents. Melissa and James sat on one side of the rickety old table, Gary, Hayden, and Jennifer on the other.

"Relax, Val," Melissa said. "It's been less than an hour."

"I thought they'd be here already."

"I'm sure they'll be here soon."

"So what's taking them so long?"

The question was met with a communal shrug and varying looks of dismay.

"Where the hell are they?" Val asked after another fifteen minutes had passed.

"They're probably just getting all their ducks in a row," James offered.

"What ducks? Don't they need to talk to us before they can start arranging any dumb ducks?"

"I'm sure they're on their way," Melissa offered.

"They've probably issued the APB on Tyler's car by now," Jennifer said. "Maybe they're waiting to see if anything turns up."

"And what if nothing does?" Val asked. "What if Brianne and Tyler have already left the area?"

"Where would they go?"

"I don't know. Maybe they went back to Brooklyn."

"I can't imagine they'd drive all the way back to Brooklyn," James said. "Not in that storm."

"Then where is she? Why hasn't she come back here?" Val was trying—and failing—not to hear the sound of tires screeching as she pictured Tyler's black Honda Civic sliding out of control on the wet highway and slamming into a tree. She was trying—and failing—not to see Brianne's mangled body in the car's smoldering wreckage. "Do you think maybe she ran away?" she asked almost hopefully, the question managing to temporarily dislodge the horrifying sound-and-light show in her brain. "I mean, she was embarrassed, she was angry, and after what happened with Hayden, she was probably too afraid to come back here. You're sure she didn't say anything to you?" Val asked Gary's son, knowing she'd already asked this question at least half a dozen times already. "Give you any clue where they might be headed?"

Hayden shook his head as Val sank down on the bench between Melissa and James.

"Look. Why don't I go back to the office and try your house?" Jennifer volunteered, standing up as Val was sitting down. "In case she's there . . ."

"That would be great," Val said. "The number is . . ."

"I know the number."

Val nodded, said nothing.

"And while I'm there, I'll try getting in touch with Henry again. Maybe he knows what's keeping everyone."

"Well," James whispered as Jennifer disappeared from sight. "Looks as if the Slut is proving to be quite useful."

Val spun sharply toward him. "Don't call her that," she said.

*   *   *

JENNIFER WAS JUST about to hang up the old rotary black phone when she heard Brianne's voice on the other end of the line.

"Hi," Brianne said sweetly.

"Brianne. My God, we've been worried sick . . ."

"This is Brianne," the voice continued, as if Jennifer hadn't spoken. "I can't take your message at the moment, but if you'd leave your name and number . . ."

"Damn it." Jennifer slammed the receiver back inside its carriage.

"Careful with that," Carolyn Murray warned from behind the reception counter. Then, softening slightly, "Still no luck?"

"If she's home, she's not picking up."

"Teenagers," Carolyn said, as if that explained everything. "I'm sure she's fine. You'll see. You'll all have a good laugh about this later."

"Somehow I doubt that." Jennifer picked up the phone again, dialed Henry's number. "Just this one last call," she told Carolyn. "To find out what's keeping everybody." The phone rang once, twice, before being picked up in the middle of its third ring.

"Henry Voight," the voice said instead of hello.

"Henry, it's Jennifer. I'm really sorry to bother you again . . ."

"Did Brianne come back?" he interrupted.

"No. And the rangers still aren't here."

There was a slight pause before the ranger spoke again. "Look, Jennifer. I know this is hard, but you need to tell everyone to be patient and sit tight. You have to understand that a girl who sneaks off with her boyfriend in the middle of the night isn't exactly the rangers' top priority. The sergeant has assured me he'll have someone out to see you by noon."

"Noon?"

"In the meantime, they're on the lookout for Tyler's car, and I'm doing a foot search of the area."

"I'm sorry. I don't mean to sound unappreciative, I really don't. It's just that everyone is so worried . . ."

"I understand completely."

Which was when Jennifer heard a scream shoot through the phone wires, like fire through oil. The scream was followed immediately by another, and then another, each one building on the last, each one more horrifying than the one before. "Dear God, what is that? Is that Brianne?"

Then suddenly, the screaming stopped.

Jennifer stared at the receiver, knowing the line had gone dead in her hands.

TWENTY-FOUR

BRIANNE WAS RUNNING AROUND in hapless circles, screaming into the brittle, early morning air. Her screams bounced between the trees, ricocheting off the sprawling sides of the mountain, before being swallowed by the indifferent mist. "No, no," she continued, sobbing now. "This isn't happening. It can't be happening." She grabbed on to the nearest branch, feeling it break off in her hands, and she lost her balance, lurching forward and closing her eyes as she stumbled toward the ground. "No, please. I'm still asleep," she moaned as her bare knees scraped against the jagged surface of a rock, the sharp stone cutting into her flesh like a knife through butter. "This is just a bad dream. I'm still asleep. I'm still asleep." Please, she begged silently, her eyes remaining tightly closed as she struggled back to her feet. *Please let me be dreaming. Please don't let this be real.*

Except it *was* real. She knew that. She'd known it the minute the cold sun had awakened her almost two hours earlier, as rudely as if someone were shining a flashlight directly into her eyes. She'd sat up abruptly, watching the sun instantly retreat behind some clouds, as if on purpose, only to reappear seconds later, only to disappear again, as if engaging in a sadistic game of peekaboo. *Catch me if you can,* it seemed to taunt her, sneaking in and out of her line of vision, shining a spotlight on her surroundings one minute, blinding her the next.

Damn that stupid Tyler Currington, she'd thought in that moment, peering through the trees and hoping to see him vaulting toward her, a rescue team following immediately behind. Where the hell was he? Hadn't he promised he'd be right back? Hadn't he told her the cottage he'd seen was only a mile away, and that he'd break into it if he had to, get help, and come back for her?

So where was he, damn it? It had been hours since he'd left. Had the idiot gotten lost again? Had he turned right instead of left, then left instead of right, becoming increasingly disoriented as he groped his way through the dark, misplaced pride his only guide? Had he finally given in to the hopelessness of his situation and his own overwhelming fatigue and lain down, falling asleep in a clump of leaves, as she had? Was he only now just waking up, realizing he was more lost than ever, and trying to determine the best way back to her?

Or had he managed to find the cottage, only to discover nobody home and the phone disconnected? Faced with the choice of being either noble or comfortable, of venturing back into the unfriendly woods or waiting till morning, had he, quite understandably, Brianne was loath to admit, given in to the temptation of a warm and empty bed? Was he even now curled up peacefully on its bare mattress, inhaling its pleasant mustiness and dreaming of better weekends ahead? And would the owners of the cottage come home later in the day to find him snoring softly? Would he awaken to a chorus of "Who's been sleeping in my bed?"

A persistent rumbling in her stomach and an even more persistent swarm of mosquitoes finally convinced her it was time to get up and get moving on her own. She couldn't just sit here all day and hope Tyler would come back. The moron was probably long gone. He'd probably had the dumb luck to stumble upon the main road and hitch a ride back into the city, leaving her to fend for herself.

Her mother would never have left her, she thought, pushing herself gingerly to her feet, feeling her joints unfolding stiffly one at a time. Her mother would have carried her on her back, if necessary, even if her back were breaking, even if she had to carry her to the ends of the earth.

"Which is probably where I am," Brianne said out loud, looking around, hearing the muscles in her neck groan as she glanced from side to side. Everything ached. Her left shoulder and arm were numb from lying on the hard ground, and both legs were cramped and wobbly. Her mother would kiss her assorted aches and pains and make them magically disappear.

She looked down at her feet. Having spent the last few hours with her bare feet encased in the earth for warmth, dried mud now covered her from her ankles to her toes, so that it appeared as if she were wearing short black boots. "I'm nothing if not fashionable," she muttered, and laughed, relieved when she realized she was able to put some weight on her ankle, that Tyler had been right about one thing at least—it didn't seem to be broken.

She started walking, the clouds that circled overhead following after her, growing increasingly heavy with the renewed threat of rain. "Well, at least I'll have something to drink if nobody finds me soon," she said, wondering if her mother was awake yet, if anyone had even realized she was gone. Good thing she'd drunk so many glasses of water last night, the water serving as a convenient excuse for all those trips to the bathroom before she'd snuck off to meet Tyler. "Oh, God," she moaned, once more picturing Hayden lying unconscious at the side of the road, and praying he was all right. "I'm so sorry, Hayden. I never meant for that to happen. I'm so sorry." Then, crying softly, "Please find me, Mommy. If you find me, I swear that from now on, I'll be the best daughter ever. I'll pick up after myself and I'll keep my room neat. I'll do my homework and return my library books on time. I won't lie to you ever again, and I won't go out with morons like Tyler Currington. And I won't have sex again until after I'm married." Well, maybe not that, she amended immediately. Surely even her mother wouldn't expect her to go that far.

"Mommmmmmy!" she yelled as loud as she could, stretching the word as if it were an elastic band, until she ran out of breath, her cry sending shock waves through the surrounding stillness. "Can you hear me? Please! Can anybody hear me?" She stopped and waited, listening for even a hint of acknowledgment. Surely there had to be other hikers in the area by now. Surely someone would hear her. "Mommmmmy!" she called again, realizing she hadn't actually called her mother that in years, and how much she liked its reassuring sound. "Mommy," she repeated softly, wishing she could disappear into the comforting softness of her mother's arms.

Why was I so mean to her? she thought. Why did I give her such a hard time? The things I said to her! Comparing her to Grandma, for God's sake, when she's nothing remotely like Grandma. What was that all about? And sucking up to Jennifer instead of being loyal to the woman who's loved me unconditionally my entire life; ignoring her, defying her, embarrassing her, all but wishing she were dead.

Which was when the thought suddenly hit her that she might never see her mother again.

What if a bear gets me, or I starve to death? she thought, panicking. What if nobody ever finds me and I die out here, and my mother never knows how much I loved her? What if I never get to tell her? What if . . . ?

What if . . . what if . . . what if . . .

"Help me!" Brianne screamed, collapsing to the ground in a torrent of tears. "Somebody, please help me!"

What was the point in going any farther when she had absolutely no idea where she was? Hadn't she read somewhere— maybe even in one of her mother's travel articles—that when you get lost, the best thing to do is to sit tight and wait for someone to find you? Because eventually someone *will* find me, she told herself. James would wake up and realize she wasn't ensconced in the sleeping bag beside him. Hayden would return to the campsite and tell everyone what had happened, that she'd gone off with Tyler, leaving him unconscious by the side of the road. "I'm so sorry, Hayden," she whispered again. They'd find stupid Tyler's stupid car in that stupid ditch. They'd send out a search party. They'd start searching the woods.

Except they'd been searching the woods for David Gowan for days without any luck.

Although he'd probably just gone back to New York, Brianne decided in the next second, wondering if that was what everybody would assume about her. That she'd run off with Tyler, that they'd most likely hitched a ride back to New York

SHADOW CREEK 293

after his car got stuck in the ditch. And what then? Would they call the police or simply say "good riddance to bad rubbish"? Would they shake their heads in disgust and head back to Brooklyn without her? "Shit," she said, making a silent promise she'd never swear again if only somebody would find her before the deer flies and mosquitoes succeeded in eating her alive. "Crap," she settled for instead.

She sat on the wet ground for several more minutes before deciding it was probably better to keep moving. Hopefully at some point she'd run into some hikers or park rangers. Yesterday, every time she turned around, it seemed like the rangers were there, with their stupid uniforms and their stupid frowns and their stupid lectures. So where were they now? Where were they when you actually needed them?

At least she'd have some funny stories to tell Sasha when she got home. *If* she got home.

Thinking of Sasha now, Brianne realized that the pretty blonde was probably the last person she wanted to see. Initially, she'd been flattered by all the attention Sasha had shown her, Sasha being older, more experienced, less inhibited. It had been Sasha who'd initiated their friendship, Sasha who'd introduced her to Tyler, who'd encouraged her to go out with him, later pressing her for all the intimate details of their encounter, enjoying each salacious, if largely fictional, tidbit Brianne tossed her way. So clearly, Sasha's taste in men was dubious at best. No, the sad truth, Brianne realized as she reached down to the ground to push herself up, was that beyond a shared taste in expensive exercise gear, the two young women had almost nothing in common and even less to talk about.

"I could really use something to drink," she said aloud, trying to pull some saliva into her mouth as her hand brushed up against something at once foreign and familiar. Her fingers grasped what felt suspiciously at first like a bunch of worms, except these worms were cold and thick and seemed to be attached to one another at their base. Snakes? she wondered, feeling her stomach lurch. No, that was impossible. Snakes wouldn't continue to lie immobile and stiff in her hand. They'd be slithering around and trying to crawl up her arm. And even the smallest of snakes would be longer than whatever it was she was holding. "Don't look," she told herself. "Just drop it, start walking, and don't look back."

Except, of course, it was already too late. Even without looking, she knew what it was.

Which was the moment she started screaming, loud, unearthly sounds she could scarcely believe were coming from her mouth. Sounds she didn't think she was capable of making, as she ran blindly from one tree to the next, hurling herself over rocks and stumps, shouting, crying, screaming. "No, no. This isn't happening. It can't be happening. No, please. I'm still asleep. This is just a bad dream. I'm still asleep. I'm still asleep."

If she kept screaming, maybe they would pierce through the confines of her awful nightmare, catapult her into consciousness. She'd awake to find herself back in her comfortable king-size bed at the lodge, Jennifer asleep beside her, her mother in the next bed beside Melissa, James sprawled out on the sofa in the adjoining room. Or better yet, they wouldn't be in the Adirondacks at all. She'd be snug and safe in her own bed in Brooklyn, having dreamed up this entire unfortunate excursion. There'd be no lodge, no campground, no stupid car in a stupid ditch, no being lost in the woods, in the rain.

No severed hand dangling from her fingertips.

She screamed again, even louder this time. Leaning against the trunk of a tall tree, she shook the memory of the severed hand dangling from her fingers, as her body convulsed in a series of painful dry heaves.

When she looked up, he was standing there, not more than twenty feet away. His face was flushed, as if he'd been running, and sweat stained the front of his uniform. He wasn't quite as good-looking in the daylight as he'd been in the darkness of the previous night, but at that moment Brianne thought him the handsomest man on earth. "Henry," she cried, running toward the park ranger and falling into his arms. "Thank God you're here."

"WHAT DO YOU mean, you heard screaming?" Val immediately jumped to her feet, causing the picnic table at which they'd all been sitting to shake and sway.

"I *think* it was screaming," Jennifer qualified.

"Was it Brianne?"

"I don't know. I couldn't tell. I just heard what sounded like a scream, and then the line went dead."

"That's it. I've had enough. I'm not waiting around anymore."

"Val, please," Jennifer cautioned. "Henry said we have to be patient, that the rangers might not be able to get here before noon."

"That was before there was a scream, before his line went dead," Val said, reminding Jennifer of what she'd just told them. She tried to curb her growing panic. "Brianne's in real trouble. I can feel it."

"I'm sure Henry would have called right back if he found Brianne."

"Maybe he can't call. Maybe there's a problem with his

phone. Or maybe something terrible has happened to Brianne and he doesn't want to call . . ."

"Don't do this to yourself, Val," Gary said from somewhere beside her.

"Something's very wrong. I know it."

"That's good enough for me." Melissa pushed herself away from the picnic table, grabbing James by the hand and pulling him up along with her. "Come on. We're getting out of here."

"Where are we going?"

"Wherever Val wants," Melissa said.

"I HEARD YOU screaming," Henry was saying, holding Brianne an arm's distance away and looking her up and down, as if checking for signs of injury. "Are you all right? You're not hurt, are you?"

Brianne tried to speak but only sobs emerged.

"It's okay. It's okay. Slow down. Take your time."

"There's . . . there's . . ." She tried pointing, but her hand only flopped around ineffectually.

"Breathe," Henry advised. "That's right. Take deep breaths. More. From the diaphragm. Good. That's much better."

"There's . . . a . . . a . . . *hand*."

"A . . . *what*?"

Once again Brianne felt the bile rising in her throat. "Over there." She lurched forward, retching violently into a cluster of pine needles.

"Okay. Okay. Take more deep breaths. Thatta girl." Henry waited while she wiped the spittle from her mouth, then the tears from her eyes. "I'm sorry. Did you say, there's a . . . *hand*?"

Again Brianne pointed, this time with greater success. Then

she clasped both hands over her mouth to keep from screaming again.

Henry crouched down and began sifting through the earth until he found what he was looking for.

"It looks like it's been hacked off with an axe," Brianne said between gulps of air.

"No, I don't think so." Henry lifted up the offending object by its cold, dead fingers, his voice measured and calm. "More than likely, a bear did this."

"Oh, God." Brianne shot a wary glance over her shoulder. "Is it still here?"

"I don't know. But it's probably best not to wait around to find out."

"Do you think the hand could belong to that guy, David, the one who disappeared from the lodge the other night?"

Henry shrugged. "Hard to say how long this has been here." He tossed the hand down on some leaves.

"Are you just going to leave it there?"

"I'll take care of it later. Now come on." He took her by the elbow, began leading her through the dense foliage. "It's time to get you someplace safe."

THE HEADQUARTERS FOR the local branch of the park rangers was located in Bolton Landing, a charming little village that was approximately a twenty-minute drive from the Starbright campground. The small, boxy, redbrick building stood out like a proverbial sore thumb among the otherwise quaint architecture of the town, and was located at the foot of a narrow bridge that connected the village to a nearby island, on which stood the historic, green-trimmed, white-clapboard Sagamore Hotel.

Val pulled her SUV into the parking lot. Aside from a few

ranger vehicles, there were no other cars. What the hell were they so damn busy with that they couldn't have sent some- one out to interview her earlier? she wondered, running up the three front steps and into the main office, her companions struggling to catch up.

"Can I help you?" the young man behind the front recep- tion counter inquired as they converged on him, Val the obvi- ous leader, Melissa and James at her right shoulder, Jennifer and Gary at her left. Once again, they'd left Hayden behind in case Brianne returned to the campsite.

The ranger's name was Steve Severin. He was of medium height and weight, with dark hair and a pleasant, if unmem- orable, face. Val noted there were two desks directly behind him and a large glassed-in office at the back. Four other rang- ers were mulling about, including the older of the two officers who'd escorted Brianne and Tyler back to the lodge yesterday afternoon. She had a vague recollection that his name was Leo, but she wasn't sure. He recognized her immediately and nodded in her direction, approaching cautiously. "We've been waiting all morning for you guys to show up," Val admonished before he had a chance to speak.

"Show up for what?" he asked, opening the small gate to allow Val and her friends entry into the inner sanctum as the other rangers gathered around them. "Suppose you sit down and tell us what this is about."

"You should *know* what this is about," Val insisted impa- tiently. "Henry Voight called and explained everything to you first thing this morning." She looked toward Jennifer for con- firmation.

It was only then that she realized that Jennifer was no longer part of the group. She'd remained on the other side of the counter, and was seemingly engrossed in the long line of rangers' photographs decorating the hallway to the left of the front door.

"You've been speaking to Henry Voight?" Steve Severin asked.

"Well, no. It was Jennifer who actually spoke to him." What the hell is that woman doing over there? Val wondered impatiently. Looking for a new recruit? "Jennifer, could we bother you for a minute, please?"

"Officer Voight didn't report for work this morning," Leo said as Jennifer turned toward them.

"Didn't you say it was his day off?" Val asked Jennifer.

"This can't be right," Jennifer said, her face drained of its natural color.

"What can't be right?" Steve Severin asked.

"The name under this picture. It says this man is Henry Voight." She tapped the photograph directly behind her.

"Yes, that's Henry," Leo said as the others nodded their agreement.

Jennifer looked warily toward Val, who already knew without hearing the words what Jennifer was about to say. "That's not the man I met last night," she told them. "I've never seen this man before."

TWENTY-FIVE

HOW ARE YOU DOING?" Henry asked after they'd walked about a quarter of a mile. "Am I going too fast for you?"

"I'm okay," Brianne said, although the bottoms of her bare feet were under constant attack by the sticks and stones that covered the ground, and the uneven terrain was causing her calves to cramp. Amazingly, her ankle didn't hurt at all.

"What happened to those nice shoes you were wearing?"

"I threw the stupid things away."

He laughed. "Good move. They weren't exactly built for hiking in the Adirondacks. Although, I have to admit, they looked pretty fantastic."

Brianne smiled. "Thanks."

"And they probably cost a small fortune."

"Not so small." She sighed, the smile quickly disappearing. "My mom's gonna kill me."

"Yeah. Something tells me she's not going to be too happy about any of this."

Brianne sighed again. She'd already told the park ranger about having snuck off with Tyler—she'd left out the part about their having been discovered in flagrante delicto earlier in the afternoon—and about how Tyler had subsequently driven his car into a ditch—she'd left out the part about Tyler's drinking and his subsequent fight with Hayden—and about how they'd then managed to get themselves lost in the woods, and how Sir Galahad had left her, supposedly to find help, and never returned.

Yes, she thought. Henry was right. Her mother wasn't going to be too happy. "Maybe you could speak to her first, soften her up a little."

Henry grinned shyly. "I can try."

Brianne thought how cute the ranger looked when he smiled, and she found herself wondering if he had a girlfriend. Although her mother would undoubtedly insist he was way too old for her, she thought, irritated with her already. Still, he was responsible and hardworking and he'd rescued her from nearly being eaten by a bear, for God's sake. Surely that should count for something. "Are we almost there?" she asked after another ten minutes, trying to keep the whine from her voice.

"Shouldn't be much longer."

"You're sure you know where you're going?"

Henry laughed. "I'd say I know these woods like the back of my hand," he joked, "but I wouldn't want you to throw up again."

Brianne scowled, trying not to feel the waxy, dead fingers

of the severed hand in her own. "As if there's anything left in my stomach to throw up."

Henry's eyes narrowed. "When was the last time you had something to eat?"

"Not since breakfast yesterday morning."

"You haven't eaten anything in twenty-four hours?"

Brianne shrugged, as if this was no big deal. She'd refused to eat the hot dogs being grilled last night at the campsite, even though they'd smelled delicious. "I'm a vegetarian," she'd reminded her mother testily, although they both knew this wasn't, strictly or even remotely speaking, true. The truth was that she liked the idea of being a vegetarian far better than she actually liked being one. The truth was that she liked nothing better than a good, juicy piece of red meat. The truth was she was starving. "I *am* pretty hungry," she admitted after several more minutes had passed.

"We'll get you something to eat when we get to the cottage," Henry said.

"Cottage?"

"You should be able to see it any minute now." As if on cue, a dirt road suddenly materialized behind a row of thinning trees, a small log cabin appearing, like a mirage, at its far end.

"Oh, my God," Brianne exclaimed. "That must be the cottage Tyler was talking about."

Henry came to a sudden stop. "Tyler told you about a cottage?"

Brianne quickly filled in a few of the details she'd left out of her story the first time: that she and Tyler had been fighting and he'd gone off in a huff; that he'd returned later with the news he'd spotted a road and a cottage about a mile away; that she hadn't been able to walk on her sore ankle, which was the reason Tyler had gone on alone. "Whose cottage is it?"

"Mine," Henry said.

"Yours?"

"Well, it belonged to my parents. They left it to me when they died." He resumed walking. "Car crash," he said, tossing the words casually over his shoulder before she could ask.

"That's terrible. I'm so sorry."

"Thanks. But I guess that's life, you know. Sometimes terrible things happen to good people."

Brianne slowed her pace, wondering if she'd be so cavalier if something were to happen to her parents. "So, were you there last night? In the cottage, I mean."

"Yep."

"And you never saw Tyler? No one came banging on your doors and windows?"

"Must have been a different cottage he was talking about," Henry said as they trudged up the dirt road toward the cabin.

"I guess." Brianne looked around. She didn't see any other cottages. So where the hell was Tyler? "And you never heard anyone calling for help?" she asked, watching the ranger shake his head.

"No one but you." Henry laughed. "That's quite a set of lungs you've got there, girl."

But if Tyler hadn't reached the cottage, and if he hadn't miraculously found the main road, that meant he was still out there somewhere, wandering blindly through the woods. And if Henry had heard her screaming from more than a mile away, surely Tyler had heard her, too. Why hadn't he responded to her screams? "Oh, God," she said, stopping suddenly. "What if that bear gets him?" And then, an even worse thought: What if it already had?

"The hand isn't Tyler's," Henry said, as if reading her mind.

"That hand's been there longer than a few hours. I promise you, Brianne. It's not his."

Brianne nodded, although she wasn't completely convinced. She continued to look warily over her shoulder as they drew nearer the cottage, which she saw was made of large pine logs painted dark brown and trimmed in white. A row of orange and white impatiens ran around the base of the cabin and a set of copper wind chimes hung from an overhead brown canvas awning, tinkling in the breeze. The sound of a creek babbled playfully in the background. All that's missing is the gingerbread, Brianne found herself thinking. "You like living out here all by yourself?"

"Love it. Besides, I'm not alone."

"You're not?"

"I've got the birds and the deer and the flowers and the creek. And, of course, there's Nikki," he said as the door of the cottage opened and a young woman wearing a scowl and a floral dress that was at least several sizes too big for her stepped outside.

"SO WHAT DO we do now?" Val was asking.

"*You* do nothing," the senior ranger told her in no uncertain terms. His name was Mike Jones, and he was as straightforward as his name suggested, tall and barrel-chested and square of jaw. Everything about him screamed "hero," from his brown wavy hair and large chocolate brown eyes to his straight nose and full, if unsmiling, lips. Only a faded mustard stain on the cuff of his neatly pressed beige shirt reassured Val he was human after all, and not a refugee from a Disney cartoon. He'd appeared sometime in the last half hour, seemingly from out of nowhere, but more likely from one of the rooms at the back Val hadn't noticed until now, and had effortlessly assumed control of the investigation. Although what exactly he was investigating still wasn't clear. "We'll take it from here."

"What exactly are you taking?" Val asked.

"We'll do everything we can to locate your daughter, Mrs. Rowe. I've assigned a team to start searching the woods . . ."

"Have your search teams been successful in their search for David Gowan?"

Mike Jones looked toward the other rangers present. "We're pretty convinced that Mr. Gowan is no longer in the area."

"So, the answer is no, you haven't found him."

"We're pretty certain that come Monday morning, he'll be back at work . . ."

"Just like Henry Voight showed up for work today?"

"We're getting off topic here, Mrs. Rowe."

"I don't think we are," Val said forcefully, continuing before he could object. "Look. Three people are missing: David Gowan, Henry Voight, and my daughter, all of whom have mysteriously vanished in the last few days. What's more, there is someone patrolling the woods impersonating a park ranger and wearing a uniform that likely belongs to the missing Henry Voight. Which, I don't know, kind of suggests the possibility of foul play to me."

"I don't think we should be jumping to conclusions . . ."

"This man actually talked to my daughter and my friend here," Val interrupted, indicating Jennifer, "last night."

"And Miss Logan has given us a description of the man she talked to," Mike Jones interrupted, "and we'll be circulating that description . . ."

"Fine," Val said, realizing this was the first time she was hearing Jennifer's maiden name, that she'd gotten used to thinking of her as the other Mrs. Rowe, that they were, in some perverse way, related. "What else are you doing? Have you called the FBI?"

"I really don't think that's necessary at this point."

"When *will* you think it's necessary?"

"Mrs. Rowe, I understand your concern," Mike Jones said. "I really do. I have teenage daughters of my own, so believe me, I know the kind of hell you're going through right now. But let's look at the facts. The first fact is that yesterday afternoon your daughter was found by our rangers having sex with her boyfriend in a public place."

"Yes, thank you for reminding me of that."

"Fact number two is that she snuck out of the campsite last night at midnight to go meet this boy. Quite willingly, from what I understand."

"Yes. I'm not arguing with you . . ."

"Fact number three is that there was a fight with this man's son," Mike Jones continued, nodding toward Gary, who was standing ramrod straight at Val's side. "A fight that left him unconscious at the side of the road."

"Brianne wasn't responsible for what Tyler Currington did to Hayden," Val said, looking to Gary for support. Gary quickly looked away, unwilling to hold her gaze. What did that mean? she wondered. That he *did* consider Brianne at least partly responsible, that he might decide to press charges against her after all?

"Be that as it may, Mrs. Rowe, your daughter then drove off in a car with this boy. So, at the very least, you can see why she may not be in a hurry to come back and face the music. She may be afraid . . ."

"Brianne's not afraid of anything," Val said.

Fearless, she heard Gary say. Again, she glanced in his

direction, wondering if he was thinking the same thing. But he was staring at the floor, and didn't look up.

"I'm just saying that the odds are that your daughter is just too embarrassed to face you at this time. Just like David Gowan is too embarrassed to face his wife . . ."

"And Henry Voight? What's he embarrassed about?"

"We'll be looking into that."

"And, in the meantime, we're supposed to just sit around here and wait?"

"Actually, I'd suggest going back to the campground office. That way, you'll be there should your daughter decide to return, and I can reach you by phone as soon as I hear anything."

"And if you don't hear anything?"

"Suppose we give it to the end of the day. If your daughter still hasn't turned up, we'll notify the state troopers."

"Why can't we do that now?" Val pressed.

A phone rang. Seconds later, Steve Severin approached, leaning in toward Mike Jones. "They've found Tyler Currington's car," he announced.

"I KNOW YOU, don't I?" Brianne said to the girl, taking several steps forward and shielding her eyes against the sudden reappearance of the sun.

Nikki looked from Brianne to Henry and then back again. "I don't think so."

"Yes, I do. I saw you at the lodge," Brianne continued, recognizing Nikki as the young woman who'd plowed into her mother at the elevators when they'd first arrived, almost knocking her down, then giving them all the finger.

"No. I don't think so." Again, Nikki looked toward Henry.

"It could have been you," Henry said easily. "We go there sometimes for dinner."

"Yeah. Sometimes my grandmother gives us money, tells us to go live it up. She's cool that way."

"Your grandmother?"

Nikki indicated the cottage behind her with a lazy flick of her thumb. "This is her place."

Brianne's eyes shot toward Henry, watching him flinch. Hadn't he said this was *his* cottage, that his parents had left it to him when they died?

Sometimes terrible things happen to good people, she distinctly recalled him saying, although it was entirely possible she'd misinterpreted his remarks. She was beyond exhausted. Not to mention weak from hunger and dying of thirst. Under the circumstances, it was easy to get confused.

"Anyway, I don't remember seeing you there," Nikki was saying now.

"I was with my mother and her friends."

"Sounds like lots of fun." Nikki made no attempt to mask her sarcasm. "Come on in." She opened the cottage door and stepped inside.

Brianne followed the girl into the cottage, Henry right behind her. Immediately she became aware of a vaguely unpleasant smell. She tried to identify it, but failed. "What's that smell?"

"We think it's a dead animal," Henry said, glaring at Nikki. "I thought you were going to spray."

"I did," Nikki said testily. *"English Garden."*

"A bunch of raccoons were fighting with each other last week," Henry said. "We think one of them might have crawled under the cottage to die."

"Kenny keeps saying he's going to go under there and dig them out but—"

"Who's Kenny?" Brianne asked.

Nikki paled.

"Friend of mine," Henry said. "He doesn't mind doing that sort of thing. He's just been a little busy lately."

"We don't really notice the smell so much anymore," Nikki said. "It's worse when the wind blows a certain way."

"You'll forget about it in a few minutes," Henry added.

Brianne's eyes skipped across the room. This place is a mess, she thought in her mother's voice. There was dust everywhere. Dirty dishes filled the sink. Cutlery was scattered everywhere, including the kitchen floor. The pillows on the sofa were hopelessly askew. A large rug had been rolled up and left in front of a stone fireplace that was filled to overflowing with ashes, the underside of the rug filthy and covered with stains that looked fresh, even damp. She couldn't imagine anybody's grandmother living in such a mess.

Not even her own.

Of course her mother paid a woman to come in once a week to keep her grandmother's apartment relatively neat and clean. Neat and clean were clearly not priorities in this cottage, where everything appeared more than slightly *off*. Including this girl, Nikki, Brianne thought, in her oversized floral dress with the old-fashioned rhinestone brooch pinned carelessly into the folds above her left breast. "Do you think we could try calling the campground?" she asked. "My mother is probably half out of her mind."

"Already on it," Henry said, holding up his phone and punching in a series of numbers. "Babe, you think you could get our guest something to eat?"

"There's not a whole lot of stuff left," Nikki said.

"That's okay. I don't need much." Brianne's appetite had pretty much evaporated the instant she walked through the door. "Actually, just a glass of water would be great. I'm dying of thirst."

Nikki laughed, as if Brianne had just said something very funny, and walked slowly into the kitchen, searching haphazardly through the cupboards for a glass, as if she wasn't quite sure where to find them.

Please let there be a clean one, Brianne prayed, relieved when the girl finally retrieved one from the back of a cupboard directly over the sink. She watched Nikki fill the glass with water, then return to the main room, arm extended, a thin, wriggly red line snaking from the underside of her elbow to her wrist, like a tattoo. Or dried blood, she thought. Had Nikki cut herself?

"Don't know how cold it is," Nikki said as Brianne raised the glass to her lips, drinking the water down in one gulp.

"Easy there," Henry advised. "You don't want to get sick again." Then, into the phone, "Yes, hello. Yes, this is Henry Voight with the park rangers. I'm trying to locate a Mrs. . . . ?" He looked toward Brianne.

"Valerie Rowe," Brianne told him quickly. "R-O-W-E."

"Valerie Rowe," he repeated. "I believe she and her friends stayed with you last night. Yes. R-O-W-E. That's right. Of course, I'll hold."

"Do you think I could have another glass of water?"

"Why don't you make Brianne some of your cranberry and peach tea?" Henry suggested. "Tea is very good for you."

"No, that's fine. Really. I don't want to be any trouble."

"It's no trouble. Water's already boiled," Nikki said. She pointed toward the sofa. "Sit down. Make yourself comfortable."

Brianne didn't have to be asked twice. Despite the mess and the smell—or maybe because of them—she was having trouble staying upright. She collapsed onto the sofa, fatigue settling across her shoulders like a heavy blanket, weighing her down. Had she ever been so utterly exhausted in her entire life? Her head swiveled toward the bedrooms at the back of the cottage, wondering again what had happened to Tyler and thinking how nice it would be to stretch out in a nice soft bed, get a few hours of uninterrupted sleep before having to confront her mother. "Is your grandmother still sleeping?" she asked.

"My grandmother?" Nikki dropped a tea bag into a mug and filled it with water from the kettle, surreptitiously slipping three Percodan into the mix.

Brianne wondered absently how long the water had been sitting there, if it was still even hot. "I'm sorry. I thought you said this was her cottage." For the second time that morning, Brianne was starting to think she might be hallucinating, that this whole interlude was part of another vaguely sinister dream.

"She's away for a few days. Here," Nikki said, handing her the tea. "Drink up." She watched closely as Brianne swallowed most of the tea in one long sip. "How is it?"

"Great," Brianne said, although in truth, the tea was merely lukewarm and tasted more bitter than sweet. Still, she was so thirsty she finished the rest of it without further prompting. "Thanks." She glanced toward Henry. "Have they located my mother yet?"

"They have me on hold." It was several minutes before he spoke again, and when he did, his voice was barely above a whisper. "Everything's going to be all right, Brianne," he began, lowering the phone to his side. "I don't want you to go getting all upset . . ."

"Has something happened to my mother? Has she been hurt?" Brianne tried getting to her feet, but it was almost as if weights had been attached to her ankles, and she fell back against the pillows, unable to stand.

"Your mother's fine."

"Then what's the matter?"

A slight pause before he spoke, then, "Apparently she and her friends checked out of the campground an hour ago."

"What do you mean, they 'checked out'?"

"They left first thing this morning, said they were going home early. The director said they seemed very angry . . ."

"I don't care how angry they were," Brianne protested. "They wouldn't just leave me."

"I'm really sorry. It looks as if that's exactly what they did."

"What? No. There's been a mistake. They probably just went back to the lodge to wait for my father."

"Do you want me to call the lodge?" Henry immediately punched in another series of numbers without waiting for her response.

Brianne tried to tell herself that it wasn't unusual for a park ranger to know the telephone number for the Lodge at Shadow Creek by heart, just as she tried to tell herself that he hadn't flinched when Nikki had said the cottage belonged to her grandmother, and that there wasn't something very strange about this girl in her too-big dress and her bitter-tasting tea. She tried to tell herself that her head was spinning because she was so tired, and nothing more. She tried to tell herself she was indeed hallucinating.

"The manager at the lodge says he hasn't seen or heard anything from your mother since she left the premises yesterday," Henry was saying in a voice that floated in and out of Brianne's consciousness in waves.

"So what do I do now?" Brianne asked. She barely recognized her voice. Her eyes were fighting to stay open.

"First, you're going to have a little nap. Then you're going to take a shower, fix your hair, and brush your teeth. Make yourself nice and presentable for Mommy. Then Nikki and I will drive you back into the city."

"Couldn't we just go now?"

"No, you're way too tired for that," Henry was saying, drawing closer, until she felt his breath warm against her lips. "Brianne," he whispered as her eyes fluttered to a close. "Brianne, can you hear me?"

Brianne opened her mouth to speak, but no sounds emerged.

And then she saw and heard nothing.

TWENTY-SIX

V AL WAS THINKING OF her mother. Not the woman she
was now, broken and befuddled by too many bottles
of booze, and not the confused and unsure woman from her
teenage years, when her self-confidence was being pummeled
by her husband's ceaseless womanizing and her own ceaseless rationalizations, but the strong and resilient mother of her
childhood, the woman who'd taught her to follow her instincts
and stand on her own two feet.

"I don't want to go to school today, Mommy," she recalled
telling her mother when she was four years old and enrolled in
the nursery school at the local Y.

"Why don't you want to go, sweetie?"

"There's a boy who's mean to me."

"How is he mean to you?"

Little Valerie had straightened her back and puffed out her chest. "He says I'm a stupid little girl," she'd announced, her tiny voice resonating with indignation. "I'm not stupid, am I?"

"You certainly are not."

"Will you come with me and tell him not to call me a stupid little girl anymore?" she'd asked.

"Oh, I think you're smart enough to handle him all by yourself," her mother had said.

And handle him she had, returning to the school that afternoon and punching the little boy smack in the mouth the second the word *stupid* left his lips.

"They're having a 'Swim for Your Life' meet at school next month," eight-year-old Valerie had announced to her parents some four years later. "It's to raise money for charity, and I need lots of sponsors. You make money for how many lengths you swim, and I'm going to swim the most lengths and raise the most money."

"Put me down for a dollar a length," her father had offered from behind the newspaper he was reading.

"How about ten?" her mother had countered. Then, with a wink in Valerie's direction, "If you don't ask, you don't get, sweetheart. You have to speak up in this life."

Little Valerie had repaid her mother's confidence—and shocked the entire school—by swimming an astonishing seventy-four lengths. Her mother had stood by proudly as her father grudgingly wrote out a check for $740.

Serves you right, Val thought now. You never believed I could do it. You never even paid attention.

Even now she could see the look of boredom stamped across her father's face, how after the first couple of lengths, he'd lost interest and drifted over to where Ava McAllister's attractive, young mother was standing with a few of her equally young, attractive friends, and how they'd all spent the balance of the swim meet engaged in flirty banter. Only occasionally had he glanced over at the pool where his daughter continued to swim length after length, determined not to come up for air until she had her father's full and undivided attention. She'd stopped—exhausted and on the verge of total collapse—only when she finally caught him looking her way, although when she replayed the scene later in her mind, she realized he'd probably just been stealing a glance at the clock on the far wall. She also understood, with a child's instinctive grasp, that she was no match for any of these other women, no matter what she accomplished, no matter how many lengths she swam. She simply wasn't interesting enough to merit his attention. She was just a stupid little girl. That boy in her nursery school class had been right.

They'd gone out for dinner that night to celebrate her success, and her father had spent most of the night talking to the waitress. "Really, Jack," Val could still hear her mother admonish as they left the restaurant, "do you have to be so obvious, especially in front of the children?" At the time, she didn't know what her mother was talking about. Nor did she remember her father's response. She did remember waking up that night to her mother's soft cries, and coming into the kitchen to find her sitting alone at the kitchen table, her gaze loose and unfocused.

"What's wrong, Mommy?"

"Nothing, sweetheart. Go back to bed. It's very late. You have school tomorrow."

"Are you sad?"

"No, sweetheart. Why would I be sad? My daughter just swam the most lengths and raised the most money in the entire history of John Fisher Public School. I'm proud as punch," she'd said with a smile, swiping at her tears with the back of her hand.

"Proud I'm such a good swimmer?"

"Proud you're such a good *you*. I want to be just like you when I grow up."

Little Valerie giggled. "You're silly."

"I adore you," her mother said.

"I adore *you*."

"Then go to bed. Get some sleep."

"Aren't you going to bed?"

"In a little while."

Valerie suddenly became aware of the bottle on the table and her mother's half-empty glass. "What's that?"

"Just a little something to help me sleep."

"Can I have some?"

"No. You don't need this stuff, Valerie. You're a strong girl. Strong enough to swim seventy-four lengths. You're going to rule the world."

"No, I'm not."

"Yes, you are. And I'm going to watch you."

So when had her mother stopped watching? When Val was ten, thirteen, fifteen, twenty-one? When had a little something to help her sleep become a little something to help her through the day, then something more, and something more again, until it was everything? When had she started sleeping until three o'clock each afternoon, and slurring her words, and tripping over her own feet when she was awake? When had she started falling down, and worse, staying down?

"Please, Mom. You need to see a doctor," Val had insisted when she was still denying the obvious, even making the appointment herself when her mother refused, then making another one when she failed to show up for the first. "I think maybe she might have a brain tumor," she'd told her father, freshly returned from honeymooning with his new wife.

"She doesn't have a brain tumor," her father had said, laughing dismissively. "She has a hangover."

"What are you talking about? She doesn't drink that much."

"Open your eyes," her father said, effectively ending the discussion and leaving her standing at the front door.

"Well, you shouldn't have just shown up like that," her sister had argued when Val filled her in later on what happened. "You should have called him first."

"Why should I have to call him? He's our father."

"You know he doesn't like surprises."

"I think you're missing the point here, Allison."

"The point being . . . ?"

"Dad is implying our mother is an alcoholic."

"I don't think he's implying anything. I think he's saying it outright."

"And you're saying . . . what? That you agree with him?"

Allison met Val's question with a shrug and a defeated shake of her head.

"He didn't even invite me into the house," Val said. "Told me they were in the middle of dinner."

"Should have called first."

"Why are you always defending him?"

"Why are you always attacking him?"

"I'm not attacking him."

"What is it you expect the man to do, Valerie? They're divorced."

"Did he divorce us, too?"

"What are you talking about? Don't be ridiculous. He didn't leave *us*. He left *her*."

"*Her* is our mother," Val reminded her sister.

"Well, *her* has a major drinking problem."

The words hit Val like a sucker punch to the solar plexus, brought tears to her eyes. "At least she didn't abandon us."

"Didn't she?" Allison asked coldly.

Was that the defining moment, the moment the two sisters could point to later as the precise instant the invisible lines of loyalty were drawn in the sand and the sides were irrevocably chosen, the moment they understood they'd lost not only their parents but each other as well?

What difference did it make? Val wondered now, feeling herself being pulled back into the present. Over the years, nothing had really changed. Allison was still fighting for their father's approval; Val was still fighting for their mother's sobriety. Both were losing battles.

"Val?" a voice interjected, sending her fragile family scattering in all directions. "Val, are you okay? What's happening?"

Val looked toward Jennifer, momentarily surprised to see her behind the wheel of her SUV, then remembered having taken her up on her offer to drive. "Nothing. I'm fine. Just frustrated. I'll be okay."

She felt James's hand on her shoulder. "So, what do we do now?" he asked from the crowded backseat as the SUV pulled into the campground's parking lot.

"We do what the man said," Gary answered. "We go to the office, we sit, and we wait."

"For how long?" Val was restless already. "I can't just sit here all day and wait for something to happen."

"I don't think we have any choice," Gary said.

"I don't think you know Val very well," Melissa said with a smile as they climbed out of the car.

"Maybe Evan's here." Jennifer looked hopefully around the parking lot for his black Jaguar, but it was nowhere in evidence.

"I'll try his lines again," she said as they entered the office. "I mean, this is crazy. Why isn't he answering his phone? Why hasn't he returned my messages?"

Gary held back. "I'm going to go check on Hayden."

"Of course," Val said, watching him leave.

Carolyn Murray was standing behind the reception counter in pretty much the same posture and position as when they'd last seen her. The frown on her face hadn't altered; the coffee stain on her shirt was still there. Only a slight stiffening of her shoulders convinced Val she was real, and not made of wood.

"I'm afraid we're going to have to impose on your hospitality a little more," Val began.

"Yes, so I hear. Mike Jones called."

"Has something happened? Have they found my daughter?"

"Not as far as I know. He said he'd be checking in with you periodically, so you can either wait here or at your tents. I can send someone to get you when he calls."

"We'll wait here," Jennifer said for all of them. It was obvious that the last thing she wanted was to return to those damn tents. "Can I use the phone?" she asked, lifting the receiver of the rotary phone and proceeding to dial Evan's number without waiting for Carolyn's okay. Seconds later, she slammed the phone down in disgust. "I got his voice mail again. What do you think it means, that he isn't answering his phone?"

Val said nothing. She could think of any number of things it might mean but decided it was best to stay silent. Jennifer would no doubt discover those things soon enough without any help from her.

And maybe he *was* really busy, Val thought, trying to give Evan the benefit of the doubt. Maybe his latest deal really had been about to blow sky-high, maybe he really had been working round the clock to salvage it, and maybe he really was at this very moment driving like a maniac around the twists and turns of Prospect Mountain, the white knight in his black Jaguar, rushing in to save the day, even though that day would likely be over by the time he got here.

Typical, she thought. Hadn't she been waiting almost two decades for him to rush in? And he still wasn't here. He was still taking detours.

And she was still waiting.

What's wrong with me? Val wondered.

You're just a stupid little girl, came the familiar taunt.

You certainly are not, her mother's voice immediately countered. *You're a strong girl. Strong enough to swim seventy-four lengths. You're going to rule the world.*

When had her world gotten so small?

Val leaned against the wall, trying to figure out her next move. She checked her watch, then checked it again. Not even lunchtime and already she was exhausted.

"You're not going to pass out, are you?" Carolyn asked, watching her from behind the counter.

"I'm not going to pass out," Val affirmed. Haven't you heard? I'm strong. I swam seventy-four lengths. I'm going to rule the world.

"SHE STILL ASLEEP?" Henry asked impatiently as Nikki returned from the bedroom.

"Snoring like a little piglet."

"Shit. How many of those pills did you put in that tea?"

"I don't know. Just a couple."

"The point was to relax her, not knock her out."

"Yeah, well, suppose next time you be a little clearer about what exactly the point is," Nikki argued, trying to put a lid on her growing anger. She'd never lost her temper with him before. Of course, he'd never given her any cause to lose it. Until now.

Until this girl came into the picture.

"Look. I didn't mean to go off on you before," he was saying. "It's just really important we get our stories straight."

"How was I supposed to know you told her this was your cottage?"

"What'd you think I was gonna tell her?"

"I don't know. How do you expect me to know anything if you don't tell me?"

"You should have seen the expression on her face when you said the cottage belonged to your grandmother."

"Well, she got me all flustered when she said she recognized me from the lodge. And then you said we'd been there for dinner. I had to think of something."

"You called me Kenny, for fuck's sake!"

"It just slipped out."

"You could have ruined everything."

"Ruined what exactly? What difference does it make what I call you? We're gonna kill her anyway." Nikki paused. "Aren't we? Aren't we gonna kill her?"

"Of course we're gonna kill her." Henry ran an exasperated hand through his long hair. "Just not right away. We're gonna have a little fun with her first. You know. Like we talked about."

"Like *you* talked about."

"What are you saying?"

"Kenny, please . . ."

"The name is Henry."

"*Henry*. We don't have time for this. You murdered a fucking park ranger. Sooner or later, they're gonna come sniffing around here. We've got to get out of here."

Henry's gaze flitted nervously around the room, stopping on the door to the bedroom where Brianne lay sleeping. "Okay. Okay. You're probably right."

"I *am* right."

"Okay. I know."

"So what are we going to do with her?"

"We'll take her with us."

"What?"

"We'll take her with us," he repeated, as if he actually thought she hadn't heard him.

"What are you talking about? That's nuts."

"Why is it nuts? She's unconscious. We'll throw her in the trunk of the car, drive up to Lake Placid, find an empty cottage where we can relax and take our time with her."

"Since when do we take our time?"

"Since this is a new experience. Brianne's young, she's pretty. She's malleable."

"What's that mean?"

He sneered.

Nikki might not have understood the word *malleable* but she understood the meaning of that sneer. It meant "dummy." He might as well have screamed it.

"You never know," Henry was saying. "She might even decide she wants to join us. We could form, like, this whole group . . ."

Oh, God, no. What was he saying? "So, what—I'm not enough for you anymore?"

"I didn't say that."

"Then cut the bullshit. I say we kill her now, and get the hell out of here."

"Come on, babe. She's unconscious. What fun would there be in killing her when she's out cold?"

"A lot more fun than life in prison," Nikki argued. "I'm telling you it's not worth the risk." Then, to placate him, "There'll be other girls."

A slow smile crept back onto Henry's lips. "You promise?"

"I promise," she said.

"WHAT'D HE SAY?" Jennifer asked as Val lowered the phone's receiver back into its old-fashioned carriage.

"He said they went over Tyler's car with a fine-tooth comb," Val told the assembled group, "and there's no sign that anyone has been hurt. No blood or anything . . ."

"Thank God," James said.

"So that's good news," Melissa added.

"The bad news is that the storm washed away any footprints, so Brianne and Tyler could be anywhere. They're going to start searching the surrounding woods, but . . ."

"But?" James asked.

"Well, he didn't say it, but I don't think finding Brianne is their major concern. They're more interested in finding out what happened to Henry Voight."

For a minute nobody said anything, no one giving voice to the thought they were all sharing: What if the disappearances were in some way connected?

"Val, can I talk to you for a minute, please?" Gary said. He'd returned to the office a few minutes earlier, while Val was on the phone with Mike Jones, and had been standing by the door, waiting.

Val followed him wordlessly outside, stopping on the bottom step when she saw Gary's son, Hayden, sitting in the passenger seat of the white Buick parked a few feet away.

"I'm leaving now. Taking Hayden back to Connecticut,"

Gary explained before Val could ask. "There's really nothing much we can do here at this point, and I want a doctor to check him out, make sure he doesn't have a concussion."

"Of course. I understand completely."

"Hayden insists he doesn't want to press charges . . ."

Val suppressed a deep sigh of relief. "I'm really so sorry about everything."

"Me, too," Gary said. Then, when both realized there was nothing more to say, "You'll find her, Val."

"Yes, I will."

"You're fearless."

"Yes, I am."

"I'll be in touch," he said.

"No, you won't," she whispered, watching him climb behind the wheel of his car and pull out of the parking lot, out of her life. And that was all right, she thought. Despite the way things had turned out, she was grateful for their brief time together. Gary had awakened something in her she'd thought was lost forever, shown her that not only could she be attractive to other men, but that she could be attracted to *them*. All she had to do was let it happen. All she had to do was let go of the recurring dream that was Evan. *The impossible dream,* she thought wistfully, imagining James belting out the song from the Broadway hit.

Except the dream had become a nightmare.

It wasn't just time for a new dream, she decided, watching Gary's car disappear in an explosion of dust. It was time to wake up.

Val turned around, about to reenter the cabin when the door opened and Jennifer stepped outside, her face flushed.

"What's the matter?" Val asked.

"I just remembered Henry said he had a place in the area."

"What?"

"The man I met last night, the man pretending to be Henry Voight, he said he had a place around here."

"Did he say where?"

"No. Just that it was close by. Where are you going?" she called as Val began racing toward her SUV.

Val's answer bounced off the gravel driveway and ricocheted off the nearby trees. She was through waiting. It was time to start swimming. "To find my daughter."

TWENTY-SEVEN

DO YOU REALLY THINK this is such a good idea?" James was asking from his usual place in the backseat. "I mean, didn't the park rangers say that we should stay put and let them handle it?"

Val ignored the rhetorical question, speeding up the highway, her eyes on the alert for Tyler's black Civic. Mike Jones had said it was only a few miles up the road from the campground.

"He's right. Maybe this isn't such a good idea," Melissa said from beside James.

"Look," Val said. "If you guys don't want to come with me, that's fine. I can stop the car right now . . ."

"We're not leaving you," Jennifer said firmly from the seat beside her.

"Of course we're not leaving you," Melissa echoed.

"I was just suggesting we let the park rangers know what we're doing," James tried to explain. "You know, in case we need backup."

"I'm sure we'll see some rangers when we get to Tyler's car," Val said, grateful her friends had opted for loyalty over common sense. She knew they thought she was being reckless and irrational, rushing off blindly, without a plan, without any idea where she was going or what she was going to do when she got there. She also knew they were absolutely right. Still, she couldn't just sit around and do nothing when her daughter might be in jeopardy. Sitting around waiting for things to happen had gotten her precisely nowhere.

Still . . .

She should probably listen to her friends, turn the car around, go back to the camp. The rangers were doubtlessly already canvassing all the cottages in the area. Although if the man pretending to be Henry Voight had lied about being a ranger, he'd probably lied about having a place nearby. On the other hand, if he actually did own property in the vicinity, it was doubtless better to let the professionals investigate, instead of having a bunch of amateurs running around like chickens with their heads cut off. She wasn't being fearless. She was being stupid.

"There's the car," Jennifer suddenly shouted, pointing toward the black Honda nose-dived in a ditch by the side of the road.

"I don't see any rangers," James said as Val pulled her SUV to a stop behind the old Civic and turned off the engine.

"They've probably sent for a tow truck," Melissa said as they emerged from the car, four doors opening and slamming shut in unison.

Val approached Tyler's car slowly, peering into the window of the driver's side, hoping to spot her daughter curled up asleep in the backseat, then opening the car door when she saw nothing.

"Should you be doing that?" James glanced over his shoulder at the steady parade of oncoming cars.

"Probably not." Val's eyes scanned the interior of the car for any sign of Brianne, her nose sniffing at the stale air for traces of her daughter's scent.

Nothing.

"So what now?" Jennifer asked.

Val pointed to the woods beyond the ditch. "We go that way," she said, hurrying on before anyone could stop her.

"WHAT ARE YOU doing?" Nikki stood in the doorway, watching Henry rifle through the dresser drawers of the master bedroom.

"Just looking for a little extra cash."

"We've already been through all the drawers."

"We might have missed something. Like this." He held up a red-green-and-blue rhinestone brooch in the shape of a butterfly. "Bet this is worth something."

"It's a piece of junk, like all the others," Nikki said, knowing exactly what Henry was doing. Which was stalling. They should have killed the girl by now. They should have killed her and taken off. Instead, he'd found one thing after another that supposedly needed taking care of: first, he had to make himself a sandwich; then he had to take another shower, and then a "power nap" to get his strength up, not just for the kill but for the drive to Lake Placid; then he had to check the cottage for valuables, which was supposedly what he was doing now, although they'd already searched through every drawer in the place at least half a dozen times and taken whatever cash and valuables they'd missed the first six times. There wasn't even a television to steal, for shit's sake. Just that stupid computer, which was old and wouldn't be worth very much.

A vague memory intruded on her thoughts. Something about that stupid computer had been nagging at her since this morning, although she couldn't put her finger on what it was. She had a hazy recollection of going through Ellen's e-mails the other night when she was stoned on Percodan and weed. There was a letter from her son, she remembered. Something about not being able to come to some stupid party in the fall.

And something else.

Something else, she repeated, waving away the troublesome thought as if it were a mosquito buzzing around her head. Whatever it was, it couldn't be very important. What was important was to kill the girl now and get out of here.

"We're wasting time," she told him, knowing that's exactly what he was trying to do. He's giving Brianne time to wake up, she realized. Why? So he could kill her, or have sex with her? And then what? Was he really going to try to persuade the girl to join them? Did he plan on forming his own little band of merry men and women to populate the forest, a modern-day Robin Hood, except they didn't just steal from the rich, they killed them? More like a modern-day Charles Manson, she decided, thinking of the special on the murderous clan she'd seen recently on E! Admittedly, they'd seemed kind of cool, but she much preferred things the way they were now, with just the two of them. She didn't want to have to fight for her lover's attention or affection. She didn't want to worry about who was his favorite or if she was in danger of being replaced. She wanted to go back to what they did best, which was ridding the world of useless old people.

Old people, she thought, glancing toward the computer. Something on that computer about old people.

"We gotta wipe down the place for fingerprints," Henry was saying.

"We can do that after we kill Brianne."

"No," he said adamantly. "We're saving the best for last."

She was about to protest but thought better of it. Arguing with him just meant delaying things further.

"Maybe you should go get gas," he suggested.

"You want me to get gas?" she repeated incredulously, wondering what he was up to now.

"Yeah. That way we don't have to stop later."

"Forget it. I'm not going for gas," Nikki said. Was he still harboring hopes about taking Brianne with them? Was it possible he was actually thinking of letting her go?

"Suit yourself. It was just an idea."

"If you want gas so much, you go get it."

"You're the one who's in such a hurry to get moving," he reminded her with a shrug and a knowing raise of his eyebrows. "Come on. We gotta start wiping everything down."

"Why don't we just torch the place?"

"Oh, yeah, that's really smart. Why don't we take an ad out in the papers while we're at it, huh? Let the cops know exactly where we are."

Nikki felt herself surprisingly close to tears. "Why are you being so mean to me?" she asked in the little-girl voice of her childhood. It was a voice she barely recognized, one she thought she'd buried long ago.

"What are you talking about? I'm not being mean to you."

"Yes, you are. Ever since you found out about that girl, you've been acting . . . I don't know . . . all weird."

"Hey," Henry said, dropping a bunch of beaded necklaces

he'd found in the top drawer of the dresser to the floor, sending beads spraying in all directions. He walked slowly toward her, cocking his head to one side, like a mischievous puppy. "Is that jealousy I'm hearing?"

"Don't be ridiculous."

"'Cause you're acting kind of jealous."

"I just want to kill the stupid girl and get out of here."

"You sure you're not just a tiny bit jealous?" he asked playfully, his hand creeping up underneath the oversized dress she was wearing. "Is that why you're in such a hurry to kill her?"

"I'm not jealous."

"You're not wearing any underwear either." His other hand moved to her breast.

Nikki smiled. "Glad I finally got your attention."

"Oh, you got it, all right. The question is, what are you gonna do with it?"

Nikki fell to her knees in front of him. "I'll show you."

"ISN'T BLACK FLY season supposed to be over?" James asked, slapping at his neck.

"It *is* over. These are *deer* flies." Melissa scratched behind her ear. When she withdrew her hand, she saw blood underneath her fingernails.

"Lovely," James said. "A fly for every season."

Jennifer was bringing up the rear. If the deer flies were bothering her, she gave no sign. "Does anybody have any idea where we are?"

Val spit an errant mosquito out of her mouth into the back of her hand. She marveled that anyone could continue to look so lovely under such trying circumstances. No wonder Evan had been so smitten. "The creek should be around here somewhere," she said, recalling the times she and Evan had hiked through these very woods. "I think we should keep going in this direction . . ."

"Where are the rangers?" James asked accusingly. "Aren't they supposed to be searching the area?"

"Like I said, I don't think Brianne is their top priority." Then, in the next breath, "Brianne! Brianne, can you hear me?"

"Brianne," Jennifer echoed. "Brianne . . . Brianne!"

The chant was taken up by Melissa and James, but even after five minutes of continuously shouting out her name, there was no response.

"What's this?" Jennifer asked, suddenly stopping.

"What?" The others quickly gathered around her.

"Look at the way the ground is flattened down over here, kind of like somebody was lying down . . ."

"Someone or some*thing*," James said with a noticeable shudder and yet another glance over his shoulder. "Like a bear, maybe?"

"Oh, my God!" Melissa was pointing at something several feet away. "Is that a shoe?"

"What?" Val lunged toward the mud-covered object on the ground, one hand lifting it into the air, the other furiously scraping the caked earth from its thin, high heel. "It's Brianne's. It's her shoe." She spun around. "Brianne . . . Brianne! Where are you? Can you hear me? Oh, God. Where is she?" She spun around, holding the shoe close against her chest, her eyes scanning the surrounding trees. "I know there are cottages. There has to be a road . . ."

"How far are we talking?" James asked.

"I don't know. Maybe another mile. Maybe less. Maybe more."

"Then I've got to have a little rest." James looked around,

finding a log on which to perch, then gingerly lowering himself down. "Sorry to be such a diva, but these legs are definitely not what they once were."

"You're not a diva." Val sat down beside him. "You're wonderful." She looked toward Melissa and Jennifer. "You, too. All of you."

Jennifer's eyes filled with tears. She quickly turned her head away.

The scream started slowly, building gradually, before exploding into the air. At first Val wasn't even sure what the sound was or where it was coming from, and it wasn't until she saw Jennifer's face, and her eyes wide with terror, that she realized the scream was coming from her mouth.

"What is it? What happened? Jennifer, what the hell happened?" she repeated when Jennifer failed to respond.

"Oh, God. Oh, God."

Val began spinning around in circles, trying to pinpoint the cause of Jennifer's outburst. And then she saw it.

"Please tell me that's not what I think it is," James whispered.

Val's throat was suddenly void of all saliva. The words scraped painfully along the sides of her larynx as she moved closer. "It's a hand."

"Is it . . . ?" Melissa asked, unable to finish the sentence.

"It's a *man's* hand," Val said, crouching down to examine it, and then bursting into tears. "It's not Brianne's."

"Thank God."

"Don't touch it," James said. "Whatever you do, don't touch that awful thing."

"What does it mean?" Jennifer asked.

"It means we're getting out of here right now," Melissa said.

Val pushed herself back to her feet, one hand still clutching

Brianne's shoe to her breast, and they started walking, slowly at first, and then faster, faster, until they were running, barely aware of the twigs snapping underfoot or the overhanging branches slapping at their faces.

"Do you think the hand could be David Gowan's?" Melissa asked when they stopped to catch their breath.

"Do you think a bear got him?" James asked. "Or, dear God, something worse?"

"What do you mean?" Jennifer asked. Then, as if she could read his mind, "No. No. That's impossible. It's impossible," she repeated, looking to Val for confirmation.

Val didn't have to ask what impossible she was referring to. She knew exactly what Jennifer was thinking, what they were all thinking. She'd been thinking the same thing all morning, ever since Jennifer had announced that the Henry Voight she'd met the previous evening didn't match the Henry Voight whose picture was hanging on the wall at ranger headquarters.

They were thinking of the murders in the Berkshires.

Was it possible the killers they'd been hearing about on TV and on the radio, those monsters responsible for the murders of those elderly couples in the Berkshires, had left Massachusetts for the higher hills of New York state? Were they even now roaming the Adirondacks in search of more prey? Had they killed David Gowan and the real Henry Voight? Had Brianne and Tyler met a similar fate?

No, don't be absurd, Val castigated herself. Even if the killers *were* in the area, and the likelihood of that was beyond remote, their targets were old people. What would they want with David Gowan or Henry Voight? Surely they'd have no interest in Tyler or Brianne.

Except what of that poor young man whose body had been found—in pieces, dear God, in pieces—near the site of one of the slaughters, a young man the police suspected had been a victim of nothing but circumstance, someone whose extreme bad fortune it had been to stumble onto the scene of the crime, and paid the ultimate price? What if Brianne had stumbled upon a similar scene? What if she'd . . . ?

What if . . . what if . . . what if?

Stop it, Val told herself before she could finish the thought. Stop it right now. "Okay, look," she said to keep from screaming. "We can't let our imaginations get the better of us."

"You're right," Melissa agreed. "We're getting way ahead of ourselves here."

"Brianne's just fine," James said, with perhaps a bit too much conviction. "Once she got rid of those damn high heels, she'd have had no trouble making her way out of here. She's probably back at the campsite, wondering where the hell everybody went."

"God, I hope you're right."

"There's no reason to suspect foul play," Jennifer said. "That hand . . ."

". . . has probably been there for weeks," James continued.

"Some poor slob got eaten by a bear," Melissa said, with a nod of her head for emphasis.

"We should go back to the camp," Jennifer told them. "We have to notify the park rangers about this right away. We have to tell them what we found."

"Yes," Melissa said.

"We have to let them do their jobs," James agreed.

"Val?" Jennifer asked, looking to her for confirmation.

"Yes. All right," Val said. "Okay." After all, what choice did she have? The discovery of Brianne's shoe had been one thing, confirmation that Brianne had indeed been wandering these woods. It was a reason to keep searching. But finding the hand had changed everything. Whatever the cause, animal or human, it was too dangerous for them to continue. They had to inform the rangers of their grisly discovery immediately. They had to let the professionals do their job.

"Maybe we should go back to the car," James suggested.

"That'll take too long," Val said. "It'll be faster this way."

"You sure there's a road?" Jennifer asked.

"Evan and I used to hike through these woods all the time," Val told her, watching the younger woman wince, although not for the reason Val initially suspected.

"He should be here for you," Jennifer said, catching Val by surprise. "It's not right that he's not here."

They continued walking in silence for another ten minutes, Val clinging to Brianne's shoe as if it were a lifeline, as if it were keeping her upright. And perhaps it was, she thought, as she noticed bits of sky filtering through the trees. "I think that might be the road through there."

"Thank God."

In a few more minutes, they found themselves out in the open, at the side of a long, winding dirt road, Shadow Creek perhaps a hundred yards in front of them, stretched out lazily, like a serpent in the sun.

"What's that over there?" Jennifer squinted as she brought her hand to her forehead and pointed. "Is that a cottage?"

"I say whatever it is, we forget it and head straight back to the camp," James said, reiterating their earlier decision.

But Val had already turned and started walking—a silent prayer on her lips, Brianne's muddy shoe in her hand—toward the cottage at the far end of the road.

TWENTY-EIGHT

S OMEBODY'S COMING."

"What?"

"You heard me." Nikki pressed her forehead against the cottage's front window. "Down at the end of the road. Looks like a whole bunch of people."

Henry was immediately at her side, yanking on her arm to pull her out of the way.

"Ow," she said, noting that he'd changed out of his ranger uniform into a pair of better-fitting jeans and a T-shirt bearing the craggy likeness of Keith Richards, cigarette dangling from his lips. The dead ranger's gun lay discarded on the sofa where he'd tossed it earlier.

"Get down," he told her now, peering through the front window. "Shit."

"Is it the cops?"

"I don't think so." He snuck another peek through the window. "They're too far away to tell for sure, but one of them looks like Jennifer."

"Jennifer? Who the hell is Jennifer?" Was there yet another woman she had to worry about?

"The one I met last night. The one who called here this morning to tell me about Brianne."

"You told her where to find us?"

"Of course not. Don't be stupid."

Nikki felt her entire body bristle. How many times had she begged him not to call her stupid? He was the dummy in the group, not her. If he'd listened to her, they would have been long gone by now. "Who's she with?" she asked, returning to the window.

"I don't know. Probably Brianne's mother and her oddball friends. They're definitely not cops."

"So which one is Jennifer?" Nikki asked as the ragged-looking foursome drew closer.

"What difference does it make? Get down," Henry ordered again. "Do you want them to see you?"

"They can't see anything. They're still too far away. Is she the one with the long blond hair?"

"I don't remember," he said, but his tone said otherwise. "I told that bitch to stay put."

"Doesn't look like she was paying much attention."

"If she's talked to the park rangers, if she told them about talking to Henry Voight . . ."

"You think she's pretty?" Nikki asked.

"What the fuck difference does it make?"

"She doesn't look like anything special from here. Looks like a million other girls. Pretty ordinary, if you ask me."

He waved aside her assessment with an impatient hand. "Nobody's asking you."

"I'm just saying . . ."

"Shut up for a minute, will you? I gotta think."

So now he was telling her to shut up. Nikki bit down on her lip to keep from crying. "It looks like they're heading right this way. Shouldn't take them more than a few minutes to get here."

"Shit."

"I'll go lock the door."

"Nah. Don't bother. They aren't going to go away, and a locked door isn't going to stop them." He glanced toward the gun on the sofa.

"What—you're gonna shoot four people?" Nikki asked incredulously. "Have you ever even fired a gun before? What if you miss? What if one of them gets away? It's way too risky."

"Since when do you get to decide? Now shut up and let me think."

That was twice he'd told her to shut up. "I'm just saying," she said, trying to still the anger building inside her, "that they're almost here. And the state troopers could be right behind them. If we take off right now, we can be gone before they get here."

He seemed to consider this for several seconds. "What about Brianne?" he asked.

"What about her? We don't have time to deal with her. We just go."

"Or we take her with us." He was already sprinting toward one of the bedrooms at the rear of the cottage.

Nikki was right behind him. "What? No. We decided this already."

"Change of plans." He approached the bed where Brianne lay sleeping on top of the quilted spread, a handful of leaves still clinging to her dirty clothes. "Come on. Give me a hand."

"The hell I will."

"Suit yourself." He scooped the sleeping girl into his arms. Brianne stirred slightly but didn't wake up.

"This is nuts. We don't have time for this. They'll be here any minute."

"Then let's get moving."

"I'm not going anywhere with her."

"Don't be stupid," he said, returning to the living room.

That's three, Nikki thought, plopping down on the sofa and folding her arms across her chest. What was that saying—three strikes and you're out? She wasn't sure why she was being so stubborn, why she just didn't go along with him, as she usually did, but there was just something . . . something about this girl, something about the way he looked at her, the way he acted around her . . . But surely if he had to choose between them . . .

"Suit yourself," he said again, pausing briefly at the front door to toss Brianne over his shoulder. Then he opened the door and exited the cottage.

"What are you doing? They'll see you!" Nikki shouted after him, knowing he was protected from view by the surrounding trees.

Nikki pictured him running around to the back of the cottage, where he'd hidden their car. She heard the car's trunk creak open, then slam shut. This is ridiculous, she thought. That dumb girl is ruining everything. I should have slit her throat the second I laid eyes on her.

Which is exactly what I'm gonna do, she decided. Just as soon as I get the chance. If Henry, or Kenny, or Matthew, or fucking Ishmael, whatever the hell he wants to call himself, if he thinks he can just replace me that easy, that he can yell at me and call me stupid, well he doesn't know me nearly as well as he thinks he does. As soon as we stop for gas, as soon as he gets out of the car to take a leak, I'm gonna open that damn trunk and slice a blade across that stupid girl's jugular.

Now that's what I call a plan, she thought, full of fresh resolve as she unfolded her arms, placing both palms on the cushions beside her, about to push herself up and go after him, when her hand brushed against something cold and hard. The gun, she realized, as her fingers curled quickly around it.

Which was when she saw them standing in the open doorway, looking like a bunch of motley circus rejects: an attractive, middle-aged woman with dirty blond hair and a slightly crazed look in her eyes; a short woman with bangs that covered the top half of her face and glasses that covered the rest, dressed head to toe in black; a skinny, somewhat effeminate-looking man with spiky, carrot-orange hair; and last but not least, Jennifer, with her big tits and legs that went on forever. She recognized them as the group she'd seen arguing in the lobby of the lodge the previous afternoon.

"Hi," said the first woman before Nikki had a chance to speak. "Sorry. We didn't mean to startle you."

Nikki slid the gun into the side pocket of her dress without anyone noticing. "What do you want?" She wondered where Henry was and what he was doing, whether he was watching them and biding his time, or if he was getting ready to drive off and leave her here alone.

"My name is Val. These are my friends," Val began. "We're looking for my daughter. We were hoping you might have seen her."

"No," Nikki said, eyes traveling warily among them. "I'm afraid I can't help you."

"She's a pretty girl. Around your age. About five feet six, slim, long brown hair."

"Sorry. Haven't seen her."

"Her name is Brianne," Val continued, tears filling her eyes.

She looks like she's going to pass out, Nikki thought, wondering if her mother had ever worried that much about her. "Pretty name," she said.

"You look familiar. Have we met before?" asked the woman in black. She took several steps into the main room, uninvited.

"No, I don't think so."

"I'm Melissa. This is James. And Jennifer. You are . . . ?"

"Nikki," she answered reluctantly, not wanting to arouse undue suspicion. Probably she should try to get as much information out of them as she could. And what was it her grandmother used to say—you catch more flies with honey than with vinegar?

"Is there someone else here we could talk to?" Jennifer asked. "Maybe your parents have seen her."

"My parents aren't here. This is my grandmother's cottage," she added when it seemed more explanation was required. "I'm staying with her for the summer."

"Is she here? Could we talk to her?"

"She's sleeping. She hasn't been feeling very well."

"And you're sure you haven't seen or heard anything?" asked Val again, swaying unsteadily.

"Like what?" Where the hell was Henry? What was he doing?

"Like maybe somebody crying or calling for help . . ."

"No. I'm sure I would have heard something like that. Are you all right? You look kinda funny."

"I'm just exhausted." Valerie suddenly collapsed in the doorway, crumbling to the floor like a piece of discarded tissue paper.

"Val, are you all right?" the others cried, almost in unison.

Nikki hid her budding smile behind her hand. Under more

normal circumstances, she might have found this fun. "Did she faint?" she asked, not moving.

"Do you think maybe we could get a glass of water?" Jennifer asked, although it was more command than question.

Nikki walked quickly to the sink, grabbing a freshly rinsed glass from the counter. All that time spent wiping the area clean of fingerprints for nothing, she thought, noticing James sniffing at the air. "What's that weird smell?" she heard him ask as she was turning on the tap.

Nikki peered out the small window above the sink, hoping to see Henry, but all she saw was trees. Where the hell was he? What was he doing? Was he even still out there? Surely she would have heard the car pull away, she decided, shutting off the tap and carrying the glass of water over to Val. Jennifer immediately snatched the glass from her hands and held it up to Val's lips.

"Would it be all right if we sit down for a few minutes?" James asked.

"My grandmother's sleeping," Nikki reminded them.

"We won't disturb her," Jennifer said.

"It's just that we didn't get much sleep last night, and we've been walking for hours," Melissa added. "We need a few minutes to catch our breath."

Nikki motioned toward the sofa. "I guess it's okay."

James and Jennifer led a still wobbly Val to the couch, sitting down on either side of her, as if propping her up. Melissa balanced on the sofa's arm, staring at Nikki through huge, black-rimmed glasses that did nothing to diminish the intensity of her gaze.

"So, what happened to your daughter?" Nikki asked, then watched Val struggle with how much to tell her.

"She went hiking with her boyfriend yesterday," Val replied

slowly, "and they haven't come back. We think they might have gotten lost in the woods."

"Or maybe they just took off," Nikki said with a grin.

"You find that funny?" Melissa's voice was an accusation. "Her mother is worried half to death. We all are."

Nikki tensed at Melissa's tone. I could shoot you right now, bitch, she thought, feeling the barrel of the gun in her hand. What she said was "Sorry. Didn't mean to sound insensitive. Have you reported her missing to the park rangers?"

"Yes. We were down at ranger headquarters this morning. They're organizing a search party."

"And what—you're the advance scouts?"

"It's hard to just sit around and do nothing," Val said.

"So the rangers don't know you're here?" Nikki asked, trying to read the expression on Val's face.

The question struck Val as odd. The pursing of Melissa's lips told her she was thinking the same thing. Something was seriously strange here. Say something, Val's eyes urged her friend. *Anything* to keep the girl talking.

"That's a beautiful pin you're wearing," Melissa said obligingly. "Is it an Eisenberg?"

"What?" Nikki glanced down at her chest. What was this woman talking about?

"The rhinestone bow you're wearing. It looks like an Eisenberg."

Nikki shrugged. "Does that mean it's valuable?"

"It could be. I'd have to have a closer look."

Nikki immediately unfastened the brooch and dropped it into Melissa's hand, watching as Melissa turned it over and studied it.

"Yes. It's an Eisenberg, all right. See? Here's his signature, etched into the back."

"So, how much would it be worth?" Nikki asked without bothering to look.

"Well, I don't think this is really the time to be discussing . . ."

"There's lots more," Nikki said, interrupting her. "My grandmother's got a drawer full of the shit."

"In that case, perhaps we could talk to her . . ."

"I told you—she's sleeping. Would you give me something for it right now?"

"I don't think your grandmother would be very happy . . ."

"She won't mind. I'll get it." Nikki immediately headed for the bedroom. "Don't move. I'll be right back." She stopped suddenly, a big smile filling her face. "And then I'll make you some of my special peach and cranberry tea."

"OKAY, IS IT just me or is there something very wrong here?" Val whispered underneath her breath as soon as Nikki was gone. She was squeezing Brianne's shoe so tightly, she could almost feel the leather starting to dissolve.

"There's definitely something not right. That girl . . . ," Jennifer said.

"And that smell," added James, fanning his face with his hand.

"Okay, the girl is definitely peculiar," Melissa agreed, "but do you think she knows something about Brianne?"

"She's definitely hiding something."

"We need to check the other rooms," Val said as Nikki was exiting the bedroom, her hands full of sparkling baubles, half a dozen necklaces slung carelessly around her neck. She kicked the bedroom door shut behind her.

"That oughta wake up Grandma," James muttered behind his hand.

"Ta-da!" Nikki dropped about two dozen pins to the coffee table, then pulled the necklaces roughly over her head. "I thought it was junk. You really think it's worth something?"

Val gave Melissa a look. The look said, take your time. Stretch this out as long as you can.

"Well, I'd really have to examine the pieces more closely," Melissa said, lifting one of the brooches into her hands and turning it over, as James did the same.

"Are they an Eisen . . . who you said?"

"Well, this one here looks like a Coro," James said.

"Is that good?"

"And I think this one might be an original Chanel."

"You're shitting me. Chanel? That's gotta be worth plenty."

"Excuse me," Val said. "Do you mind if I use your bathroom?"

"Go ahead." Nikki motioned vaguely over her shoulder toward the rear of the cottage, her attention focused solely on the jewelry. "It's back there."

"I'll come with you," Jennifer said, helping Val to her feet.

"So, would you give me something for the whole lot?" Nikki asked as Val and Jennifer were leaving the room.

"Well, I'll need a little time to go through everything."

"How much time? I mean, I'm kind of in a hurry."

"Maybe another ten minutes or so?"

"How about that tea you offered?" James said.

"What's she doing?" Val asked Jennifer as they neared the bathroom, realizing she'd been holding her breath. "Is she looking this way?"

"She went into the kitchen." Jennifer quickly opened the bedroom door and the two women ducked inside.

The bed was unmade, the dresser drawers open, their contents strewn across the floor. There were stray beads everywhere. "God, what a mess."

"No grandmother."

"No Brianne, either," Val said.

"Look under the bed," Jennifer directed. "I'll check the closet." Her eyes quickly scanned its contents. "There's women's *and* men's stuff in here," she announced, glancing toward the bedroom door. "So where's Grandpa?"

Val reached into the mess underneath the bed and pulled out a man's rumpled shirt. There was a tin badge clinging to its front. "Oh, God." She began tapping Brianne's shoe against the badge, trying to wrap her mind around this latest development. The shirt had to belong to Henry Voight. What did it mean?

"Let's check the other rooms," Jennifer said as Val dropped the shirt to the floor.

The women quickly ducked into the hallway.

"You check. I'll keep watch," Jennifer said as Val opened the door to the second bedroom.

This bedroom was smaller than the first, the sun pushing against the olive-green curtains covering the window. The double bed, whose quilted spread matched the curtains, was neatly made and looked as if it had never been slept in, although the drawers of the dresser on the opposite wall were all open and their meager contents—some linens and a few towels—dumped on the hardwood floor. Val took a quick peek under the bed, then inside the closet. What few clothes were hanging there— an old housecoat, a few pairs of women's slacks, all much too big for Nikki—had been pushed off to one side, as if to make room for company.

"Anything?" Jennifer whispered as Val emerged from the room.

"No." She entered the third bedroom, a basic replica of the one she'd just left. Except for one crucial difference. "Oh, God."

"What?" Jennifer was suddenly right beside her. "What is it?"

"Brianne was here," Val said, feeling Brianne's shoe burning a hole in the palm of her hand.

"What do you mean? How do you know?"

She pointed wordlessly at the bed, whose quilted spread was noticeably crumpled, as if someone had recently been lying in the middle of it. Dirt and stray leaves littered its surface. "It's still warm." Instantly, she was on her knees, checking under it as Jennifer vaulted toward the closet.

Nothing.

"Shit. Where is she?" Jennifer asked, returning to Val's side.

There was a sudden, noticeable stirring in the air. The women turned. Nikki was standing in the doorway.

"Sorry. We turned the wrong way," Val said quickly.

Nikki smiled. "Tea's ready," she said.

TWENTY-NINE

W E DON'T WANT TO put you to any trouble," Val was saying as Nikki led them back into the living room and handed them two mugs of tea.

"No trouble at all. It's herbal," she said. "Peach and cranberry."

"Smells delicious."

"Drink up."

Melissa and James were sitting side by side, sipping their tea while sifting through the costume jewelry spread out across the coffee table in front of them. Val squeezed in beside Melissa, mug in one hand, Brianne's shoe in the other, as Jennifer perched on the end of the nearby chair. Val leaned toward Melissa, pretending to be tucking some stray hairs behind Melissa's ear. "We found Henry Voight's uniform. Brianne was definitely here," she whispered. Straightening up, she said, "Find anything interesting?" She took a sip of her tea, and then another, feeling it warm against her throat. Despite the outside heat, the hot liquid felt surprisingly good, even though it tasted slightly bitter. She hadn't realized how parched she was.

"Almost everything is interesting." Melissa separated a few beaded strands from the rest, lifting one long necklace over Val's head and then pretending to admire it. "What do you want to do?" she muttered underneath her breath.

"We should probably get out of here."

"Agreed." Melissa removed the necklace and turned back to Nikki. "There's really some very good stuff here. Eisenberg, Coro, Weiss, Trifari."

"And there's quite a rare signed Coro Duette, dated 1950," James added, his eyes as wide as the jeweled centers of the vintage owl clip-on earrings he was holding. "Who'd have thought?"

Val tried to catch his eye, but failed.

"So, how much will you give me for the lot?" Nikki shifted restlessly from one foot to the other.

Melissa hesitated. "How does a thousand dollars sound?"

"A thousand dollars! Are you serious? You'll give me a thousand dollars for this stuff?"

"Shouldn't we speak to your grandmother first?" James asked.

"She won't care."

"Still, if she's here . . ."

"She isn't."

"I thought you said she was sleeping," James persisted.

Shit, Val thought, her eyes pleading with James to shut up. They had to get out of here. They had to alert the park rangers, the state troopers, the FBI.

"She is. Sort of." An indifferent shrug. "Okay. She's not exactly sleeping. The truth is . . . she died. A few months ago."

That does it, Val thought, lowering her tea to the coffee table and looking toward the still open front door. We have to get out of here *now*.

"I didn't tell you before because I didn't know who you were and I didn't want you to think I was living here all by myself. Anyway," Nikki continued, "she left me the cottage and everything in it. So there's no problem about the jewelry. Can you give me the money now?"

Melissa looked toward Val, her gaze strangely unfocused. "Well, I only have a few dollars on me at the moment."

Nikki's eyes flashed anger. "So . . . what? You were just bullshitting me? This is, like, a joke to you?"

"No, of course not. It's just that I'd have to get to a cash machine."

"Where's your car?"

"At the campground," Val interjected quickly. Brianne had definitely been here, she was sure of that. Just as she was certain this girl knew where she was now. But Nikki was also clearly crazy and Val doubted there was anything to be gained by sticking around. They'd found the real Henry's uniform. The man who'd stolen it might still be lurking. They had to contact the authorities. "Look, we'll go to the car, get the money, and come right back. How's that?" She pushed herself to her feet, felt Melissa struggle to get up beside her. "Are you all right?"

"Now *I'm* the one who's dizzy," Melissa said.

"How long do you think you'll be?" Nikki asked.

"Shouldn't be too long," Val answered, watching James stagger when he tried to stand, his empty mug falling to the floor and bouncing toward the fireplace. Val grabbed his arm before he could fall over.

"What's happening?" Jennifer asked.

"Why don't you ask him?" Nikki said, looking toward the open door.

A young man stood in the doorway, a smile on his lips, a picture of Keith Richards on his chest, and a bloodstained machete in his hands.

Val gasped, a sound immediately echoed by Jennifer and Melissa.

"Oh, God," moaned James, fighting to stay upright.

"I don't think you're going anywhere." The young man kicked the door shut behind him with his booted foot, waving the machete in front of him as he walked into the center of the room. "Enjoy your tea, everyone?"

"It's my special blend." Nikki pulled the gun out of her pocket.

"Oh, God," James said again.

"No need to be so formal. You can just call me Henry." The young man laughed. "Hello, Jennifer. Nice to see you again. And you must be Brianne's mother," he said to Val. "I can definitely see a resemblance."

"Where's my daughter? What have you done with her?"

"Nothing." Henry's smile widened. "Yet."

"They have money," Nikki told him. "That bitch just offered me a thousand dollars for this shit." She looked from Melissa to the jewelry spread across the coffee table. "They were just going to go to a cash machine."

"You really are stupid, you know that?" Henry's voice resonated disdain. "The only place they're going is straight to the cops."

Nikki's cheeks flushed pink with embarrassment. "Don't call me stupid."

"You gotta learn to read between the lines, sweetheart. They know everything. Don't you?" he said to Val. "Of course you do," he said, answering his own question. "They've already talked to the park rangers. They know I'm not the real Henry Voight. In fact, I think they probably have a pretty good idea at this point just who I really am." He pointed the machete at Val's throat. "If not, I'd say this here's a pretty good clue."

"You killed those people in the Berkshires," James whispered.

"Bingo."

"And the real Henry Voight?" Jennifer asked.

"Don't forget about David Gowan," Nikki said with obvious pride.

Val fought back the fresh tears she felt forming behind her eyes. "What have you done with my daughter?" she asked again, her focus starting to blur.

"Like I said, nothing yet. I'm saving her." The young man winked. "For later."

"Don't count on it," Nikki muttered, not quite under her breath.

He spun toward her. "What are you saying? That I can't count on you anymore? Is that what you're saying?"

"No, of course not."

His gaze shifted to Jennifer. "Should have listened to me when I told you to stay put," he admonished. "Instead, you come snooping around, filling poor Nikki's head with nonsense . . ."

"It's not nonsense," Melissa said, her words bumping up against one another in their rush to escape her mouth. "Vintage costume jewelry can be very valuable. It's my business. I know. And I can get you the money."

"Save it, Mrs. Magoo. Nikki here might be too stupid to see through you, but I'm not."

"I'm not stupid," Nikki said.

"No, you're a regular Einstein. Or should I say 'Eisenberg'?"
He laughed.

So he'd been listening outside the door the whole time, Val
realized, patiently waiting for them to finish their tea. What
was in it anyway? How much of that damn stuff had she drunk?
Where were they hiding Brianne?

"I guess we should get this show on the road," he said.

"You don't have to do this," James said, his words barely
audible.

"Don't have to," the young man agreed. "But oh, I really,
really want to. Ready, babe?"

A car honked from somewhere down the road.

"Wait." Nikki looked toward the window, paling noticeably.

"What now?"

"Someone's coming."

Please, God, let it be the park rangers, Val thought, straining for the sound of tires on gravel, praying for the cavalry to
come riding to their rescue.

"You're imagining things," the young man said, vaulting
toward the window and peering through the trees.

Nikki looked confused, her eyes darting back and forth
without focusing on anything in particular.

"There's no one there," he told her, impatiently.

"Are you sure? I remember . . ."

"You remember what?"

"There was something . . . something on the computer.
Something about . . . shit, I don't know . . . Quakers? Is that
possible?"

"Quakers? What the hell are you talking about?"

"There was something. Wait. It was a name. Quaker? Was

that it? No, no. *McQuaker.* Yes, that's it. Fran and Wayne McQuaker dot-com."

"Fran and Wayne . . . what the hell are you talking about?"

"Fran and Wayne McQuaker. I remember now. They're coming to visit. Saturday."

"Someone's coming here *today*? And you didn't think to tell me about it before?"

"I was stoned. I just remembered when I heard the car honking."

"You just remembered," he repeated, shaking his head. "Shit. Your grandparents were right about you. You're just a stupid little girl."

The familiar words jolted Val out of her growing lethargy, clearing her head as if she'd been slapped in the face. "Are you going to let him talk to you that way?" she snapped, knowing time was running out, that she had to do something before it was too late. Maybe if she could pit one against the other . . .

"Somebody ask for your opinion? For fuck's sake, just shoot the bitch," the young man ordered. Then, when Nikki didn't react fast enough, "Well, what are you waiting for, dummy? Christmas?"

Nikki steadied the gun in her hand and slowly raised it.

"You're not stupid, Nikki. So be smart," Val urged, holding her breath as she watched Nikki turn around slowly, pointing the gun at the young man's chest. *Pull the trigger,* she prayed silently.

"Come on, babe," the man said, his voice suddenly soft and conciliatory. "You know I don't mean any of that shit. You know I love you."

"What about that bitch in the trunk? You love her, too?"

"She means nothing. You know that. You know you're the only girl for me."

"So we're not gonna take her with us?"

"We'll do whatever you want with her."

"He's lying," Val said, understanding they were talking about Brianne.

"Shut up," Nikki said, swiveling toward her, so that the gun was now pointing directly at Val's head.

Was that all it took to get women to surrender their power—a few sweet words, even when they knew them to be false? And was she really so surprised? *Hey, you,* was all Evan had to say, and she'd been ready to forgive him anything.

Val understood in that second that Nikki would blindly follow her man, no matter what, that there was no point in trying to talk sense into her. She wouldn't listen to reason any more than Val had listened when people had tried to talk to her about Evan. She was just wasting whatever time and breath she had left.

Her eyes shot to Jennifer, who nodded, as if she'd heard Val's thoughts. There would be no handsome princes riding to their rescue, they both understood. They were on their own.

They moved quickly and in unison, Jennifer hurling what remained of her tea into Nikki's face as Val ferociously swung Brianne's shoe at the girl's head. The shoe caught Nikki smack between the eyes and she pitched forward, Jennifer knocking the gun from her hands as she fell, sending it skating across the floor toward Val's feet.

"You dumb cunts!" the young man yelled, rushing at them, his last words before a succession of bullets ripped through his chest, tearing apart Keith Richards's sneering face and sending the young man crashing back against the window, the machete in his raised arm arching gracefully back over his head to slice through the glass, sending it shattering in all directions. Jagged shards fell around his head, like icicles dropping from a rooftop.

Val stared down at the gun in her hands, her index finger pressed firmly against its trigger.

"Bravo! Bravo, Val!" James was shouting from somewhere beside her, clapping his hands as Melissa sleepily tossed a handful of the beaded necklaces she'd been clutching into the air, like so much celebratory confetti.

"Are you all right?" Val asked Jennifer, now sitting firmly on top of Nikki, who was moaning but not moving.

"Never better," Jennifer said.

Which was when they heard a car pulling up outside, followed by a door slamming shut, and then another.

A woman's chirpy voice cut through the ensuing silence. "Hello, Ellen? Stuart? Yoo-hoo! We're here. We finally made it!"

Val looked toward the door as an elderly couple walked cheerily up the front steps, the woman carrying a large potted plant, the man cradling a bottle of champagne.

"Ellen! Stuart! Come out, come out, wherever you are!" They stopped, staring wide-eyed at the scene in front of them.

Val stared back. They were all still staring at one another when they heard the sound of police sirens approaching in the distance.

THIRTY

THEY LEFT FOR HOME first thing the next morning.

"You're sure you're okay to drive?" Melissa asked.

"I'm fine." Val smiled toward the three occupants of the backseat, then stretched her arm across the front console to where her daughter sat staring out the side window, a steady stream of tears cascading down her pale cheeks. She'd been crying from almost the minute they'd discovered her, more or less unconscious, in the trunk of Matthew Stabler's car. "How about you, sweetheart? How are you doing?" Even though her daughter had emerged miraculously unharmed and had thankfully witnessed none of the carnage, the news of Tyler's fate and the knowledge of what would have likely happened to her had her mother not found her had been traumatic enough. She'd slept fitfully, her backside curled into her mother's stomach in bed, holding tight to her mother's hand as it draped across her hip. The manager of the lodge had been eager to cooperate with the state police when informed of Val and her friends' heroics in apprehending the monsters who'd slaughtered so many, and had happily provided them with their original suite for the night.

Brianne felt a fresh gathering of tears behind her eyes. She didn't deserve her mother's concern, she was thinking. If she'd listened to her mother in the first place, none of this would have happened. Tyler would still be alive.

"It's not your fault," Val told her, as if reading her mind. "You didn't kill Tyler."

"I'm the reason he was in that cottage."

"Maybe initially," Val reminded her. "Let's not forget the things Nikki told the police." Nikki had made a full confession, providing details of all the grisly murders she and Matthew had committed, as well as a full description of her romp with Tyler just prior to his death. "You made an error in judgment," Val told her daughter now. "Trust me, sweetheart. We've all been guilty of that."

"He didn't deserve to die, Mom."

"No, he didn't."

A small cry escaped Brianne's lips. "I ruined your birthday," she said plaintively, sounding all of ten years old.

Val smiled sadly and squeezed her daughter's hand. She'd arrange for Brianne to see a therapist when they got back to the city, deciding it was probably a good idea that she go, too. "Let's just say you made it one we'll never forget."

"Ain't that the truth," James said.

"Are you guys comfortable enough back there?" Val glanced over her shoulder at James, Melissa, and Jennifer. Melissa nodded; James gave her a thumbs-up; Jennifer looked up and smiled, then returned to rereading the message that had arrived last night from Evan. Surely she had it memorized by now, Val thought, feeling Jennifer's disappointment as keenly as if it were her own. After all, it was a feeling she knew well.

Val watched as the Lodge at Shadow Creek receded in her rearview mirror. Another turn and it would be merely a memory, one she could only pray would fade with time. Would it? she wondered, reliving yesterday's events as if they were still happening, disconnected images flashing before her eyes like a strobe light. Flash: they were running through the woods. Flash: she was holding up Brianne's mud-encrusted shoe. Flash: they were walking toward the cottage. Flash: they were in the bedroom. Flash: a young man was standing in the doorway.

One second, a blood-caked machete had been pointed at her throat; the next instant, she was emptying a gun into a young man's chest.

Matthew Stabler, she thought, silently mouthing his name. The police had identified him from the driver's license they'd found in the back pocket of his jeans, although according to his young accomplice it was a name he rarely used.

Val pictured Nikki in her ill-fitting cotton dress, politely handing her a mug of hot tea. Val could still taste the sedative-laced liquid on her lips. She could still feel the sting of shame in Nikki's eyes when Matthew called her stupid. She could still hear the thwack of Brianne's shoe as it hit the girl's forehead. She could still feel the awful vibrations that traveled up and down her arm as she repeatedly pulled the trigger.

Val pictured Nikki, still dazed and bleeding, as the state police led her away. Her real name was Janet Richardson, they told her later. She was seventeen years old.

Val knew the police still had questions, that the fallout from their ordeal was far from over, and wondered how long it would be before the story hit the front pages. It wouldn't be long before reporters and cameras started gathering outside her door. She wondered if Evan had already heard the news.

As if on cue, her cell phone began ringing in her purse. "Well, what do you know? We finally have reception. Can you get that, sweetheart?" she asked Brianne, who immediately began fumbling inside her mother's bag. "Is it your father?"

"Is it Evan?" Jennifer asked simultaneously.

"It's Grandma," Brianne said, unable to disguise the surprise in her voice.

Val took the phone from her daughter's hand, raised it to her ear. "Mom?"

"Happy birthday, darling," her mother said. "I know I'm a few days late, but you know what they say—better late than never."

Val brushed aside the pesky, unvoiced corollary: but better never than too late. "It's never too late," she said forcefully.

"So how does it feel to be forty?"

Val laughed. "Actually, pretty damn good."

"Do you feel any different?"

Val nodded, tears filling her eyes and streaming down her cheeks. "I do, yes. Very different."

"Well, you'll always be my little girl."

"A girl who really misses her mother," Val said, her words barely audible.

It was her mother who'd taught her that if you don't ask, you don't get, her mother who'd counseled her to speak up, and assured her that she could do anything she set her mind to do, that she was not a stupid little girl. If she was indeed as fearless as Gary had claimed, it was in large part because of her mother.

And while Val recognized she might not be able to save her—her mother was ultimately the only person who could do that—she was no longer prepared to simply give up on her without a fight.

Husbands were notoriously unreliable, she thought, thinking of Evan. Men came and went, she thought, picturing Gary. Mothers were forever.

Was there anything she could say or do to persuade her mother to get the help she needed? And if she refused to get help, could Val possibly learn to accept her for who she was and love her anyway? It had been so easy to just feel sorry for herself, to simply give up on her mother and look the other way.

"I love you, Mom."

"I love you, too, darling."

She decided to contact Al-Anon as soon as she got home.

It would be her birthday present to herself.

JENNIFER LOWERED THE e-mail she'd been reading to her lap and closed her eyes, still seeing the neatly handwritten message the receptionist had given her when they'd arrived back at the lodge. "Mr. Rowe e-mailed first thing this morning," the receptionist had explained. "Said he couldn't get through to your cell and that you'd probably be checking in with us for messages. He asked me to give this to you." She'd smiled as she'd slipped the brief message from Evan into Jennifer's hand.

So sorry, Jen, the note read. *By now I'm sure you realize that I won't be able to join you, and I apologize for being so completely unavailable. You probably thought I disappeared off the face of the earth, but please be assured you were never far from my thoughts, however derelict I've been about returning your messages. I know nothing has worked out the way we'd planned, and I hope it hasn't been too awful for you, but I promise I'll make it up to you. This working round the clock is for the birds. The good news is that the deal is almost done. I'm in meetings again all day today, deter-mined to get this thing signed, sealed, and delivered, so you won't be able to get ahold of me. You might as well relax and enjoy the fresh mountain air, and I'll see you when you get back to the city later tonight. I love you, Evan.*

Jennifer shook her head. *The good news*, she thought, silently repeating his words, is that you won't have to tear yourself away from your important meeting to drive all the way up here to identify the various body parts of your daughter, your ex-wife, and your fiancée, assuming you'd know the dif-ference. The good news is that we're alive. No thanks to you. *That's* the good news. And I've had enough fresh mountain air to last a lifetime, thank you very much. I just want to go home.

She'd call her sister when she got back, Jennifer decided, see if they couldn't find a way to get back on track, to work together to determine the best way to look after their father. It might not be possible. But then again, it might. At least she had to try.

She reached over the front seat to give Val's shoulder a reas-suring pat. "Let me know if you'd like me to take over for a little while."

"Thanks. I'm good." Val smiled into the rearview mirror.

Jennifer returned her smile. "I know you are."

IT WAS JUST after three o'clock when they reached Manhattan.

"Just a few more blocks," Jennifer said, directing Val to turn right, then right again. "There. That building over there." She pointed toward a fifteen-story white brick building on the southwest corner of the tree-lined street. A uniformed doorman stood waiting outside. "Home, sweet home."

"Mom," Brianne said as Val watched Jennifer stretch her impossibly long legs toward the pavement, and for once not immediately picturing them wrapped around Evan's head. "Look. Over there." She pointed to the other side of the street at a bright orange Mustang parked at least three feet from the curb. "Isn't that Sasha's car?"

"It most certainly is," Val muttered, the pieces of a familiar puzzle suddenly falling into place as Jennifer grabbed her overnight bag from the trunk. "Jennifer, wait." Val climbed quickly out of the driver's seat. You prick, she was thinking, her eyes traveling up the building's white brick exterior. You lying, self-serving, selfish little prick. You just can't help yourself, can you?

"Is something wrong?"

Val tried to find the words that would keep Jennifer from entering her apartment, that would protect her, keep her safe. Will wonders never cease? she marveled.

"What is it?"

"I just remembered that you left your car at my house."

"That's okay. I'll come by tomorrow to pick it up. Hey," she said in the next breath, her eyes wandering across the street toward Sasha's orange car. "Didn't I see that car at your place the other day?"

Val held her breath.

"It's Brianne's friend's, isn't it? The pretty blonde from Lululemon." There was a long pause while the meaning of her words registered on her brain. "Oh, God."

"It might not be her car," Val said quickly.

"Yes. I'm sure there are hundreds of bright orange Mustangs in the city."

"Even if it is hers, it doesn't mean . . ."

"Yes, it does." Jennifer's eyes glistened with the threat of tears. "Oh, well. What is it they say? Turnabout's fair play? I guess it's no less than I deserve."

"No," Val said adamantly. "You deserve so much more. We both do." Once again she heard echoes of Evan's seductive murmurings on the phone, the sly hints and vague innuendos. Had any of it meant anything? Or had his words been designed solely to keep her hanging on? Was she his fallback position in case his current deal fell apart? *Hey, you . . .*

Was he really so deliberate? Or was he just easily distracted? Did it matter?

"I really should get upstairs," Jennifer was saying. "Wouldn't want to miss the fireworks."

"Do you want me to come up with you?"

Jennifer laughed. "Much as I'd love to see the look on Evan's face, I think it's best if I go alone."

"Will you be all right?"

"Absolutely." Jennifer looked down at the sidewalk. "I'm in control of my feet," she said, taking a long, deep breath.

"You can call me, you know," Val told her. "Anytime."

Jennifer suddenly threw her arms around Val, hugging her tight. They stood locked in this embrace for several seconds, before slowly pulling apart. Jennifer waved a quick goodbye to the others watching, slack-jawed and open-mouthed, from the car, then walked purposefully toward the door the doorman was holding open. Then she turned around and waved again.

"Good luck," Val whispered, watching her disappear inside the lobby.

"Is it true?" James asked, leaning over the front seat as Val returned to the car. "Has Evan really been holed up here all weekend with Brianne's friend?"

"She's not my friend," Brianne said pointedly.

"And, fortunately, Evan is no longer my problem," said Val.

"Amen to that," Melissa said.

"Amen," echoed James.

"Amen," Val repeated, pulling the car away from the curb. Then again, because she liked both the finality and the hope inherent in the word, "Amen."